FIRST

FIRST, YOU'RE BORN.
You don't ask for it. No one asks for it, but the moment you break through that threshold you cling to life. Hunger for it. Fight for it. Grab hold of it with all the intensity your chubby little baby fingers can muster.

And then you learn what you've been fighting for.

***

Sometime in the future, after the year 94 O.O.

"PHRIN!"
Kris yells. But it is a prayer, I promise. We humble ourselves before you.
Where there was nothing, something. Before us, opens the phrinway—the shifting tunnel of colors and consciousness. May it carry us safely. Olorun, protect us as we use your highway to navigate the place between places.
"Cartagena, too? What in the name of Eshu..."
Ruins.
Ogun, walk with us.
Shango, protect us, O. Let us escape those who seek to do us harm, even as they shadow our every step.
Please, please show us the Miracle was real....
Footsteps
"PHRIN!"
Colors. Accra City. Ruins.
Footsteps, the steady sound of those who would end us
They can't keep this up ... we can't...
"PHRIN!"
Colors. Linton City. Ruins.
"Kris! You okay?"
Why's he so slow? I wonder ...
"I'm fine, Dara—PHRIN!"
Colors. Southern Icelands. Ruins.

Footsteps
How are they finding us? Olorun, how are they still latching?
How
   "Dara! LOW!"
Too close. Was that funny to you, Eshu?
   "Fleer beam coulda killed you, bisa! Coño!"
   "But it missed—Kris, just PHRIN!"
Colors. Lagos?

Footsteps

   "Dara! Spikes in the rubbl—"
   "I know—I see, PHRIN!"
Todirb. Ruins....
Footsteps closer ... no—
   "BACK OFF!"
*Could've wiped us. Turned us to ash and memories. Ogun, do you smile
in moments like this?*
I only wanted to wound them. I hate feeling sympathy for their fallen.
   "You slowed 'em, Dara. Had to. We don't got too much
time."
   *"We're here; this wall this is it—one more phrinway and we're free,
I can feel it."*
   "They look so alive on this mural ... feels like they right
here. Whatchu think? Probably think they're watching over us
somewhere?"
   *"I don't know. But I know that on this wall they're immortal, all
of them." They did well for nobody kids from Todirb. Orunmila, did
you foresee?*
More footsteps...? How—
   "PHRIN!"
Colors. Blood. Rubble... trash, ruins.
   "This was...?"
   "Yea."
   "Necesitas un minuto?"
   "We don't have one, PHRIN."

Ruins. That's what they left us; this is what they did after the gods spoke to them.

   "PHRIN"

I'll never understand, Olorun. How could you let them?

Miracle or Mirage?

   "Phrin"

No more footsteps. Is that your answer?

I hear you. For now,

Free

64 O.O.

"I-978 panel log entry. All previous statements and IDs fully
confirmed, current and applicable. Today's date is Tuesday,
April 16, 64 O.O. The time is 1215 hours, Central Union
Base Time. Updating progress on Program Irunmole: attempt
to synthesize igioyin cure from antibodies of individuals
possessing extranormal ability. There's been a setback.
Extranormals' perceived immunity to igioyin appears to be
limited by a range of variables; most notably, use of their
abilities. Usage results in a rapid acceleration of the virus'
maturity. Resultant mortality rate is far greater than baseline
for highly vulnerable *Normals*. We believe the selection of
antibodies from higher usage Extranormals may be the root
cause for the failure of the current iteration of the formula
S1-91-978. After the initial success of trials with patient set
11.1 without the adverse effects seen in prior Normal groups,
it appeared we had a viable treatment for the igioyin virus.
Today the last member of set 11.1 died. Symptoms observed
were identical to all members in the patient set. Autopsy and
blood samples indicate a rejection of the formula by the
body's immune system after initially accepting it without
incident. This is a grave development—worse than
anticipated. However, I have arranged for testing of extracted
antibodies from low usage Extranormals prior to returning to
the nascent phase to re-diagram. The time is now 1217 hours
Central Union Base Time, on Tuesday, April 16, 64 O.O.; this
log is complete."

DARA

Present Day

"I'M GUESSING YOU DON'T AGREE, Miss Adeleye."
Dara stared out a window into a sea of lifeless permafrost. It was early May in the year 93 O.O. (*La ti Odun Oluwa* or Years Since the Miracle). In generations past, the warm weather this time of year would've likely inspired countless students to disappear from within the confining walls of Ron Ed Instructional for the remainder of the day. Grateful to be indoors, she turned up the heat setting on her thermer and played with the small blue crystals on her lanyard, thinking of the next moment she'd be able to paint.

Instructor Bivins was droning on about the "Wonder" of verus, and how it saved the population from the igioyin virus. He held its creation and distribution up as a fine example of the Ministry's efficiency, implying it was successful because the union's constituents allowed it to be. "Some want to get in the way of the process," he pivoted, turning the lecture in her direction. "Too busy complaining instead of trusting in what's kept us safe."

Dara didn't mind finding new ways to challenge the indoctrination which took place daily in Bivins' classroom. Often it meant being able to—at least briefly—avoid thinking of the frigid gray mess outside that served as an appropriate backdrop to her life. His persistence with this particular topic *did* however, anger and annoy her as she thought of all the ways her closest friend Nicole's condition refuted his statements. *He's nothing more than an instrument of propaganda. Just like the others. Don't let him get to you.* She caught herself squeezing her lanyard a bit too tight and relaxed her grip.

"You know me so well," she said, without moving her gaze from the winter wasteland burying the once carefully maintained artificial grass that marked the campus' borders

2

and wondered why they bothered. Surely whoever mapped out the curriculum had to know it was being squandered on the already defeated, the apathetic. Ron Ed, like all instructionals, functioned as low budget daycare for the dispirited.

A few of her classmates groaned, some snickered. The remainder continued sleeping, uninterrupted.

"Dah-Rah, you 'bout to get another detention today," said a short but menacing kid who sat next to her. He probably had a name, other than "Shut-the-hell-up." Today a frosty glare would suffice. She turned away from the kid to look at Bivins, making eye contact for the first time since class began.

The instructor's eyes lit up, his trademark disdain for her reappearing in his smile. "Oh? And what argument could *you* have against the Ministry saving millions of lives? Tell me, child. I've grown quite fond of your comedic genius."

Dara thought it insulting of him to claim efficiency on the part of the Ministry, but maybe it was easy for Bivins to see it that way; he lived in the cloud of a blue vane. "I may be a child but I'm old enough to remember the Ministry's wastefulness causing countless Todirb deaths long after relief should've arrived. Maybe efficiency means something else to you. Instructor Bivins, are you *aware* most of us who live outside the clouds can't afford the weekly inoculation? We still walk around in fear *every day* not knowing if…." She hesitated and looked around. "Yeah, you call it a 'Wonder' and hail it as some miracle but you love omitting key facts whenever you lecture us. Pretty hard to push the lies when the truth is always hovering in the background, isn't it?" Dara said this, barely making it through before sarcasm could give way to palpable irritation.

"Ahhh, Dara … are *you* the truth that's hovering in the background?" Instructor Bivins laughed exaggeratedly and shook his head, locks flying as if ridding himself of an infestation. "For one so potentially intelligent, it's surprising you insist on lazy conspiracy theories over easily accessible facts. It's common knowledge the Ministry has made

3

available alternative options for those in the predicament you've mentioned. It's been well documented verus need not be administered weekly to be effective. Sure, potency varies due to a multitude of factors, but socioeconomic status is *not* one of them. If you paid any attention during your science courses, you'd be aware of this, no doubt!" He sighed. "Perhaps your thoughts will one day escape the fantasy land in which they reside and you can return to focusing on appropriate things, like the latest Miren dress or float-shoe. You're not unattractive. Properly groomed, you could make a decent wife to a blue marlsonne willing to step down a few rungs—perhaps even one from New Stuyvesant! Feel free to dream."

His grin was especially wide on the last suggestion. Dara smiled in kind, her irritation now gone. Despite his unbothered act, he'd added a deeply personal insult. She'd managed to rile him up a bit and his grin was a poor cover for taking the bait. Dara wasn't naïve. She knew the Ministry wasn't entirely to blame; a lot of things could be traced to the terror the Nth had inflicted on all of them. Igioyin *wouldn't even exist* if it weren't for the Nth. Still, it was worth it to see Bivins like this.

She felt the urge to turn her gaze back towards the window and regain her aura of disinterest but realized such a move could be mistaken to suggest the opposite. With Bivins, these little battles were often won and lost on body language alone. She maintained her gaze and chose instead to see if she could bait him further.

"Insult me all you want Instructor Bivins, but I promise you I *will* be Minister one day. And I won't turn my back on my roots and leave the poor suffering, as Minister Corlmond has done. And, sir, on that day if you're lucky, I may choose to help *you* … because, it almost seemed like there was a note of reverence in your tone when you said 'marlsonne.' Or maybe it was embarrassment." She'd heard the rumors of his failed career as one of the nobility's fabled singers.

"Unlikely." The detachment which Instructor Bivins had nearly abandoned moments earlier returned in full force.

Dara backed off. There would be no detention for her today.

She returned her attention to the window, the instructor's words fading further into the background as her gaze caught and focused on a group of animated kids—laughing, chasing each other, throwing things—in the distance. They were from Ron Ed Preparatory which had let out twenty minutes earlier. A smile crossed her face as she thought back to a few years ago. *That was me and Nic, once. Playing around, saying we'd become things everyone told us we were silly to imagine.* She allowed her smile to linger as she watched, knowing that with her successes each passing day she was becoming greater proof that *everyone* knew squat. Suddenly, one of the boys began convulsing. The other kids ran to hold him and one ran off, presumably to get help. Within seconds his convulsions had stopped, and he lay still. Two adults in medic suits arrived at the scene and picked up the body.

Some of the kids tried to follow, but Dara saw them being waved off. With their heads down, they plodded across the landscape until they were out of sight. She touched her forehead as if massaging a headache and quickly moved her hand down her face, removing a few droplets of water from her eyes. *Wimp.* Whenever she saw another fall, she questioned if her tears were from genuine sadness or the reminder her moment could be as random. She'd recently tested negative for igioyin, but it seemed like it would be only a matter of time before it chose her too.

This was life in the world after the gods descended to earth in a vision: "The Miracle of Elegua (sometimes derisively referred to as "The Mirage of Elegua")," disabled weapons of mass destruction and promised to save mankind from itself. In the ninety-three years since, there had been The Nightfall War—a twenty-six-year worldwide attritional nightmare ending with the tattered remains of civilization crawling multilaterally towards peace and agreeing to a global alliance in order to survive as a species; the rise of the Nth, self-proclaimed freedom fighters who brought destruction and chaos in the name of the gods; and igioyin: the tachy-degenerative disease that was a ticking time bomb for anyone born of low stock. "Miracle of Elegua," "Wonder of Verus," it didn't matter; adults put names to things and then chose whatever meanings justified their atrocities.

The lights in the classroom changed from white to red to signify the end of the school day.

"And now back to the gray," Dara whispered to herself.

Her classmates got up and showed their first collective signs of life all day. Dara remained in her seat for a second longer, allowing the crowd to clear. She gathered her things and trudged along behind the rest of her class, barely acknowledging Instructor Bivins' self-satisfied "Till Monday, Miss Adeleye!"

"Actually, Miss Adeleye, I need to see you for a moment. Miss Adeleye!"

Startled, she jumped slightly and turned to Bivins. "Yes?"

"Don't think I've forgotten about that work of yours for Monday. I can't wait for us all to be underwhelmed and disappointed. I will *personally* put the finishing touch on your file. Then we can lay your foolish ambitions to rest and you can aim appropriately for your true lot in life." He snickered. "Minister eh? And *I'd* love to teach the bright children of the nobility in the wondrous Lyteche-sponsored academies of the clouds instead of wasting my talents here in instructionals with you lot, but we *all* must be realistic."

"Oh, Bivins, you always say the sweetest things to me," she replied dismissively, walking away.

Dara had a lot riding on Monday. Yearly, three exceptional students, juniors, from each red vane were picked to be recipients of the Carbo Scholarship, allowing them to attend one blue vane university of their choosing. It was a lottery ticket of sorts, sponsored by popular TV faith healer Darcen Carbo, and in most cases, the only way to a better life for its recipients. Any other path likely condemned them to a life of low wages and no chance of upward mobility. The difference between the Carbo and the *actual* lotteries was, with this, the contestants had some semblance of control over their destiny, and there were people who won. Dara had done everything in her power thus far to be a frontrunner for a selection, with the exception of her provocations with Bivins—which had threatened to unravel her entire candidacy on more than one occasion. A finalist, her work Monday would make her a lock as a rep for the class of 94 O.O. and Instructor (and unfortunately, also Vice Chancellor) Bivins practically powerless in her march to a better future, and eventual rise to Minister of the North Emerian Union. The only problem was she hadn't finished her submission yet.

As she shuffled past the weapons detectors and through the school's switched-off doors, Dara inhaled deeply, reacquainting herself with a world she'd have little respite from for the next three days. Burning icicles formed in her nose. The gelid air in Todirb Wall was no different than in any other red vane: sooty and reeked of sulfur—quite different than the green or blue vanes. She envied those who lived their entire lives under the protected atmosphere of the clouds and envisioned herself as a beaming student at Stuyvesant University, imbibing the celestial New Stuy mist.

Weekends were the worst in "The Wall" because they passed excruciatingly slowly. One could link up with friends for some outdoor mischief, but unless they had money and an approved pass for a trip to the blue vanes, reds were better off staying indoors, or within the immediate proximity of their residences. It didn't take much to start street fights, and the medics weren't exactly clamoring to make their way to the chaos of such events. With this, plus the number of students who died from igioyin, local instructionals were permanently short a few attendees each Monday.

Dara's living circumstances barely made staying indoors a better option. Although it meant she'd only briefly get to see Nicole, she decided right then as she stood outside it was best she grab her project from home and spend the majority of the weekend at school working on it.

She descended the steps. It hadn't snowed for weeks now, but the sidewalk and street were perpetually carpeted in a crunchy gray crust. It often seemed the ground was a reflection of the sky, or vice versa and the vagrant crowd milling about outside the school hoping for leftover lunches or unwanted snacks was a daily reminder of what the future held for many of her classmates. She sighed.

The place where we dwell.

Still, things could be worse, though thinking of those possibilities was of no real comfort. As she deftly avoided any contact with the crowd and headed up the block on Kane Street, Dara pushed such thoughts out of her mind. Instead, she played the game that always brought her comfort on the walk home. She would count how many already snow-imprinted footsteps she'd stepped in before she had to make her own. Once done, she'd start again. In this manner she often got home without incident, save for the cursed she'd occasionally pass as they were convulsing before death. Stragglers and goons could obstruct only if they were given an opening.

As she passed the cages of Pratt Correctional Facility and neared her home on Lee Way, the routine that helped many times before proved useless. Red vanes such as Todirb Wall, much like their blue and green counterparts, were secured by way of shiny, dark obelisks (tinted slightly with the color of their vane), known as *towers*. Draped in molten black pearl, they rose ambitiously from the vision of a landscape that wasn't; against the archaic red vane architecture, their beauty made them an eyesore. These immovable, impenetrable structures monitored criminal as well as potential terrorist activity allowing the state to send Pro-Ts to bring swift and decisive justice to those caught in the act. Their scope covered a wide radius and due to their phallic shape, they acquired a variety of unsurprising nicknames—none similar to the official names given by the Ministry. Utterance of the phrase "Rick's watching," was enough to jettison an illicit deal of any kind. No one knew quite how they worked, only that they did—with chilling efficiency.

There were, however, places even the prying eyes of the Ministry couldn't reach, as well as activities to which it turned a blind one. Left were a variety of vices for willing and dedicated career criminals to make a comfortable living from without drawing the attention of the Pro-Ts. They took full advantage, turning other red vane inhabitants into unwitting victims and unwilling participants at a rate that should have been alarming. In Wall slang, these professionals were called *lawyers*. Such was their ability to avoid the inside of the cages.

That was why Dara could make little sense of the scene emerging less than a block from her home. Ahead, there was a large crowd, but it was different from the homeless zombified masses usually collecting around a block. They were surrounding something (or someone) with a unifying frenzied energy. As she attempted to make her way around the horde, a brilliant white streak leapt from its center, reaching towards the sky. Falling woefully short, its descent and the accompanying boom managed to splinter the gathering enough for Dara to see what had caused the swarm.

Impossible.

Her disbelief carried her through the crowd and she found herself in front of a downed tower; Brouder Tower, the *central eye* of Todirb—made somehow more menacing as it watched her from the ground, its power to intimidate unaffected by its damaged state. Nonetheless, she stared. It was smooth, seamless; gorgeous. There was no mark from the lightning, no visible fissure or crack from which it could have escaped. The crowd struck a strange equilibrium; desperate to leave, yet drawn by the unknown, they froze, waiting.

Dara—who suffered no such paralysis, backed away, wondering who or what could have caused such a thing to occur. The lawyers' domain was far away from the watchful eyes of the towers. Such a brazen act of vandalism would only bring attention to Todirb leading to unwanted Pro-T scrutiny to their dealings. While criminal, they were businessmen, not idiots. Swarms of Pro-Ts drove down profit margins. Was this some sort of attack by the Nth? But that would be stupid—wasteful. *They'd never do anything like that here. We're nobody—*

From out of nowhere, swarms of tall, broad-shouldered, masked officers clad in all-black form-fitting garb appeared and began dispersing the crowd. Dara's curiosity gave way to terror. These weren't officers; they weren't dressed like Pro-Ts. These were the Nth! Every news panel story she'd ever heard or seen, every nightmare she'd had of them was laughable in comparison to this, the real thing. They moved like gods, vengeful ones; each step towards the crowd rung out with the finality of fate. They held fleers—beautiful, slender, skipping stone shaped silver weapons—and opened them, emitting radiant glows searing the flesh of those unlucky enough to be transfixed by the sight.

Fortunately, Dara's earlier movement away from the crowd had given her a head start. She now found herself running side by side with a little girl who couldn't have been older than six. They were being pursued by an Nthn who'd noticed them break away from the larger throng. Dara saw him reach for his fleer and ran faster, nearly slipping on slick patches, ducking into an alley alongside the little girl and a few other escapees to avoid the fatal beam that would surely follow. Coming to a stop at a wall after weaving through a maze-like series of side streets and alleys during which the others fell away, she was surprised and relieved to see the child still next to her, perhaps even a half step ahead. She was crestfallen to see they hadn't managed to shake their pursuer. The Nthn stood facing them less than twenty feet away, fleer aimed. The Nth emblem of Ogun, the Yoruba God-of-War, was visible on his breastplate. Dara stepped in front and shielded the little girl, laughing, wondering which smile Bivins would choose upon getting word of her death. As she laughed, she felt herself being lifted by tiny hands and casually thrown against a wall. Her back struck the wall. She fell.

The Nthn who she'd thought only moments ago was pursuing her paid no attention to her jumbled form and remained in his menacing stance, fleer trained on the child. Dara, conscious but woozy, was confused by what occurred next.

Dara had heard the horror stories about the Nth growing up. She'd heard the urban legends of mystery Nthns seizing red vane youngsters, disappearing them into the darkness, but she'd never had the good fortune of personally seeing one in action. She watched in dismay as the Nthn fired his weapon at the girl. She was astonished when the incandescent beam bent around the girl and destroyed the wall behind her. The girl, seemingly out of nowhere, produced an object resembling a *glowing!?* sprezen—a dispenser often used for graffiti—and she responded with a similar beam of her own. This beam made contact with the Nthn and he was replaced with a pile of dust. As the scene went in and out of focus, Dara saw the girl, glowing sprezen in hand, turn towards her with an expression she couldn't decipher. As the girl pointed the sprezen at her, Dara felt her helplessness and fear return.

Eshu if these are my final moments please protect my soul and give me safe passage through the crossroads.

A bright pink light engulfed her. She was conscious in that moment of whatever force held her together because she felt its pull weakening. Her eyes remained open, but they were rendered visionless and she soon lost consciousness.

She came to in a large, soft bed in a windowless room dimly lit with blue hue. Across from the foot of the bed, to the side, was an empty wooden chair pushed under a matching desk. On the desk, she could make out a thick stack of old-style reads. Directly across from her and the bed was what had to be the door, a light green rectangular slab with an over-sized golden marble fixed near the center on the edge. It looked overweight and inefficient. Dara had seen its like in history panels from time to time. To the other side of the door was what appeared to be a small translucent statue with black and red engravings, but she couldn't make out its features. It hid in a corner created by the doorframe and the end of a couch. The bed was a cream island atop a calm sea of dark blue carpeting. As she surveyed the room, not daring to move from this foreign bed where she felt strangely safe, she wondered if she'd somehow awoken in the distant past, was still asleep, or in the alley, littering the frost with her disintegrated carcass.

She heard a slow creak as the primitive, cumbersome door opened, laboring on its hinges, loudly threatening her feeling of safety. In a panic, she gasped with the absurd and desperate hope that somehow the act of taking in all the air in the room would make her invisible as the air itself. A glance at her hand showed she'd failed and she slowly exhaled. In stepped the little girl from moments, hours or *days ago?* It was impossible to tell how much time had passed in this room.

"Relax," the child said. She hesitated as if struggling with what to say next. "You're safe," followed. She held out a small light-yellow flask. "Drink." Dara, not moving or saying anything, stared. The girl had dark brown wavy hair, platted into a single braid, which ran down her back. Her olive eyes were kind but looked aged and weary, out of place against the vitality of her soft, honey skin. Dara had seen those tired eyes before—in the mirror and on the faces of her peers—but they had at least twice the years of suffering under their belts. Glancing at the flask in the tiny hands, Dara was reluctant to obey.

She knew she had the girl to thank for her safety, but was that enough to trust her? She did not know the motives of this child. As she thought it over, pain shot through her body. A shriek of agony too grotesque to manifest audibly welled up inside her, emerging in her look instead. The little girl stepped forward quickly, while opening the flask and forced a bittersweet syrupy substance from it down Dara's throat. Within seconds, Dara felt a gentle warming sensation throughout her body. The pain ceased. Words tumbled out of her mouth.

"Thanks so much."

The little girl nodded.

"Why was that Nthn after us?"

"Not Nthn. IPU" the little girl replied.

"IPU? Huh? No, that wasn't IPU ... they were wearing Nth—"

"IPU. Not. Nthn."

"Then why? Who *are you*?" What would the Institute for Preservation of Unity be doing in Todirb? They were the royal force of the (ceremonial) emperor, dealing primarily with international peacekeeping affairs. Dara was confused. She set a foot off the edge of the bed and tried to stand up, but wobbled, lost her balance and fell back.

"Soon, every ..."

As Dara faded into the cocoon of a dream, the girl's words dissipated and all at once she was aware of a flood of colors. Colors leaned their heads back and belched other brighter colors. Colors held hands and jumped over landscapes, leaving trails on the horizon. Colors she knew. Colors for which no words existed. Colors that took the drab reality in which she resided and made *that* the dream, a woeful, slapdash attempt at replication falling far short of this new realm she wanted to stay in forever.

She was moving—no—she was being moved. Was this only in the dream? Was her physical body in motion? There were shapes. Some colors would die and leave odd, unfamiliar outlines in their wake before newer ones sprang to life. Each outline moved towards her, enveloping her for a split second before disappearing behind her, a parade of disfigured doorways. The shapes appeared with increasing frequency and speed, moving towards, around and eventually past her and Dara was abruptly airborne through a rainbow tunnel. She reconnected with her physical body—it traveled in sync with her visions, seemingly unveiling them as more than a mere dream. She couldn't open her eyes to confirm this, as she had no control whatsoever; she could only trust her intuition. She sensed, but didn't feel wind, was aware of, but couldn't see clouds, and felt, but did not hear sound. She was free: from responsibility, from worry, from fear. It was exhilarating. Was this death? If so, she was grateful to Olorun to have discovered it early.

She felt herself being angled downward, mind and body resisting the inevitable pull of gravity, dragged off the ether like trees failing to remain on the hillside during an avalanche. There was momentary acceleration followed by a decline in speed so sharp she felt she'd come to a full stop. She soon realized she was still descending, albeit slowly. When she finally stopped moving, Dara opened her eyes. She was surprised and disappointed to find herself in the same bed and the little girl in the same spot, standing there, static—save for the flask in her hand which was now closed. It dawned on Dara that time and space hadn't revealed any intimate secrets, she hadn't traveled to undiscovered worlds, and she was not capable of flight. Whatever it was this child had given her to drink simply put her in a hallucinatory state. She did, however, feel the strength return to her body as she stood and stretched. Naturally, she followed with a flood of questions ranging from the child's identity and origins to what she'd been given to drink. The child watched, unmoved.

Dara, overwhelmed and out of breath, took a moment, and then came the statements of her importance (threats), followed by demands to return home. "Please! You don't understand I need to finish. I'm gonna be the first kid from Todirb to become Minister and this is my shot at the scholarship—this is how! This is my chance to change things; I'll miss it if I don't make it back home in time. You *have* to take me home now or I won't make it! I'll be like everyone else—I can't let Bivins be right—I won't!" Dara, teary and unable to control her gesticulations or the volume of her increasingly cracking voice during this torrent, was uneasy about the way the girl stood calmly, letting her vent, not saying a word, not changing her expression. It was enough to stop her barrage. She studied the little girl's face once more.

Well?

The girl, returning Dara's curious stare, pointed to herself and said, "Vida. Seven." She took a deep breath. "Safe here." Another breath. "Please, stay. Urgent. Much to discu—"

Dara, not calmed by the kid's seeming inability to form complete sentences, ran over to the door, fought with it a bit before it gave, and in flooded bright light from the hallway. She stepped into it and as her eyes adjusted, looked for an exit. Finding a stairwell ahead, she rushed to descend it. She reached the bottom of the steps and found herself in a living room, furnished like ones of eons ago with shelves of old-style reads, pictures hung up on the walls and floral pattern seats and couches. Directly ahead of her was another primitive door—windowed, leading outside. She turned back, expecting to see the child in full pursuit.

Dara threw the door open and a brighter light than that of the hallway upstairs invited itself in. It was unusually brilliant, a light so rare as to be unfamiliar. It soaked her, catching her off guard, making her aware of little else. Déjà vu washed over her before she connected the warmth of the rays to the feeling she had after consuming Vida's concoction.

The Sun?

Praise Olorun!

As her eyes adjusted, she was now certain she'd never left the alley, and was enjoying some pleasant afterlife, for what she saw was surreal.

Spread out beyond the edges of the wildest reaches of her imagination was green. Beautiful fields reclined effortlessly on top of the land, open as the possibilities in a starlit sky, dotted with trees whose forms swayed in reverence. On the horizon were hills—mountains, rivals in ascent, each a jealous shade as they kissed the unblemished belly of the crystal blue heavens. And the air … her lungs ballooned and decided against limits. If she ended up floating away, so be it.

"Beautiful?"

Startled, Dara turned to look over her shoulder, and there was Vida, as if she'd been beside her, staring the whole time. "Yeah. But it's not real."

The little girl said nothing and smiled.

Dara turned back to look at the house, a yellow two-story cottage. The door was a spotless ivory. There were flowers in all manners of color, most of them presumed extinct, obliviously socializing with one another on both sides of the door. She had to be in another universe, world; *another life.*

Sure, blue vanes she'd been to on occasional field trips had vegetation, better air quality, warmth, and were cleaner than the slums of the red vane she hailed from, but they were nothing like this. She turned back around and sat on the pillowy earth, her legs outstretched in the grass, looking into the distance of what had to be a wondrous lie, and let Vida explain. A tranquil breeze accompanied by the lightest of drizzle, gently touched her face as it wafted between them. This small, subtle gesture from the elements was life affirming. She couldn't shake the feeling she'd somehow come to this place before. Wherever they were, maybe it *was* real.

Vida spread her arms wide, as if preparing to hug the air. She looked around and said simply, "Hidden."

"I don't follow." Dara questioned how this much land and open space could fit such a description. The house was one thing. She had figured it had to have been somehow concealed to be "safe," as Vida put it. But the suggestion its hiding place was also hidden ... Dara thought of a cosmic nesting doll and gave a quiet laugh.

Vida stood and put two fingers from each hand on the back of her head and brought them forward simultaneously, flicking them at the moment they reached her temples. A panel then appeared in front of them with an image of other people, considerably older than Vida, performing the same movement. Dara failed to understand. Vida motioned her to keep watching.

From the temple of each person shown, a holographic image of a beautiful land with green hills, trees and a cottage became more vivid. The image did not, however, show them sitting in front of the cottage.

Vida then said, "Together." Motioning to everything around them, "This. *Igbo Oluwa.*" She pointed to the people in the panel and pointed to herself: "Us."

Dara after a lengthy pause said, "But ... out of nothing?" Her limits of belief had already been stretched quite a bit already. She wasn't sure how much more she could take.

Vida replied, "Found. Not made."

Dara relaxed her shoulders, her brow unfurrowed. "This place already existed."

Vida smiled. "You. Here before."

Dara was unnerved by the certainty in Vida's tone. "What? No ... no. I don't know what you mean."

"Yes. You do. Re. mem. ber. Soon."

"Why did you bring me here?"

"You have. Great. Path. *Olorí-iré.*"

"I know. To get out of Todirb. To be Minister, I told you already. Thanks for saving me, I'm thankful, but I have to get back."

"No. Much. Greater. Ogun. Walks. With you."

"Greater than Minister of the NEU? I don't think so. This has been fun but please, I don't know what time it is and my friend needs me."

Vida smiled and again said nothing.

Dara groaned.

"Soon, clear. You, too. This." said Vida. After pausing again, she added, "Soon, home. Trust."

With that, Vida closed the panel, stood and went back into the house.

As Dara dragged her feet, following a girl who could've been her baby sister, she had the silliest thought of *how wonderful it would be to live in a place like this.* She dismissed it and stepped through the cottage doorway. She lost consciousness once again.

* * *

Dara found herself at Nicole's doorstep, backpack in tow, filled with a bag of food she'd pilfered from the cafeteria and the meds she'd picked up in the morning before school. Her lungs burned and her nostrils were raw, having had no time to readjust from the strange dreamland she'd just been unceremoniously booted out of by Vida.

When Nicole opened the door, she smiled saying, "What took you so long? I thought school let out like a couple hours ago, I got worried." Before Dara could answer, Nicole's eyes lit up and her face grew wide as if she'd stumbled on some well-hidden secret. "You finally have a boyfriend, don't you? How was the kiss? Tell me he's a marlsonne and you have a forbidden love! Spill it, bisa!"

Dara smiled and said unenthusiastically, "Yeah, you got me there." She'd decided she didn't have the strength to explain the madness that had occurred in the (*two hours!!???* *Impossible!!!*) between leaving school and seeing Nicole. Going along with the imaginary boyfriend was easier; once she'd thrilled her friend with the inside scoop on the day's events, she handed her the meds.

"Verus: Take once weekly to neutralize igioyin." Nicole tossed the package on the couch. "Fantastic if you're a New Stuy siren with Daddy's easy money. Or you can be me and get a handful every few months, hoping you don't die before then."

Dara wasn't going to let her go down this road again. Nicole was prone to spells of deep depression, leaving Dara fearful she might beat the illness to the punch and punch out. *No, not with me around.* It made Dara feel guilty each time she tested negative. "Hey Nic, what about Jess? He said he could get some extras from work, right?"

"Nuh, that's not gonna work, Dara. I know he thinks it would change my life—that I'd get off this couch and go out and go be something but who knows? I can't let him risk it."

18

"He's right though, you can't keep missing school and staying home all the time; I think getting out will help with your mood." Nicole laughed at this suggestion. "Oh yeah? Like how you usually look super happy when I see you after school? No point wasting whatever time I have *there*."

"I'm serious. I don't want you hurting yourself."

"I have a disease where the first symptom is death. If I hurt myself it'll be to feel alive."

Nicole's brother, Jess—a sanitation analyst at Macon Medicine in New Stuyvesant, had told her scores of verus were stored in the facility, but Nicole explained how she could never bring herself to let him take anything. If he got caught and lost his job, they'd have nothing. No place to live, no food, and they wouldn't have been able to get even the small number of pills she did now. It was best she get by in her current state until they could find a better solution. Dara, frustrated but understanding, was reminded again of her multiple failed attempts to land a part-time job at Macon.

Nicole laughed. "I know that look, Dara Adeleye. It's okay! Forget about it, I won't hurt myself, I promise. I'll be fine! let's talk some more about your life. How's the mural coming along? You done yet!!? I can't wait for my best friend to get into Stuy U!!! You know I'm gonna visit you like every weekend, right?"

Dara laughed. She jumped on the futon and wrapped Nicole in a headlock, and upon releasing, pecked her on the cheek. "Of course, you can be my roomie. As long as you don't mind sleeping and watching movies while I spend every waking hour studying."

Nicole stopped laughing, but kept smiling. "Booooooo! How's that different from now?! Wait, you're serious? You're too much lose!" She threw a pillow at Dara.

Dara, knocking the pillow away and still chuckling, got up and stepped into the kitchen. "Nope. Win forever. Grabbing a drink, you want anything?"

"Nuh."

Dara filled a pitcher with water while continuing their conversation. "Nic, how's Auntie Modupe?"

"She's fine! You know how things are. She tries to help, send spends and stuff but their part of Lagos is a difficult place and she has her own children to worry about too. Daniel tested negative last we spoke but she's terrified especially for the little ones."

"You guys ever thought about moving out there?"

"What? Halfway across the world to be a burden to her in person? No. A red vane in Lagos is still a red vane." Nicole went quiet and Dara wondered if her visits did more harm than good.

"Hey there, lover," Nicole appeared in the kitchen seemingly out of nowhere. Dara jumped.

"Geez Nic! Soooo creepy."

"You were taking forever. I thought you were playing me, seducing some woman of ill repute behind my back."

"Never, you siren tramp, float-shoe Goddess. You're the only one for me …"

"That's laughably dishonest," Nicole interrupted, grinning, spinning rhythmically. "*And* it was better in the song anyway. But I'll take it."

They returned to the futon and watched part of a documentary on the scarlet macaw, a beautiful endangered South Emerian bird that was best known for its starring role as a green vane delicacy. They were enthralled until they heard the series of grating honks it used to communicate. Nicole (bless her heart) was still sympathetic. They played some games on the netlines together while Nicole caught Dara up on all the celebrity drama and gossip which was forgotten once Nicole wasn't around, and as she listened Dara wondered if she and Nicole had always been this drastically different, and realized they had. They never shared any of the same interests, didn't enjoy much of the same music and Dara couldn't be bothered about anything outside of important community affairs, art and education. It was as if Nicole possessed all the frivolity Dara lacked, but perhaps this was why they loved each other. Being next-door neighbors for much of their childhood hadn't hurt but Dara wasn't willing to give all the credit to Ministry Zoning. As she listened to Nicole, she could feel herself getting sleepy. It had been a long day; it was getting late and she had work to do. She got up and gave Nicole a generous hug. "I've gotta go."

"Aww, so soon? You never come by."

"Maybe if you'd stop lying like that I'd be by more."

Nicole, chuckling in reply as Dara switched off the door to exit, stopped as a thought popped into her head. "Dara! Remember to tell me when you finish the mural! I demand to see it first!"

"Yes, Mother!" Dara replied, smiling as Nic switched on the door to close it behind her.

* * *

"I don't understand. How by Ogun's blade is this possible?"

Institute for Preservation of Unity Captain Eaves Darcela stared into the open panel screen in disbelief as footage of a ghost ducking into an alleyway in Todirb Wall with one of her emises in hot pursuit played on loop. She kissed a scarification of Ogun, the Yoruba God-of-War on her wrist.

"We're not sure, Captain. Initial footage from Brouder Tower earlier in the day was a positive match. This loop was all we could get from the remaining tower in the area. Emis Portland's audio confirmed the match as well."

"What do you *mean* '*Emis Portland's audio*'? What about his blacker?" she asked, referencing the emises' impermeable all-black bodysuits. "His entire blacker is a cam."

"That's the thing Captain, we're not sure. No emis cams at the scene were operational. We're unsure if … well we think maybe—"

"Maybe *what?*"

"The girl may have done something to them."

"Like what? What in *Ogun's name* could she have done?"
The captain lifted a rather large mouse out of a tank
containing a few others, pet it, and began feeding it from her
hand. "Don't answer that."

"Y-yes captain." The emis quaked.

"Aw, he's so cute! Don't be so fearful of me—it's rude,
you're just giving a report. So, *Brouder?*"

"Yes captain." The emis struggled to steady himself as the
mouse sat in the captain's exposed palm while nibbling away
at the treats in her gloved hand.

"How many red-vaners were killed?"

"By us, captain? Thirteen. None by the girl—"

"But all our emises at scene were displaying Nth logos
prominently, I take it."

"Yes—"

"Good. As far as the reds know it was Nthn business as
usual and we were never there. So, destroying a tower. Quite
the entrance ... yet you let her escape." The mouse jumped
from her palm into her gloved hand for the last of the treats.
"I *love it* when they do that," She delighted.

"Um, we don't have all the details captain but it sounds
like Emis Portland nearly apprehended her in an alley before
she vaporized him and disappeared. The rest of the feed was
lost and we arrived seconds too late. It's as if she wanted to
be seen ... and then didn't. Chose the perfect alley to duck
into—the remaining tower's range cuts off at the entrance.
All we know for certain is she was there and now she's gone."

Captain Darcela froze the screen for a moment and
zoomed in. "Who are those people, the ones running near
her; what can you make out?"

"Very little, captain. We're seeing the same as you; that's
all the footage we have. We didn't think to ID the others.
They appeared to be vagrants fleeing to safety. As you can
imagine, our priority and all resources were on the girl."

The black-gloved hand of the captain closed viciously
without warning. The emis flinched at the resulting blood
spray. Captain Darcela opened the hand, letting the squashed

mouse plop to the ground. She laughed softly, motioning the emis to clean it up. "I really should calibrate that pressure-glove, shouldn't I? ID the others! Take the footage to Toley for full analysis. I don't care how long it takes, we need to know who else was near her. Find them all; question them. We need to know what they saw. Don't look so revolted. I believe mouse is a red vane delicacy."

KRIS

Present Day

"**LIFE IS DUMB**. Everyone's sitting around and waiting for the end. No one tells you that, nuh. Especially not the rich ones, the 'royals,' the 'nobility'—the ones who got infinite spends. The ones we see on the panels selling us lies. The ones sharing their big plans, bragging about their latest conquests—gassing us up—riling us up for their causes, for their 'values,' like we the same. And they try to sell that to you like they know everything—like they got it figured out and we can too if we follow them. Like we can live *their* life; sheeeit ... *they* can barely live their lives. Just look at them ... full of false hope. Full of fake energy. People who daily sing the praises of Olorun, Shango, Eshu, Orunmila—have you believing in being blessed—they want so badly for you to believe they are—that they suck you in and infect you with their intoxication. It's disgusting. It's sad. It's even funny. They done such a good job of lying to themselves, their new truth has you convinced. They're never far away from the real truth though; when they're pushing their lies on us. It seeps out through that bullshit. Their silly catchphrases give 'em away. They tell you 'tomorrow's not promised; live everyday like it's your last.' And 'carpe diem,' 'Yolo,' and all their dumb, stupid little variations like it matters.

That's cuz they know, briz; they know we're all toy huvs being pulled along that invisible field. And yeah ... they accelerating hard and to us it looks like they're going faster, but they—we all moving to the same place, the same destination. They could be gone tomorrow, like any of us. Verus may have saved them but it ain't make 'em invincible. Who cares about their titles? Who cares about their spends and houses and huvs and phrincars? Who cares that they got

24

five Lyteche panels in every room? They gotta give it up eventually when they go into that nothingness and then they'll be just like us, and they'll be kicking and screaming. They no better cuz they can afford things and we can't. They don't know any more than we do. How many of ya'll carry igioyin? Yeah. Yeah exactly, that's all of us. They're the same people that want to blame *us*, call it a curse—say the gods turned their backs on us. I say what gods? Hell, we got the advantage cuz we don't got nothing to give up and we *know* it could be over any minute. Nothing to lose. No fear, briz.

It's May, *93 O.O.*—and ain't nothin' changed! I know those who died *today*, yesterday, last week, last month. I know you all do too. And the Nth is everywhere, briz. They strike whenever and ain't nobody stopping them last I checked. Ain't nobody really in control. And it *frightens* those fake go getters, briz—those clowns in the clouds. It scares them more than it scares us: the ones who got up in the afternoon instead of the morning because we know it don't matter. So when ya'll ask me wh—"

"Is that why your lazy ass always tryna get *everyone else* to do stuff, Kill? Cuz it don't matter?"

The instant silence of tension.

Kris Arvelo looked over the crowd of his fellow teens to the back of the dimly lit space in the Quarters clubhouse, his scowl a missile, eyes seeking the bold suicide who dared address him like an old pal, using his nickname: Kill. Upon finding its intended target, all tension melted and gave way to a smile generous enough to belong to a different face. "Envy! What's love, briz?! Come up here you loser!"

A short, rail thin kid covered in tattoos up to his neck strode to the front of the room. His gait projected an assuredness distinct from the tall, chiseled Kris' confident, rhythmic stride. It was the bop of one with nothing to lose. As Kris stepped forward to meet him in the middle of the room, their embrace could have easily been mistaken for rivals attempting to strangle one another.

"*Man* … the great Tommy B. Thought you was dead or something, briz. You disappeared forever. What you been up to?" Kris spoke to Envy as if they were the only two in the room.

"Chill briz, no need to drop the government name, but yeah … gone a couple years … but I had to lay low. You know after I dropped out Grammy was trying to force me to go back to Ron Ed. I grabbed my shit one night and vimmed out. Went where none a ya'll could find me. Last I needed was somebody tracing my move back to you or Donzi or whoever. You know, getting *you* in some trouble."

Kris nodded, gnawing on a toothpick that hadn't left his mouth since he began his speech. "True, true."

Envy spoke again, something catching his eye. "Chewing on them toothies huh? Expensive ass habit—your spends must be crazy … *and* I see you still got that chain, briz, ha … some things never change."

Kris instinctively touched his necklace—links of shiny dark metal peppered with light clear blue stones. "Ha! Stop it, briz. Spends is the same they've always been."

He turned to address the gathering.

"This is Envy; he's family. Don't let his frame fool you; he's the toughest briz I know."

Envy smiled, knocking his tattooed knuckles together and nodded to the small crowd. With a brief scan he saw it was mostly gangly, scraggly dressed boys. A handful of them bore the look of the confident intense, the hungry. Most of the others possessed the hallmarks of the eager to please, the desperate to fit in; the types of kids to look around and see if everyone else was laughing at a joke before they did. All were attentive, hanging onto Kris' every word, trying hard to look like they belonged.

He recalled feeling that way once—wanting, hoping to belong. By the end of preparatory, the last bit of this foolishness left him, and he entered Ron Ed Instructional a live wire and true menace. His first day of instructional, he was suspended for fighting a senior who had about five inches and fifty pounds, mostly muscle, on him. The senior was not the victor.

No one could recall what started the fight, but that wasn't the important thing anyway, at least not to Envy. He instantly became someone only the most unbalanced kids would dare mess with; everyone else knew better. He wouldn't fit in, but he'd be left alone. In a school like Ron Ed, which sometimes resembled the cages of Rikesland or Pratt Correctional, it was a necessary start.

Kris' smile faded as his face regained the intensity of the moments before Envy's entrance.

"Chaos is the only thing that truly matters. They put all this order in place to control us. They tell us to be like so and so who studies, become scholars, and eventually we too can move into the green or blue vanes and live a better life under the protection of the clouds. Or we can keep our heads down too and get to be servants who spend the days slaving away in the clouds, seeing how great things are over there only to come back here to garbage. That's weak, briz. They tell us if we have a talent to get up early, focus, develop it, one day we'll wow them enough to join their ranks. Or join their Pro-Ts and hurt our own daily. Or join their IPU and be bottom-feeders, risking our lives to get their little, charity nobility titles. Nuh. It's all lies, briz. How many of you know *anyone, ANYONE!* Who's ever gone from this level, this un-existence, this non-existence, to the clouds? To the betters?"

He scanned the room, daring anyone to claim they did.

"Exactly! We born alone. We die alone and we could drop dead at any minute. So while we're here, it only makes sense we get together and tell them nuh, they don't control our lives. They can't tell us where we headed. This our path. Chaos is our way; bedlam is our way. I'm tired of being told what to do. I know *you're* tired of being told what to do! You're tired of being picked on by Pro-Ts, lawyers, and loser parents who take their sadness out on us! Let's do whatever

27

we want, when and however we want, cuz when we pass through to that other side, ain't nobody else coming with us anyway! Not *one* of them!"

Envy smiled. The room was restless and electric. Every single set of eyes followed Kris intently, ears perked for an order, forms poised for the next move.

Kris, now silent, made eye contact with those in the front row.

"I'm walking into the room behind that door over there. After I close the door, I want ya'll to line up outside it," he said, pointing to a brown rectangular slab cut into the wall, unlike anything most of the kids had seen. "The rest of ya'll put yourselves in rows like the front. Anytime the light above the door glows, the next man in line enters. When the last man from the row in front of you enters the door, the next row moves up and so on, until we down to the last one. You got it?"

They nodded in unison.

Kris walked into the room and closed the door behind him. The first row lined up by the door as ordered.

Envy, somewhat impressed by the scene unfolding before him, looked on in admiration.

* * *

88 O.O. *(Five Years Ago)*

"What you doing briz?"

"Huh?"

"You heard me. What you looking at? What you doing?"

"I don't know what you're asking me."

Thomas Barrington Jr. took a couple of steps towards a lanky dark-haired, pimple-faced kid who didn't seem to understand breaking eye contact was in his best interest. Moments before, Tommy (Or Envy as he was better known) had taken off his boot and used it to beat another kid to a

28

heap of jumbled limbs. As Envy moved forward, the kid with the pimples sat there unmoving, stare picking up intensity.

"You must want to get stomped out, huh?" As he knocked together his tattooed knuckles he added: "Brizzes love making moves they'll regret."

"I was reading. You were loud … don't you gotta class to go flunk?" Next to the seated kid was a panel, hovering. Visible were the lines to "Life's A Bitch," by Nasir Jones.

"Oh. Poetry. Look at you, all in the classics. You sensitive, huh? Pitiful twib." Envy chuckled. He looked at the kid's neck. "Cute necklace though. I think I'll take that."

Pimples sighed the sigh of one bored with the daily parade of preparatory bullies. "Yo, you're dumb. Nas is win, EASY. If you're gonna do something then do something, but don't come here talkin' tha—"

His words were interrupted by a stout cross connecting with his jaw. Knocked to the ground from his seat, the pimply faced "pitiful twib" slowly gathered himself and stood, clearly surprised and still feeling the effects of the punch. The pitiful twib towered over his assailant and the short, wiry Envy chuckled, as this was merely a cosmetic advantage. When Pimples fell, his upper front teeth had bitten his lower lip. He wiped it with his hand and examined the blood. He remained standing, staring at Envy, saying nothing.

Envy hit him again, this time with a hook.

For a moment the kids face swung from the impact, but unlike with the first punch, he seemed unfazed. As his face returned to its starting point, bruised from the force of the punch, Pimples stared at Envy, a smile slowly spreading across his face.

"Oh, you think you're some warrior, huh?"

The boy said nothing and this time Envy punched him in the stomach, fully expecting him to fall over and remain down. Instead, Envy found himself grabbing his own fist

29

from the pain of impact. "What the … hell? You cover your stomach with concrete or something?"

As a chip-toothed grin grew wider on the pimply boy's face, he ran his hands through his ruffled coils of hair, put them in his pockets and said, "Man, I was waiting on you to take my chain. You still got your leprechaun issues to work out you little goblin or we done now?" He turned away from Envy. Incensed, Envy grabbed the boy by the scruff of his neck, ripped off the necklace, pulled out a knife and attempted to stick it clean into his side. The boy responded by grabbing the arm holding the knife and using his free arm to wriggle out of his thermcoat to wrap it around the blade. The two of them tumbled to the floor, struggling until he was able to loosen the knife from Envy's grip and slide it across the floor. The boy then lifted his elbow above Envy's chest while holding him still with his other arm and bodyweight, and came down with the full force of his upper body. Envy felt all the air leave his body at once, and frantically began flailing his arms as if by doing so he could somehow grab it and return it to his lungs. As Envy struggled, his victim turned attacker sat him up and said quietly, "Don't panic man, breathe slowly. It'll come back. Slow breaths. C'mon now, there you go. There you go. There you go. You got it." Pimples got up to get his necklace which had been thrown a few feet away during the struggle. The clasp had been snapped. He was angry, but it could be fixed.

Envy coughed a few times and spoke. He attempted his normal frenetic pace of speech but it only resulted in grunts and more coughs.

"What was that you said? I can't hear you," The pimpled boy chuckled.

"That was weak, briz," said Envy, with the hint of a smile. "And you're still a pitiful twib."

"Or," the pimple-face boy replied, "You can call me Kill."

30

* * *

93 O.O. *(Present Day)*

The entire first line had emptied into the mystery room. Only one kid, a tall, dark-skinned dreadlocked boy called Brink, had exited. As he stepped out, everyone in the room looked to his face for some sort of clue or sign as to what exactly went on in the room. They got nothing.

Brink walked over to a group of chairs to the far corner of the room where Kris had been speaking earlier and sat in the first one. He stared straight ahead making eye contact with no one, and the next row of boys quickly gathered and formed a line at the door.

* * *

90 O.O. *(3 Years Ago)*

Kris was going to be late for class again. He sped up his stride, trying to see if he could get there without exerting excessive effort or looking like he had. For a moment, he even broke into a power walk.

Shit. Not now!

He broke the toothpick in his mouth.

He felt a stabbing sensation throughout his body. It seemed like there had been an increase in these periodic waves of intense pain ever since he'd tested positive for igioyin. His symptoms and results were abnormal; Kris hadn't so much tested positive for the virus as *active,* the doctor advised. The pain and occasional bleeding were signs his body was fighting the virus, which was unheard of. When the doctor told him and his mother that Kris should have been dead long ago, Mrs. Arvelo praised it as a miracle, predictably thanking Osanyin—the god of healing—and leaving tribute for continued blessing. But Kris didn't think it was a miracle, just a slowing of the inevitable and the pain was a reminder. He tried to ignore it and kept up the pace until he got to the door.

As he coasted into instructor Bivins' classroom, interrupting the start of a lecture, all he could think about was his mother's request he make the most of his blessing and start Ron Ed on the right foot. "This is quite the note you've chosen to begin your instructional career on, child. I can see you have a bright future ahead of you. I'm thinking sanitation analyst. Or, perhaps you want to skip earning a living all together and become a caged bridesmaid." Bivins chuckled and the class followed suit. "Ah yes! I can see it ... now have a seat!"

Kris scanned the room until he saw an empty desk in the far corner of the front row by the window. He made eye contact with a familiar face in the seat behind his, smiled, shook his head, and sat.

"As I was saying prior to the intrusion," Bivins glowered at Kris. "Welcome to Ron Ed Instructional. You may think it simply a continuation of your preparatory years, but I assure you it's not. Many of you got away with quite a bit at the prep level. You'll find there's no such leeway here. You are expected to be on time to class—"

He shot another glare at Kris.

"Hand in class work and homework on time, study and excel on your exams, keep illicit behavior off the school grounds, and when off school grounds, no illicit behavior as you are all representatives of Ron Ed!"

Kris didn't know what planet this instructor came from, but from what he'd heard and seen in his days on the prep level, the instructional was worse, and far graver and illicit goings on occurred all the time. Perhaps this was a new company line. Perhaps it was always the company line. He figured he could try to stay out of trouble though. It was the least he could do for his mom. He pulled out his history panel as Bivins moved on to the lecture.

"And today we discuss how the Great Sino-Persian Conflict brought about The Nightfall War, and the geopolitical consequences and fallout, 173e9 in your panels please."

As he entered the coordinates, he felt a poke on his shoulder. Donzilana Yang, his best friend since the first grade leaned over and whispered in his ear:

"Faster, Pussycat! Kill! Kill!"

"I swear by Obatala! Donzi, I'm trying to be good this year, become something. Shut up!" He whispered.

"You should start by getting rid of that thermcoat, Kill! Kill!" She chuckled, tapping on the graphic of a busty woman with a menacing grin, dressed in all black spandex with nails out like claws, looking ready to pounce off the back of his jacket onto foes real or imagined. "You've had that thing since sixth grade. It was win then but now it's draw; let it go."

He couldn't see her, but he knew she was grinning like mad and twirling her hair. Donzi was always twirling her hair when she knew it would annoy him.

"Donzi, seriously chill—" he whispered again

"*My name* is Donzilana not Donzi; Kill, stop being a punk. You see my dad anywhere around here?"

"Since when? You never minded before."

"Since now because I feel like it—like really, *Obatala*? You don't even believe in the gods like that. Unless Carbo made you a believer over the break."

Kris snickered. "Ha-ha, yeah … like I'd ever pull up a panel to watch that *fake healer*. Every once in a while, I like to throw around the name of your false deities for entertainment value."

Donzilana gasped, "Savage! You're going to hell!"

Kris smiled. "Shango will protect me. Have you seen Shango? He wields an axe of thunder and lightning and controls FIRE. I'm good. Don't worry about me."

"You're so confusing."

Instructor Bivins hissed.

33

"Goodbye, Kris. Chancellor's. NOW!"

Kris shook his head, closed his panel and cursed Donzilana every which way under his breath, "Coño!" He strode out of the room without looking back, hands playing with his necklace, the continued needle stabs overshadowed by thoughts of how he'd disappointed his mother in record time. He turned down the hall and headed for the chancellor's office. As he entered, a familiar voice said, "What took you so long, you pitiful twib?" He shook his head and unsuccessfully tried to avoid smiling.

* * *

Present Day

Donzilana stood in the midst of the Quarters crowd with her thermcap on in a loose fitting unisuit. Her cherry wine hair was cropped short and styled plainly to avoid drawing attention. It hid well under the thermcap; she could have easily been mistaken for bald. She watched Brink take a seat. She tried not to stare at Envy. Hiding in plain sight, for once thankful her chest was easily concealed, she was one of the boys.

The next group lined up three rows in front of her, and she could feel the nervousness amongst them. She didn't blame them. After all, no one knew what was going on in that room. She asked the kid next to her to see his flyer. He obliged. Her eyes grew wide and she became as nervous as those around her.

As she scratched the thin layer of false facial hair on her chin, she distracted herself listening to the surrounding conversations. The boys argued about the best futbol player, which one of them was a greater fighter than the legendary Boom Ba-Ye and the flashiest neck panel displays. They talked about girls and what star's thermcoat they wanted. They spoke about everything except what was on their minds.

34

She found this amusing, but shifted her attention from the conversational game of keep-away to Envy, who was going through old-style reads on the bookshelf near the spot Kris had stood speaking to the boys earlier. As he held each one, studying the faded dusty covers, looking through the pages, she wondered if they truly held Envy's interest, or were mere curiosities to be satisfied as quickly as they arose. As if reading her mind, Envy stopped on a burgundy covered beauty with gold script and edges. She saw him read the wording on the back cover, open it, examine a few pages, sit with it and begin to read. Donzilana had no doubt it was the striking beauty of the read and not its content that had lured him in.

She heard a collective shuffle of feet. Amongst loud whispers, her attention was diverted back to where she stood and she noticed everyone, save for Envy, fixed upon the door. The fourth row had begun to line up as the light was now on, and they'd all noticed no one from the previous row had come out into the room to join Brink in the far corner seats. *What's happening to the others?* Her thoughts mirrored the whispers around her. Two more rows still had to go before she found out. She looked over at Envy once more. Envy was oblivious, lost in his new toy.

* * *

90 O.O. (Three Years Ago)

"Damnnnnn, who's that? Is that *Yang*?"

"Eh, you need to calm down. That's baby sis right there. And nuh, it doesn't matter that we the same age."

"Oh, look at you being all protective, briz; ha-ha, that's love. Chill, Kill! I'm just a man who likes quality, admiring from afar. Still can't believe this the first I noticed her."

"Probably cuz you liking humans is a new thing, llama licker." Kris ignored Envy's protest. "I ain't telling you stay away from her. Do what you want, but your tries will be fun for everyone except you." Kris flashed his wide chipped-tooth grin.

"You cold for no reason, briz. I should slap that expensive-ass toothpick out your mouth. In all honesty, I'm burning for *that*," Envy pointed to a seemingly door-less sleek, graphite colored vehicle with neon green headlights. It was floating inches above the glaciated street in front of the school steps.

A trumpet blared twice.

"You boys gonna waste my time zizzing around there or get in?" The trumpet blared again.

"King-side!" yelled Envy. Kris laughed, pushed him, and beating him down the steps of Ron Ed, hopped in the front seat. Envy grumbled and settled into the back.

"Thanks for the ride Donzi … lana?"

"Yeah, that's right. Cool. People always screw it up. You can call me Donzi though." She ignored Kris' look of disbelief.

"I'm Envy."

"Yeah, I know."

Envy turned to Kris, smirking. As the vehicle began its weightless glide, he turned back towards the driver:

"How you get a huv but live in the Wall? I shouldn't be in this; it's gotta be stolen. All I've ever seen out here are wheelies."

"A huv's okay, but a phrincar would be the real. Thing so fast its two places at once."

"I don't care about no phrincar, Kill. They exaggerate the speeds anyway—"

"How would *you* know?"

"Whatever, briz. Donzi, how'd you get it?"

Donzi smiled. It was clear she enjoyed the question.

"Back in the day my dad used to traze tags on anything he could get his hands on. Trains, wheelies, choppers, whatever;

if it had any type of space, it was a wall. And if it was a wall, it was a face."

"Face? I don't get it," said Envy,

"You look at a face, what you see?" Kris chimed in.

"I dunno. A face."

"Expressions, man. Whatever the person who controls that face wants you to see."

"Ehhhh … okay …" said Envy. "Whatever, go ahead."

Donzilana rolled her eyes. "*Anyway,* when these came out, they were impossible to traze, because of all the security features; the cams, the sensors, the alarms, the notification system that went straight to the owner's cles. Some had surfaces built to immediately wipe clean any markings. It was a nightmare for a trazer; it wasn't happening. It's the same thing that makes it impossible to steal." She shot Envy a disdainful glance.

"Alright, so?" Envy impatiently asked, ignoring her expression.

"Well my dad never told me how he did it. He would always say vague things like 'The clues are all around you, sweetie.' But anyway, the guy whose huv he trazed ended up being some famous art collector. Dude was so impressed he gave him one on the spot, in exchange for being able to keep the one Pops trazed. Dad never really messed around with the mainstream scene like that, but it was hilarious to him that someone would give him a new huv in exchange for being able to keep his own."

"And now it belongs to his little princess," said Envy, playfully mocking.

"Yeup, something like that," said Donzilana, turning to Kris. "Where to?"

"Willoughby and Myrtle. We gotta drop this clown off," he said, motioning to Envy. "Then I gotta go see moms for a minute and we can head to your place to study."

"You're never moving back in, huh?"

"Nah, Donzi. it's better for both of us that way. Moms will never admit it, but she knows. Plus, my spot is stupid nice!"

Envy laughed. "It's def stupid, Kill, I dunno about the nice part … it's an abandoned buildin—"

"Yeah, and it's *mine*, Envy. We all live in the Wall anyway, don't act your place is any better—*plus* you got parents hovering over you. I got freedom. I don't wanna hear you whinin' and trying to come over when you tired of havin' no privacy either—go stay in one of the deserted ones nearby with no furniture. Mines is now officially off limits!"

"Okay children, calm down—you're both doing *the most* right now." Donzi chuckled, and spent the rest of the drive casually ignoring Envy's advances ("So pops was a trazer huh … that's dope. You were his best creation though. Is that a tattoo on the back of your neck? What of? I got one on my neck too"). Twice they were stopped by Pro-Ts who claimed to have heard reports of a stolen huv and were looking into the situation. Each time, Donzilana had to demand Kris restrain himself, while she handed them spends.

* * *

Present Day

Envy found *The Forest of a Thousand Daemons* to be a rather strange but engrossing read. The world he found himself in the space of a few pages was a pleasant dream. The history panels in class during his preparatory days had spoken of a time when preservation of wildlife, trees and forests had been a reality. In the post-Nightfall War world, it was an afterthought as the remaining nations and their citizens had placed their focus on immediate survival by any means. The Forest, with its lush greenery, talking animals and mythical characters—presented a cozy alternative to his reality—the one where he was currently lying to his closest friend about the reasons for his disappearance and return. The one where he abandoned the girl who understood him. *Sorry, Donzi.* He rubbed his neck, fingers skittering over a still healing tattoo. An author from a few centuries ago knew what it was he needed at this moment. It was remarkable. As feet shuffled into the room where Kris held court and the main clubhouse space dwindled down to a couple handfuls of people, he read on.

"What you doing here?" Kris' voice was devoid of emotion. All trace of expression was absent from his face. He nibbled at his toothpick, rolled it from side to side between his lips. He sat relaxed and his surroundings were startlingly bare, the black couch from which he stared and a bookshelf nearby were its only furnishings. The room could have easily been in a different building from the one next door, as it was spotless with soft clean blue carpeting and pristine white walls. This contrasted sharply with the greater clubhouse meeting space which seemed as if someone had dropped mud walls and a roof onto a vacant lot. Kris allowed over a minute to pass without requesting an answer, and he changed nothing about his expression or stance. The combination became overwhelming for Donzilana, and she feared Kris had seen through her disguise. She began speaking to take her mind off her fear. In her voicer-modified voice, Donzilana told Kris how he'd inspired her and the other dudes out there to realize there wasn't nobody looking out for them, and whatever this was, it was at least a chance to do something for themselves.

When she was finished, Donzilana stood there, teeth chattering slightly, drops of sweat forming, breathing irregular. *Did I give the wrong answer?* Would she be shuttered away into the unknown with the mystery masses? She wondered if she'd been careless and had left clues for Kris as to her true identity. Maybe her mannerisms had given her away or maybe her attention to detail when creating her disguise hadn't been meticulous enough. *He knows. He did that flyer to draw me out and expose me.* The silence she met with in the aftermath only served to heighten her self-awareness. She summoned all the composure left in her being, making every effort to avoid a panic attack.

Kris sat there unmoved, silent as before. Then, to Donzilana's relief, he spoke again. "Laran, right?"

She nodded.

"Interesting name—how you spell that?" Donzi obliged, her voice sounding much steadier than she felt.

"Hmm."

What? What is it!? He was impossible to read.

"Cool. Aight. Turn and look at the wall to your right. Close your eyes. Imagine a place you'd love to be this moment—*the place* you'd love to be. There's no limits. Imagine you're there now. Imagine the sound of it. The smell. The colors. What else is there? Why this place? Who else is there? Don't tell me—but know why."

As Donzilana got lost in her imagination, she felt Kris open her right hand and place an object that felt like a sprezen in it.

"Hold this and keep your eyes closed. Imagine going to that place right now."

Donzilana did as she was told.

Seconds later, Kris yanked the sprezen from her hand. "Head out into the clubhouse and have a seat in the corner."

Donzilana still didn't know what this meant. She only knew she wouldn't be one of those no one out in the clubhouse knew what happened to. She opened the door and headed over to the corner seats to join three others. There was one last group of boys getting ready to line up at the door, staring at her. Though as far as they knew, she was one of them, Donzilana felt self-conscious, and had to remind herself the gawking was for a different reason than usual. She sat next to a mop-top fire-haired kid named Flick, and stared

straight ahead as he, Brink and the others did, awaiting the
end of the last procession filing into the room.

She noticed Envy out of the corner of her eye, read
clasped under his arm, strolling over to the group.

"Whatever ya'll got, it must be win. Let Kill know I'll see
him around. I'm keeping this read." Envy left in the same
fashion he'd arrived.

Donzilana's heart sank for a reason she couldn't explain,
but she remained steady. After some time, the door opened,
and only Kris walked out. He surveyed the group before him.

"Envy said to—" Donzilana began, but Kris raised his
hand and she stopped. He addressed the group.

"I know you all wanna know why I chose you. I'm sure
there's been mad guesses why we're here, why the others
weren't chosen and where they are now. We won't talk of the
others. They don't matter. You four are here cuz you're
rather unique. And you got a skill nobody can mess with.
Ya'lls minds are capable of some crazy things and that's good.
In that room, I saw the potential to really create … it's
special. Things I can't define … things beyond the walls of
intelligence. The energy coming from your imaginations is
pure and captivating."

He took in their blank expressions.

"Ya'll don't know what the hell I'm talking about, huh.
Okay, watch." He singled out a short, skinny cedar-skinned
kid with freckles, dreadlocks and a bookish demeanor.
"Trevin, close your eyes. Everyone else keep yours open.
Trev, imagine this room, every detail of it. Where I'm
standing right now. What I'm doing."

Kris produced a sprezen and tossed it to Trevin, who
caught it without opening his eyes. "Trevin, you remember
what I asked you to do when you were in the other room?"

"Yeah."

"Okay, repeat that. And keep your eyes closed."

Trevin stood with the sprezen in his hand and held it out
in front of him. The sprezen began glowing, taking on an

orange reddish hue. Donzilana let out a small gasp. The others leaned forward as if it would make what they were seeing more believable. Trevin pressed on the valve and made a motion in the form of a square. Particles from the sprezen began grouping themselves together as if alive and soon there was a panel in front of Trevin showing a three-dimensional moving image of a futbol match taking place from the vantage point of an empty stadium hallway. By the colors of the unis as well as a few flags present, it appeared to be in the Southern Icelands. There was a collective groan, the letdown evident.

"It's a motion panel ... that's it. You brought us here to check out some new motion panel thing? C'mon briz...." The one called Flick said this as he got up to leave.

Kris laughed. "Walk out and miss it, Flick, and never come around again. That's a choice you're free to make, but you'll miss out, and trust me, you don't want to." Flick stopped, sat and Kris replaced a toothpick. "Okay Trev, now."

The panel widened and lengthened until it was the size of a doorway. It was now glowing and resembled a tunnel.

"Open your eyes."

Donzilana watched Trevin's total bewilderment at what was in front of him.

"I don—I don't get it," he stammered.

"It's a phrinway."

"How?!"

"Trev, I need you to trust me. Step into it. It leads exactly where you think it does. This is your test right here. This tells me whether you belong with us. You got my loyalty if you do this; don't moog out. I'll guide you through, alright briz? I got you."

Trevin slowly nodded.

"Then let's go!"

Trevin nervously tiptoed through the phrinway, sprezen in hand no longer glowing.

"You got it, Trev, keep moving."

Once he was all the way through, it closed after him and he was gone. There wasn't a trace left behind of him. Donzilana felt sick. *What did you do, Kris?* All the time she'd known him—he could be mischievous, but he was never ever sinister. *But this* ... Donzilana couldn't help but feel something quite scary was happening. People weren't supposed to move through phrinways. Vehicles were built, *with protections*, specifically for such movement. How would he come back? *Could* he? Was that what had happened to the kids who hadn't made the cut? No one spoke or moved, likely for fear of contributing to some upset in the balance of the universe. Chaos was good and well when they were kids in a clubhouse listening to an entertaining leader; it was quite a different thing when the uncertainty of it slapped them in the face.

Right as the group's uneasiness was increasing, the phrinway reopened, and Trevin came charging back through, sprezen in his pocket, Southern Icelanden flags in tow, futbol at his feet. "Ballgame!" He exclaimed, laughing. He looked at ease.

Donzilana relaxed. Brink, the massive teen who was first out of the secret room, let out a cry of astonishment. They all looked at Flick, who watched unmoved, ignoring their attention. "That's impossible," he said.

"What makes it impossible, Flick?" Donzi wondered if Kris *ever* talked without a smirk in his tone.

"First off, we're supposed to believe that Trevin—*a human*, not a phrincar, not a phrinjet, not a phrincopter—can open phrinways? Without any of the tech? And on top of that bullshit, you want us to believe Trevin here, went to the Southern Icelands—a couple thousand miles away—and came back in a matter of minutes? When phrincars, jets and copters can only jump miles at a time? C'mon briz."

Kris laughed. "Yeah, better believe it—you'll be doing it soon too."

"Doubtful."

Kris, having solidified both awe and trust (in those not named Flick) with the return of Trevin, and smiling wide as ever, moved forward. "Laran, come on," he said as he motioned Donzilana forward. "Yours is gonna be a little different from Trev's." Donzilana strode up betraying none of the nervousness she was feeling. Each second she stayed in disguise she felt as if everyone, especially Kris, was closer to seeing through it, or worse; they'd already seen through it and were screwing with her. *Oh well, too late now anyway.*

"Sprezens."

"Huh?"

"Laran, there's sprezens in front of you. Pay attention or you're out. We'll get someone else."

Donzilana, back to reality, standing side-by-side with Kris, looked to the ground in front of her and saw two sprezens at her feet. One was blue, her favorite color; the other was green, her second favorite color, but that had to be coincidental. She held her mini panic at bay.

"Close your eyes. Clear your mind." Seconds of silence passed. "Remember where the sprezens are. Imagine the one you want. Reach out, but don't move from where you are. Imagine the one you've chosen coming to you. Imagine it in your hands."

Suddenly, Donzilana felt the cold metal in her hand as if pulled by some invisible force and was amazed, though not surprised. After having witnessed Trevin, plenty seemed possible. She heard laughter and a "Do you think he possibly could have bought it, that trickery?" from what sounded like Trevin. She opened her eyes and saw Kris grinning, his hand still on the sprezen as it had been moments ago, when he placed it in hers. "I know you saw Trevin do some special shit but we're not wizards . . . ha-ha. Close your eyes again."

Asshole. She closed her eyes.

"Let go of your embarrassment. Clear your mind. Think of a time you were terrified, when your life was in danger, or

44

you were scared of something happening. Remember that
fear. It's a terrible, horrible feeling but let it take hold. Let it
wash over you." Donzilana's hands shook, a few beads of
sweat took a trip down her forehead. She tried to steady her
hands with marginal success. "The sprezen in your hand,
spray it, NOW!"

Donzilana jumped slightly and what she did next was
more out of reflex than the following of an order. She felt her
index finger pressing down on the sprezen with surprising
strength; at one point she thought she might break it.
Suddenly she stopped, eyes still closed.

"Why'd you stop?"

"I dunno."

That was a lie. She'd stopped because all her fear of
moments before had left her. Relieved, she'd returned to
being curious about where this was all going and what tricks
this magic peddling friend of hers was up t—

"CLANG!" Donzilana was startled by what had to be a
large piece of metal dropping near her. She opened her eyes
and was confused by the applause and laughter and exhales as
Kris asked her to put the sprezen down.

Around her was a thin, translucent blue bubble at least a
foot taller than her and a couple feet wider around. On the
ground in front of her was a bent crowbar, nearly snapped in
two. As she pieced together what happened she became
infuriated with Kris. It took everything she had not to lunge
at him and start yelling intimate obscenities from their
childhood roughhousing days. Instead she said, "You lunatic!
You could have killed me," while picking up the blue sprezen
again and stepping towards Kris menacingly. The bubble
disappeared. The sprezen glowed. "I don't know who you
think you are, but that's sick. I'm done." Donzilana tossed the
sprezen and walked away.

"Hey, Laran! You don't want to know how I knew I
wouldn't hurt you?"

Donzilana stopped. "I don't believe you knew. I think these are guesses to you, and you're high-key surprised as we are to see the results."

The amusement that had been a constant in Kris' voice was gone. In its place was stern condescension. "I *specifically* had you remember the feeling of being scared." Kris turned to the rest of the group. "You're smart. Why'd I tell Laran that?"

"Adrenaline, why else?" Flick barely waited for Kris' question to finish before he replied.

Kris chuckled. "That was quick, briz. Almost sounds like you believe in me—go on though."

"When you remember trauma or something scary, your senses can't tell the difference between your memory and the real thing. You relive it. You get sweaty, your heart rate goes up, natural body defenses kick in."

"Damn Flick, you a genius! I'm glad you didn't leave. Laran, I waited for that bubble around you to form. I touched it to make sure its composition was right. Some of you—all of you are gonna have to start trusting me. Otherwise why'd ya'll come here? I know what I'm looking for—it's something unique, special … wonderful. Ya'll got some oyas, briz. Real oyas. I found 'em in each one of you."

Oyas. Donzi thought it was interesting Kris was using the Yoruba term that had come to mean gifts, or power. Not *ebun* which literally meant gift, or *agbara*—which quite literally meant power or strength—but *oya(s)*—which came from a form of tribute to Oya, the Yoruba goddess of wind and storms. While a relatively common term, it could be damn near superstitious—occult and the Kris who laughed at the gods at every opportunity didn't have to use it. So why? Did he see some sort of divine blessing in what they could do?

"And together we gonna do great, fun things. Lovely, scary things. But ya'll gotta trust me. You gotta trust me with your lives. Cuz last I looked there's not another person out there, who truly gave a damn about any of us. Flick, when we

46

were in the room, I asked you why you came here. What'd you tell me? It's okay; we're all fam. No secrets between us."

The last bit of Flick's hesitance dissipated. "I'm tired. I told you I'm tired of being picked on. I wanna be able to get up and come to school without always getting that sick feeling in my stomach. Without using viz just to get through the week. Half the time I can't eat, I lose focus, have problems with my gra—"

"Maybe if you weren't such a twib, people wouldn't bug you though," Brink said, snickering. The rest joined in the laughter, save for Donzilana.

Kris descended upon Brink, grabbing him by the neck and shouted "I DON'T WANT TO HEAR YOU SAY THAT AGAIN. YOU UNDERSTAND ME?"

Brink stopped laughing and nodded. Kris released him.

"Look, in case none of ya'll knew, everyone here's a trazer. A couple a ya'lls work I'm actually familiar with—that's why I decorated the flyers with it—but that's only part of why I picked you. We come here to be safe and watch out for each other—be a family. If anyone here feels you can't do that for every person in this room, leave now."

Kris waited a few minutes. Nobody moved.

"Okay. Then everyone here is *in*. Trust, loyalty, *love*. The last will come with time after the other two, but I love y'all already, for real. Support each other, watch out for each other, tease each other sometimes, but we don't diss each other. We'll explore the beauty of turning things upside down. We'll get out of this universe everything they told us was out of reach. We'll use our oyas—a word they used for a goddess but we don't recognize that. We only recognize the havoc of the storms it wreaks and we harness that. Our oyas are chaos and we'll use 'em to get the things they told us were within reach if we only bought into their lies. And we'll do it the way they told us it couldn't be done."

The last of Donzilana's anger left, as she realized Kris was exactly who she'd thought he was, and she felt a sense of pride. She returned to her seat, faith restored in the friend she'd put her trust in for so many years.

TRIAL RUN

Present Day

DONZILANA CLIMBED OUT of her bed around midnight. She'd been asleep since she got home from school. She tucked away her short hair, affixed hair strips to her face and the area above her top lip for a convincing scruff, applied skin shade and attached her voicer to the back corner of her mouth. She smiled while saying "Laran, perfidious prince of the paupers!" and adjusted it until it matched the appropriate deep setting. Then she flexed her biceps and laughed. Since the gathering, she'd found herself even more upbeat and energetic than usual.

Kris had caught her smiling off into space during lunch some time ago and gotten suspicious, asking if she'd met a new guy or girl. "Yeah," she giggled, and then he was asking her questions about this new guy or girl he knew she wouldn't answer. "Shut up, Kill." She smiled and went back to inhaling her food.

"Whoever it is, I hope things turn out better than they did with Envy ... waaaaaaaaaait ... is that what it is? You know he's back right?! You two catch u—"

"Shut it!"

She was glad he had no idea she'd been at the Quarters clubhouse meeting playing dress-up, and after a while he stopped bugging her altogether. She was thankful for this, knowing Kris would never have allowed her to join them, and would've instead given her a million weak excuses about how dangerous it was.

School in the days since the meeting had been nothing short of a revelation. She kept running into the "other guys" from their little gang, guys she'd never noticed before, guys she'd never previously been aware of. Guys like Flick and

49

Trevin, as it turned out, she had classes with. She caught herself smiling at Trevin without realizing what she was doing, and made a better effort to avoid doing it again in case he got the wrong idea, although he was cute in his own bookish, clumsy way. She did, however, feel the joy of knowing they all shared a secret (although it came by way of the secret she kept from them) and it made her giddy—this no effort could hide. Kris had called them the "Kids of Stolen Tomorrow" or KoST, and she dug it. It was dramatic, but it was what they'd wanted it to be.

She smiled to herself and ordered her panel to play music, dancing as she got ready. She lived alone—no mom or dad to wake up as she fully transformed into Laran. She strolled out the door, bopping where peers would normally tiptoe. As she descended the stairwell outside the apartment, she didn't even attempt to avoid eye contact with a few lifters gathered at the base.

"Vision?" A lanky one with rotted teeth, sunken eyelids and razor marks on each cheek spat out. It was a command posed as a question.

"Nuh I'm good," she replied, and pushed her way past the lifter—who'd clearly been abusing his own supply—and the rest of his crew.

They laughed as Donzilana disguised as Laran made her way out the door of the building, and the lanky one called out, "You know you need the viz! You'll wish you'd chosen the escape. They always do. Midnight is eternal in these vanes of the unforgiven!"

Donzi felt a chill as she stormed into the twilight shadows, ashen terrain crunching beneath her Laran trod. She knew it wasn't from the temperature, but she turned the heat higher on her thermer anyway and kept moving. As she weaved through neighborhood after neighborhood, she was reminded as always that late night was the ultimate adventure, though adrenaline junkies were smarter taking on one with a more favorable survival rate, like jumping from a phrinjet

without a parachute. Amongst the night perils were whispers
of Nthns who snatched red vane kids up never to be seen
again, save as corpses. She suffered no such fate and made it
to the clubhouse relatively unscathed. Kris was putting items
into a backpack while Brink and Flick were taking turns
throwing things at each other's protective bubbles.

"Laran, glad you could make it. Waiting on Trevin and we
out," Kris said as he looked up.

Donzi nodded and adjusted her pack.

"Masks and packs only—leave your thermcoats." The
kids exchanged baffled looks. "You'll get it soon enough briz,
no questions." They shed the thermcoats. He had them shed
their boots as well and provided each of them with lighter
footwear, increasing the puzzlement. "Damn, Laran I thought
I was seeing things at first but you really got some tiny feet.
Shopping for kicks must be a relief huh? Probably still get
kiddie prices…." They laughed as he handed Donzi her
replacements, still confused, but relaxed. "I know ya'll scrap
and scrounge before you head to Spike's Joint to cop your
sprezens. Some a ya'll hit up Rob's Emporium. And they
hook us up and that's win, but I know a blue vane spot where
we can load up for zero and they won't notice. After that,
we're gonna eat like kings … swooping the finest dishes."
Kris smiled. Everyone looked at each other wondering what
was next. "For now, we only go through the phrinways I
draw. It's the safest way to keep us together, plus I'm the only
one who knows tower blind spots. Ya'll ready?" He tossed a
backpack to each of the Kids of Stolen Tomorrow. They
reached into their packs and put on their masks and they
were off.

Donzilana, flanked by Brink and Flick, followed Kris
through the first phrinway. Trevin was close behind. When
they came out on the other side, they were underground
somewhere in front of a metal ladder mounted into a stone
wall. They shivered.

Great plan taking away the thermcoats, Kill. Donzilana, crossing her arms, looked down and noticed she was standing on railroad tracks which now led nowhere, clearly a remnant of the old subway system that once breathed life into the city.

Looking at her, Kris smiled. "Chilly huh, Laran? We gonna do a lot of moving around the city from here—get used to it. Some places are better for opening phrinways than others, and this might be the best place in the city for it. It's more useful to us now than it was to those old deads before us." He climbed up the ladder, stopped on the fourth rung and climbed back down, pulled a can out of his backpack and trazed on the wall next to the ladder "Pu$$ycat KILL!" followed by "KoST." He turned to the others and told them to traze their tags.

Brink and Flick stayed the same, but Trevin became "Tre Traps" and Laran became "Larceny 81." They all traced over and added flourishes to Kris' "KoST" which was still glowing and grew brighter with each tag. Feeling pleased with themselves, they looked to Kris, who was already halfway back up the ladder.

"Let's show the world what we got!" He called back to them as they scampered up behind him. As he neared the top of the ladder, Kris pulled out his sprezen again and drew a circular window on the roof of the tunnel to see through the ground above. As a soft light shone through, he previewed the premises and called back to the crew "Yup! We in the right place." He erased the window and in the once again dim light he waited, looking around the roof of the tunnel as the others caught up. In the place of the window he'd erased, he drew a phrinway. "When you get to the top, if you need help coming through, reach your arm through the phrinway and I'll pull you up! Except you, Brink. You're too heavy. Climb all the way through."

They followed him through into a warehouse containing an assortment of paints and shelves upon shelves of spray paint alone.

Kris chuckled at the collective "Whoa," of the gang.

"That's cute guys, I'm touched—but fill your packs with the sprezens and let's get the hell outta here—doesn't matter the color."

Following his lead, they grabbed as many sprezens as possible—filling their bags to the brim, and made their escape. Back in the subway they emptied out the packs, sending the sprezens through a phrinway Kris opened to a storage closet in the Quarters. Seemingly pleased, he closed the gate and walked back towards the ladder, climbing it once again. Opening another phrinway as he neared the top he said, "You ready to swoop in style? Follow me." It was an unnecessary command.

Trevin, followed by Donzilana, Flick and Brink, climbed through the phrinway and found themselves in the empty kitchen of a closed Mike's Diner. "No way," Flick said. "There's always a line to get in this place. You don't get in here unless you're a big-time lifter or a politician. You gotta have spends on disc to step in here . . . man wait til I tell my boys they'll never beli—" Kris shot Flick a look implying he wouldn't be telling his boys a thing. Flick nodded, and went back to appreciating his surroundings. Mike's was the only place in the red vanes with meals that looked like the movie food in the panels.

Kris had often heard—they'd all heard, it tasted like the food before Nightfall, long before their time. He wondered why people always wanted things that were no longer around, as he looked at the astonished faces before him and smiled. "You're welcome. There won't be anyone here for a few more hours, but they have a yeller, so swipe what you want to swoop and let's be out before they try to catch us! We got a couple minutes."

They ran through the cabinets, the refrigerators, the freezers and grabbed every bite they could lay their hands on—chicken, salmon, potato slices, Southern Icelanden meat patties, pastries—and tossed them into their packs. "Brink what are you doing?" Donzilana asked with a snicker. Brink was currently attempting to fit three packs worth of vegetables into his one.

"Sheeitttt, Brink," Flick said, toothy grin on his face. "You think there's a phrinway at the bottom of your bag or somethin'?" Brink ignored them but eventually gave up and closed his pack.

Kris opened a new phrinway as the alarm in the restaurant went off. "Let's get outta here."

"Wait, hol' up!" Brink quickly trazed "KoST because you owe US!" on the wall by the oven and ran after the others through the phrinway, packs securely on their backs. They found themselves back underground on a platform in a different part of the old subway system.

"Good job back there, Brink, real slick, that was win," Kris said as he took his pack and mask off and walked to a massive dining table a few yards away from them on the platform under a faded, moldy sign which read "Atlan Av Barc a Cen." The table and the seats were pristine, unlike the surroundings. Kris unpacked the contents of his haul on the table, and after unmasking, everyone else followed suit.

They ate ravenously, devouring the foods as if they hadn't eaten in ages. In a way, they hadn't; the food their families could afford was abundant precisely because it was low quality and rarely, if ever, filling. Donzilana, full, stopped midway through a turkey leg and put it down on her plate, watching the others.

"What up Laran?" Kris asked.

"Nothing, but now everything else is gonna taste shitty."

Kris laughed. "Like it didn't already. I guess we gotta keep grabbing this whenever we're hungry then. Swipe to swoop." It was hard to tell whether or not he was joking. As the gang finished eating, Kris pulled up a map of the vane on a panel, circled a spot and closed it. He smiled. "We're about to do something crazy tonight. You gotta be brave for this one. If you're scared, if you're not built like that and you don't want no part it's cool; you can go home and we never speak again—we never gotta so much as look at each other. But if you choose to go with me tonight, to share in our adventures and our journey, we bonded for life. We watch out for each other when things get—"

He coughed hard and wiped something off the back of his hand. Laran looked alarmed.

"Ain't nothing but a little cold, relax. But yeah, see? We watch out for each other when it gets rough and we'll never let anyone suffer alone. We go through the highs and the lows together as a family, and we may not always get along but we'll always be there for each other, alrigh'?" He looked at each one of them, stood and opened up a phrinway. "Whoever wants to leave, feel free," he pointed to the opening. "This phrinway will take you outside the Quarters, you can head home from there." He waited as everyone looked around at each other.

One minute passed before Flick spoke up. "No one's leaving."

Kris, after seeing the nods of agreement, closed the phrinway to the Quarters and opened another. The group put their masks back on, a couple leaving some of the contents of their packs, as well as reluctant leftovers on the table as an offering to the god *Eshu*, at Laran's suggestion. Kris did not acquiesce to this and said with a smirk, "I know no gods but havoc and disorder, but you can be foolish if you want, briz."

They ran through the phrinway and came to a wall in a place with air so clean and clear, they momentarily had difficulty breathing. They were stunned at the solid ground that did not crunch, but rather, pattered. Donzi felt overdressed in the warmth, as did the others, judging by the loosening of their clothes. Kris, bemused, said, "I can see ya'll never been outside the Wall before. Redrats no more—you're welcome." The area was well lit, but they found themselves in a shadowed corner, one of the "blind spots" chosen by Kris. "Okay briz we don't have much time, let's get to work!"

They proceeded to splash the wall. Laran drew a smiling skull-and-crossbones on top of a man's body with middle fingers extended. Kris drew two hunched over trees with the branches withering and leaves turning into dollar signs as they fell down a black hole. Trevin kept trazing "Trev Traps" tags all over the wall, Flick trazed "Because Never" and Brink trazed "KoST Because You Took, KoST Because You Never Cared, KoST Because You Owe Us." Their splashes and tags glowed in a variety of different colors, resembling moving lights captured in a freeze frame against the wall.

"Time's up!" Kris yelled, as Laran was putting the finishing touches on a piece. A hole opened in the wall, over the piece and Donzilana felt herself being pushed through, tumbling to the other side of the phrinway, ending up back on the platform beneath a heap of the rest of the gang.

"Anybody wanna say what just happened?" It was Brink, who was presumably higher up in the heap than Donzilana and could both breathe and speak.

"When you get off me!" It was a muffled reply from Flick as they sorted themselves out.

Kris, who was clearly never in the pile, said, "I saw Pro-Ts coming around the corner from the distance. Couldn't tell if they were for us but we can't take that chance in a blue vane so I pushed everybody through. It would have been a matter of time before the towers caught on to us anyway."

"I hate towers, briz," said Flick. "They're always watching everything, following us around always in our business."

"Ha-ha shut up, Flick, they don't give a crid about your life. You don't even notice they're there. I know I don't," said Donzi, barely stifling a cough as she readjusted to the poor air quality.

"Psshh! Yeah you do. But you don't pay attention because you don't think you can do anything about it."

"*Oh,* like *you* can do something about it, Flick? That's funny."

"Probably. We can jump through phrinways—"

56

"Yeah, and that's win but there's a difference between Kill rounding us up to steal restaurant food and whatever it is you're suggest—"

"I should be offended, Laran! You cast me as a common thief?" Kris interjected, bemused look on his face. "What you thinking, Flick?"

"Maybe we traze the watchers? Blot out their eyes, show them what's what?"

Brink nodded. "Exactly."

Donzi shook her head. "Bad idea, briz. No good can come of that."

"Uhhh, I don't know, Laran," Trevin weighed in. "I think we should at least traze *one*. It's a tower! Something no crew's ever done, right? Plus, Kill keeps saying we special … and we are right? And it's not *that* dangerous. It is certain we could escape unscathed from the premises in the immediate aftermath, correct?"

"Ha-ha Trev with that—I have no idea what you're talking, briz! I never know when you're gonna go full professor on us but eh, I think Laran's right. A few cookies from the jar without getting your hands smacked, and suddenly you're planning missions? Slow down kids, slow down. Trazing *a tower*?" He snickered. "You're not ready for the pressure that comes with trying to pull that off. May as well run up into the Ministry and start slapping everybody. And I mean … why would we wanna do that?" A smile spread slowly across his face.

Donzilana knew that look. They'd be trazing a tower tonight.

Kris made eye contact with Donzilana and smiled in a manner that made her again fear he knew who she was, but he simply donned his mask, drew a phrinway and said, "You wanna mess around with history, huh? Alrigh'. Watch a pro do it first," before jumping in. They tried to follow but each one of them bounced off the phrinway entrance as if it were Laran's force field from earlier.

"Now what the hell?" said Flick, clearly exasperated. The opening expanded and took on the shape of a large panel. Soon they could see Kris in front of Brouder Tower beginning to work as they helplessly watched events unfold, reduced to moviegoers. "Damn. He picked Brouder? Pro-Ts are gonna come after him hard."

"Yeah well, that's *your* fault, Flick." To Donzi this was *infinitely worse* than Flick's idea. At least as a group they could have looked out for one another. Her fear for Kris' safety grew as each moment passed.

Kris trazed hunched trees over a hole, leaves plummeting, with the line "Spends all day but it all falls down." He trazed "Pu$$ycat Kill! Kill!" followed by "Trev Traps—Professor," "Larry Larceny" and "Buffalo Soldier on the Brink." He wrote "What Flick Dares, Beware" at the base. He concluded by spraying at the top of the piece "You never gave a CRID, so WE NEVER DID. KoST Because You Owe US."

"Beautiful ain't it?" Donzilana was surprised to hear the voice of arrogant amusement next to her, half expecting to still see Kris in the panel.

"That was weak, Kill. We coulda gone too."

"I don't wanna take that risk yet, Flick. We got a lot of big things to do together. Don't need ya'll getting snatched by the Pro-Ts this early in the game. Don't worry, briz, I got you."

Donzilana, still angered by Kris' audacity was about to address it, but was distracted by what she saw on the panel. "The tags are still glowing," she said. "Do they always do that? Glow after we've left?"

Kris looked at the panel. "Oh yeah ... I see ... not usually for too long, they tend to stop glowing within a few minutes though they still have a little um ... sparkle left afterwards, I guess?"

"Luminescence," said Trevin.

"Right on time, professor," chuckled Kris.

58

"No but look though, it's still glowing; it's getting brighter," said Flick, having forgotten his annoyance of moments ago. The letters and pictures were beginning to not only grow brighter, but they seemed to be getting larger as well—until they formed a coat, covering the entire tower. Everyone was glued to the screen, unsure of what was to follow. The coat turned to tags once more, the tags returned to normal size, dimmed, and there was nothing more to see.

"Damn. I guess that's why we never see tags on towers. What a waste."

"Laran you kidding me? We do this for the thrill of it. Never forget that." Kris closed the panel and turned to the group. "We'll leave our packs down here. This is our real base, the abandoned unwatched, untouched blood vessel of our city. The Quarters are the Quarters, but this is home." Flick raised his hand. "And no, we can't take the leftover food back with us; we gotta be smart about things. Don't need people who normally don't give a crid asking questions about where we got it." Flick put his hand down. Kris drew a phrinway back to the Quarters. Before jumping through, he turned back to address Trevin. "Hey Trev, when we get to the Quarters, hang back. I wanna talk to you about somethin'." Trevin nodded and Kris jumped through. They hopped in after him, and save for Kris and Trevin, everyone returned home.

Donzilana lay awake in bed glad she told Kris ahead of time she'd be missing school to get an early start on the weekend and visit her cousin. The last thing she needed was him coming by later. It was just before the break of dawn when she got home, and she'd need a lot of time to absorb what she experienced overnight. She smiled, exhilarated by both the fear she felt earlier, and the sense she *was doing something*. This was so much more than her sporadic solo runs. She couldn't help but feel she'd made a leap towards

59

becoming like her dad. Even if she wasn't the great trazer he was, even if this was a little different and something he never would've wanted for her, she could feel closer to him through the KoST. It was as if he was still alive and guiding her each step of the way.

69 O.O.

"I-2437 PANEL LOG entry. All previous statements and IDs fully confirmed, current and applicable. Today's date is Sunday, January 15, 69 O.O. The time is 1411 hours, Central Union Base Time. Updating progress on Program Irunmole. After introducing the antibodies of a high-usage extranormal—the only of her kind who never—for at least several years—developed igioyin symptoms, there have been some promising findings over the last four-hundred and sixty-seven sessions. Myself and Dr. Ali ... we've made significant progress on the purification process. Of 368 mutating strains, 22 have been combated effectively. Additionally, we have observed residual effect in the aftermath of treatment: Some of the other strains become dormant in the human body upon the neutralization of the 22, at least 7 additional thus far. It appears the host recognizes what's occurred and triggers immunoprotective response. While the other active strains eventually overwhelm the immune system and the subject's body shuts down, this is a significant result, one we can build upon. Potential is shown for daily administration as a possible long-term solution. Further research necessary. The time is now 1413 hours on Sunday, January 15, 69 O.O.; this log is complete."

THE PLACE

Date Unknown

THE BOY SAT still on the edge of the pond as he had done many times before and closed his eyes. It was a noisy afternoon. Sometimes it was like that, or started like that at least. Entering a trance, he projected himself to the center of the clear blue pond as the sounds—the birds chirping, gnats, bees, and all sorts of other insects buzzing, whirring, whizzing, and squirrels rustling—faded away. It was him and the water now. Here he could be alone, think.

His thoughts turned to Mom and Dad. They yelled a lot at each other that week, and he tried to help but Daddy would always tell him to "go away, not now, mi pequeño mundo," and Mommy would always cry. It made him sad to see her that way, and he always asked her what was wrong whenever she was like that, but she would shake her head, say nothing, and keep crying. So he'd hug her until he couldn't anymore, until he fell asleep with his arms around her and would wake up later, alone in his room, holding on to his teddy bear instead. It made him sad. He didn't want to think about them anymore.

He wanted to think about being happy. Here he could think about the cool stillness of the water. The sun patted him gently on the back as he sat quietly in the center of the pond, a tacit approval of his quest for peace. He sat, unmoving, until he was aware of only himself and his thoughts, and then only his thoughts. When he opened his eyes, he was in the grass at the edge of the pond and looked out across the pond and saw himself still sitting there, in a raft at the center of it, tranquil and undisturbed. He got up as he did each time, shook the branches and grass out of his clothing, and began to wander through the forest.

$* * *$

Present Day

Dara stared at the mural for what felt like hours. She wasn't sure the idea she began with made much sense to her now. *But it's not about making sense to you. It's about what makes sense for them.* Besides, she was already halfway through it. Starting over would require either a different location or wiping over her work thus far. Both things took extra time and resources; they weren't happening.

She'd already had an uphill battle to be the muralist this year, upon being voted by her classmates, due to Instructor Bivins telling Chancellor Francis "She's subversive. I can think of many others better suited for the honor." Only after multiple firm lectures and promises made to the administration was she allowed to accept the role for which she was chosen by her peers.

Now she stood, oils in one hand, wondering why they needed to see trees or the sun or flowers, and other scarce things. Why hadn't she drawn the ravages of famine? Or the pain of loss brought on by war? Or the doomed so commonplace people hardly reacted to them? These were things familiar to her class; things they could relate to more than this impossible dream she was creating for them. *Because this was what they wanted,* she said to herself. If they were anything like her, left to their thoughts and desires, the kids of Todirb Wall yearned for the real thing. They wanted to feel the sun wake them with its warmth, not read about it and wonder or hear about others' brief encounters with it in the clouds. They wanted to sit in the trees and watch foxes hunt down rabbits, or see a deer escape a cougar. They wanted the things their world would never give them, with its endless grey days under red vane skies. They wanted the things they'd read about; the past they'd studied; the present taken away from them when their ancestors chose not to care. They didn't need a rabble-rouser. They needed a messenger of beauty and of innocence lost. They needed a glimpse at paradise. Reminding herself of this, she was once again inspired, but she still didn't know where to resume.

* * *

Sometimes, the sun could be harsh, but that was why the boy liked walking in the wood. The trees were always his shield whenever his warm friend El Sol got to be a little rude. The grass and dirt beneath his feet yielded presents. Slingshots! Bows! He had a little backpack with him, typically filled with his toys when he was at home, but out here he needed the space for everything the woods gave him. He picked up Y shaped twigs for slingshots, straight sticks for arrows, and pretty little blue crystal fragments that sometimes served as arrowheads and put them all in his little pack. As he was bending down to pick up a sturdy curved stick for a would-be bow, he heard a rustling ahead of him and looked up. "Hey squirrel," he said, quite happily to a gold colored creature with a bushy, green striped tail. "Señor Squirrel, no se escapan, por favor. Regrese! Come back!" The boy dropped his bag and began chasing after the squirrel. As the squirrel scurried up the nearest tree, the boy followed, climbing as if he had paws with claws for hands and hooks for toes. "Señor Squirrel! I see you." He did, but the squirrel, too fast for him, leapt to another tree and scampered away. The boy, now slightly winded, though not at all tired, sat on the branch he'd been standing on and decided to enjoy the view, until he saw her: someone else in *his* place where he came to be alone! He was angry. He climbed down to tell her to go away because this was his!

* * *

Present Day

"You shouldn't stare. It's impolite."

"That refers to people not objects, and certainly not paintings. I could say the same for you, and mean it correctly." Dara said this nonchalantly without turning to look at the boy who dared try to break her concentration.

"How would you know, when you're trying so hard not to look at me?"

"You're funny. No, wait … you might take that the wrong way—you're annoying. As you can see I'm working and would like not to be bothered. Besides, shouldn't you be out roaming the streets making your life and everyone else's miserable?"

"I don't know why you'd assume I'm the type to do such a thing."

"You go here; you all are."

"Sooo you mean we? Or do you not count?" He said this with a hint of a smirk in his voice.

"No, I mean *you*; the guys who go to this school, who are here on the weekend because they were obviously in detention otherwise they wouldn't be here at all; meaning for two or three hours a store was saved from being robbed, or someone's property was stopped from being vandalized, or someone made it home with his wallet and all its contents and praised Olorun or Shango as soon as he got home, so grateful for his stroke of luck, that *you* were forced to be here today."

The smirk in Kris' voice turned to a smile. "I don't see the big deal with me stopping to say hello. I really don't. I was on the way out when the mural caught my eye. I'm here to observe and enjoy a delightful painting; that's all. You ain't gotta be all rude and ignorant, girl; it hurts."

"Surrrre it does. Please leave. Go rob, steal or destroy, or don't. Go disturb anyone but me."

65

"As you wish, Miss," Kris said. "But answer me this: you really think you doing a good job of hiding that glow?"

Dara's hands froze as she looked at Kris for the first time.

* * *

The girl wondered who the boy in the tree was and why he was yelling, and what he was yelling, but she didn't let it bother her. She'd become used to surprising and odd new things happening each time she had this dream, what was a new person? She ignored him and ran to the cave in the opposite direction of the tree with the crazy boy. She'd begun to explore it the last time this dream occurred, but something distracted her, woke her up. She'd have plenty of time to look this time around; she'd just fallen asleep. She thought she heard footsteps behind her, but they quickly faded away as she picked up speed and got nearer to the cave.

As she got closer she saw someone waiting for her at the entrance, but she was too far to make out the person's features yet. Was it the boy from the tree? How'd he get ahead that fast? When? The person quickly disappeared into the cave as she got closer. "Wait! Wait!" She ran faster. She was out of breath by the time she got to the entrance, but she regained form and ran in, calling after the mysterious figure. "Who are you? Wait!" The chamber was surprisingly well lit for a cave and the light seemed to come from everywhere and nowhere. There were no torches on the walls and there were no other openings save the entrance, but there was a perpetual ethereal blue-white glow distributed evenly throughout, as if the cave possessed an internal halo or inverted aura. The girl saw a flash of the figure again and heard a shrill laughter (a little girl's laughter?) as the figure ran down a flight of stairs. She pursued the figure down a series of winding staircases and through a tunnel which had to be far beneath the cave's entrance until she cornered the

cloaked, hooded figure against a dead end. Tired and out of
breath, she said exhaustedly "Who are you?"

There was the loud playful laughter again, then the figure
pulled back its hood and Dara found herself facing her mirror
image.

* * *

Present Day

"Oluwadara, I'm guessing? I'm Kris—Arvelo. You mind
if I call you Dara?" he said, extending his hand while smiling
and looking directly into her eyes. "I'm sure you heard all
great things about me, and I ain't trying to ruin your
impression, robberies and all."

She *had* heard a few things about him; everyone had. His
family used to live in the clouds some years ago but then
something happened and now he lived in Todirb Wall.
Elewon. Elewon was what Dara's father called the rare, cursed
cases who fell from the grace of the clouds into the red vane
slums. It meant prisoner in his native language of Yoruba.
Besides that, Kris was unremarkable; he mostly tended to get
in trouble for arguments with teachers and clashes with the
administration. A lot of fighting, stealing. All in all, typical
Ron Ed stuff.

His eyes though … they shook her. They were intense:
black bayonets that opened her up and made her feel as if she
couldn't hide anything anywhere, not with him around. Laid
bare in front of him, she was simultaneously drawn in and
uncomfortable. On the copper skin of his cheek, he had a
narrow cut running down to the corner of his lip. His lips …

Nope.

She decided they were stupid lips. His stupid smile gave
her the opportunity to notice he had a chipped tooth in the
front, accentuating his stupid face. She regained her
composure. She would not shake his stupid hand.

"No. You can't call me Dara. Go back to what you were saying about my hands glowing."

He laughed. "It's the tips of your fingers when they touch the paint brush, at least they start to, but then it's like they're stifled immediately or spark out or something. I can't tell. Do your paintings glow sometimes?"

Dara had felt such an imaginative rush following yesterday's incident. After Vida sent her back home last night, she'd spent hours drawing and painting all she could, trying to make sense of everything without letting inspiration go to waste. Within her first few minutes of painting, "the glow" began flowing from her fingers into her brushes into the drawings. She tried switching brushes. She tried switching paints. It didn't affect her when she used charcoals, but that didn't help as she still had to finish painting the mural. She stayed up all night (with her father passed out and none the wiser), and worked to control the glow until she got it down to practically invisible. She had no doubt in her mind this was the result of her strange run in with Vida, but knowing didn't slow the flood. Who knew to what extent she was affected? This guy before her with the piercing eyes and the stupid face seemed to have some idea, but she'd decided she could not trust him.

"Go away, please."

* * *

What she saw made her turn around and run, run, run, back the way she came, through the tunnel up all the winding stairs, through the strange glowing cave, and far, far away from her twin's laughter. She ran and ran until the cave was distant enough to be a fading memory then she ran some more. She ran and ran and ran until she collided with the boy she thought had been chasing her before. Sticks and twine and sharp rocks spilled out of his backpack and he pushed and kicked her to get off him.

"Stupid!" he said.

"What?!"

"This was mine, quiet and beautiful and fun! And no one's here, only me! And you came to mess it up. You ruined it." He was fighting back tears.

He's not winning, she thought.

"Go away, okay!? Go! Get out of here! You're stupid!"

"I'm sorry; I didn't mean to mess it up alright? I like this place; it's the only place where my dreams are peaceful. Today it got kind of scary, but it's still better than my other dreams."

"You've been here before?" asked the boy after several moments of silence.

"I try to come here anytime I go to sleep. It makes being awake easier. Things are really scary at home sometimes out in the world," she said to him.

"I guess that's what I do too," he said. "Anytime Mom and Dad fight for a long time, I run to my room, hide under the bed, close my eyes and I'm here. It helps me be strong when I go back to help Mommy."

She smiled at him. "You're such a brave little boy," she said.

He sprang up. "Hey you wanna see something?" He was running before she could respond. She laughed and followed. After about a minute they came to a clearing by the water. The boy pointed and she saw it. It appeared the boy she was talking to was also sitting on a raft in the middle of the lake.

She was confused. "Is that your twin? He's here too?"

The boy laughed. "No it's me! He keeps me from wandering too far."

The girl thought about what had sent her running out of the cave. "How? Is it possible someone could do that without knowing—be two of them here? Could there be another one of me?"

"I dunno, maybe. I just close my eyes when I get here and open them again when I leave. It's easy!"

69

The girl was about to ask him another question but he was already on other things. "Hey! I have something for you," he reached into the bag and handed her one of the small blue crystal fragments he'd found in the grass. "You can keep it because you're nice. I like you."

She smiled as she took it and examined it. "Aww, I like you t—"

She felt herself waking up.

"Where are you going? I want to show you some of my favorite places. You can stay! I'm sorry I called you stupid."

"I'll be back! I'll see you again!" She said this as forcefully as she could before returning to the world of the awake. She didn't know *when*, but she believed she would.

* * *

Present Day

"Hey, I know what's going on. I can help you learn how to control it, for real. There's more to me than what you think."

"If we pretend you're telling the truth, it still doesn't help me. Please, go away. I've had an eventful enough twenty-four hours. I'd like to finish my painting and go home and go to sleep."

Kris stopped smiling. He stuck his fingers into one of the open containers of paint Dara had set in front of the mural. The paint began glowing in his hands as soon as he pulled them out. He painted "SEE?" in the palm of his hand and showed her. The letters were still glowing, as were his fingertips and the paint can. Dara slowly backed away. She wanted to run, but she needed to know why, how he was like her. What *was wrong with them.*

She sighed. "Did you meet her too? The little girl? Did she do this to you?"

"Huh?" He looked genuinely bewildered.

70

"Yesterday I met a—eh, never mind." She decided she'd let him do most of the talking. *Shouldn't be too hard, he seems like he likes to hear himself talk anyway.*

Kris noticed her smirk and took it as a cue to go ahead. "This has been happening to me for as long as I can remember. My dad was an artist ... had this small room where he would work overnight, but he'd usually be asleep during the day when my mom was out to work. Whenever he was asleep, I'd bring out some of his materials from the closet where he kept them and paint landscapes, animals, dinosaurs, dragons, and places I'd never been to. You know? Anything I could. Of course, the paintings were terrible. I never was much of an artist anyway but—What's up? What is it?" Dara's look had gone from one of rapt attention to fear. She covered her mouth with her hand, shaking as she did so.

"What, what did I say?"

Dara dropped the paintbrush in her other hand and backed away from Kris. She was now in a full-scale panic. "Where did you ... where did you ge—I don't know what the hell you're doing or who you think you are but stay away from me!"

"Hey wait, hold up! What's the deal?" He grabbed her arm. She kicked him in the groin, shook free and ran. Kris doubled over in pain.

She kept running. How many more strange things were waiting for her around each corner?

Back at the school, on the floor, Kris repeated his bewildered response. "Wait, what? I don't understand."

But she was gone.

As he lay there clutching his groin, still calling out to her, his head spun as he tried to make sense of what had occurred.

Dara, outside the school, did the same. Perhaps Kris meant well, but added to the peculiarity of the past twenty-four hours it was too much. Where did he get the necklace? *No. He doesn't mean well. He's obviously trying to manipulate me.* But where did he get ... *that?* Not *that* necklace. Not with *that* writing. It wasn't possible. Lucid memories of past dreams had come flooding back as soon as she saw it and like the first waves of the glow from the night before, there was little she could do to stop it. She saw *the place* now, crystal clear— recalled all that had happened there, as if it were not a dream. But that was … impossible. And for what reason? *What does he want from me anyway?* And from something so personal … like the dreams, she needed time, lots of time to think. She moved farther away from the school, and decided to go home. She'd left the mural but it could wait. *I'll come in and finish it tomorrow.* Besides, by being at home today she could keep practicing hiding her glow, since she was still so clearly bad at it. She'd be fine if she could keep from adding new glow or if the glowing parts faded by Monday. *Who does he think he is?* She felt bad for kicking him. *I'm not going back there now. I don't want to see him.* She needed time to think.

Kris pulled himself together well enough to sit against the wall under the mural instead of lying sprawled out in the hallway. His groin ached. He'd never been more embarrassed in his life. Being honest and open in his approach had ended up being *more* harmful, far more disastrous, than if he'd been more reserved, more covert, more devious. Worse, he didn't know why. What did she know, or think she knew? He laughed at the absurdity, clutching his groin with the additional pain of each guffaw. When he'd gotten every last bit of laughter out of his system, he sat, unmoving, staring at the blank wall across from him for several minutes. He stood, slowly and painfully but steadfastly. He turned around, stretching. That was when, for the first time, he saw the mural and froze. "Shit." He laughed again, lighter than earlier. He understood. He knew what he had to do.

Dara entered her house and cleared all the empty bottles of liquor from around her dad's feet. She removed his shoes, laid back the recliner and pulled out the sides until it formed a twin-sized bed. She got a couple of pillows from the closet, placed them under his head, and closed the panel playing old films in front of him. She went to the only bedroom in the apartment—hers, and sat on the bed, frustrated, angry and annoyed. She took a few deep breaths, got her brushes out of her pack, walked up to her easel and painted. She grew more frustrated as she noticed everything she painted was glowing, brightly. "No! No! No!" She kept painting out of frustration, but it only got brighter. She would tear up the paintings then pull out a new slate and start over, but the problem was getting worse. Panic overtook her again because the school building would be closed Sunday. If she was unable to get this under control by tomorrow and return to finish it, there would be an incomplete mural at the unveiling.

In the midst of this absurdity, Dara repeated her goals like a mantra. She had to get into one of the blue vane colleges. She had to succeed. She couldn't let Bivins win. She *would* get this under control, and she would finish the mural, and her path would be free and clear. She would put all this strange glowing and the little girl and her encounter with Kris all behind her; all would be a distant memory once she was in the esteemed halls of Stuy U. She painted deep into the night, crumpling up sheet after glowing sheet. Finally showing improvement, and unable to keep her eyes open a second more, she fell asleep.

She slept through Saturday and Sunday, waking up only in time to be hours early for school Monday. By the time she woke up she was a mess of dread, frustration, and anger. After her initial disbelief wore off, she got dressed, made breakfast for her father, and took it over to him. He was passed out on the recliner. If it weren't for the new empty bottles of liquor, she might've thought he'd slept through the days as she had.

"Get up, Dad! I have to see you eat before I go. You have to go to work!" She forced him up as he grumbled and struggled with her. She got a warm, wet towel to wipe his face. As she was wiping his face she noticed his swollen lip, a cut on his cheek, and a large bruise under his eye. As she unbuttoned his shirt to check for additional bruises she noticed something else. "Dad, what happened to your neck panel?" He grumbled in response. "Dad, I'm serious."

"I lost it," he said barely above a whisper.

She hissed.

"Omode (Uh-muh-dey), no vex," he said in the same manner.

"Why are you bruised? What happened and when?"

"I drank too much. You know your papa is a disgrace. It's my fault. I will get another one."

Dara looked at the floor as she spoke. "How, Dad? We can't afford another. Can you at least tell me who took it?"

Her father snickered. "What, you're going to go fight battles for your baba now? Go to school Dara."

Realizing she would never get anything out of him, she satisfied herself with getting him ready for work and watching him eat. When he finished she said, "I'm leaving now. Please get to work on time for me, okay?" He nodded. She kissed him on the cheek, hugged him and left.

A couple extra hours, maybe I can pull off a miracle with a couple extra hours. As she raced towards school she prayed the faculty hadn't seen the half-finished piece yet, least of all Bivins, who, no matter the final result, would lord the manner of its completion over her. Dara struggled to regain her breath as she burst through the school entrance barely slowed by the weapons detectors and the guards at the doors. She had a feeling—*no* was confident—*no* was absolutely certain—she'd be able to complete the mural in the time she had left without any problems. Her weekend hibernation had given her a healthy boost of energy and an irrational level of confidence. When she got to the senior hall however, she found the mural had been covered and sealed as if completed for the unveiling later that morning. Her heart sank as she saw a figure coming over to her from across the hall. It was Bivins. A knot formed in her stomach.

Bivins smiled as he neared her. "Miss Adeleye, why so early? I would've thought you'd skip my class and show up just in time for the unveiling!"

He wants to ruin me. He did this. He sealed it on purpose. I'm going to be disgraced in front of the entire school ... the administration. She knew she had to choose her next few words carefully. She forced a smile. "I wouldn't miss your class for the world, Instructor Bivins. But I'd like to reopen it to do a once-over and last-minute touch up."

Bivins smiled, and Dara thought she noticed a faint self-satisfaction. "Now, now, don't be modest. Perfection needs no improvement. I believe the work in and of itself should stand as an example, a reminder of what your presence has meant for us here. There'll be no more tweaks, no, no. I won't let you ruin such great use of space with last minute panic. Now off to the cafeteria with you." He motioned to a guard a few yards away from them. "Melsin, please watch Miss Adeleye while she's in the cafeteria and make sure she makes no attempts to return here? Thank you."

Dara sank into a chair in the cafeteria with the guard Melsin hovering less than a yard away, feeling thoroughly beaten by Bivins. Despite all her hard work, it had come down to this weekend, this moment, and now she would have nothing to show for it because she'd gotten spooked by something stupid. She remained there, lost in her thoughts until the lights changed from green to white to signal the start of the school day.

She headed to Bivins' class for homeroom, and the hour dragged as Dara spent the entire time trying to read Bivins, attempting to gauge what he might be up to. She got nowhere. She didn't expect to, but her anxiety still made her overanalyze every vocal inflection and facial twitch. He made no attempts to bait her, instead reminding everyone of the unveiling of her work which would occur after class. He generously congratulated her which set her further on edge, the knot in her stomach growing. When homeroom was over, she rose reluctantly and crept wearily towards the senior hall, the weight of impending failure growing greater with each closer step.

"Soaking in the moment beforehand, eh?" Bivins said, while seemingly in lockstep. His jovial manner annoyed her and made her certain he'd matched his pace to hers to do precisely that.

She ignored him, instead thinking of how she could explain her way out of the half-finished painting. *I can say it's like our futures, unfinished but hopeful despite the odds. No, that's stupid. They'll see right through it ... no one's gonna endorse me after this....* Lost in her thoughts, she was startled by the raucous applause which greeted her when she reached the senior hall.

"There she is!" Exclaimed Chancellor Francis, flanked by Bivins (who, Dara swore, had been by *her* side the whole time) and a few other faculty members. Chancellor Francis motioned for Dara to come up and stand next to her. "This year's mural unveiling features an exceptional young lady, an artist who's taken special care to create an image of inspiration, a mural worthy of the honor you, her classmates, bestowed upon her by choosing her to paint it. Dara, before we reveal the beautiful piece you've worked so diligently on throughout the term, could you please say a few remarks?"

As Dara made her way up to the podium placed next to the painting, the knot was now her center of gravity, stringing her extremities together, the pain torturing her with each step. It reminded her of the dread she'd felt in the alley. Last Thursday seemed like a lifetime ago, but maybe Vida would pop up out of nowhere and whisk her away again? She realized she'd have no such luck when she got to the podium. She looked at everyone and no one before choosing to focus on a cap atop someone's head in the middle of the crowd rather than make eye contact. She began her speech. The one she'd memorized was useless now; instead she improvised and attempted to lower expectations.

"When you guys chose me, it was an honor and an opportunity I was both shocked and extremely grateful for. I'd get to represent the hopes and dreams of our rising senior class as we head into our last year and look to our future. For a while I struggled with what to paint. I thought it made sense to show the struggles we face as the kids who've grown up outside the clouds, the poor living conditions, the fear, the depressing environment, the things we see every day." The faculty looked visibly uncomfortable. "But when I thought about what surrounds us, I got an idea. I thought it would be better to show what we're missing from our lives and should strive to find, to *reach*, to be *inspired by*. So ... I painted a place that came to me in a dream. It's unlike anything we've seen growing up here, there's color; bright, deep, hopeful color. It's the most beautiful, extraordinary place, and like us and our future, the place in that dream is ... um ... is . . . unfinished." She cringed internally. "But it's worth striving for!"

Chancellor Francis and faculty began clapping, and the students followed suit. Dara's fear of the next moment froze her, as Instructor Bivins, in what seemed like the slowest motion ever, pulled back the covering and revealed the painting. Dara's fear quickly turned to shock, then astonishment as the applause grew louder, and there were gasps of awe from the crowd.

No way.

Before her was her painting—*wait*—the? No—her painting. It was her painting. It was painted exactly as she had, but ... but ... it was ... complete. It was impossible. *It's impossible!* It was as if someone had tapped into her brain and finished it precisely as she'd seen and envisioned it.

No way.

As she attempted to make sense of things, her body interacted with the faculty and crowd on autopilot. It was during this moment as a passenger she realized she'd sleepwalked during her weekend hibernation and must've

77

finished the painting Saturday. She felt increasingly relieved as this plausible explanation took hold. The knot dissolved. Somewhat relaxed, she was able to appreciate the moment. She'd done it! Now, she could look forward to the bright future she'd pointed her schoolmates towards. She shook hands with members of the faculty, posed for panel clips with them and the painting, and shot Bivins a few victorious smiles.

After she posed for the last of the pictures, she headed over to her calculus class and got on with the rest of her day. The remaining hours passed by uneventfully. She was periodically bothered by thoughts of Kris, but she would quickly push them away. She similarly ignored the doubts that crept in about how she finished the mural. A few minutes before the end of her second to last class, she was sent a message on her panel, inviting her to the chancellor's office for the last period. As she walked down the admin hall, she couldn't recall the last time she'd gone without being sent by Bivins and she welcomed the change. Secretary Liscardi smiled as she came in and nodded her towards the chancellor's office. Seated was Chancellor Francis with an unreadable expression. In the chair across from her desk, and with his back turned to Dara, was Instructor Bivins who turned around as soon as she entered and acknowledged her with an eerie smile.

Of course, he'd be here.

"Please Dara, have a seat." Chancellor Francis' expression did not change, but Dara was certain she a heard a hint of disappointment in her voice. "We won't be keeping you too long, but Vice-Chancellor Bivins has brought a matter to my attention I believe is necessary to address. As you're perhaps our brightest student and in the running for the Carbo prize, I'm sure you'll understand the need for clarification."

"What's going on?"

Chancellor Francis nodded to Bivins, who stopped smiling and adopted a neutral tone to address Dara. "Earlier this morning, I asked the security staff for the usual Monday morning logs of weekend activity. I asked if they'd noticed anything odd apart from the usual post detention shuffling on Friday and Saturday. They noted suspicious behavior from a kid who was here for detention on Friday." Bivins then pulled up a panel and swiped across the bottom of the screen, allowing all in the room to view footage of an empty senior hall. As Bivins moved the frame forward and zoomed closer she grew impatient. What game was he playing? He zoomed in until the frame came to the wall where the mural helped secure her future hours earlier; it was empty. Though she could not quite make out a smile, Bivins face gave her enough to indicate he was enjoying this moment. He looked at her for what felt like a second too long.

"I don't get it. That's the wall before I brought in my work Friday. It's a marouflage piece—it's for the whole wall, you know this, Instructor Bivins. What's the problem?"

"If you'll look more closely, Dara, you'll find this stamp is from *Saturday*. But let us proceed. I promise you it gets more intriguing. Why don't we go back to Friday?"

Dara's mouth went dry. As Bivins shifted the frame, an individual she recognized as Kris came into focus. The knot returned to her stomach. He was detaching her unfinished work from the wall—the work she came back to finish Saturday! This was obviously after she'd stormed off.

Stupid.

She watched in disbelief, attempting to hold her swirling emotions in check until she fully understood what was happening. Bivins stopped the panel briefly to gloat.

"It gets better, Miss Adeleye. I promise you, it gets better." She had no choice but to ignore Bivins' remark and watch. The panel resumed play, and he pointed to the timestamp. "Saturday afternoon." The next frame was of Kris placing the perfectly completed mural back on the wall, every single inch of it meticulously, flawlessly painted. It was as if he'd been in her head and removed the painting from it. Or maybe he'd followed her home and stole ... *no, there's a million things wrong with that theory.* But what then? How could she accept that everything, her future, all she'd worked for was in question because of this guy? That he was the one who'd finished the mural and not her? She found herself speechless after emerging from her thoughts to Bivins' grumblings. "What do you have to say for yourself?"

After a long period of silence, Chancellor Francis called Secretary Liscardi on her cles. "Please send Kristano Arvelo in here, thank you."

"If you won't speak up, we can at least hear the confession from your co-conspirator," said Bivins. It didn't take Dara long to be overwhelmed by the hopelessness of the situation as she realized Bivins likely had footage of them interacting by the mural Friday as she was painting it and Kris stood, pointing, talking, bothering her. She knew the footage would be silent and exactly what that scene looked like, *even* if the footage of her kicking Kris were included. There would be no escaping, outwitting, or outthinking. Bivins had won.

Kris walked in and sat in a third empty chair on the other side of Instructor Bivins. Dara wanted to stab him, but that would have prevented her from knowing why and *how* he did what he did. He'd have to live for now. He did not look at her, instead acknowledging only Chancellor Francis and Instructor/Vice-Chancellor Bivins.

"Do you know why you're here?" Chancellor Francis said.

"To be honest, I'm a bit confused," said Kris, the smile from when he walked in growing wider. "Dara did all the work. I'm merely the delivery guy, unless y'all are now in the habit of recognizing errand boys as well. But if that's the case why didn't I get a speech at the ceremony too?"

Dara wasn't sure of what she was hearing, and by the looks of it, Bivins wasn't either.

"What exactly are you babbling on about, Arvelo?" Bivins played the footage he'd showed Dara earlier, as well as the footage she'd feared, and correctly guessed, was in his possession. "This clearly shows the mural which Dara has taken full credit for was finished by *you* Kri—"

"No, it doesn't."

"How dare you interrupt me? It clearly shows the mural was finished by you Mr. Arvelo, and as a result, we're rewarding you for your efforts, and making sure you don't go unrecognized for your part in its completion."

Kris laughed a loud, disturbing, arrogant laugh, eyes wide as he looked from Instructor Bivins to Chancellor Francis. "You guys are good, man, I swear. I thought I'd seen it all but the nonsense you wanna pull, ha-ha, man, credit for trying. Adults think we're stupid for real."

"Tread carefully, Kristano, you're on hazardous ground." Dara had never before seen a look of menace such as she was witnessing on Chancellor Francis' face. It was as if the muscles around the chancellor's eyes and mouth were so used to smiling and neutral expressions, they struggled to cooperate from a lack of exercise. It had the effect of being more chilling.

Kris was undeterred. "You don't think I see what you're doing here? You guys make up some story about how I finished the mural for Dara, based on footage that only proves I took it down and put it back up there the next day. You try to give me credit, thinking I'll get all happy and ask for recognition. Like I don't know you wanna set us up—get us in trouble? Ha-ha, I ain't dumb, briz. When I got outta detention Friday, I saw this bisa doing her thing, painting as I walked down senior hall on my way out. I thought it was cool so I started asking her questions about it or whatever, and she answered some but made it clear she was trying to concentrate. I asked her out because I thought she was pretty and talented, you know—just my type, and I guess she ain't like my approach or nothing cuz she kicked me and got outta there. I mean my pride was hurt, I ain't gonna lie. BUT as I sat there trying to ease the pain, I figured since I'd creeped her out, I'd get the mural to my cousin who lives in the same neighborhood to get to her, and she could finish it in peace or whatever. So whatever ya'll trying needs to cease, because all that vid says is that I got it to her, she finished it, and got it back to me."

"Enough of this!" Dara had never seen Bivins' blood vessels quiver so. "If she finished it why did she not bring it back herself? Especially seeing as she's clearly repulsed by you. This doesn't add up. Arvelo, you are a liar and an idiot."

"I dunno, maybe she was tired? You gotta ask *her*, Bivins. All I know is my cousin clessed me Saturday saying Dara was done but couldn't bring it back to school herself, so I picked it up and brought it back here and put it back up. That's it. That's all. I'm telling the truth."

"A likely story," Bivins sneered, turning to Dara. "What's your take on the tale of your new best friend … and apparent errand-boy?"

Dara was silent as she took everything in. *Why is he lying for me?* She didn't have time to process what it meant about him, though she was trying to anyway.

* * *

There wasn't anyone there when she returned. She'd hoped to find the little boy; he'd seemed sullen when she had to go. She felt like she'd let him down by waking up, and thoughts of returning to the dream to comfort him had often distracted her during her waking hours. She looked in the tree where she'd first ignored him; she looked in the clearing where she'd knocked him over as she barreled out of the cave. She looked by the river. She saw no trace of anyone. She sat down to enjoy her surroundings and reflect. Eventually she dozed off. She felt a light tap on her forehead and startled awake. "Who's that?!" she looked to one side and saw no one and was looking to the other when he yelled.

"Surprise!"

She slapped him. A boy who looked slightly familiar sat next to her, smiling. Gone was the baby fat round face replaced by a long, lean, bony pre-adolescent one, dotted with acne. "What happened, are you shrinking? You used to be much bigger than me." But then she was gone again. This time she didn't get a chance to respond or say goodbye, she simply faded away into the early morning. Try as she might in all her dreams to follow, she never saw him after that.

* * *

Present Day

"Miss Adeleye?!"

"Yes? Oh. Sorry." Dara had done everything in her life right, up to this point. What was wrong with going along with what Kris was saying? *No.* She caught herself. She'd wanted the Carbo more than anything—worked so hard for it the desire had defined her—but she couldn't. She didn't care for a future that came with the price tag of a lie. She knew her next words might destroy everything, but she was strong. *I'll recover. I'll find a way and it will be the right way.* The school footage and Kris' lie had made it clear her sleepwalking completion theory was what she'd thought it was: mumbo-jumbo she'd placated herself with to avoid the disturbing truth. She would own up now, no more delusions. Besides, maybe Chancellor Francis would take her track record into account and things would be alright after all.

"No. It's not true what he's saying. After I left I went home to clear my head. I ended up falling asleep for several hours and woke up Saturday diagramming exactly how I was going to finish. I took what I thought was going to be a quick nap. By the time I woke up it was Sunday and the building was closed. I rushed here Monday morning to finish it, and that was when Instructor Bivins harassed me and prevented me from putting on any finishing touches. The first time I saw the painting in its final form was at the ceremony after homeroom this morning. I took credit for it at the time of the unveiling but it's not my work. To sit here now and say it is would make me a fraud."

Kris looked at Dara for the first time since he'd stepped in the room. *You don't have to do this,* his eyes seemed to say. She ignored him and waited for Bivins and Chancellor Francis, who were both silent, staring at each other.

After a long sigh, Chancellor Francis nodded, stood, and turned away from the three of them to stare out the window behind her desk. "There was a time when an opportunity such as the Carbo Scholarship would've been unavailable to students who lived outside the clouds. We know what the usual options are for those of you who attend Ron Ed. However, it's not a bad life—the path you're set on if you at least do reasonably well and stay out of trouble here. You can carve out a respectable living working in the food services, or janitorial and housekeeping in the blue vanes. Some of you may get picked to work these areas in the green vanes. Daily living wage, protection under the clouds during the workday, it's a fantastic existence. All we ask is you follow the plan. The exceptionally attractive of you may even work in the pleasure industries, or entertainment, or marry up. I know for one as intelligent as you, Dara, it will feel as if your talents are being wasted, and you may be right. I believe in time you'd come to realize things are the way they are for a good reason, and you would embrace this path that differs from what you wanted or expected. I understand what led you to lie up until this moment. I understand the terror of the moment you realize your dream may not come true. I too was once a girl who dreamt a different dream. But it still turns out okay." She turned back around to face them. "Luther, thank you for bringing this to my attention."

"I only want for our students to do what's right, Chancellor," said Bivins.

Chancellor Francis looked from Bivins to Kris to Dara. When she came to Dara she stopped and stared, nodding slowly three or four times. "Dara, I strongly considered expelling you for this offense. But in light of the remorse and understanding you have shown, I now believe that to be excessive. You are however, suspended for the rest of the year. The few other students here as bright as you must learn intelligence doesn't place them above the repercussions of deceit. You will return here at the beginning of your senior year, hopefully more focused and ready to work towards a respectable life. We will certainly recommend you to quality employers, provided you do your part."

She turned to Kris. "Mr. Arvelo, your tenure here has been nothing but constant clashes with authority, arguments, fights, distractions, pranks, and with a mere double-take one could often find your fingerprints on a litany of mishaps. Then for the cherry on top you pull *this* stunt. I'd remark on your audacity, but that would likely thrill you. Instead I'm going to thank you for making this the easiest decision I've had in my time here as chancellor. You're expelled. This being your last year, we never have to see you again. I can only say I'm bewildered it didn't occur sooner. I'll forever question if it was some sort of testament to my ineptitude, or a nod to your slippery, manipulative, conniving nature. Either way, goodbye."

Dara had known it was coming, but the full force of it didn't hit until she heard. *Suspended.*

She felt as if everything said to her had been said to someone else, as if it had all happened to another person. The ache in her gut had yet to subside. It would've been unbearable by now if it was happening to her, but it was happening to this other person. This other person's face opened to mouth the words "Thank You."

As Kris got up, he laughed, said, "Coño. What a joke, you're all morons," and strolled out. This other person got up and followed. He noticed and broke into a full sprint out the building.

Dara called out to Kris but he didn't slow down. "I want to talk about Friday and why I left!" Kris came to a full stop. They were both outside now. She was out of breath as she caught up with him.

"Okay, TALK," he said. He was breathing as if he'd been on nothing other than a light stroll.

"I want to know what exactly it is you know about me, and how you know it." Kris laughed as she said this, but it was a dry, mirthless laugh. He shook his head.

"Unbelievable."

"What?"

"Can't thank me, huh."

"I didn't ask you to finish the painting. I definitely didn't ask for or need you to lie for me. Don't expect my gratitude for actions I didn't ask for, you prick." She was herself again.

Kris laughed coldly and resumed running. Dara, anticipating this, responded with a short burst of speed, getting a foot in front of him long enough to trip him. "Shit. Yo! Why can't you leave me alone?" He said this as he got up and wiped the dirt and slush from his thermcoat.

"Don't be like that! Like I said, I want to talk."

"What for? We did, back in the chancellor's office."

"I want to know *how* … and why. Why'd you finish the painting? How? Why didn't you leave things, and *me* alone? You saw how I left. I *told* you to stay away. I told you I didn't want to be bothered."

He was unmoved. "All I hear is more questions, but it's not like … I'm the only one who has a story to tell." He turned away from her and walked instead of running this time.

Dara stayed where she was for a full minute, watching him walk away before running after him. "Okay," she said as she tugged his shoulder to get him to turn around. As he faced her, her eyes fell on the pendant around his neck, catching part of the inscription "… *fire on the wind.*" She quickly looked up to meet his gaze and those eyes of his that did not allow her the luxury of hiding away. "You're being misleading, you know," she said softly. "If there's anyone here who's known what's going on, it's you. You know why I left Friday, or have some idea. I'm not mad but I'm still trying to figure things out and I need straight up answers and playing these games doesn't make me feel confident you're looking to give me those."

"I think I've been as honest as I could be without freaking you out, which you seem to do a good job of anyway."

Valid point, but whatever. "What happened with the painting?"

"It's a place from a dream I had as a kid. After you left, I got to look at what you painted and it triggered things. I finished it based on what I remembered. I didn't know if it was your memory too—I wasn't sure. Did I hope? Yeah. But I think we gotta lot of common memories anyway—you know, people do. Inner experiences we share more than we let on."

As she let his words sink in, she studied his face. She could kind of see it: the eternal smirk of the smart-ass pre-teen, boniness and baby fat replaced with a chiseled jaw, pimples cleared up, smirk offset by those intense eyes. That was what was off. She didn't recall his eyes being as piercing, she definitely would have remembered, but then again it was a dream. It was always a dream.

"Anything else?"

"No … I mean yeah, the necklace, who gave it to you?"

"I made it." He played with the links around his neck. She froze, then nodded.

"You looked surprised," he said.

"Nope," she said clinically.

It's you. He wasn't going to push, but he knew she was *the* girl; it made sense—the half-painting of "The Place," her reaction to his necklace. They walked side by side in silence until they passed a construction crew that made Kris do a

87

double-take. "Wait, is that … is that *Brouder Tower?* Being *repaired?*"

"Yeah, why?" Dara was curious. He looked perplexed.

Kris thought back to his failed attempt to traze the tower during the KoST trial run a few weeks prior. "Nothing, just I didn't think towers could be … I mean … they don't even get *scratches*. Never mind. Hey, being a disgrace to the school as usual has made me hungry—feel free to join a fellow rogue for a meal." He stopped as if her response would make an eatery appear, and Dara looked at him and looked around, confused as to why.

After she nodded "Sure, whatever," Kris smiled and reached into his backpack and his entire arm began to glow. He pulled his also glowing hand out and in it was a familiar object whose appearance chilled her to the bone. *Vida*…. With a glimmering sprezen he sprayed the wall in the alleyway next to them where he'd stopped and there was suddenly a slim passageway barely wide enough for both of them with a Burger Palace on the other side. She recognized the eatery. It was all the way uptown in the Riverdale red vane. She'd gotten lost in that area once while visiting a friend. *A phrinway? Did he just …* Kris, grinning and nodding (clearly impressed with himself), asked her if she was still hungry, striding through the phrinway and out of an alley across the street from the Burger Palace as he asked.

She didn't answer, but watched him step in first, and satisfied that he hadn't caught fire or otherwise turned to dust in the phrinway, she followed. She tried to maintain an air of indifference though she knew disbelief had to be all over her face if his grin was any indication. They ordered and as they sat awaiting their meals, she took it as her opportunity to find out what he knew about the glow and why he was using a sprezen that belonged to a seven-year old girl named Vida.

"You're gonna have to start at the beginning and leave nothing out. I want to know how you learned to control it. I want to know how you got it. I want to know how in Eshu's name you opened a phrinway. I want to know what else you can do. I want to know what you think *I can do*. Tell me everything."

* * *

The boy had looked and looked for her every single time he returned, but never found her again. Each time he went back, he left something for the girl. These little gifts disappeared invariably, without a trace, without the sign or slightest hint they'd made it to their intended recipient. He became convinced Eshu intercepted them for his own various ends. In the boy's final attempt, he left something he hoped Eshu would disregard, a message carved in stone on a large slab outside the cave entrance where he'd once chased her:

You appeared,
Like fire on the wind to draw me out of the sky
And I ran you down
But being with you sometimes
Was sometimes better than being alone,
and
I know that now,
Find me.
The next time you appear,
I hope you do
A boy only has so many gifts to share
And I do think it's a bit unfair
that your share goes to
Eshu

ALÁRÀBARÀ

Present Day

IPU CAPTAIN EAVES DARCELA QUESTIONED whether it
was more merciful to tell someone she was going to kill them
before torturing them or after. She thought this as she
listened to Emis Ptolemy Kabore (or Toley as she often
called him) provide her with a status update on the search for
the young girl with a single braid who was urgently at the top
of the emperor's (and her personal) wanted list.

"I've been able to isolate images of her and the vagrants
running from Emis Portland down to a single individual she
kept in lockstep with but I don't know how in Eshu's name
we've ever caught anyone outside Brouder's radius, heh. That
other tower's bloody useless. We have rear composite but no
side or frontal image of this other person. I can't give you a
proper ETA—heh-heh—on when—*if,* I'll be able to get a
positive match."

Captain Darcela smiled as she walked towards Toley,
leaned over and whispered in his ear: "You'd better figure out
something my love because I will get that ponytailed demon
child or I will get *someone*—" she put her hand around Toley's
chin, turned his face to hers, and held eye contact "to take her
place." She kissed him slowly and bit his tongue *hard* before
letting him go. The captain then kissed the Ogun mark on her
wrist.

Emis Kabore, look of terror plastered on his face, blood
seeping out onto his lips, nodded and began typing at a pace
twice as furious as before.

"Thanks, love." Captain Darcela turned to the other
emises who wore expressions similar to Toley's. "You've had
a month. What have you found?"

After a moment of silence in which each emis peered at one another as if willing the others to come forward, the losing one spoke up. "We believe from the interviews she may have been running with an older school girl, either from the local prep or instructional but—"

"But what?"

"But the people we were interviewing—they wer-weren't reliable ma'am."

"Stop stuttering. Elaborate."

"Well the ones we spoke to couldn't describe height or color or what the person was wearing. And … and I believe a few of the witnesses were high on vision ma'am. Couple of them said Vida was running away alone, a couple said she was running with a boy from a nearby instructional, others said it was a girl. We gave them all the year test—only two of them answered correctly *ninety-three* O.O.; only one of those two knew it was June."

Captain Darcela, who'd been smiling throughout the emis' report, stopped. The emis, shaking, aware of his error, backed away although the captain hadn't moved. "Don't you say her name. Don't you *ever* say her name. Only *I* say her name. Understand?"

"Ye-ye-yes, Captain."

"Stop stuttering. Why are you petrified? That was a fine report." The smile had returned to her face. "Dismissed, all of you."

"Yes ma'am."

"Except you Toley—keep working." She shrugged. "I haven't the slightest idea why they're always nervous and jittery around me." As she said this, Captain Darcela put down a large dagger she'd been holding in her pressure-gloved hand. She had managed to crush the handle.

* * *

Dara finished another shift at work, changed into her street clothes, greeted her manager ("Try not to kill anyone, Sal!") and headed home. It had been a month since her suspension (and her demand for answers from Kris), three weeks since Kris had shown her what the glowing meant she could do and since she'd told him to stay away from her, and one week since he'd listened and left her alone. As she embarked on what appeared to be another relatively peaceful walk—free from Kris badgering and pressuring her to go traze with him, her racing pulse, flushing extremities, and intermittent trembling—as if she were constructed of fault lines—told a different tale. She wondered if the constant storm inside her would ever subside. She didn't want to feel angry at Kris (she would have preferred to feel nothing towards him—*to not think of him at all*), but every time that smirk and those blade-point eyes found their way to her head she couldn't help but stew. And then there was Vida—Vida who'd started this mess. Dara had planned out her entire future, doing well despite obstacles every step of the way to get to the point where it all seemed possible and then Vida....

"ARGH!"

If she hadn't decided early on to expand her hours at the library organizing and dusting the old-style reads and generally anything else needed to keep her from being home during the day, she wouldn't have been able to get out of bed. She still hadn't told her dad she'd been suspended. She knew eventually, during one of his sober moments he'd ask her about how the "Carbo thing was coming along," and she dreaded what she'd have to say. She feared that moment—whenever it arrived—would send her father into a spiral from which he would not recover. As long as she could keep putting off the day he'd find out (between her not being home and him being passed out from work and drink) she would. He would have been so happy ... *so proud*, but now....

"ARGH!" in between sobs had become her daily ritual to and from work. Each way she got enough out of her system to be okay at her destination. It was during one such sob on the way home she allowed herself to be distracted and found herself pushed through a phrinway. By the time she put up any defense, she was staring at the familiar yellow cottage and Vida in front of it.

"YOU!" A furious Dara charged towards Vida with all the energy and rage she could muster. With no thought beyond her fury, a glowing sprezen formed in her hand *all on its own* and out shot a large beam which knocked Vida back. Stunned at first by the continuous burst, Vida recovered, appearing to *absorb it?* Dara—still not sure she was in control—exhausted the beam and collapsed into the grass. When she awoke, she found herself in a familiar room, in the same bed, but this time the door was open, and Vida was seated across from her. "You destroyed my future. You ruined my life. Who are you? Who do you think you are?" Dara sobbed.

Vida said nothing. When Dara was finished, Vida stood, replying: "I. Must. Train. You." Vida then went down the stairs with Dara chasing.

"Train me for what?"

"Your. True. Path. Olorí-iré. Ogu—"

"Shut-Up! I don't wanna hear about my true path or olorí—whatever or Ogun walking. I want to know why you ruined my life. Why you ruined my father's life—he was waiting for me to get that scholarship—to get into New Stuy, to ease his burdens ... now I'm nothing ... nothing but another reason for him to be depressed. I'm useless to him. I'm useless to my friends. I can't do anything for anyone. They only give you one chance, you know, and it's a shitty one at that. They stack everything against you. It's not even personal; it's just how they did it ... to catch as many as they can. To stop everyone. And I was *still* gonna show them ..."

"Please. You. Need. This. I. Can. Help."

93

Dara could have sworn she saw a tear in Vida's eye as she responded. "No. NO! Please, just take me home."

* * *

Dara found herself at Nicole's doorstep and Nicole opened immediately. "Hey! Where've you been the past few weeks? Sending meds without swinging by—it's almost like you've been avoiding me." Nicole paused. "*Have* you been avoiding me?"

"Nothing like that, Nic." She looked around. "Listen, what I'm going to tell you—you can't tell *anyone*. Okay? Not your brother, not your aunt—no one."

"Okay. Promise"

"I got suspended."

Nicole looked bewildered. "From?"

"From school, Nic. It's a long story but it's my fault. I allowed myself to get swept up in things … things I had no business being caught in."

"Like … *drugs*? Have you been using viz?"

Dara smiled "No, nothing like that." Nicole was silent for a while as she let the gravity of what Dara was saying sink in. *Trust me, Nic. I know. It hit me like that too.*

"Well … what are you gonna do? Can you fix it? I can't live in a world where you don't end up at Stuy U or become minister you're the smart one you're supposed to accomplish your dreams you've given so much this isn't how it's supposed to b—"

Dara caught her. Confronted with Nicole's helplessness, she felt forced to be tough and not allow herself to wallow in her own sadness any longer. "Don't worry Nic," she said as she hugged her best friend. "I can fix it, and I will. I will. I promise." *In a different way.* She realized then, maybe there was something greater; something here. Something *now*. Maybe it was helping the people in her community who had no voice, people who had no way to fight back. People like Nicole, people like her father. And Dara could do it; without the Carbo Scholarship, without Stuyvesant University. She would not give up—Olorí-iré, just not in whatever way Vida had in mind. Dara would make her own way, as she always had. *Many thanks, Ogun. If you indeed walk with me, you've made my path clear this day.*

HER

"I WANT TO LEARN. *Really learn.* And go trazing with you." Dara found herself at the Quarters clubhouse in front of a Kris who seemed way too cool, considering the extent to which he'd begged and badgered her to keep trazing with him a mere week ago.

"Okay," he casually tossed out, in between chews of the toothpick he spat to the ground and replaced with another as if they weren't a coveted cloud luxury. "Do you remember what we last worked on?"

I'm not fooled by your cool, Mr. Arvelo. I know what you really are. "Don't be silly, Kris. That easy thing? The parlor-trick?" She avoided his eye contact. He reminded her of the scarlet macaw—all colorful feathers and raucous honks.

"You can downplay it all you want bisa, but you gotta set the tone with the easy stuff and work your way up. You'll never be able to open phrinways at will to wherever if you can't get that down." He smirked. "Unless … that's why you stopped showing up." He was laughing now. She punched him. "Ow! Unnecessary …"

"I'm setting the tone."

"Maybe I *shouldn't* help you." He rubbed his shoulder.

Dara grabbed a green sprezen from a nearby table and drew a phrinway. She walked through it. It closed and reopened on the other side of the room and she stepped out. Kris clapped. "Yo! Impressive! And on your first try? That was like 45 feet this time!"

Dara rolled her eyes. *You patronizing ass.* "Are you gonna be this annoying the whole time again? If so, I can just try to figure this shit out on my own."

96

"Damn, bisa. Don't be cold … I can't help it. When I see you get better it fires me up."

She looked at him—moving his macaw beak and clapping his kaleidoscope wings; there wasn't a false note in his demeanor. He appeared genuinely excited for her. *Hmm. Maybe I was wrong. Maybe he isn't the most dreadful creature ever.*

"Plus, it reminds me of how amazing of a teacher I am. Bet you I'd be running things if they gave me a job at one of the academies."

(HONK!) *Oh. Never mind. I was right, he is.*

They practiced until the late twilight hours. Dara progressed to opening a phrinway to the Kids of Stolen Tomorrow underground tunnel and returning; Kris accompanying her each time until they were certain she could go to-and-fro instinctively. When she returned from her first solo trip to the tunnel, Kris smiling, giggling, *giggling? He's giggling! Ugh*—embraced her. "That was crazy, Dara. You're incredible, bisa."

His zeal—even after a long day of training, and the unexpected embrace took her by surprise. It was a pleasant one; though she was drained from all the work they'd put in, she wasn't sure her progress was adequate. His embrace and tone were reassuring. Sure, he could be a bit over the top, but he was nothing if not sincere. She allowed a slight smile to escape. She returned the embrace.

"Uh, oh, let me find out you might have enjoyed yourself out here tonight!"

"Goodnight, Kris."

"When you stopping by next?"

"You'll know."

* * *

She startled him one day in July, a few weeks after their last meeting. "What are you writing?"

"Huh what?" He jumped. "How'd you get in here?"

"I just walked in. You left the door switched off. No bioscan needed or anything. If I hadn't been here before I would've thought you didn't have a door."

Kris pulled up the security panel. The door was on and there was no indication it had been opened recently. "That's weird. I didn't feel any cold air coming in either." He locked the panel screen, turned up his thermer and walked to the main entrance to double check. "Yep, definitely on." He returned to his seat, unlocking the panel. "Oh well. Whaddup?"

"Oh. So you're avoiding my original question." Dara moved closer and began reading aloud. "Hushed in sightless daw—waiiit is that a poem?"

"Stop it, whatchu you even doing here anyway?" Kris locked the panel screen.

He writes friggin' poetry!? She wasn't sure if she was mortified or mystified. The Kristano Arvelo she knew was too conceited, too external. "I came to learn some more, oh great teacher, but *that's* far more interesting. Let me see the rest."

"No way."

"Pleeeeeeeease?"

"No. If you came to learn we can get started now."

His unwillingness only increased her determination. "How about … if I can phrin one-hundred miles in our session today you show me?"

"*Sheeeeeit*, maybe a hundred miles at once."

She gave him a look. She was thinking it over. "Okay, if I can phrin one-hundred miles at once today you have to show me what you were writing."

Kris cackled. "Sure! It's a deal."

Dara puckered her lips. "Have you so little faith in me?"

"I've got all the faith in the world in you, but seeing as I couldn't pull off a hundred miler until a couple years of doing this and I'm basically the Boom Ba-Ye of phrinning, I'm pretty confident you won't be seeing—"

Dara opened a phrinway and returned wearing a thermshirt with a picture of NEU Minister Janine Corlmond on it that read "Hometown Girl, Carolanda Proud," *and* with time-stamped footage of her purchasing the thermshirt in Blackbern, Carolanda, moments ago.

Carolanda was six hundred miles away.

Dara bent over to pick something off the floor and walked over to Kris. "Here's your jaw, Kristano Arvelo. I figure you still need it, right?"

"Womp, womp, wohhmmmp—whatever." Despite his attempt to downplay it in his initial response, Kris shook his head, wondering how he got played so easily. "Boca de trapo. Jabladora, you set me up!"

Dara smiled. "Oh Kris, I'm flattered. Why wouldn't I talk shit when I'm the new Boom Ba-Ye? I never lied ... but someone *did* set you up—you. If memory serves, I believe you owe me something?"

Kris, grumbling, began unlocking the panel.

"Chop! Chop!"

"Yo, you're insufferable."

Dara read the poem aloud:

Keep the cries of
The bear cub
Hushed
In sightless dawn
Where strongest conviction
Saps
And scatters over mist that
Never settles.

She was quiet for a time. "What does it mean?" She asked, softly.

"Nuhhhhh bisa, the deal was you got to read it. We ain't say nothin' about me explaining it."

"Please?" She tugged at the elbow of his thermer. She wondered what could make this guy she'd figured out write poems about creatures that no longer walked the planet.

"Um. Okay."

He was bashful. It was strange. "Bears were my favorite animal to read about back in the day. I um—learned everything there was to know about 'em. The different species or whatever. I found out when they were born they were blind and had to depend on their moms for everything so when they were hungry, um—they would cry and that's how the moms would know to feed them."

"What made you write it?"

"I dunno I was just thinkin' or whateve—yo, Dara I'm not talking about this no more, aight?"

She smiled. "Okay. I really like it."

"*You do?*"

"Yeah."

* * *

She's a funny girl.

Dara had splashed a wall in half the time it took Kris and had done so with such control and mastery he wondered how he could call them both trazers without shortchanging her.

He still couldn't believe it when she came by the Quarters three months ago—looking for him—after she'd sworn she'd kill him if he bothered her again the last time they saw each other. A week later she showed up, smiling like things had been great between them all along, and she was sweet enough for him to suspect a trap. Now they'd been hanging non-stop for the better part of three months and her presence had

100

been nothing short of a gift from her nonexistent gods. It was almost enough to make him believe again.

Almost.

"What are you doing, Kris? You gonna zizz around or you gonna join in?" Dara's sprezen was no longer glowing as she waited for him to answer her call.

"I don't know what I could add to it; looks complete as is."

Dara laughed in response. "Suddenly, the great Kris Arvelo has nothing to add? You sure you don't want to drop it off with your cousin and bring it back later?"

Clever. Kris was glad she'd taken to the constant movement and improvisation inherent to the trazer lifestyle, but what surprised him the most was how quickly she'd picked everything up. She could open phrinways to anywhere with relative ease and her use of the sprezen was second nature. Once she got it down, her natural artistic talent shone through wherever they trazed—transforming walls into worlds, such as the beauty before him. A mischievous grin took hold. "Oh actually, I do have an idea." Kris went up to Dara's piece and sprayed "Pu$$ycat Kill!" in giant red block letters over the mural. He felt stones whiz by his head, one pelting him in the back of the neck. "HEY!" he yelped while laughing and opened a gateway to escape through. Dara chased him through phrinway after phrinway, until he tired and stopped. "Damn girl," he said through heavy breaths, "How you still got all that energy?"

It was nightfall where they were, but she hadn't been chasing him for *that long*—they had to be on the other side of the world somewhere. *Are we in a blue vane?* He was suddenly nervous and looked around, they were in a large field with no sign of civilization as far as their eyes could see. The warm air welcomed them, cradled them, and then he realized where they were. And she might have too, but she pushed him playfully as she said, "Don't be such a child."

101

He laughed. "But *I am*. AND, this may come as news to you, but you are too. You can't control everything. Stop trying."

Now was her turn to laugh. "Oh, is that the lesson you've appeared in my life to teach me? Because I can think of a few non-permanent ways you could have done it."

Coño—she'll always hate me for that, but he noticed she was moving towards him. Her smile nearly disarmed him, but as she got closer he noticed she had another rock in her hand. This time as she threw it, he was ready. He used his sprezen to produce a shield and the rock bounced off the bubble and fell to the ground.

Dara, surprised, clapped slowly. "Impressive, Mr. Arvelo. I suppose."

He could see a bit of awe in her eyes as she processed his new trick, try as she might to downplay it. She stood facing him, trembling with her lips parted slightly—too tight for words to escape but open enough to invite. It was he who now moved towards her, closing the remaining distance between them, and he—now close enough to her to feel both her nervous energy and the magnet pulling him to her—who looked into her eyes one last time for confirmation she felt it too and saw everything he needed. As their lips touched he felt her nails dig into his back and all awareness of their surroundings dissipate. His heart rapped with increasing fervor, knocking harder the tighter his chest pressed against hers, as if requesting—demanding to abscond with this presence that returned its fervor and matched its passion beat for beat. They swallowed each other up in that moment— phrinway opening up into phrinway—one he wouldn't be forgetting anytime soon.

* * *

What was happening didn't make sense to Dara. She knew precisely why she was hanging around Kris, and she'd already learned the things she needed to help Nicole and her own father. She'd been out with Kris alone many times before—in fact it was how they usually traveled—how she'd usually learned from him. But this trip, the chase—the accidental trip to the place of her childhood dreams overwhelmed her. She tried remaining calm, remaining herself, in control—*grounded,* but around him ripple after ripple of warmth spread from within throughout, pulling her away from all reason, her panic as she fought it only serving to tug her under. And then she was *hot. Cold. Hot* and enthralled to be so alive and in the moment, so able to take in each and every bit of the time they'd spent there. That place where the trees grew down from the sky comfortably into the soft earth around them, where she and Kris had lain next to each other, looking up, straining to make out the leaves somewhere at the top that kept them shaded and let just the right amount of sunlight in.

She'd laughed as he trazed her and ran, leaping over rocks, daring her to tag him back like a primary schoolboy at recess without a care in the world. She did. And chased him, chased him even all the way into the cave that had once given her nightmares.

She could only smile as she thought about it now. She smiled and again tried to stop herself. *What is wrong with me? He's a guy, that's all. Nothing special.* But she didn't believe that, even as she thought it; even as she fought the waves that betrayed her and stirred in his presence. She thought of his hands, kept seeing them, imagining what they could feel like against her skin. She thought of the way his hands picked up things and the way they threw things, the way they glowed and trazed things and even the way they were when they'd sit there, idle, unused. She wanted to be held with those hands; she wanted to be thrown about the way he carelessly discarded what he didn't need, then rediscovered by him and thoughtfully held again. She now thought about each moment they'd spent together no matter how short or insignificant,

KIDS OF STOLEN TOMORROW

recounting the words, the smiles, the glances they'd both pretended meant nothing but knew better. She remembered the mercurial boy she'd met in her dreams—capricious, joyful. He had changed more than a bit but hadn't she *always* known him? Hadn't she once she spent her nights trying to find him? And her days trying to break into those dreams where he, as a sweet pudgy little boy, had begged her to stay? Sure, preparatory felt like ancient times, but it wasn't *that* long ago.

And the kiss…

Stop.

Stop it!

She struggled with the fact that one moment he was a nobody to her, an aimless loser from school, and suddenly she went to bed consumed with the anticipation of seeing his face the following day. She woke up thinking about him, wondering where he was. He laid waste to her thoughts— turned her landscape into his personal playground and she was mad at him for it, angry he could have such an effect just by being who he was and being around her. But it was too late to change anything; the adventure had already begun and she had to see where it led.

* * *

Trevin was ecstatic to receive a blacker, a cles—one of several picked up for the crew—and an isolated panel band from Kris. He was a little disappointed Kris hadn't yet trusted the others enough to join his blue vane gadget raids, and that *he* couldn't go because it would look highly suspicious or like favoritism. Trevin had to seem like one of the gang so they'd feel comfortable opening up around him with their true views about Kris and KoST. In reality, Trev and Kris first met a few years ago, when Kris was trying to chase down the "pathetic twib" who kept trazing "TRE TRAPS" tags around every "Pu\$\$yCaT KILL!" he put up in the city. Kris had set

104

upon Trevin ready to play out his "Kill" nickname but as he approached he saw the tag and the can from which Trev constantly disrespected him were glowing. It was almost too good to be true for both of them. Kris had no idea others like himself existed in the city (or anywhere for that matter), let alone the kid he'd angrily been playing tag with for months and Trev had no idea the extent of his own oyas until Kris showed him how to phrin; but he had known there was one other trazer with the "magic glow" tags, and thought there could be others. And so it was Trevin who suggested, after a year of trazing and phrinning together, that they recruit. Kris had the more magnetic personality and it would be easy to hold an audition of sorts with him at the helm, but he resisted the idea for months before flipping it back at Trevin and jokingly presenting it as if it had been his *own idea* all along.

Both Trev and Kris felt responsible for all the KoST, but Kris was overprotective. Trevin wasn't surprised at this; he understood where it came from. Plus, the gadget raids were a bit more dangerous than the "trial runs" Kris liked to call the quick trips for food and (mostly) red vane trazing, and *What, four months in? Yeah. It's September now*—they were still evaluating everyone's strengths and weaknesses.

Trev felt the crew needed more variety, and they had yet to recruit a girl to join. The others, especially Flick and Laran, were annoyed by Kris' side trips with the girl Dara, who wasn't a part of the group even if she *did* share their oyas. She was too polished; she put them to shame. When it came to the group's phrinning, he felt as if they'd taken the training wheels off a bike but still needed to wobble the front wheel a bit for balance. If Dara joined, they could learn a thing or two.

The complaining didn't bother Trevin or raise any red flags; quite the opposite. It showed they were invested in KoST and worried about how much their leader still was. Their complaints gave Trevin ample opportunities to refocus them and voice his vote of confidence.

When Kris asked if Trevin knew anything of the netlines
and scarnet a few months ago, Trev thought his friend had
either been kidding, or didn't know him. When the shock
subsided, it dawned on him: though Kris had seen him typing
furiously on the occasional netline, they hardly ever talked
anything that wasn't traze or phrin-related (and they'd both
gone through *many* phrinways separately over the past couple
years). That said, Kris couldn't have asked a sillier question.
Trev had spent every extra bit of time he'd had since he could
remember *being aware*, on the scarnet; it was the only way to
access information free of the Ministry's firewalls. It was how
he'd initially discovered there was at least one other "magic
glow" trazer out there, and had considered reaching out to
that trazer but it was dicey. The person hadn't wanted to be
found, and he felt outing them was a dark path to go down
for the sake of not feeling alone (not long after, he met Kris).
Trev had *thousands* of aliases, all of which could be traced to
various blue vane household members around the world.
Routing to green-vaners was far too risky and routing to red-
vaners could bring more trouble to people who suffered
enough daily, but no one worried about the online activities
of isolated blue-vaners dotting the planet.

"Yo Trev, I thought it would be win if we found new
places to phrin to, without anyone being onto us, but I don't
know crid about the net. Is that something you can help me
do? Don't say you can if you can't, *pendejo*. You're under no
pressure fr—"

Trevin chuckled. "Kill."

"What up?"

"Shut up, briz. You're going on like I'm one of the others
and you need to charm me and it's embarrassing. I got you—
we're good."

Trevin told Kris what he'd need in order to help; showed
him diagrams, pictures and specs on his panel. At the time, he
wasn't sure Kris had understood anything he was saying. Yet

here he was now, playing with some of his favorite toys and using them to find new places to play.

As he sat alone in the Quarters in the early Sunday twilight hours searching for multiple safe netline connections buried deep and hidden far from the Ministry's eyes, he thought back to how Dara had been received during her official introduction to the group. He knew of her from school as the artist who got kicked out or something for lying about the senior hall mural. Kris forbade further mention of "that bullshit" and explained to him (and the others) they'd be seeing her more often around the Quarters, especially on missions. Unsurprisingly, the group chose not to make their private grumblings public. Trevin, like the others, had wondered if the two were dating. No one dared ask though, not even the frequently brazen Flick, and Kris volunteered nothing. Even when Trev tried to broach it privately, Kris played it off. No matter; the haul they brought in together was remarkable. Aside from everything Trevin needed to get them online without being tracked, Kris and Dara had also managed to grab a full course dinner including chicken, beef, goat, bread, fruit pies, and all sorts of other exotic cuisines which made the items the KoST picked up on their other runs seem artificial. They ate heartily. A few offered-up sacrifice to Eshu as always and as the others left, Dara walked over to the corner where Trevin had been getting set up.

"Hey, Trevin, right? Or Trev?"

"Trev's good."

She extended her hand, "I'm Dara."

"I know who you are," Trev responded as he shook her hand.

"You mind if I ask you a couple questions?"

He nervously looked over to Kris who was on the other side of the room doing chin-ups. Kris paused in mid pull-up to nod and smile. Trevin nodded to Dara.

"No, I don't mind." She was dazzling. He was jittery and he tried to avoid staring at her, but he also didn't want to be

107

rude and look like he was ignoring her while he was setting up the equipment.

His awkwardness must have been obvious because she said, "You can keep working while you answer. I don't want to disturb you or make you feel like you're being interrogated."

"Yeah."

She proceeded to ask him why he'd joined the KoST, when he found out he could phrin, and things about his parents he'd never given a second thought to. Somewhat relieved when it was over, he noticed she was silent, but hesitant, as if she wanted to ask him something else.

"What is it?"

"Kris said you're good with netlines and hacking and stuff. If I give you the serial number to a panel would you be able to locate it?"

Trevin smiled. "Yeah, time varies by type—some are more difficult than others, but nothing is untraceable, *for me*. If it's general use, absolutely. It would be win, easy."

"Thanks."

And that was it. He had no idea why she'd gotten so personal or why she'd asked him the questions in such a formal manner. Maybe she'd wanted to get to know him better without seeming *too* friendly? Perhaps she and Kris *were* dating. If so, Trevin was sure they hadn't discussed how Kris knew him, because Dara didn't seem deceitful. *Oh, well I give no crid about it anyway.* "And we're online! Yes!" Trevin looked around to make sure no one had suddenly returned through a phrinway, then did a dance with his shoulders. He stopped as the wave of shame and regret that normally protected him from potentially embarrassing himself publicly kicked in. He put his head down and shook it. *Nerd.* With the entire KoST crew now having clesses, he was able to set them to a frequency tied to an encrypted network he'd built within the scarnet. Now they'd be able to communicate from anywhere with practically zero chance of anyone listening in. They'd also be able to zero in on a place to jump to from wherever they were, as long as they had a password into the network at the Quarters to select a location. *Well, at least I'm a cool nerd. Maybe.* He sent Kris' cles a message: "WIN!"

Seconds later, his cles buzzed with Kris' voice saying "Ha-ha! Love you brother."

He knew it was the excitement of the moment, but for a split-second, Trevin felt what he'd left out in his answer to Dara about why Kids of Stolen Tomorrow: the kinship.

* * *

"Captain Darcela?"

"Yes, Toley?"

"I've found something. It's far from exact but it should help us ID the girl who was with …"

"It's okay, Toley; you can say it."

"Vida, after we run it through our databases. The bad news is there's no telling how long it will take. I know it's already been five months—WAIT! There's good news, Captain, I promise!"

"Go on."

"While I was running the composite algorithm, it was interrupted by the alert I set up for motion signature changes in the dungeons. I pulled the feed and … look what I found."

Captain Darcela smiled. "Oh Toley, you beautiful boy. Let's go greet the Nth."

* * *

"What are you smiling about?" Dara said this eyeing Kris up as he strolled out of the bathroom in the motel chamber where they were staying. She had trouble moving her eyes to his face at the moment as they remained transfixed on his chiseled stomach. Every muscle on his body looked so taut, so tightly wound; it was a *miracle he doesn't come bursting apart at the seams when he runs . . .*

"Eyes over here *mi bellita*, you'll miss my beautiful face," he said with the most conceited smile, as he got back under the covers with her.

"Annnnnnnnnd it's gone." Dara turned away from him as he leaned over for a kiss while getting into bed, leaving him to kiss the back of her head. This did not stop him.

"Tasty hair ... so delicious," He said with a lisp as she felt his tongue penetrating through her curls until he reached her scalp. "I think you should get *all of it* braided. Then things will get interesting."

"You're ridiculous." She said this as he turned her back around to face him. Her smile did a poor job of hiding her amusement. He pulled her face close to his, looking in her eyes before closing his and kissing her slowly, biting on her lower lip and pulling it out gradually, deliberately lingering for a moment too long before letting go. When he did, she returned the favor by spitting out strands of her hair into his face.

"Thanks."

"Anytime, Señor Arvelo." As Dara responded, Kris played with one of her three braided strands when he noticed a lanyard with little blue crystals weaved into one of the other braids. *How did I miss this?!* "Where did you get these?"

"The crystals?"

"Yeah."

Dara laughed. "We can say my share didn't go to Eshu. I tied it in just now—while you were in the bathroom."

"So ... you got *everything* I left you? Why didn't you let me know?"

"I just did."

Kris did not look amused. "Damn. All that time, you let me be a dummy writing on a rock in the middle of nowhere."

"What are you talking about? One, I wasn't entirely sure the crystals were being left for me. Two, I thought that *if* you

110

were the one leaving them you knew I was getting them since
I was finding them and keeping them somehow. Three, it
never felt real. I never had much control there; it was a dream
for me. I would wake up and think I sleepwalked somewhere
and suddenly ... stones. I still kind of think that. I guess
seeing your poem on the slab clued me in a little? But that
was the last time I was ever there, and it wasn't for long. I
haven't been able to get back in years. I kept some of the
crystals on my lanyard and locked the rest away. Eventually it
all faded, and all I had was vague memories or feelings ...
things that came out in art—"
    "Ah, like the mural."
    "Or fragments would come back like lines"
    "Of the poem. Oh, yeah, so Trevin called. We're plugged
in."
    "That's nice. Sooo, Kris Arvelo, God of Chaos; Leader of
the Domain of the Directionless ... you gonna at least
consider what I've been saying?"
    "I have been; it's ..." he sighed. "Let's talk about
something else for now." He laid back, facing the ceiling, his
head on the pillow. Dara placed her head on his chest and
rested her palm against his stomach.
    "Okay."
    "How did you learn to open phrinways? I get the trazing
and the dream-world, but phrinways?"
    "It was a complete accident, actually," he chuckled.
    "Oh really?"
    "Yeah. I was climbing the HubHorn building—"
    "Deathwish much?!" She slapped his stomach.
    "Hey no big deal—I lived, right? My plan was to get to
the top of it and make some kind of grand statement. But
truth is—I'd left my thermer at home, and I hadn't decided
what the statement was! Winging it—you know, the fly shit-"
    "GO ON, KRIS."
    "Okay! So the higher up I got, and the tireder I was and
the more I froze, the less conviction I had about what I was

gonna do—but still, I couldn't climb all that way and not do nothing righ'?"

"Riiight," Dara responded, eyes rolling.

"So I get to like halfway up, with like 20 or something like that more stories to go. And I look back down and I look up. And I'm realizing I probably won't make it either way," he chuckled. "But for a few moments all I can think is 'well shit, pendejo you gotta draw something.' So I just start trazing a door—mind you, I'm hanging on for dear life on one a them window panel bar things—and on the door I write 'LET ME IN' and start trazing my Pu$$yCat Kill tag and as I'm leaning forward to put the 'Kill' I lose all balance and fall. And for a second I think *that's it* right, bisa? Fall forward, hit my head— it's a wrap I'm empanadas on the street. But when I open my eyes I'm actually in the building! Like on that floor in the Hub! Of course, Pro-Ts arrested me and shit as I tried my daring escape out the lobby. I guess the old lady's apartment I ran outta—she called em' told them I was a burglar. But that was it. Then I just kept trying after that. Every day, hours on end for months until I cracked the code."

"I see...."

"What?"

"Nothing. Just interesting." *So he can be dedicated. If he really wants something.*

They were both silent for a few minutes, breathing each other in.

"I'm glad Nic likes you." That wasn't entirely true, Dara had wanted Nicole to hate him hate him *hate him,* at first, in hopes she'd be able to pull herself away from him with such ammo. But Nicole had picked up on what she had; that Kristano Arvelo, for all his bluster, was a big softie.

"Good, I'm glad. I like her too. She's sweet." He yawned. "Whaddup with the interrogations? Flick, Brink, Trevin...."

"KRIS, we already talked about this. I told you—"

"Right, I know, but we were phrinning at the time. Forgive me if I was distracted jumping to the other side of the world."

"That's bull, you could phrin with your eyes closed and still get where you want to. Nope, you were ignoring me. Maybe next time you *should* close your eyes instead of putting your fingers in your ears, toothpick boy. You might have better landings."

"Wow! You're clearly jealous and emotional because my landings are *phenomenal*. I think you're just upset I don't take you on more runs, but maybe I would if you didn't always crash for like a whole day after phrinning."

"Which, unfortunately, keeps me from missing out on your great and noble acts that significantly balance the scales of justice, like pastry theft."

Kris smiled. "You can try to downplay it bisa, but pastries are delicious. I'm a national hero out in these streets." Dara feigned puking and he ignored her, continuing: "I just want a little more detail alrigh'?"

"Nothing crazy. I'm trying to figure out why, how. What's the common thread between all of us?"

"You found it?"

She tapped his chest. "No, not yet. I wondered if it was the fact you guys were trazers. You said everyone you recruited was one."

"Yeah, but I recruited alotta kids at that first meeting and all of 'em were trazers. Only a few had the oyas."

Dara nodded. "Yeah, and there's the fact that I'd never trazed a day in my life before mine showed ..."

"Oh well. Best to enjoy our travels, not question why. There's way more important things you could be focused on."

"I agree. Like why you won't help me if you like me so much."

"Again? Give it a rest, bisa." He flicked his toothpick into the waste-bin and placed another between his teeth. "Like you so much, eh? You're ever the confident one Miss Adeleye."

"Why wouldn't I be? When you've paid for a crash-house chamber and an expensive dinner, despite the fact I'd have been perfectly happy if we'd phrinned somewhere, stolen food, and had fun at your place or in the clearing by the lake."

Kris smiled. "Well, if you'd told me before—" Dara's warning glance cut him short and he wisely changed the subject. "I don't see the point of it, *mi bellita*, of doing anything to fight things as they are. If you think there's control, you're fooling yourself. We're all on a wave … peaks and troughs without a rhythm."

"*What happened to you?* The little pudgy boy in my dreams was protective and fiery. There was destiny in his waddle. He spoke of the gods in a tone of true belief. *Even then* you gave off the air of purpose."

A melancholy smile crossed Kris' face. "One day, if you're unlucky enough, I'll tell you what changed."

EAVES

March 74 O.O.

SHE WASN'T PREPARED for what happened that day. The
first thing she remembered were sun rays tickling her back.
Blue laid there next to her, curly black mane, piercing
sapphire eyes, the thin layer of facial hair forever keeping him
from being clean-shaven. He had that half smile on his face
letting her know *how long* he'd been waiting for her to open
her eyes. She smiled back at him, then she kicked him,
because it couldn't have been *that long*. He laughed. For a
moment, they were everything.

Her cles rang. It was a call from work, and they needed
her in earlier than usual, on her *day off*, no less. "Eee-
yahhhhhh-vehzzzz ..." he said, tugging at her, dragging her
name out in that smooth drawl of his—usually a convincing
argument. She reluctantly kissed him goodbye though she
would see him later, because they could never spend too
much time together.

Quickly getting dressed, Eaves put on her blacker and
adjusted it to nine. She had a feeling she'd need it to be pulser
proof; it was a Monday. Looking in the mirror, she scanned
for marks on her neck in case she had to darken the clarity
setting of the blacker around it. Blue could be quite
aggressive when she let him. Satisfied, she left it on "skin."
She pulled her hair to the back and tied it. She was sometimes
surprised it wasn't stuck that way, after years of doing little
else. She undid it for a few seconds, tried a few different
looks, laughed and tied it back again. She put on her
helmet—maybe another time. She left the clarity setting on
the helmet-mask transparent as well. Hurrying out of the
brownstone, she smiled at her neighbor's niece, Vida—who
was sitting on the steps watching cartoons on her panel—and

115

reminded her girls don't run the world by being late for school. Vida rolled her eyes and said, "I know, Miss Darcela," closed the panel and shuffled along. *When did I become a Miss?* Eaves smirked at Vida while briefly removing her helmet and jokingly checking her face for wrinkles.

Eaves was greeted outside Unity International Bank by the crowds who always seemed to think change came through standing across from places where decisions were made and yelling angrily. Although the crowds were always fiercest on Monday, she thought she could make it up the steps and into the UIB building untouched and she almost did. *Almost.* She felt the pull of a claw at her back, then nothing. The feeling then repeated on each of her arms, and her chest where she saw the usual flash of a low power pulser before the feeling was gone. Eaves turned to peer at the crowd, laughed and shook her head. "Try working for a change!" She marched up the steps.

Two guards, dressed like her, except their blackers and helmets from the neck up weren't see-through, nodded knowingly as she reached the top step. They opened the door. "Good morning, Emis Darcela," said one. The other jovially muttered something about Mondays and she nodded in return before heading in.

She greeted their receptionist Juanes. He was one of those people who was always smiling but you were sure they were never quite certain why. She smiled back. Marc, her secretary, noticed. "You smile? Since when?" He asked as she breezed by his desk on the way into her office.

She switched on her door and sat. She stuck her hand under her desk and felt around until she found the reason she'd been called in. She pushed the temporarily installed button and held for fingerprint scan. An oversized bright red panel appeared in front of her with green markers lighting certain columns throughout. "Always so dramatic aren't you, Ruben?" She said to no one in particular. He would soon be in the room to guide her through the panels but Eaves began deciphering them anyway. Midway through the last one he showed up. He scanned himself in. Marc didn't have a chance to buzz her on the cles.

"Eave—" She heard him yell as the door slid open.

"There you are, beautiful." The smile was in Ruben's voice and not on his face. He made himself comfortable in the chair across from her desk. "Can you stop entering through the front? You're the only one who still does it, I swear. You're royalty. What are you proving? You wouldn't have to wear the blacker and you could dress normal."

"Normally," Eaves corrected, though she knew he'd done it to annoy her. "And I don't need to dress normally. It's far more important those protesters know at least one of us isn't going to be intimidated by them."

Ruben rolled his eyes. "The fact they're allowed in a blue vane is silly. They have no business here whatsoever. Anyway, I take it you've looked through everything? Good, here's what I want you to pay attention to."

He talked while she sat quietly, nodding, for about fifteen minutes. When he took a breath, she showed him she was already close to finished.

"By Shango, so you are." The smile was on his face this time. "Okay, what can you tell me?"

Eaves walked Ruben through the activity of a flagged client—Lorzan Industries—who seemed to be using one of Unity International Bank's subsidiaries to launder its money. In a vacuum, the money might have been clean enough for Lorzan's officers to fly under the radar, but taken in context with cycle time and other factors, things were too suspicious and they warranted further observation. Eaves realized Ruben didn't need her services for that; anyone could monitor the file and investigate Lorzan's officers.

"Eaves, I need you to find out the owners of Lorzan."

And there it was. Emis Darcela froze momentarily, not quite believing what she'd heard. Ruben had asked her to perform the highly illegal task of determining a private corporation's owners. Meaning he couldn't trust anyone else to do it. Something was definitely up. *Maybe he wasn't granted the emperor's permissions.* But what if it was the opposite—was this a command from the crown? But it couldn't have been; it was the current emperor who made it treason—the current emperor who'd sealed all records.

"You'll need to carry out the order in secret, using your own personal gear and resources, reporting only to me. Use your old untraceable panel for netline access—no Lyteche equipment, okay? Understood?" She nodded, slowly. "This one must be important, huh?"

"No more so than any others, sweetheart."

"BS. I can count on one hand the number of times you've called me in on my day off and still have four fingers left."

Ruben stared at her. He was quiet for a few moments. "What can you tell me about the purchases?"

"They're buying small scale finance houses. They vary from red vane loan sharking, to lower blue vane lending houses. They're not just here in the North Emerian Union either, they're in red vanes throughout the globe. They don't purchase stakes in anything too big or flashy, only controlling and outright full ownership in regional and locals. They've been moving down the east corridor. Carolanda looks like its next and I think they're gonna target red vanes in the RDC triangle. I'll need more time for the other thing."

"I'm aware. You've done well, Eaves. In the meantime, I can run with this."

She smiled. "You're still not going to tell me what's going on, are you?"

He gave her a stern look, and Eaves knew what was coming next. "If you'd listened to me, then maybe I could tell you." He got up to leave.

"And there it is! Of course, how did I know we were going here?"

"Move out to Bushwall Heights; the palace awaits. Work domain. We love what you do here. But if you want to start getting great recognition, if you want to start moving up, you've got to get out there and show them what you're worth. You're bright, but even better, you're Decalaoba. You could be *emperor! I* know you're more than just a brain. Let *them* see it."

Decalaoba. She hated that word right then; the way he used it. That word that denoted her birth into one of the ten ruling houses of the corporate class—the only houses from which an emperor could be selected. It was a grand distinction, a term that set her apart from even the other nobility; a mark of high royalty. Yet in that moment, it felt like a slur. Usually, she let him continue without responding. To her it had become something he had to do so he could feel satisfied he'd pushed her. That day she didn't. At the time, she tried to act like it wasn't anything in particular setting her off, but her response showed that to be a lie.

"I think I've done more than enough for the palace."

"That? *Still?* If that's what's bugging you, kid, you've got to let that go. Your sister will eventually forgive you."

"Will she?! Mariela trusted me to keep his secret and now he's—"

"Unity before family when family threatens unity; greater good always. To serve the crown is a privilege. Your sister has the same lineage as you and she'll get it someday. If she doesn't? Well ... some never understand but you always have. It's why you're perfect for—"

"Why? I'm perfectly happy *here.* If I keep producing the crown will take notice. They know what I've contributed. The last two ascensions Lord Charris gave me, they saw my name and signed off without a single question. Why do you always think I have to go somewhere else to make my way in the world? I don't get it! Besides, a lot of good it did for you. Are you not royalty too? Are you not Decalaoba? You were a *Lord! Next in line to be emper*—you know—"

"You're raising your voice Emis Darcela; don't be insubordinate. And you know nothing of what happened with me. Speak only of things you understand."

"I'm just saying there are different ways to ascend, and you always act as if I'm not doing enough or I—"

He saw it. In that split-second she *knew* he saw it before she heard it. He saw it before he—they felt it. And then she heard it. For a split second. And then she couldn't hear.

And then she couldn't see.

The pain awakened her. She didn't know how long she'd been unconscious, but the pain told her sharply, cruelly she was alive. It's said life is a gift, but she begged for that cruel reminder of her good fortune to be a trick. She prayed to Eshu that it be one of his illusions, and she would soon pass through the crossroads. She prayed to Shango to give thanks for her life, and to Ogun to wield his sword and bring her a swift and merciful end. Then, somehow overcoming the pain and prayers for death, panic took hold of her. "Papa! Papa!" She screamed, frantically trying to move. She was covered by what was once her desk, chunks of the ceiling, and she had a piece of metal the size and shape of a baton lodged in her arm. Her blacker was damaged by the blast, but it had kept her alive.

She forced her way out from under the remains of her desk and debris and crawled over to the doorway where the one-time lord had been standing. She screamed again. She couldn't stop—she couldn't control it. His body was there, but … she couldn't look—not at first. She sidled up to him, crying irrepressibly and held him, cradled him, talking to him as if it was going to bring him back. She tried to make his face the way it was before as she sat there, sobbing for what felt like hours. "Please, please I'm so sorry. Please, I promise. Please Papa … I'll do what you wanted me to do and it will be alright, okay? I promise I'll work domain and I'll ascend, and you'll be proud and we'll be happy …"

"Is anyone here?"

The sound of another voice startled her. The medics had made their way to her office. One of them saw her and three others quickly moved to help get her onto a gurney. They pulled her away from Ruben—from her father and covered him with a sheet. She screamed again. A red headed medic with a face like a wooly mammoth removed her lodged metal, pulled up a panel, located unbroken exposed skin near the wound, then pressed a slant against her wounded arm and lifted it as she mustered a miraculous amount of strength and struck him in the chest with the other. She screamed. "Take my dad; bring him with you—he's a lord you hear me?! He must be treated! The crown—please, please, ple ..." The anesthesia from the slant took hold and everything went dark again.

* * *

Blue didn't show up that day at the hospital. Eaves missed him more than ever and wanted him by her side. She needed him; her father was *gone;* she needed somebody. He didn't show up Tuesday either. She was afraid to cles him and she went through all sorts of explanations as to why he didn't show. *We were never serious anyway. It's not like we'd planned for a future or anything, so he's not obligated....* In her state—constantly sedated, in and out of consciousness—she knew attempting to reason or think was foolish. After her Tuesday surgeries, she slept until Saturday morning. The deep sleep was brought on by drugs designed to help her heal faster, but she doubted she'd have slept any less without them. In the moment before she awoke, she felt a warm presence, and could sense Blue by her side, scraggly from having arrived Tuesday night and having never left the hospital. She smiled, and finally opening her eyes, looked to the chair by her bedside. Seated there was her sister, Mariela. Eaves heart sank. Mariela looked at her with something almost resembling pity. Eaves cried.

"Your boyfriend's dead, hermanita."

121

Deep down, she'd already known.

Mariela got up from where she was seated and put a key on the stand by the bed. She leaned forward and kissed Eaves on the forehead, whispering "It doesn't feel so great when it happens to you. Does it, puta?" Eaves felt some of Mariela's lipstick come off. Her perfume was nauseating. Without saying another word, Mariela turned around and left.

Later that afternoon, a doctor with two nurses by his side came in to tell Eaves her surgeries had been successful. She'd had three broken ribs, a fractured collarbone, a broken ankle and an infection caused by the metal lodged in her arm. They would keep her for two weeks to rule out brain damage, despite the fact she miraculously showed few signs of head trauma.

Eaves had questions about what happened; but first, she had to hear from someone else what happened to Blue. Was there any chance cruel Mariela had gleefully whispered a lie? The doctor insisted he didn't know anything yet and that Eaves needed to rest. She raised her voice in response. She struggled, trying to get out of bed; she would have either run or fought him. The nurses came to her bedside to restrain her but she didn't need to be; for all her efforts, she'd barely moved. The doctor pressed a slant on her arm. Eaves stopped struggling. Darkness again.

* * *

BOOM.

The sound rocked, crumbled and shattered everything. In one moment, the once unshakeable buildings were no longer pillars of anything—the physical devastation almost an afterthought to the symbolic destruction. People, scattered in the streets, scurried instinctively towards safety. Reza Shirazi, Emperor of the Global Union Alliance and High Commander of the IPU—Institute for the Preservation of Unity, had heard the explosion even deep within the fortress

that was the IPU palace in Bushwall Heights. Once intel
flowed in, he discovered his organization, charged with the
safety of the citizens of the North Emerian Union, had been
targeted and suffered crushing losses. As he hovered in a
phrincopter above the scene of the biggest target (and one of
the many buildings to fall in the blast), Unity International
Bank, he had an idea who was behind the chaos he observed
beneath him. *How* they had managed to carry out this feat of
terror was another matter entirely.

"Emperor?" Grace Ife, a tall woman of regal posture
attempted to get his attention.

"Yes, Captain Ife."

"I've received word one of our emises from this site
survived. Eaves Darcela, a funding analyst."

"Good news. Is she ready for questioning?"

"No, Oba. She's critical. Doctors say it may take up to a
week to bring her to full consciousness."

"Well, inform them she must be ready faster than that.
Whatever resources necessary will be made available. We
need to know what she saw … Darcela … *Ruben's* daughter?"

"Yes, Oba."

"Unfortunate. Express my sympathies to him."

"Sir, Ruben Darcela died in the bombing. He was onsite,
killed immediately by the blast per the account from the
medics."

The emperor let out a long exhale. "Be sure to make the
proper arrangements for his memorial. His service to the
crown will not go unnoticed. Did we have any survivors apart
from Eaves? What of the civilian nobles employed by the
bank?"

Grace shook her head and gave the emperor a heavy-
hearted look. "No word of any other survivors so far, Oba. It
appears living quarters of multiple personnel were also
targeted."

The emperor nodded. "This was a deliberate attack on
the gentry, a shot across the bow of our union's ideals. Place

a band of emises on the ground. I want them to go through
the ruins, go where the safes were stored. Notify the Pro-Ts
they are to let only those with emis' passcodes and IDs
through. Understood?"

"Yes, sire."

Emperor Shirazi looked at his cles showing a summon
from Minister Janine Corlmond and declined the call. The
Minister would be upset, but there were far more pressing
matters requiring attention than constantly briefing the
elected leader of the NEU. Hopefully the young emis Eaves
would provide some insight upon regaining consciousness,
but in the meantime swift action had to be taken. Referred to
in whispers by some in the Ministry as the "Emperor of
Shadows," Shirazi didn't appreciate the foolishness of people
who refused to understand what it took to not only survive as
a union, but to thrive and be more than a mere going
concern. Especially the elected—those who had less stake in
its future than its ruling class. There were, as tragic as this
incident was, benefits to be had from it, as certain measures
he'd often received pushback on from the Ministry would
perhaps now receive a warmer reception. It wouldn't be long
before the emises rummaging through the ruins of the bank
would strengthen his position by confirming his suspicions.

"Captain Ife,"

"Yes, Oba?"

"What's the final tally on how many buildings were hit?"

"Seven total."

"Okay. Take a look at the other locations. Have our
analysts pull feeds from all towers within a ten-block radius
of each blast for twenty-four hours prior. I want them to
comb through every inch and provide you with a point by
point summary of all suspicious activity."

"Yes, Oba."

Emperor Shirazi smiled at Captain Ife as she left the
room. His cles lit up with another summons from Minister
Corlmond. "Good morning, Madam Minister. Yes, I

apologize, but as you can understand, I have been at the scene assessing the severity and working to apprehend those responsible. At least four hundred casualties. I can assure you, Madam Minister, that we will be meeting shortly. Of course, I agree. There are critical security measures we must discuss." He sat and made himself comfortable as the carrier phrinned to the scene of the other blasts.

* * *

Nearly a week went by before Emperor Shirazi received word the young emis Eaves Darcela had fully regained consciousness and was now responsive. In that time, he'd been notified by his emises on the ground that corlypses— light blue crystals more important to national security than anything else lost that day—had been stolen from the underground vault at Unity International Bank, confirming his suspicions about the perpetrators of the attack. But there were still missing pieces, and anything Emis Darcela could provide would go a long way.

He called Grace into his alcove at the palace. "Captain Ife, alert the twins. Advise them we're traveling via gate to Carter Royal Hospital. Captain Ife returned, flanked by two tall, bald identical twins with muscular builds. Aged bruises and scars wrote combat on their faces, and both were armed. "Ready?"

Captain Ife smiled in response to Emperor Shirazi's query and her hands, glowing, created a phrinway out of thin air. Within moments, the four of them were at the hospital, at the foot of Emis Darcela's bed.

"Superb gate, Captain Ife. Thank you."

"My pleasure, Oba."

The doctor, who'd been expecting them looked rattled upon their arrival, but quickly composed himself. "Good afternoon Emperor Shirazi. She's been placed in med-induced sleep to aid her recovery, but we can wake her now."

KIDS OF STOLEN TOMORROW

* * *

The next time Eaves came to, three men and one woman
were standing at the foot of her bed, all with blackers on and
helmets tucked under their arms. She recognized one of them
as the High Commander of the Institute for Preservation of
Unity. Emperor … something. *Her emperor;* her *Oba.* She
couldn't recall his name, and was suddenly glad she was under
observation for head trauma. They stood, silently studying
her. The woman activated a panel and walked over to her.
"Identity confirmed as Eee-yah-vez Dar-say-lah," the panel
vocalized.

The woman, tall and silky-skinned, was a high-ascended
captain—Eaves had seen her before, but like the emperor,
names did not materialize. The intensity in her eyes belied
how effortlessly her presence intimidated; she could easily be
mistaken for the most royal of the four. Overall, their
presence as a group triggered the first hint of relief she'd had
since her horrific nightmare began last Monday. She'd start
getting some answers.

"Eaves, I am Captain Grace Ife. We understand this is a
difficult time for you. Your dad was sincerely loved and
respected by all of us; we can't imagine the pain you're
suffering right now, but we want you to know you're not
alone. We want to apprehend those responsible for this and
prevent such a tragedy from occurring in the future. What
Emperor Shirazi and I would like from you—"

Ah, Emperor Shirazi—that was it.

He took over. "We must know about events leading up to
the blast. Tell me everything you remember about your day—
during, before and after it. Even anecdotal, seemingly
unrelated details may be critical, as I'm sure you understand.
Can you help us?"

Answers were coming later, she guessed. Teary-eyed, she
nodded. "My father—" she wept. Captain Ife touched her on

the shoulder; it helped. "It was my day off. My father—
Captain Darcela called me in to work. I assumed it was an
emergency, said goodbye to Blue—wait, where's Blue? I
haven't seen him since ... she said he was dead but she lied,
right?" More tears.

"Please, Emis Darcela—"

"Okay ... I put on my blacker and headed in. When I
arrived, I entered through the front—there was a crowd of
protesters across the street—"

"Did you notice anything suspicious?" Emperor Shirazi
interjected.

"No, sire, a light pulse blast hit my blacker from the
crowd but that was it; it was weak and barely noticeable.
Nothing compared to what those crowds have thrown in the
past. I entered without further disturbance. When I got to my
desk I started reviewing the file he—" she stuttered and took
a few deep breaths to compose herself. "The file he left for
me. I was able to find some patterns. But some things didn't
make sense ..."

Captain Ife pulled up a panel twice as large as the one she
used to scan Eaves earlier. Eaves immediately recognized the
files she'd deciphered that Monday. She fought back tears and
took a deep breath.

"What do you need to know?"

"Your opinion of what you found."

Eaves hesitated. Captain Ife looked at Emperor Shirazi.
"Eaves, we—"

"No, no, no ... how could I not see this ... How am I
just now realizing this?" Eaves, suddenly remembering
herself, looked at Grace. "Sorry to interrupt, Captain."

Captain Ife looked back at Eaves encouragingly.
"Realizing what? Go on."

"The file—the history. It wasn't an accident I was looking
at it, not that morning. There were a lot of red flags. The
pattern shared some consistencies with money laundering.
But things didn't make sense—everything was incongruent."

"Like?"

"Well, for example, I thought it was strange they went through one of Unity International's subsidiaries, Unico, for this stage of laundering. They'd been clients for five years with only small transactions here and there, but over the past year, there were huge spikes in the size of deposits out of sorts with their business model ... and what was stranger was the regularity of cycle time involving the spikes—shortly after they made the larger deposits they purchased assets, every time. In this case, lending houses ranging from red vane level loan shark filth, to fairly respectable blue vane regionals. I checked their books and the deposits were from pure, clean profits."

"Finance. Curious," the emperor interjected.

"Yes, Oba, but there was more. The lion's share of their lending is in the red vanes, where there's far less regulation; rational. But the size in combination with the frequency—it was exact, predictable, perfect. No profit cycle is *that* consistent, and no smart money launderer is going to go for such impossible consistency. It was daring. Doing that at *any* institution will trigger alarms after a while. It may take ages but it'll eventually be caught if the staff is half competent. But doing it at *Unico* or anywhere affiliated with Unity International is like wearing a neon blacker and running a pulse through it in the dark in a crowded room. Their file couldn't have possibly been that way the whole time or we'd have caught on long ago. Our algos automatically detect such anomalies. Something changed, someone altered it. They *wanted* to be seen. They wanted the files to be found. They wanted us to know, *that day*."

"And your guess as to who's behind it?"

"Not sure, Captain," she answered. "Lorzan's officers were predictably a dead end in the little time I checked ... but ..."

"*Emis Darcela*," the emperor sounded impatient.

128

"Muh-my dad asked me to trace the owners ... he must have had some idea, right? Only the worst kind of enemy, someone—people consumed with hatred would be so bold and this particular brand of daring ... the Nth maybe? But this doesn't fit anything we know about them ..."

"*Did* you trace the owners, Emis Darcela?" Emperor Shirazi's voice was suddenly chilling. Eaves looked to Captain Ife. She couldn't decipher the captain's look but it was not comforting like before. This confirmed her suspicions her father hadn't gotten clearance for the owner trace.

"Did you?"

"No. No, sire, the blast happened and ..."

The emperor nodded and shot a glance at Captain Ife. The twins moved, each to opposite sides of her bed, one at her feet, and the other by her shoulders. Captain Ife closed the panel Eaves had analyzed and brought up another one, but Eaves was unable to make out what was on it. She swiped across it once, and one of the twins came forward and pressed a slant against her arm and all the pain she'd felt was gone. Her eyes grew wide. "What was that? I can't move. What did you do?"

The emperor smiled. "It's okay, Eaves. You've been temporarily paralyzed from the shoulders down. It will wear off soon and you'll feel better. We're taking you to a medical wing at the palace where we can more closely monitor your recovery." Eaves was carried by the twins through a phrinway opened by Captain Ife. The emperor and Captain Ife followed them, and together they entered a room in the palace infirmary. The twins placed Eaves on a bed as the emperor addressed her. "You have several sensitive injuries that are healing well, but would be aggravated by excessive motion. Once the effects of the slant wear off and you're fully rested, we'll require more of your help. You'll come to agree with me it was better for you to hear the news in this state." The twins sat her up. "Monday morning, March 3, in this year 74 O.O, around 7:49 AM, Unity International Bank,

129

Unico Bank, and the residences of any personnel who were scheduled to be home at that time, were simultaneously rocked by explosions. We received an untraceable panel stream with a cloaked, masked individual claiming this was the 'Will of Olorun by the glory of the Son Ogun, and that all who still hold to the false gods of old shall fall.' We have reason to think the Unico client, and by extension, Unity International client Lorzan Industries whose file you analyzed, is a shell for the Nth and they are behind the attack. The bomb detonated was a pulse-bomb—limited in range but especially powerful and easily synchronized. You're aware of them, yes?"

"Yes, Oba," Eaves responded weakly

"Then you're also aware pulse bombs are powered by corlypses—those rare crystals long coveted by the Nth for that very reason. Lorzan's CEO has issued a denial of any involvement, sends condolences, and promises full cooperation. He, several executives and other employees, have been placed under arrest until further information can be extracted. We believe and agree with your suspicion you were meant to discover that file, those breadcrumbs were left intentionally. We believe the analysis of their file activated a trigger they'd planted ages ago. Furthermore, all the inhabitants of your Brownstone at home at the time perished. We recovered the bodies of your neighbors in the rubble."

"No ..."

"Aaron Simondson, or "Blue," as you referred to him, was in your apartment at the time of the blast. Medics were sent to the scene in the immediate aftermath but all attempts to revive him failed. We are truly sorry for your loss, and will see to it you have ample time to grieve. There will be a commemoration for your father. As you're well aware, there's much to attend to so we must get going. The staff will be here to watch over and return you to full strength. You have served the crown well and are a shining example of nobility. I can only hope once you're healed you can find it within yourself to help bring to justice those who've committed this heinous act."

Eaves was quiet for several minutes, weeping. As the emperor turned to leave, she said, weakly, "Vida"

"What was that?"

"Vida, sire. She was … she's my neighbor's niece—a child. She was in school, supposed to be … please make sure she's okay, Oba—please."

"We'll do our best, Eaves."

Eaves lay there barely able to translate any of what she was feeling, cycling between deep sadness, anger, guilt and pain. Her temporary paralysis had made a true release of these emotions impossible and she nearly choked in her frustration. She felt pity for the little girl orphaned by the actions of savages, and that brought her back to anger. *They'll suffer; they will know my agony.* She felt fortunate to be in the palace, a place whose very idea she'd fought. Now she saw it as a fortress from where she could channel her pain. Ruben wouldn't get to see her but she'd fulfill his wildest dreams. She would prove her worth in the domain. She'd find every last Lorzan Industries "employee" and let them feel the pain she felt, forever and ever. *They'll never hurt anyone again.* Ruben's death pushed her in a way his whip-cracking in life had not.

Immobilized in bed, Eaves understood what now drove her, and it was nothing as superfluous as "Making Papá Proud." All she saw was revenge. Revenge for Aaron, revenge for her father. Revenge for what the Nth did to *her* life. Who were they to act as the mouthpiece of the gods? Did they not know that the crown was the true voice—that the nobility were the arbiters on earth? She cursed the gods for what they'd allowed to happen to her loved ones, save for Ogun. He would be her guide and avenging salvation.

* * *

IPU High Commander and Global Union Alliance Emperor Reza Shirazi sat across from Minister Janine Corlmond and waited. After a while, Minister Corlmond smiled at him, and looked at Grace. "Captain Ife, your background is not unlike others who may protest. Do you agree with this measure?"

Captain Ife opened her mouth to answer, but Shirazi interjected. "The same could be said for all of us in this room. With all due respect, there is little relevance, Madam Minister. The safety of our nation is greater than such concerns."

The Minister could have sworn the outer edges of his mouth twisted up into a smirk as he said "all of us," which made her slightly angry and half amused. She held a holographic ball in her hand which she twirled with a finger as she sat at her desk. She stood while pressing a button on the side of the ball, increasing its size. Facing a wall, she threw the ball against it, effortlessly catching it, throwing it again. She continued quietly like this for several minutes, back turned to her guests.

"You realize what you're suggesting I do? What we do? You know once we hop into that little rocket ship and take off, there ain't no comin' back. No return visits, no nothin'. Once we cross this line, that's the way it's gonna be." Turning around to face them, she bounced the ball, but against the floor now, pace steady, uninterrupted. "You sure? You ready for this? Can ya'll live with that? We are amongst the last of the unions to be without such a measure for good reason and it's a point of pride!"

"I find it helps to have a healthy hatred for the present and its prisoners. We must look to the future now more than ever. With all due respect, Madam Minister, the belief our avoidance of this has been anything other than cosmetic is a false one. I'd say we began this expedition long ago. This is merely terra forming." Emperor Shirazi was smiling now, a full-on grin, a thing which made her uneasy. He nodded to Captain Ife who exited the room.

"I'm not so sure I know exactly what you're referring to, Emperor. My main goal is a safe and strong unio—"

"And I assure you, you will have that, Madam Minister. We have the same goal. The difference is I do not worry about focus groups and public opinion polls and second guess my steps. I have *real* information readily available to me. I deal only in facts. I oversaw this process with great success in the West African Union and the South Emerian Union. My strength comes from knowing what I do is right, that this union will be protected as a result of the IPU's actions and my convictions. The entire North Emerian Union is afraid. Those in the red vanes are no different from their counterparts in the clouds in this regard. As long as the poor have a common enemy with the nobility and others of means—the threat of a *real*, foreign, boogie man, they'll accept whatever measures we put in place for their safety. They'll *beg for them.*" The hairs on the minister's neck stood on end. "They'll forget their struggle for precious, scarce resources, follow what we tell them and be *grateful* to still be considered part of the North Emerian Union. Because, make no mistake, the Nth want us *all* gone. Nobility, *elected officials,* red-vaners, NEU, AU, WAU, SEU—they won't stop until the little civilization left in this world is destroyed. And that's no scaremongering, Madam Minister. The Unity bombing was the culmination of terrorists being able to take advantage of lax zoning procedures resulting in the detonation of a weapon powered by corlypses. Corlypses—that in the aftermath of that bombing, they were able to get their hands on *again.* You've heard the threats, read their mission statements. We're seeing the results of inaction. We cannot continue to leave ourselves exposed."

At a gala a few months before she took office, Corlmond was told by the outgoing minister that Emperor Shirazi's manner of speaking wasn't deliberately insulting. *I never did give Minister Zhang credit for his sense of humor,* she thought as she listened to the emperor ooze condescension. "Emperor, can you guarantee our stores of corlypses will be protected? That they'll no longer fall into the wrong hands? That our citizens will be kept safe if we go down this path?"

"Of course, Madam Minister. Contrary to what you may believe, the IPU's umbrella extends beyond the ruling class."

And you're sure all the 'real information readily available' to you is enough to pull this here trigger?"

"Unequivocally."

"You sure seem mighty sure of everything, Emperor."

Shirazi smiled. "Madam Minister, a late, great emperor once told me that humility is for 'men in the face of gods.' Everything else, is just pretend."

Minister Corlmond shivered. She wished there were other—*any* other viable options. She wished the best available plan didn't come from someone so arrogant and disrespectful and opaque, but he was correct. Only facts mattered and the fact was the North Emerian Union needed to survive, no matter the cost. She remained silent for several minutes.

"Alrighty, Lord of Darkness, take me through what we're lookin' at here. I need *everrry* detail before I take this to the council. They'll eat it up, but only if it looks right."

Minister Janine Corlmond had been a three-sport star at the collegiate level, president of her graduating class, and a two-time world champion swimmer. She ran seven miles a day, worked-out before bed, and did not believe a problem existed that couldn't be solved by "putting our heads together and barreling through that summabitch." She wore stunning float-shoes but they were always powered off, the minister preferring the strength of her "God-given two" feet to walk places. The middle child of nine, she learned the benefits of connecting with several different types of personalities long before she learned the uselessness of long division.

She was born and raised in Blackbern, Carolanda, and her campaign machine had filled the panels with tales of her difficult red vane-like upbringing in this small impoverished town. She'd sold the populace a dream of achieving the

134

impossible and ridden it to the halls of Glory Tower. In reality, her family owned six *million* acres of Carolanda land through various trusts and holding companies, a *tenth* of the entire landmass. Didn't matter though, it was both illegal and impossible to trace it to them, and Minister Corlmond was the right woman at the right time.

The "poor country girl" overcoming the odds to reverse the fortunes of a once proud empire brought the union together in a way not seen since the beginning of the Nightfall War. She was a throwback to a time when the center of the North Emerian Union had a strong singular identity that overrode all the other disparate voices. Maybe, the active electorate thought, she was what they needed. Her holographic ball now deactivated but her hands still moving as if it never left, she sat again, about to enact legislation that could divide that same union if not handled with the right amount of care, finesse and charisma. She smiled, knowing such things were as easy for her as breathing in the purified green vane air. Her daddy had always said she could "talk a dog off a meat wagon." This particular dog would require the minister's most brilliant performance to date, but she was ready.

Emperor Shirazi outlined his plan to form fully regulated, monitored and enforced divisions between the vanes. Until the Unity attacks, vanes had been an understood but non-explicit concept amongst the NEU's populace, thanks to the differences in temperature and air quality between them due to the Lyteche-built Climate Limitation Atmospheric Organic Devices—simply called clouds—that enveloped and protected the blue and green ones, enhancing and magnifying the sun's stifled rays, leaving the red vanes exposed to the deteriorated environment. However, red-vaners, many of whom worked minimum pay jobs in the blue vanes, and a select few who worked in the green had become, as he explained, "a security threat and liability that will be exploited continuously by the enemy unless we seal the vulnerability."

Shirazi is a funny little man, thought Minister Corlmond as she listened to and watched him. How did *he* become the most powerful of the royals? His build and stature reminded her of an over-sized penguin. Even the way he raised his arm from his side to adjust his spectacles (who still wore those?) reminded her of a penguin flapping its wing. Yet the chills his presence elicited killed the impulse to laugh. She peered at his infamous indentation—a burn mark that opened below one eye and ran down the side of his face to the base of his neck. She'd asked him about it once, and he'd only said—smiling— that he had it before he became a soldier. She accepted that as a dead end. If Emperor Shirazi wanted something to stay hidden, no force on earth could expose it. Formidable as Minister Corlmond was, coming into contact with him—as always, gave her the sense that she wasn't quite in control and made her wonder if she should've left politics alone and gone for *real* power, as her mother had once advised. But it also reminded her that whatever the emperor was, she was not. And she was glad for that.

Emperor Shirazi's demeanor convinced Minister Corlmond she'd need to exclude him from the selling of the plan to the Council. She'd initially thought it necessary he be present but her doubts about his presence helping resurfaced during this meeting. It was one thing for a man to look like he had a few secrets—another to look like he was always hiding something and that subtle difference could easily wreak havoc on the reverence his presence demanded. *No, I've made the right choice. I'll use his notes, but I go this alone.*

* * *

"My final assessment is we, effective immediately, create solid fenced and armed borders between the vanes, and increase both emis and Pro-T presence at all checkpoints. Furthermore, red vane inhabitants who work in either blue or green vanes are required to scan in upon entry and out upon exit at the end of their work days. Any non-worker red vane inhabitants who wish to enter either the blue or green vanes must apply for a pass beforehand and undergo an extensive background check before approval. This process may take several months. They must also keep their vane pass at eye level during their stay. Red-vaners may be stopped at any point in time by any green or blue vane inhabitant and asked to produce IDs. Any resistance will be met by immediate arrest and quarantine. I think if you review the document in your panels provided by the emperor, you'll find it's rather fair considering the heap of cow shit we find ourselves in."

"So how exactly does this solve our situation, Minister?"

Oh, lovely, Councilman Portnick. Aren't you always a dear? Why don't you put that half-assed "people's college" education to work and read? The Minister beamed. "As outlined there in the panel, blue and green vanes will receive maximum concentration of security. Forces will be focused on making sure attacks don't occur in these vanes. Traffic in and out will be screened. The regular folks who live there are scanned daily anyway. This'll make attacks extremely difficult, virtually impossible. Red vanes won't be targeted because there are little to no targets worthwhile in them."

"You're saying our neglect of these people will keep them safe!?"

"Your words not mine, Portnick, but there'll be far less incentive to attack red vanes. It's worked resoundingly in our sister unions throughout the globe and we're *behind* in adopting it. In addition, anyone who's followed history knows recovery time in such areas is relatively swift compared to more developed ones, due to the low replacement cost of primitive infrastructure. But you were the educator. *I know you know that."* Minister Corlmond exaggerated her drawl for emphasis. Chuckles and guffaws filled the room.

Councilman Dean Portnick, now a shade of red that undermined his attempt to appear unbothered, waited for the ruckus to die down. "Humor me, Minister. What if the so-called impossible happens? What if there's an attack in the red vanes?"

"You know as well as everybody here any blast or chemical attack would be deflected by the clouds and wouldn't spread. Emergency response protocol would handle the rest. I'd accuse you of being a few circuits short of a full grid, but I'm sure there's some angle or game you're playing here, Dean."

"I want to hear you acknowledge you're treating these people like they don't have the same rights, like they're second class citizens. You cannot do this! You can't. You're using lives, *people* to divert away attacks! You can't use human lives this way. You can't funnel terror away from one group of lives to another!" A collective groan arose from all present.

"Minister, I don't understand for the life of me why we humor Portnick at all. Why don't we reach out to someone like Carbo, someone with real power—real *oya* and influence amongst these people to make this more palatable?" Councilman Williams, who represented a blue vane district bordering a red, had previously been curiously silent.

This is good. He's engaging, the minister thought. *He's a true barometer.*

"That puppy-turned-prophet for profit? *Power?* Councilman Williams," she replied; "Darcen Carbo may be an impressive young man, but he has *oya* in the way a chicken has wings. If you need to get some helpless, hapless downtrodden family to give up their life savings to increase his fleet of huvs in exchange for some back-end promise of eternal miracles, sure he's the guy, but I doubt his influence extends beyond that. What we need here is lasting commitment to be in these communities from someone we can *trust.* And someone *they* trust simply because they've already been doing it for so long. We all pile on Dean, but he's fine at what he does and is indeed a necessary . . ." she stopped there and smiled.

Laughter from the gathering.

She returned to Councilman Portnick's question. "Dean, no one here's funneling anything, no one's rights are being taken away. But can you cut the crap? We all know the survival of this union is predicated on one unassailable fact: the haves will be the ones who push us forward into the future and allow us to regain our dominance on the world stage. And that benefits everyone. Just because nukes are gone doesn't mean we can't all still be annihilated. Do you *even remember* the EU? What about the EAU? I'm sure they thought they'd still be around. Look at what's taken place in the heart of our union, in a place we believed to be secure. Would you rather have us all destroyed? With nothing and no one left to move us into that great tomorrow where we return to the grand throne that's rightfully ours?"

"I think your rousing jingoist rhetoric and monarchy reference tells us what we need to know about your true intentions and loyalties, Madam Minister. But I want everyone here to remember I did not agree to this wholeheartedly, I objected to many points—"

"We get it, Dean. That's enough now. Let's vote." A voice like a boulder rumbling down the side of a mountain silenced Portnick. It belonged to Councilwoman Rafferty. Janine stared at her. *It's about time,* her look said, twinkle in her eyes. *I figured I would make you sweat a little,* Rafferty shot back, menace in hers. Shortly before, an aide from the minister's office confirmed Councilwoman Rafferty had secured additional funding for Councilman Portnick's oft ridiculed Helping Hands Initiative, the joke being Portnick's hands were the only ones being helped. The biggest potential roadblock to a smooth implementation was out of the way.

The Unity Protection Act of 74 O.O. (more commonly known as the Vane Act) passed unanimously. Eaves watched the announcement on a panel from her hospital bed at the IPU. As Minister Corlmond (surrounded by the noble marlsonnes literally singing praises in the background) and popular red vane councilman Dean Portnick explained how the act was necessary to protect the future and would save countless lives; she wondered why the emperor wasn't up there. It had his fingerprints all over it. Then again, that was probably why he didn't need to be.

Eaves closed her eyes. She had a long path to recovery ahead of her. Her mind and spirit needed recovery more than anything else; physically she was nearly healed. She saw an image of Ruben sitting with her as a little girl as she argued with him about the method he used to solve a differential equation. He teased her as she grew more frustrated with his quicker but slightly less accurate way. In her anger, she discovered a way both faster and more accurate than either of their previous tries. He had the widest, proudest smile on his face when she showed him. He was always pushing her to think outside the box, even then—especially then. That was the first time in her life she understood what people meant when they spoke of adoration; that moment, that day, was *it*. As the memory floated across her mind, the numbing agent used on her earlier began to wear off, and she felt warmth and a peaceful strength as she went quietly to sleep.

80 O.O.

I-4822 PANEL LOG entry. All previous statements and IDs fully confirmed, current and applicable. Today's date is Tuesday, March 19, 80 O.O. The time is 1332 hours, Central Union Base Time. Updating progress on Program Irunmole. Of 368 mutating strains we have been able to effectively combat 368, with minimal to no side effect, discoloration, or the former wild fluctuations in bioavailability. With the changes made in the dormant strands of the Alvir77, we were able to refashion it into a chameleonic micropeptide encoded for infiltration. Since entry I-3915, strain 187, it has effectively mutated along with igioyin and neutralizes its effects each iteration. But all is not perfect. There is at this time a limitation to the potency. 1500 milligrams appear to be the max dose the human body can ingest at a time without grave side effects. As suspected and indicated in earlier logs, igioyin remains neutralized only with persistent application, however; we have been able to increase the period after ingestion to 171 hours prior to destabilization. Application at 1500 milligrams is thus required every seven days. Normals have consistently shown a full recovery at this schedule with little if any negative effects. Extranormals have had varying results with side effects ranging from death, to full recovery with dramatic reduction in extranormal ability. Further research must be conducted to determine if treatment can be modified to a single dose. The time is now 1335 hours Central Union Base Time, on Tuesday, March 19, 80 O.O.; this log is complete.

OJUJU

THE MAN WORE *a long, white, loose fitting lace top with ornate designs and gold, was it gold? Yes—it was, weaved into the wavy patterns of the long sleeves. The top, which stopped below his knees, appeared to blend into his trousers of the same fit and design. The sparkling sandals which adorned his feet cost more than enough to be worthy of his agbada, as his garb was known. A quick scan of the audience in the panel showed a crowd of what was likely mostly red-vaners with a few blues mixed in, faces rapt with attention. Around his neck were assorted beads that met in a black leather pouch on his chest. He smiled at the audience, removed his sandals and walked backwards to sit on a mat on the stage, crossing his legs in front of him. He closed his eyes and motioned to a man near the front of the audience.*

A short, rotund, peach hued individual who looked to be in his early forties stood. He wore a similar outfit to the man on the stage, save his—a light, grassy green color—appeared to have been tailored for the skinnier twin he'd devoured in the womb. His surprisingly spectacular head of hair was out of place enough for viewers to suspect he was planting. Tucked under his arm as he approached the stage was a box in purple wrapping paper with gold trim. He was motioned by the man in white to stop before the top of the steps at the center of the stage, and set his gift down at its edge. The rotund man shook with each step, and what began as a few droplets of sweat coming down his forehead had now turned the once dry, grassy green of his top into lush marshes and dark swampland. Without opening his eyes, the man in white spoke.

"Raymond, it's okay. Tell them."

Unable to commit to fully facing the crowd and also reluctant to turn away from facing the man on stage, Raymond settled for the sides of his now reddened face towards each. He continued to shake, yet managed to string a few sentences together to everyone and yet no one in particular

142

about how he'd had some issue or another and the man on stage in white had cured him.

"What an idiot." Eaves Darcela snickered as she watched the audience clap and the man waddle back to his seat. She pulled out a large dark cloth the same shade as her blacker and wiped a glob of coagulated blood off her blade.

"Want me to turn it off, Captain?" This was asked by a young musclebound emis accompanying her, as he stepped over two bodies and a pond of blood.

"No. It's always nice to have something going in the background while we work. The best part is coming up right now." She looked at him then nodded to the panel with her eyes. "You watch Carbo?"

"Not much now, a lot when I was little."

"Ah … so last week?" she said, half kidding, wholly amused. Each year, her staff got younger.

"Yes. Wait—No, no I'd still be—" He realized she was joking and laughed. "No, back in 79. About fourteen years ago or so."

And dumber, apparently.

It always seemed she, on the other hand, was going in the opposite direction. Despite all the charges she'd found herself leading in the domain over the years and the losses she'd endured, battle weary drag was still a foreign concept to Captain Eaves Darcela. Her attributes were in a state of perpetual ascension and ceilings were trivial constructs, meant for cowards who gave up communion with the sun for protection from the rain. It wouldn't last forever though; it couldn't. She knew it would end someday—that she'd be brought down to earth in a spectacular blaze, likely at the moment she least expected it, at the worst possible time.

Like Dad.

Like Grace.

"You little bastards love making me feel old, don't you?"

Four months ago, Captain Darcela had been told of an impossible thing—the reappearance of Vida, the girl with a single braid—her deceased neighbor's niece—who'd disappeared the day of the Unity bombings. Vida, then a little girl, hadn't aged a day in the 19 years since. Worse still, she'd managed to kill an emis in pursuit before disappearing yet again, and interviews of the remaining witnesses yielded nothing.

But things were looking up.

Eaves turned to a haggard looking man drenched in sweat, bound by chains, and examined a trail of rubies encrusting a large gash down his bicep. "That's not looking too good you know. You don't have to meet the same fate as your buddies over there. We know you're the one who has the information we're looking for, so of course I'd prefer you keep living. But you have to give me something. Why'd you try to steal the corlypses? How did you know they were here? Are you working with Vida? The little girl. Is that what you call her, Vida? I know she's part of your organization. What do you know about her, where is she?" Eaves pressed down on the wound with her blade. The man winced as the scabs fell and fresh plasma sprang forth, but he remained silent and sneering, defiance plastered on his face like a panel for martyrdom. Nthns had no names, only numbers. They were encouraged to have no familial ties as well and often did not—a result of smart recruiting (orphans were targeted) and cultish dedication. This often made obtaining leverage and information impossible and this one was likely as dead an end as his late comrades. But they *were* human, and the captain had a hunch.

The emis who'd made Eaves feel old walked over to the captive at her beckoning. He leaned the Nthn's head back and forced his mouth open as he struggled, fear finally taking residence in his eyes as he anticipated his end. The emis smiled, placed a slight cut inside the Nthn's cheek, swabbed it and nodded at his captain.

"Give it to Ptolemy." Darcela motioned to the corner. "Toley, come take a look at this."

The perpetually giggling Toley of ample, ever-present overbite—resembling a pitiable pre-teen, matchstick limbs precariously supporting his bowling ball noggin—got up from the corner where he'd been viewing a netline panel with ear phones and timidly wobbled towards the brawny emis to take hold of the crimson swab. He noticed the blood streaming from the seated Nthn's open arm wound and pulled out a cloth from his blacker, covering his nose and mouth. As he got closer, his cheeks resembled the chests of some birds when threatened. Eaves laughed. Ptolemy turned away from the scene and vomited. Eaves motioned to a third emis to wipe up the mess.

"C'mon, this isn't your first time out here Toley. Get it together," her laughter tapered to a snicker and she added: "no chuckling that time, eh? Now, *that's* funny."

Ptolemy, ignoring her, wiped his face and collecting himself, took the swab from the emis.

"Can you use it?"

Ptolemy, seemingly recovered, giggled. "If there's a positive match anywhere, I'll find it."

"No! No …" the Nthn withered as he realized what was taking place.

"You'd better get to work then." The captain turned to the Nthn. "I didn't want to do it, but you've given me nothing to work with. Maybe you have something else to say to me now?"

Suddenly rebellious again, the Nthn spat on the ground. "You won't find a thing, go ahead."

Eaves cocked her head to the side while viewing the Nthn quizzically. She shook it. "Remember, you chose this."

"Your arrogance—to believe you can just do what you want. Your nerve. You think being born into the IPU makes you exalted? *Makes you noble?*"

"Yes."

As Ptolemy Kabore placed the swab in a Petri dish, connected the dish to his panel, put his earphones back on and logged into the secure netline of the IPU to get to work, Eaves returned her attention to the panel where Darcen Carbo was now addressing another audience member. One could make out the fading bits of audible disappointment of the audience members who weren't chosen.

"What's your name?" he said to a tall, bald-headed adolescent.

"Sunday," said the teen. Carbo smiled a knowing smile. "You're Nigerian?"

The boy nodded.

"Nice. Where from?"

"My parents are from Enugu, where I was born, but I was raised here in the NEU."

The audience let out a gasp. Carbo's smile faded.

"I have been to Enugu a few times, a bewitching place, in spite of all that's happened. A brave and mighty people you come from. Please, omo, tell me what troubles you." Sunday stood at the top step of the stage as Carbo remained seated.

Eaves snickered again. "Note how he didn't ask him where in the NEU. He's a red-vaner. His parents are probably Nth sympathizers."

Ptolemy giggled. "Captain Darcela, you're always saying Carbo's show is staged, so why would it matter?" Eaves fired a low pulse at Ptolemy, who yelped. His smirk was replaced with a pained expression as he worked in silence.

"Babalawo," the boy began after a lengthy pause, "My mother is ill." The boy produced a photo of his mother in a panel. "We've gone to doctors everywhere, and they do not know what is wrong with her. They have diagnosed her with all sorts of ailments and provided her with all sorts of medicines but nothing seems to work, and she keeps getting weaker and weaker. We fear for her life, and my father believes this all began when a co-worker, jealous of her success, cursed her with ill-health. I told him I don't believe that, but I come to you to as a last resort."

Carbo, still seated, motioned to a man holding a large tub nearby. "Now," he said. The man began emptying sand from the tub at Carbo's feet. "Stop, that's enough." The man covered the tub and returned to where he was. Carbo reached down and from a large pile beside him, picked up a handful of what looked like smooth red and white stones.

"Kola nuts," said Eaves to no one in particular.

Carbo put them down and made a mark in the sand. He picked up and poured some of the sand on himself. He repeated this process another fifteen times as the boy watched along with the audience. After the final mark was made, Carbo stared at the sand, swaying, mouthing something inaudible to himself for several minutes. He stood up and didn't so much walk as glide towards the boy.

"What is your mother's name?"

"Deola."

"So your father, he believes?"

"Yes."

"You're prepared then?"

"Yes."

"Twenty-one."

The boy turned on a panel and shifted twenty-one in spends to Carbo's International Miracle Foundry.

Captain Darcela laughed.

Carbo nodded, smiled, touched the boy on the cheek and said, "Omo dada. Good boy. Did you bring a traditional photo of your mother?"

The boy nodded and handed a photo to Carbo with an image identical to the one in the panel earlier. Carbo looked at the photo, placed it in his pants pocket, smiled at the boy again and looked out to the audience.

"I'm going to ask Sunday to give me some items, that I may appeal to Orunmila and use the power of Osanyin to return his mother, Deola, to good health. I ask those of you who have those items in your possession at this moment to pass them forward so that in this way, today, September 16th, 93 La ti Odun Oluwa we may all take part in the miracle of healing as Olorun intended."

Captain Darcela impatiently turned to Ptolemy. "What's the hold up?"

Ptolemy giggled. "Nothing. I'm narrowing down matches; there's a waiting period while the algorithm eliminates false positives and pulls addresses. I'm working as fast as I can, Captain. I understand what's at stake."

Meanwhile on the panel, Carbo: *"The blood of a hen."*
"Mo ni O!" someone near the back of the auditorium shouted. A dark-skinned security guard dressed in a golden agbada walked briskly up the aisle to the source of the shout. He returned to the stage and handed a vial full of what could be assumed to be blood of some kind to Sunday who handed it to Carbo. The guard climbed back down to the foot of the stage. Carbo held the vial up in the bright, judgmental lights of the auditorium, turning it every which way. He shook the vial three times, held it still in front of himself and closed his eyes.

A hush fell over the crowd which, up until the moment he closed his eyes, was peppered with many others who were vocal with their eagerness to share their own vials and partake in the miracle that was to happen before them. For thirty seconds, they sat in silence as he mouthed incantations too advanced for them to lip read, and too low for them to hear.

He opened his eyes, placed the vial in his pants pocket and spoke again: "The blood of a cock." This time an audience member in the front row provided the vial for the guard to pass to Sunday. Carbo repeated the process, but this time, halfway through the thirty seconds, he smashed the vial on the ground, pointed to the one who'd given the vial and yelled "ORI BURUKU!!!" All air went out of the auditorium as the crowd froze.

The security guards in the front row quickly carried out a grey-haired man with skin like coal who struggled wildly and screamed at the top of his lungs "Iro lo nso! O puro! O Puro! Carbo ko ki nso oto O!!!!! LIAR LIAR LIAR CARBO YOU LIE O!!!! YOU—" His silence conspicuously coincided with him crossing out of the view of the crowd. As he was carried out, a wave of relief could be heard as the audience moved and whispered once more.

Eaves clapped. "Ha-ha! That's right tell him ... liar. I love it."

Carbo, continuing as if nothing had happened, repeated his request. "The blood of a cock!" This time a vial was quickly moved forward and passed examination without a hitch. It went into Carbo's pocket.

"Seven kola nuts!"

148

This item was in Sunday's possession. He reached into his trouser pockets and produced a handful of the colorful fruit, from which he counted seven aloud, and said, "Here Babalawo," as he handed them over.

"Thank you. Omo dada—good boy. Sit down, my child." As Sunday returned to his seat in the audience, Carbo held the kola nuts and placed them one by one into the leather pouch around his neck. "I have from you all everything needed to return Sunday's mother to health. I must now go into my chamber and with secret, sacred ingredients chosen by Orunmila himself, prepare the etu."

The curtain came down, and the wall panel went silent. Eaves returned her attention to Ptolemy who was tapping furiously, as codes she could barely understand moved across his panel. In the twenty-two years since she'd first walked into an IPU base, his was the first mind she'd truly considered superior. At nineteen, he currently looked like he'd barely entered puberty and in title he should've been little more than a glorified assistant, as he'd failed every exam for the rank of emis. But he was nobility nonetheless, and Toley *owned* the netlines at a level of mastery that was logical only if he were a sentient code to which the netlines themselves had given birth. *If he ever truly understands what he's capable of, we're all screwed.* She looked over at the Nthn. "Toley will be done soon. You still can control the outcome if you want. It doesn't have to be this way."

The Nthn muttered profanities in response, in time for Ptolemy to interject. "Captain, I've located a 99.99 percent match for a sister, and a 98.9 percent match for a son, with a 97.8 percent match for a partner with the son's DNA," he said after a lengthier than normal giggle.

Eaves smiled, walked over to him, and patted him on the shoulder. "You're so brilliant. I forget sometimes, Toley. I shouldn't."

"BITCH—I'll strangle you with my bare hands and watch the life leave you." The Nthn was struggling against his chains as if his sheer force of will would remove them.

"Unlikely. Toley, show him." A panel displaying holographic life-size images of the Nthn's loved ones filled the room. "Did you think because you were off the grid and without an identity, they would be? The late, great Dr. Senthil Nanda once said that 'The double helix rarely deceives.' I gotta agree. *So cute!* The little one looks just like you." Captain Darcela smiled, leaning over, looking in the Nthn's eyes. He cursed her name and spat in her face. "What I don't understand is why you would let them live in any country under the Union Alliance ... we'll soon have emises within striking distance of their locations. Oh, and your son? He's the closest. You're not-too-smart, *are you?* Look at your child. *Look At Him*—look at all of them. Imagine the pain they'll suffer because of you." She turned his hand over and ran a finger gently down his palm to his wrist, saying softly "Here, let me help you." She held his wrist steadily, and said again once more, tenderly, "Look at them." Still smiling, she produced her blade and stuck it clean through his palm, and held it there, twisting it before yanking it out. The Nthn screamed. Simultaneously, the silhouette of a uniformed IPU emis showed in the footage of the Nthn's son. "He especially will feel something infinitely worse, indefinitely. My men take their time."

As his hand convulsed and shook, the Nthn yelled unintelligible phrases interspersed between multiple repeats of "I'll talk! Leave him, leave them alone! I'll talk, I'll talk, I'll do it—I'll do anything I'll say everything; what do you want to know?!"

"He's feverish. Bring a slant over here." Eaves motioned to the brawny emis. The mild cocktail of pain killers and anti-inflammatories contained in the slant settled the Nthn enough for coherence. "This dungeon, hasn't been actively used to store corlypses—or much of anything, in years. How were you able to find it, let alone get your hands on the corlypses left? What made you think there would be any?

150

What do you know of Vida? Who is she for you guys? Why hasn't she aged in 20 years?"

The Nthn provided Captain Darcela with all he knew. A bit of it she'd already managed to piece together—there were separate teams doing different parts of whatever the end goal was supposed to be—like an assembly line. The Nthn's team was named Mefa—*six* in Yoruba language. Each team, while aware of the existence of the others, knew only of its own task; the orders they received weren't centralized and they always came from various unknown Nthns who carried the codename of Val, a distinction from the usual Nthns who bore solely numbers as names. *Val.* She shook her head. *Val, who was once one of us.* That irony of how one of the IPU's most loyal and effective captains built their most powerful enemy still mystified her, but she chose to focus on the intelligence the Nthn had provided her: the "lending houses" she'd identified years ago in the file that triggered the Unity bombings, the lending houses that had been investigated to exhaustion and found not to have any connection to the Nth, the lending houses—which were thought defunct and abandoned for years now, were currently being used by Nthns.

The Nthn and his late comrades had been given a list of three locations which matched some of the old lending houses. They were to deliver the corlypses stolen from this dungeon to one of the locations; they would be told which one hours before delivery. The Nthn didn't know why they were collecting corlypses or how the corlypses were located; his team was simply given orders and locations. The Nthn didn't know who Vida was or what she had to do with anything. Captain Darcela made him go over several details again and again until she was finally satisfied.

"Okay. You're going to deliver the corlypses as originally planned when you receive the location. We'll place a tracker in the corlypses—"

151

Fear washed over the Nthn's face again as he shook his head furiously "No—I can't."

"Did you forget about your son already?"

"No—it's just—"

"Why not? TALK."

"I only communicate with Val. That was my task. Thirty-One, his job was to deliver them. Anyone but Thirty-One and it aborts, and I don't know what happens then."

"Well, where's Thirty-One?" Asked the captain, fully knowing the answer yet hoping for a wormhole of a miracle. The teary-eyed Nthn nodded in the direction of the blood-soaked bodies.

"Shit."

Eaves decided they'd wait for the Nthn to receive the location and inform "Val" his comrades had been killed but he'd escaped with a few corlypses. If the orders changed to allow him to deliver what he had, they would place a tracker in. If they didn't, he'd be released to continue his mission but his son would be held as insurance. Either way, they'd hold off on sending any emises to the location to avoid arousing suspicion. In the meantime, she and Toley began searching for active Nth "dens" by scanning the netlines to find which of the other defunct lending houses and related abandoned properties were still drawing from a power supply. Once she had her list, they could deploy emises to raid these locations and get whatever information they could from whoever they found. The Nthn advised they had a few more hours before he was due to receive the location. Darcela kept up the hologram of his son as a friendly reminder of where his loyalties now belonged.

Satisfied, the captain smiled, increased the numbing agent from the slant into the affected area of the Nthn's hand and watched his cries halt and his breathing normalize. "Now my dear, that wasn't so bad, was it?"

"May Eshu drag you to the depths of hell."

152

Turning away from the Nthn, Eaves sat next to Ptolemy, pulled up a panel to begin the search and took a moment to reflect on the past. For years she'd been chasing a virtually invisible enemy. When she'd asked the emperor and Captain Ife if they could make sure Vida was okay after the Unity attacks, they were unable to find any information on her. They contacted the school she attended and while she was enrolled as a student, it turned out she hadn't attended any classes in well over a year. The emperor informed Eaves.

"I don't understand, Oba."

"In addition, the bodies found in the building, the ones that were supposed to have belonged to your neighbors, "Vida's" "Aunt and Uncle," found in the aftermath of the explosion, have no discernible identity match with anyone living in your vane. In fact, we've been unable to find an identity match for them anywhere. As far as IPU records are concerned, they don't exist. We've expanded the search against international bases to see if we can find anything." The emperor's statements felt like an accusation though Eaves knew better. She was still raw at the time, vulnerable.

"No . . . no."

She felt a comforting hand on her shoulder. "Do you remember anything at all about them, any clues that could help us, Eaves?"

She ran through her memories, or tried, to the utmost. Captain Ife's manner helped; it made Eaves want to remember more. But try as she did, nothing came back. It was startling, frightening. It was as if her memories of them had been removed and replaced with vague nods and smiles belonging to a generic notion of acquaintance. "Nothing, Captain. I'm sorry."

Captain Ife wore a split second of disappointment before quickly replacing it with a gentle smile. "It's okay, perhaps the memories will return with time."

Later on, Emperor Shirazi would break the devastating news to her. "It seems 'Vida' as you called her, was not only

153

KIDS OF STOLEN TOMORROW

not in school, but also apparently quite active. We've found images of her near four of the blast sites in the days leading up to the attack."

"I'm sorry, Oba, but I'm not following, what are you trying to say?"

"Isn't it clear? Your beloved little Vida was involved in the bombings."

When she eventually got over her shock and accepted the evidence for what it was, she felt used, and was angry she didn't somehow know. The emperor's information served to increase her sense of personal responsibility for the attacks. It was now irrefutably her fault, something she owned, and there was nothing anyone could say otherwise to convince her. The search carried *even greater* significance, but 'Vida' had disappeared without leaving behind so much as an eyelash. Sure, there'd been a few leads, a money trail or two, but they usually led nowhere. Grilling the employees of Lorzan Industries was a dead end. They knew nothing; they were simply terrified at the possibility of being jailed and out of work. The accountants, the attorneys, executives, janitors— everyone checked out. When Emperor Shirazi authorized Eaves to resume the ownership trace on Lorzan her late father had ordered, they found the shares of the company had been spread close to evenly amongst citizens of every red vane in the entire Global Union Alliance. Lorzan essentially had no owners. They shut it down.

Breakthroughs were few and far between. The pace of progress was glacial with leads vanishing as quickly as they appeared, and others taking so long to decipher, the intel was outdated and useless by the time they did. It often made her wonder in her weaker moments why Emperor Shirazi never enacted the Dialuz Protocol he'd revealed to her in confidence a few years ago. It was a measure the Nth would certainly have no answer for.

It would be so easy. All our problems would be solved. Ogun, would you not be pleased?

154

When Nthns began stealing IPU corlypses, the Institute found the trackers they'd been fitted with were either disabled or used to lay traps. It took *years* to figure out how they were being disabled, even with the Ministry in each of the existing unions giving the IPU access to whatever resources they needed. It took multiple failures—some disastrous, before IPU Sciences started showing improvements in the stealth of the trackers. But still, progress was progress. *What else could we call it?* Eaves thought, snickering aloud. And so here they were—she was—after twenty years of close calls and near misses, with a *proven*, undetectable corlypse tracker, and the broken down Nthn who just might give them their first chance to use it. Everything was seemingly aligned.

Was this it? She kissed her *Ogun* mark.

The Nthn received his call. He told "Val" that Team Mefa had been attacked by emises and his comrades didn't survive.

He waited. Val disconnected.

"What is *it?*"

"He … he says he'll call back."

Nothing.

A ring.

The Nthn was given the location to bring the corlypses he'd escaped with.

Captain Darcela turned to Ptolemy. She'd narrowed the search for the rest of the Nth dens down to eleven locations; he nine, all nine of them in her list as well, including the one where the Nthn was scheduled to deliver the corlypses.

"Toley, load the trackers. Run one last check before this filth leaves with them."

"Yes, Captain."

"We'll wait until the corlypses have been delivered before we move."

She addressed the other two emises. "Send the order out for these nine locations to prepare our teams. I want us at a distance, for several hours, observing only until I command otherwise, understood?" She turned to the Nthn, who appeared to be deep in prayer. "You'll be glad to know your son's in custody. You do what you've been ordered and he lives. Anything else and you receive what's left. You've got the right idea. You'd better pray to every god in existence we succeed."

* * *

Darcen Carbo wasted little time gathering items and heading off stage after the curtain fell. He did not rush; rather, each move was quietly efficient so in the absolute silence of the patiently waiting crowd, it was impossible to tell if anything at all was happening behind the curtain. As he made his way to the dressing room beneath the stage, he was flanked by four security guards, an escort he routinely refused out of polite ritual more than a lack of necessity. He had them wait outside as he entered. He walked into the dressing room where he was greeted by his assistant, Mina, who took the box in purple wrapping and gold trim and placed it at the back wall of the room, where it joined hundreds of others.

He dismissed Mina after she touched up his make-up and stayed seated at the dresser, examining his face in the mirror. "Well, look at you, old man," he said, touching creases in his skin likely visible only to him. He stared into his own viridescent eyes, shaded as unripened plantains, as if searching for some truth which eluded him. Assured the answer was not yet ready to reveal itself, he ran fingers through his mahogany beard, stopped, plucked a gray hair and placed it on the surface in front of him. He repeated the action once more, this time placing a red hair down next to the gray one. He plucked a yellow hair from his head. He closed his eyes and was silent for three minutes.

He walked over to the center of the room where there was a gourd and emptied the contents of his pockets beside the gourd. He sat, crossed his legs, and one by one picked up

156

and began dropping the ingredients into the gourd: Seven kola nuts, the vials of hen and cock blood, his grey, blonde and red individual hairs. He added these things, stirring and mashing them in the gourd as he chanted, "Orunmila, eyin te ni agbara, fun mi ni agbara yin, kin le fun mama omode yen ni alaafia yin. Orunmila, you who has strength, give me your strength, so I may show Sunday's mother your blessings." The chant had an undeniable musicality to it, though it was more prayer than song. He repeated it for seven full minutes, rocking back and forth to the rhythm it had locked him into as he slowly stirred and mashed the sacred ingredients. When he was finished, he sat still with his eyes closed in a meditative state, holding the leftover energy of the chant.

Opening his eyes, he stood, walked back over to the dresser, opened the top drawer and removed a large spotless blade. He lifted up his shirt and placed the blade in a hilt on his waist, picked up the gourd and returned to the stage, which was now clear of all sand and items.

The guards returned to their positions and the curtain opened to reveal Carbo, holding the gourd under his arm. He nodded towards Sunday who stood and began walking towards the stage. When he'd reached the top step, Carbo motioned him to stop. He handed him back the photo of his mother.

"Omode mi, joko. I want you to close your eyes and kneel." Sunday obeyed. Setting the gourd down, Carbo spoke sternly. "You will feel some pain, but remember this is temporary, and a manifestation of your mother's suffering Orunmila asks that you undergo so her condition may improve. Many times it is through suffering the path to recovery is clear to us. Sho gbo, omo mi? Do you understand?" Sunday nodded. Carbo smiled. "Good. Omo dada lo je." He knelt and poured the contents of the gourd, a grey, grainy but still moist substance, into a large wooden tray that had been on the stage since the beginning of the gathering. He removed the blade from its hilt, and cut a small slit near the front of Sunday's bald head.

The teen clenched his fist, but did not move or wince. Carbo proceeded to rub the grey substance into the small wound. "Omo dada, you are now receiving the etu. Many who do not believe will say it is juju, or voodoo. It is neither. It is ogun; it is medicine. It is the way." He proceeded to repeat the small incisions and application of the substance across the top of Sunday's head six more times and looked at it for a few minutes. Satisfied, he began. "All those who sought to bring harm upon your mother, Deola, shall find it now brought upon them. No harm shall befall her from this day forth. By the healing power of Osanyin, she shall make FULL recovery! As steadily as she regains her strength, so shall those who wished her harm find themselves growing weak. They shall wail and weep and find no respite. They shall attempt to curse her again, to revisit their evil wishes and bring them upon her head once more, but all their wishes shall return to them like a great, furious, boomerang and they shall find their evil and destruction rained upon them tenfold! And your sweet mother, your graceful mother, shall grow in health and strength and fortune. So it was in the days when the enemies of Orunmila wanted his destruction and found themselves the victims of the wrath they wished for him as he remained untouched. Your mother Deola's enemies will be unable to touch her as they now find themselves the enemies of Orunmila, and one by one to the last, they shall all fall as she rises. The wind will take one away. The water will take one away. The fire will take one away, and so on until they are no more. As it was for Orunmila, so shall it be for her. The enemy who dares raise his hand against Deola shall find it swollen, infected and useless the moment he raises it, from that day forth. The enemy who dares place a curse on Deola shall find that curse revisited upon her with the violent force of the great and furious boomerang. Deola shall be untouched. Every evil they wish upon her house shall be visited upon theirs, nothing shall touch her. As they fall, she shall rise. As they fall so shall she rise. Deola's way will be clear in all things. Ami!"

Sunday echoed the last line. "Ami sa."

"Ami!"

The crowd joined. "Ami! Ami! Ami!"

"Lagbara Orunmila, Lagbara Osanyin, Lagbara Olorun! Your mother shall find strength." Darcen Carbo then knelt again and scooped some of the leftover etu with his fingers and licked it. After this he spat on Sunday's head three times over the area of the wounds. "Rise, you are finished here. May good fortune follow you, your father and your mother, your family, wherever you go, all the days of your lives." Sunday wore a wide smile that fit his face well, though Darcen suspected it didn't occur often. As tears streamed down his cheeks, he nodded and made his way back to his seat. The audience, moved, similarly stood, clapping wildly, and some could be seen wiping tears from their cheeks. Carbo politely smiled at the applause and simply said, "And now, I regret, I must go. But I shall see you all again sometime, in this life or the other. Aalafia! May good fortune follow you all the days of your lives."

* * *

Darcen Carbo adjusted his blacker and stretched his legs in the back of the limo.

"I don't know why we act like this is an improvement over traditional wear. At some point we have to admit our predecessors got some things right. You can't improve upon *everything*."

"Is Darcen Carbo admitting our world is improved overall?" Ravita Singh, CFO of Carbo International, raised an eyebrow.

"That's not what I said."

"No, but that statement implies—"

"The statement implies nothing of the sort, Ravita. Half of our world is gone, uninhabitable. That alone renders it a worse one unless by some miracle we can restore what we lost. In fact, I'm speaking more to this *window-dresser attempt* to improve everything, the push to make us feel things are improving."

"But isn't that a good thing?"

"I don't think so. I don't know that it comes from a good place. People should be able to see things for what they are, and face the reality of it, and make their decisions instead of being babied, having the truth hidden from them and being outright lied to."

"Darcen, that's chaos. Look at the red vanes, they're the closest thing we have to people living the truth and they're a waking nightmare. We've come so far—too far to plunge ourselves back into the uncertainty brought about by Nightfall. I mean what, you want to clean-slate it all? Go back in time and live the Miracle of Elegua firsthand? Last I checked, the aftermath didn't go so great."

"Mirage," Darcen countered, smiling as he did so. "And no, I don't want us to go backwards. I'm not some sort of purist on everything old versus new. But what I am against is all the distractions—all the superficial tangential things we're allowing to pull our minds away from where our world is going. Every citizen should be taking an active part. He laughed. "If we're being honest I'm one of them—the distractions—one of the worst ones. Maybe the worst."

Ravita rolled her eyes. "As if humankind cannot focus on more than one thing at a time. In the past, we had all sorts of distractions; pornography, people like you, games. Did we not advance then? And ... you start this by singling out blackers. We wear them for protection. They're practical. Life-saving, convenient. They're one of the better innovations of our time. You're rambling, D. What's *really* on your mind?"

He shook his head and waved his hand. "Nothing. Forget about it."

"Are you sure?" She touched his forehead. "No fever."

"No, no fever. Just hot blood."

"I had to make sure. No one's enjoyed things the way they are more than *you* D, at least no one I know."

"I'll be fine. I'm tired. I didn't sleep on the plane."

Ravita laughed. "Maybe it was all the friendly people in the netline open forum and their endless questions. You never rest! You're going to run yourself ragged like that."

"I'll be fine. It had to be done. How often do they get the opportunity? You'd think the NEU would have a major Babalawo of their own by now but well...." His fingers danced across his sandy mane as he shifted in his seat. "You're a brilliant person, Ravita. You ever think you're wasting it?"

"Working for 'Darcen Carbo: Worldwide Babalawo, International Thief-Thief?' Absolutely," she chuckled as she closed the panel from which the headline she'd read was displayed. "I should have been a surgeon, or maybe gone to a hedge-fund but I'd be bored. Working for the IPU would have been exciting but dangerous. They tried to recruit me out of academy and my parents hated the idea. I figured with you I get the excitement of knowing people either love or hate our organization and what we represent, and still be relatively safe."

Darcen feigned shock. "Your parents, *noble as they are*, hated the idea of you defending the crown? Our exalted *Oba*? That's a first."

"Stop it, D—it wasn't like that. They were gentry yes, but we were blue-vaners—not everyone can roll out of bed a prince of the green-vane corporate class like you. Our allegiance is to the crown, always—my parents just felt there were safer ways for a noblewoman to show it."

"Oh, but you *dazzle*. Probably would be halfway to emperor by now. Makes me wonder if this challenges you. They can't possibly believe *this* honors the crown."

She laughed. "*Emperor?* You know better. And I honor the crown with my parents' fundraisers and charity balls held in the lobby of their green vane suite, all of which *this* pays for. You challenge me. Mina challenges me. And I can say you aren't at all what I expected. I always had this idea of you as a shallow, empty huckster, one of the formerly idle princes of Lagos pulling people along on charisma and good looks. I wasn't entirely right. You're different; you've got an oya. I think you *do* connect with these people. You change their lives and you enjoy it. Too bad others haven't gotten to know you. They might change their opinions a bit."

"Oh, if *they could*, they wouldn't want to, Ravita."

"Oh? Why do you think that?"

"It's the thing you've said about different—being different. People don't want to deal with anyone that's 'different.' They like their puzzles all nice and perfect like the images in this panel. They like their people in neat little boxes. Like coffins. For the living. The way you saw me before you worked with me is the way the world would rather see me. And so it'll always be...." He went pensive. "Do you believe in what it is we do?"

"Let's say I didn't. Would it matter?"

"That doesn't answer my question, Miss Singh."

"You're not looking for an answer to that right now, or any other question. You're trying to kick up dust because you're bored. People who've never wanted for anything … they do that."

"Ouch. Remind me to never get pseudo-philosophical with you again."

Ravita clapped. "See? Improvement already." The limo pulled up to and hovered in front of the entrance of what appeared to be an abandoned shed in an uninhabited wilderness. They had last passed any signs of civilization a couple of hours ago at least. "I take it you won't be joining me in the city tonight?" Her smile enticed.

162

He hesitated, for the first time that week. "You're correct on that one, Ravita. Have fun, and be safe."

She laughed and shook her head. "It's Abuja, Darcen. It *may* be the safest place on earth."

"Well, still, you never know."

"Goodnight, D. And yes, I believe in what we do."

"Take care."

Darcen stepped into the shed which housed a secure, dimly lit, full body identification scanner. Once he was verified the entryway parted, took him down to the third floor below ground, and he was home. The doors shut behind him and he strolled to the display in the center of his spotless living room, where he confirmed his safe arrival via a circular swipe on the main panel. On the screen, he connected with the limo and reconfirmed his safe entry with a wave. It was now taking Ravita to the city.

He collapsed on the couch and opened a smaller panel which showed one missed call. Tunde. "Of course," he said under his breath. "Call *egbon*," he said aloud to the space around him. Immediately the voice of a jovial sounding man in a thick West African accent could be heard.

"*Aburo!* Baby brother! The great Darcen Carbo! It is such an honor to hear from you brother!" The man laughed a laughter that demanded one join in without knowing why. "Shebi? I should tell mama a celebrity has taken time to call me, eh? Nawa O!" He laughed again. "Men. Lemme take a look at you."

On the smaller panel screen appeared a dark-skinned man with hair cut close on a perfectly symmetrical hairline and no facial hair. His neck resembled the base of a tree growing from his broad shoulders. His ursine demeanor was offset by a slight smile ready to spring fully into action at any moment.

"Aburo, O! Let me not trouble you, no! I know you are big panel superstar, international miracle worker. World healer, ah! Oga—Big boss man! Me now, I am humble CEO of international energy giant; me I perform no work O; I do

163

not go to meetings O. Me, I sit in the office and play game, come home and get the spends from thin air O. Me now, my time, my time is not valuabl—"

"Egbon, I get it, I'm sorry. Never again Brother Tunde."

Tunde laughed as if it was his last chance to in life. "Aburo! I am ribbing you. Shebi you can still take a joke. You are not too famous for humor now? We are princes, at least one should live the lifestyle, eh? It is good to see your face and be sure you are still eating well. Keep in touch and stay humble. Mama misses you. You should visit her soon. Odabo."

Darcen nodded. "I hear you egbon; moti gbo. And yes, I'll visit her soon. Odabo."

The moment he said goodbye and ended the call, the light in the room changed from blue to light green, and the center panel lit up. Tunde was at the entrance. "Allow entry," Darcen said, standing up. Upon Tunde's entry, they quickly embraced. "Long time no see, bro. I see you're still semi-handsome," He smiled and punched Tunde's arm. "And have started stealing other people's hard-earned muscles."

Tunde chuckled. "It is dangerous for a fool to believe himself witty, especially an old one. Do the girls tell you you're smart and funny, as they look in your emerald eyes and play with your pale womanly locks?" He chuckled again. "You understand it's because of the money, eh? It always was."

Darcen laughed and shook his head. Suddenly, they were both serious. "So the call looper still works then. How much time?"

"As far as anyone would know we're still talking over the line. Forty-five minutes or so, we'll aim for thirty to be safe," Tunde responded.

"Is that enough?"

"It's what we have. Let's not waste it." Tunde produced a large notepad and pen and began writing. Darcen read along in his head:

*Four movements so far. The sixth group—Group Mefa—had a complication. Nothing grave—there were casualties but we weren't compromised. The surviving Mefa member warns that Thirty-One gave locations. Fortunately, the locations are decoys. The corlypses Group Mefa obtained do not even have trackers; they can be put to use immediately. The rest of the movements have gone undetected and the first three groups have completed their missions. We must use the distraction now. I've set something big. But I need you in harmony with me for this. I cannot stress this enough. It will be something as crippling to them as the things from our younger days. Something like that first big one, the Unity International Bank one. Something that would make Val proud, something closer to what she wanted for once. We are without the magic—the child will not help this time around. Aburo, you cannot be hesitant, there is no room for error. If it weren't for that gift all those years ago, this would be impossible. We're close. The world will learn how serious we are. As igioyin widens amongst other member nations of the Global Union Alliance we must make our presence felt. I have decided on the inoculation centers but I'm not moving until we're both in absolute agreement. I'll give you a few days to think about it, but we must move fast. There is that faction of Vals who will be in disagreement with this approach but Val 3 will address their concerns. The only time is **now**. When you've decided, send word.*

Tunde produced a silver lighter from his trouser pocket, held the pad over a bowl on the table by the couch and burned it. Darcen disposed of the ashes in the kitchen. When he came back, Tunde poured him a glass of brandy, and they sat down to drink. "That wasn't a joke earlier aburo, you need to speak with Ma more."

"I know, egbon."

"So then why don't you? It is not rocket science!" Tunde said.

"She never says it, but she always sounds like she's disappointed in me, as if I've wasted my life."

"Nonsense! You are successful. She believes no such thing. Now, Papa, he never forgave you, but you made the choice that was yours to make, and as a man he at least respected you for that, even if he never understood. Mama—she wants you to be happy, aburo" He took a deep swallow of his drink.

"I never saw how that could work. Awolowo Industries with me as the head? I mean, come on. The outrage and negative press would've been insurmountable."

"So? First, that reaction is your own mental exaggeration. Second, shebi, adopted or not you're an Awolowo, like your mother, father and brother—royalty just the same. Shebi, your father was a Nigerian. Your mother is a Nigerian. Your brother is a Nigerian. *You* are a Nigerian. It is business, not public office." Chuckling, Tunde added, "Although I can see why you may have confused the two as a young man; it can be confusing even now."

"Yes; I know who I am, egbon, I didn't think others would see it that way, and that would be bad for business."

Tunde shook his head slowly and chuckled. "Ah so you were thinking of the business, how selfless. Tell me, aburo. Why didn't this complex of yours extend to your decision to become a celebrity Babalawo? A profession where it could have been a bigger hindrance? Admit you wanted stardom and easy money. You leave your poor big brother with no choice but to take over the family affairs. You know I wish I too could go gallivanting all over the globe performing "miracles" and sleeping with actresses and models." He put his head in his hands, faking distress. "Instead I must settle for singers!" They both laughed, Darcen's challenging the hearty one of his brother's.

"I do not even enjoy music!" Tunde added, and they laughed again. He downed the rest of his brandy, stood and they embraced once more. "Olumide Awolowo, be careful," Tunde said to Darcen. I saw the show earlier and I don't know if that errant audience member was planted, but there are lunatics out there. Be safe, aburo, I'll see you again soon.

"Goodbye, egbon."

* * *

"Your final ascension looms. The day soon comes when they shall call *you* emperor." The IPU insignia of Lord-High Baroness flashed across the breastplate of Eaves Darcela's blacker, replacing the Captain's insignia.

"Don't speak that way, Oba. I'm grateful for this ascension, but I'll follow you anywhere."

"Not into abdication. The quiet goodnight we mere mortals head into is not your path."

"Don't be melodramatic, Oba. Emperor Reza Shirazi, a mere mortal? Yeah, right."

The emperor smirked. "Your flattery's not a prerequisite to replace me. You were born into one of the grand corporate dynasties that built and *rebuilt* this world and so you understand why the union hierarchy and structure must remain what they are. You understand the value of the purposeful life, and you've defended the honor of this crown with great passion. When the moment arrives, there will be none who oppose your ascension. Ruben would have been proud."

"Oba, forgive me, but proud of what? That damn near twenty years later, I haven't avenged him? Yeah, sure he would. A great testament to his legacy I've grown to be."

"This demands a perfection most don't possess. You've done what you could over the years and you've persisted. After the Unity bombings I allowed for the harnessing of rage as a unit, as opposed to pushing all to remain detached, believing the resulting ferocity would extinguish the Nthn parasites. Instead it led to tactical errors in the domain. Perhaps regrettable in those instances, but allowing you to tap into your despair has, over time, made you *and us* far more formidable."

"But is it enough? Even if *we were* perfect, Oba—we're still only human. There's obviously someone out there who renders human perfection trivial, and she's working with the

Nth. I dunno … maybe they do have the will of the gods on their side." Eaves still did not fully believe her ascension was deserved; not after the raids on the nine Nth "dens" she'd uncovered with Toley had yielded nothing, unless one counted the body of the Nthn who'd led them to the discovery—and the collapsing of the buildings shortly after the emises exited.

The emperor glanced at Eaves dismissively. "You don't believe that nonsense. Gates are out there—surely—but they're nothing other than diseased humans. They happen to manifest their illness in a way that makes it momentarily appear they have an advantage, but they don't. That's all this 'child' is. You should know better, Baroness. You've seen behind the curtain; you've worked with them."

"And Grace, Oba? Was she diseased too?"

"Yes," he replied flatly. Eaves knew not to press further.

He looked at nothing in particular in the space ahead. Eaves could have sworn he sighed.

"I miss her, Oba, *they did that*. All I'm saying is we've been relentless but this … demon-girl, Vida, she hasn't aged in twenty years and she can appear and disappear out the blue. Isn't it time we looked at the one *surefire way* we have to kill or at least flush her out? It would be a game-changer. It would even render moot the reason I came to see you. The Nth would have nowhere to hide, the Nth would have nothing to fight for … the Nth would ceas…. "

Eaves' audacity nearly caught the emperor, who'd been leaning on the palace balcony's edge, off-guard. He stepped away from it. "Dialuz is merely a concept, Baroness. It's not yet ready. And, even if it were," he said, smiling strangely, "We would not use a buzz-saw where a scalpel will do."

"A *scalpel?*" Eaves was incredulous. "We can't even catch her, Oba. It doesn't seem like she has any weaknesses."

The emperor laughed. "Well she does. As the others did. And we'll find her and break her and control her the way we need to. As we did the others like her. We'll destroy the organization she works for, reveal them for what they are and remove them from the world forever. Remember Lorzan Industries? Because no one else does. Whatever you want to call what she has or is, the worst mistake she ever made was reappearing." He tapped the trench below his eye. "Enough of the memory lane. What do you need?"

"It's the trackers we placed on the corlypses. They've finally stopped moving and now appear to be settled in at locations spread throughout the Global Union Alliance. I want to send teams to each of the locations simultaneously to observe. Not to move on them. Not yet."

The emperor raised a brow. "You've been dying for this chance, Eaves. Give me a good reason for your hesitation."

"Oba, you saw what just happened when I moved in too fast. Who knows how long that might've set us back? This seems like it might be a sure thing, the only one. I want to be right. I need to figure out a better approach."

"You can't wait forever. One does not emerge victorious by continuously licking wounds."

"I understand, Oba, but I don't want to take down part of their operation and watch the rest disappear into the ether. I want them gone, sire, all of them, forever."

"And if you're incorrect? If this is indeed the chance you have and you've waited too long and lose the trail? Or perhaps this is another decoy; better to know now, is it not?"

"No, sire. This is the real thing. I know it. I can feel it. This isn't like before. I didn't know how different until I saw the look in that Nthn's eyes when he believed his son was about to die. He was *still* struggling with his imminent betrayal. This one's big. They all believe—they're invested down to the last. *Too* invested. Those dens may have been a setup but these corlypses aren't. Whatever this is it's bigger than the Unity bombings, but I know we can stop them, Oba. We would know we did everything we could and it was for something. After all this time, wouldn't that success mean everything to you?"

Shirazi smiled. "Were you able to get any information on Vida?"

"No, sire. Dead end. The people we were able to recognize and locate from the tower footage were vagrants running for their lives. The usual clueless stragglers. In my interrogation of the Nthn, it was clear he had no idea what I was talking about. Whatever part she has to play, my guess is only those at the highest level are privy."

"Well, you have my authorization to conduct this as you see fit. However, when you *do move*, I want them captured. That means *alive*. No room for personal feelings. Understood?"

"Yes, sire."

"Good. There's only one *oya* whose will they need concern themselves with, and I am merciless."

84 O.O.

"TODAY IS THURSDAY, September 30, 84 O.O. I-6897 panel log entry. All previous statements and IDs fully confirmed, current and applicable. The time is 0425 hours, Central Union Base Time. Updating progress on Program Odudua (formerly the discontinued Irunmole). I had been dissuaded from continuing research on the defunded Irunmole on the basis of inefficiency and impracticality, however; I would be doing the scientific community, the IPU, the Ministry, and the world a disservice if I did not preserve my findings this day. For the last four years I've secretly made additional modifications to Alvir77. With a lack of viable test subjects available without arousing suspicion, I infected myself— admitting myself into the research as the test group, with the control group having been well-established over the past four years. Having discontinued seven-day verus and now shown no traces in my system of igioyin for one year, eight months, I can confidently say I believe I've found a one shot, single dose, permanent solution to the virus. Additionally, I've been able to fashion a ten-year booster for inoculation. It appears the most terrifying disease of our time now has a true cure. The biggest hurdle to production—research—has been overcome. The time is now 0428 hours, Central Union Base Time, on Thursday, September 30, 84 O.O. This log is complete."

ORI BURUKU

Present Day

Not again. Not now.

KRIS OPENED HIS EYES, stared at the ceiling in the dark and began taking slow, deep breaths. He made no attempt to move his body but took mental notes on the feeling in each of his extremities. He started repeating song lyrics of the great Fela and legendary warrior poets of his vane from the times before; Ason Unique, Kane, Black Moon, Black Star, M.O.P. and many others, as if channeling their energies to combat his agony.

By the time he'd cycled through twenty songs, the first big wave of pain had subsided.

Now the ripples.

An hour and a half after the hurt began, he slowly started wiggling the fingers on his hands. Grimacing but relieved, he lifted an arm and placed a toothpick from the top of the nightstand in his mouth. He lifted his other arm, then followed suit with his legs which still felt stiff, but ached less. Satisfied with his range of motion, albeit still limited, he got out of bed and gingerly walked to the bathroom. He took off his shirt in the mirror and saw what looked like a network of vines protruding underneath his skin all over his body, growing thicker, hugging his flesh. In that way they seemed familiar, *friendly even*—like the smiling Pro-T recruiters who constantly approached him and his peers hoping to add more fodder to the Ministry's front lines.

The intimacy demanded by parasites never ceased to amaze him.

The vines now seemed greater in number than when they'd first appeared a year ago. At the time he was mildly alarmed, but didn't pay them much mind hoping they'd

172

disappear, and they did but reoccurred periodically with increasing frequency and severity. *I'll be alright. I'll be aight.* He knew something was up—this was grave, and he could feel it. He thought about his boys seeing him in this weakened state and it infuriated him. He did pushups. He followed with crunches and planks and jumped rope, repeating these things until he could focus on the ache from the workout itself. In the shower, he wept. He got out with a clearer head. As he put his shirt back on, his hand shook. He noticed the vines slowly fading again and with them, the pain, which was supplanted by a headache. *A headache's fine. I can work with that.* He took a deep breath and looked at himself in the mirror again. He tried not to think about what was happening to him; what it could mean. He thought about the pressure Dara had been putting on him lately to help her.

"Ahhh. Not like it matters anyway."

He returned to his room and checked his cles for messages from his mother who'd called, as she did every weekend. There were two messages, both of which he marked as heard so she'd know he'd checked them. He didn't listen to either one. He hadn't seen her in weeks.

"I'll get around to it, Ma, I swear," he said as he put on his thermer and "Pu$$ycat Kill" coat. He headed a few floors up to meet with Dara at the Quarters.

"What changed your mind?"

"Stop with that, bisa ... just be happy I'm helping alright? It stops at me though. I can't pull the others in it and put them at risk, you know?" He began doing pullups on the nearby bar while Donzi and Envy watched from afar.

Dara laughed. "Don't tell me to stop. Last time we had this conversation—or last time *I* tried to have this conversation with you—"

"I know ... I know ... look I'm helping cuz none of it means anything anyway so why not give you a hand? And because if I don't help you're just gonna do it alone and get yourself killed or something." He let himself down from the bar, locked eyes with her and shrugged.

"How heartwarming and captivating, Sir Arvelo. You could have been a knight of old, so charming you are. I personally think you should pen Hall-Mark panels." Dara's attempt to deadpan in response to Kris was undermined by the slow smile spreading across her face. He would join her, and for now, that was all that mattered. She *would* have done it on her own anyway, but she couldn't help but feel some joy at her influence on him.

"Oh, hey bisa, you been feeling weird or sick lately? Like, you know, after our trips?"

"No. Sometimes I pass out for a long time after, or whatever, but you already know that. Why? Have you?"

"Nuh. I was … just wondering is all. Could you do me a favor and let me know if you start to feel sick?"

She smiled. "Ok weirdo, whatever."

* * *

Phrinning into New Stuyvesant had been a little more difficult than initially expected. Trevin had given correct coordinates, but they placed Dara and Kris at the border of the cloud, in plain view of Pro-Ts. Dara caught this right before they completed the jump and they were able to adjust, but they had to return to the Quarters to do so. By the time they safely got under the cozy cloud of New Stuy, they were already two hours behind plan.

The air in New Stuyvesant was far superior to that of Todirb Wall, but it didn't compare to the return to the forest of Dara's childhood dreams, nor the weird dreamland where Vida had taken her. It wasn't sulfuric or sooty, it was clear—but a little too much so. Back in the forest she could breathe in the exhalation of the trees and wildlife and the air itself felt alive; a vitalizing, interactive dynamic entity. Life-giving. *This* air merely sustained it. Still, she took appreciative breaths knowing they'd have to go back to the Wall soon. She looked for the Macon Medhouse while Kris followed and adjusted her Stuy U cap ("Damn bisa, look at *you* all dabbed up!"), turning her around to plant a robust kiss on her lips.

Strolling casually through the streets took a lot of effort for both of them. In addition to worrying about the placement of the towers, they had to be careful not to arouse suspicion from locals and Pro-Ts by looking lost or out of place. Dressing like Stuy U kids helped, but Kris had to consistently distract her with the overly affectionate lover routine, or her laser focus on finding the Medhouse might have drawn unwanted attention. She understood this, but it still annoyed her, because it was hard to find without the glowing holographic panels that labeled buildings during business hours. Instead she was looking for a non-descript building surrounded by other non-descript ones.

Would have been nice if we could have phrinned directly, she thought as Kris muttered "Oh sweety puddin' pop cherry pie bubblykins, you are the cuddliest in the whole world, my Queen."

I'm going to murder him.

"I wuv you too my King, and I see a place where we can engage in a little royal business," she responded through her forced smile. Then she grabbed him and pressed his face to hers like she needed him for air. People walking by averted their eyes, pretending they didn't see them, and he pulled her into a nearby alley and pressed her against a wall while they continued kissing. She motioned her head to the wall behind him and he nodded. Seconds later they were inside, surrounded by shelves of pharmaceuticals.

"We'll have twenty minutes before we're discovered. Anything in particular you need, bisa?"

"I already know what I have to get and where they keep it. Grab everything you can."

Kris enjoyed being able to take whatever he wanted, and went through the shelves choosing mostly pricey meds for

175

serious illnesses, and heavy-duty painkillers. He sent them through the phrinway to a storeroom in the Quarters and found Dara a couple shelves over. She'd opened her own phrinway back to the Quarters and funneled Nicole's pills and other hard-to-obtain meds for those she knew back in the Wall who'd been diagnosed but couldn't afford treatment. She felt a strange excitement in having a reason for doing something so precarious and smiled to herself. *You're covered for the rest of your life, Nicole. Dara's got you.* As she pushed the last of her haul through the phrinway, she kissed Kris. "Thanks," she said smiling. "You're the best." Back outside the building, they emerged from the alley holding hands and looking into each other's eyes.

"Sixteen minutes," Kris said.

"Not bad," Dara responded.

"So, what's next?"

"Something for Dad."

"Ah." Kris smiled knowingly.

Deciding it was safer than phrinning too many times and risk being seen, they walked for another forty minutes or so, moving down the blocks, twisting and turning through alleys and crisscrossing the streets, all the while looking like a young couple hopelessly in love, oblivious to the outside world. In some ways, it felt like a date, with the added thrill of unknown danger lurking.

"Here," Dara pointed to a four-story brownstone that looked like it had been built sometime in the century prior to Nightfall or at least modeled after one that was. The design was reminiscent of those in old panel pictures, but it showed none of the outward wear and tear of a building well over a century old. "Wait outside."

"No way! I'm coming in with you. It could be dangerous."

"Doubtful. Besides if you're out here you can let me know if you see someone and we have to go. You want to

176

keep me safe, tough guy? Stay here. I'll be in and out before you notice I was gone."

Kris knew the likelihood of the argument going his way no matter how long he dragged it out was nil. Best he cut his losses now. "Okay. Be safe and be quick." He tried to look inconspicuous while keeping a lookout the best he could by sitting on the curb on Wallace Avenue off to the side of the house and watching football highlights on his panel. After about fifteen minutes he sent a text. "Everything Ok?"

Seconds later a reply. "Yeah win. Be down soon."

Trevin's tracker had worked perfectly. Dara stood staring at the snoring man who'd taken her father's neck panel and now wore it without any regard or respect for the grueling months of hard work it had taken her dad to obtain it. Before she entered the man's room she'd crept through the halls and saw why her father had refused to tell her what happened: He was a Pro-T. She thought of ways to get the panel off his neck without waking him and getting caught. As she pondered, the frustration and anger and the strong urge to suffocate him in his sleep overwhelmed her. It was at that moment she received Kris' text and thought against reading it before deciding to reply. The distraction was enough to calm her and she quietly backed out into the hallway to think.

I can't kill him, but he's not waking up with Papa's panel around his neck. If I snatch it off him, I might break it, and Dad will still need a new one. There has to be something I can—she heard someone's voice and footsteps.

"Charlie, guess who's here babe!" The man grumbled and kept snoring.

Dara reentered the room and looked around frantically, plunging herself into his closet and switching on the door behind her. She turned the tracker, her cles and panels off to avoid anything that could lead to her detection.

"Hey baby, you miss me? I know you did."

Dara heard what could only be sounds of the man being woken up pleasurably.

Yuck.

She covered her ears the best she could as she wasn't interested in hearing what happened next. *You could draw a phrinway and escape right now and leave it alone. Why are you staying in here?* But the more she asked herself that question, the more she saw images in her head of her father, drunk, being beaten mercilessly, robbed by this man who hid behind the protection of his uniform. *Coward.* As she seethed, she hardly noticed the commotion going on outside the closet at first.

Kris panicked when he'd sent another message twenty-five minutes after Dara had said everything was okay and didn't get a response. He closed out the futbol highlights and phrinned into the Brownstone. Once in, he followed the noises coming from the second floor and burst into the room yelling, "Where is she!"

The naked man and woman in bed looked astonished before the woman grabbed a pulser from the nightstand. "Three seconds to tell me who you are! Three ... two ..." the first blast bounced off Kris' quickly produced shield and caused small chunks of the ceiling to fall. The man yelled and reached for his own pulser.

Dara, hearing the noise, burst out of the closet and the woman fired a pulse at her feet. Dara, paralyzed and woozy, tipped straight over. Kris caught her in time to be hit with a pulse at his feet.

"I'm calling in," were the last words he heard before passing out.

Emperor Reza Shirazi woke up almost before the ringing from the cles. Years of getting urgent calls around the time when those he kept safe were comfortably dreaming had given him a sixth sense about them. He knew the time before looking. "Yes," he said emotionlessly.

"Emperor Shirazi, there was a vane violation. We've detained the violators."

"Violators, where?"

"A Pro-T's residence in New Stuy, near the Bushwick Heights border. Captain McConnell was with him at the time."

He snorted. *"That's* why you're waking me up? For burglars? Dispose of them as usual. Torture them, find out how they got in there. Kill them. Compile and report." The emperor's voice lowered into a chilling half whisper. "Don't wake me again in the middle of the night for something you were trained to handle, or you'll find your family begging for scraps in the red vanes."

"I und-d-der-derstand sire, b-b-but you want to see this, Oba. They got in by *phrinning.*"

Impossible. "How many of them?"

"Two, sire—one male one female."

"Move them to the nearest dungeon. Search them thoroughly and confiscate any and all jewelry, no matter what it looks like. I'll be there shortly. Do not let them escape." The emperor sent a message to the lord-high baroness:

YOUR WAIT HAS ENDED.
THE RIGHT MOMENT HAS ARRIVED.
YOU WILL MOVE ON THE NTH'S LOCATIONS UPON
MY NEXT COMMAND.
DETAILS TO FOLLOW.

Kris was awakened by a splash of ice cold water. He looked around frantically for Dara.

"Get up you little shit!" He was greeted by a brawny man in a helmeted blacker with the letters IPU on the breastplate.

Oh cool. An emis. I love you too, you ass. He tried to say it aloud but his lips wouldn't cooperate. He was still feeling the paralytic aftereffects of being stunned by the pulser. All he managed was a barely intelligible "ass," and felt himself being kicked by the emis, and was then aware of the presence of several more, all masked.

"You'll speak when told," said another one of the emises.

179

"Look what I found on this one! Toothies eh? Where'd you steal these from? You crusty broke bastard! No matter, they're mine now." The brawny emis took Kris' pack of toothpicks, placed one in his mouth and put the rest away.

Kris decided he was better off conserving his energy now and gathering himself to be defiant later. His hands had been bound and he was being led—dragged out onto the main floor of what appeared to be a large warehouse. He shivered as a dark memory flashed. *It's a dungeon. One way in. No way out.* The lighting was too poor to determine what it contained and Kris thought this was deliberate. Further out in the dungeon, he could make out what had to be Dara, similarly bound, surrounded by emises, and not moving. He began struggling and screaming her name, knocking three emises to the ground in the process before they gained control and threw him against the wall next to her.

"Sorry," she mouthed to him.

He shook his head. *For what? Stop it. I said I would help you. I made a choice. It's not your fault.* He felt his head aching and his body as well. The pain had kicked in earlier during the night, but he'd largely been able to ignore it to focus on their work.

"What kind of stupid kid thinks he has a chance against a Pro-T let alone one of us?" As the emis said this, he kneed Kris in the stomach.

"The emperor said no questions."

"It was rhetorical, but really?"

"Yeah he said not to question them. He'll take care of it."

"You lucky little punk," the emis said to Kris, stepping back away from him. "Maaaan I'd love to know what these freaks have to sa—"

"Shhh shut up, he's here. He's coming over here."

Emperor Shirazi arrived at the dungeon where the would-be robbers were being held. He took a look at them: one male, one female, both children. He laughed uncontrollably as the children and emises looked at each other confusedly. When he stopped laughing, he walked up to Kris, looked him in the eyes, and squeezed his face. "Don't touch me! You'll regret this I promise you," the boy said in more of a growl than a yell. His anger simmered, smoldered. It wouldn't so much have broken the chains holding him as melted them.

Emperor Shirazi smiled. "Oh, my ... how embarrassing. Déjà vu is such a strange thing, so forgive me. Kristano *Arvelo*. I *knew* that name was familiar. You not only have his face ... but your father—I could never forget *those* eyes— your father was just as stubborn. Of course, he paid for it, and so did you and your mother I suppose, with such an embarrassing demotion; banished to forever live outside of the clouds—nobility stripped away. But you're a child; I'd say more so *now* than then. It can be forgiven that you don't understand what you lost ... that you don't understand how to treat a new friend. And that's what you need now, friends. Because the magnitude of what you've done, attacking an emis *and* a Pro-T—treason—what you've done is phrinned into a circumstance you cannot escape." Shirazi pulled out of his pocket Kris' necklace and Dara's lanyard, touching the tiny blue crystals on each. "At least Arvelo's past explains how he could have come in possession of these—but you most certainly stole yours." He walked over to Dara as he said this, regarding her unceremoniously before turning back to the boy. "Nonetheless, you have some extraordinary abilities and they're awfully rare. They will serve the crown well. For all of the late Santiago Arvelo's fire and defiance, he did not have that. You don't have to spend nearly as much time in this dungeon—or any others—as he did before his unfortunate end. What's the saying? Oh yes. One way in. No way out. Oh, calm down boy. I'm guessing from the way the girl looked at you in your little fit of rage a moment ago you're a brother and sister team?" He chuckled after pausing momentarily to look back and forth between them. "I'm kidding. It's so obvious what you are to each other; it's almost disappointing. Yet it's all the more reason for you to be *very* receptive to me."

181

The boy spat in the emperor's face. "Don't you dare talk about my father, pendejo. I don't give a damn about your dumb crown."

Shirazi coolly wiped away the gob and smiled. "Fair enough. But your resistance isn't going to save you, or her, if that's what you were hoping. It's predictable. It's cliché. Maybe brave. But it isn't smart, and while it's something I'd expect, it isn't going to help you."

The boy sneered. "You say 'treason' and 'magnitude' like that's supposed to scare us. We don't know what you're talking about. We just kids running around the city having fun. You can't do a damn thing to us."

All Dara could think was how non-threatening Emperor Shirazi seemed in person, in terms of physical stature, but something about his presence chilled—made her want to take a hot shower and it only became more pronounced when he spoke. Shivering, she avoided eye contact and chose not to speak, preferring to corral her thoughts and figure a way out of their predicament. *This mess I got us in because I couldn't let it go.* She had great difficulty doing this, because heavy exhaustion set in, threatening to take her down as it often did after extended use of her oyas. *No ... please! Not now ... Olorun, I beg of you!* Emperor Shirazi spoke and Kris grew angrier. Dara, still struggling, suddenly felt a familiar calming wave of warmth wash over her and a still, small, voice rise within her. She found herself face to face with Vida in the shaded sunlight beneath the trees of the place from her dreams.

How? Why? She said to the vision of the girl.

"It's the safest way for us to communicate. And protect you, bringing you here."

Send me back! I can't leave Kris there alone. Otherwise bring him here too. It's my fault he's in danger.

"You're still there, Dara. But you're also here. I've brought it to you. I'm doing this to protect you; restore your strength. There isn't much time to explain. Do you know what this place is?"

No. Yes, I know it. But I don't know exactly what it is. I know my dreams bring me here sometimes. And he and I, we've traveled here together ... you know this already, don't you?

Yes.

Who are you?

"It is not the time for that. But this place, Igbo Oluwa. It is important you remember the true name of it because of what is to come. It is the same as the place we went. It is home. Remember you can always return here."

You speak in complete sentences now, but still make as little sense as before. I feel lost.

The woods faded and a reenergized Dara saw the dungeon come back into clear view.

"Your path is clear. Ogun walks with you. Let go and all reveals itself ..." Vida was gone now, and Dara felt as if she'd never left the dungeon. She couldn't recall what Vida had said to her, but she was no longer in danger of passing out.

"You not a friend and we not interested in your friendship. Let us go. Whatever it is you want from us, I can promise you not gonna get it. EVER."

Emperor Shirazi stared at Kris and replied, "Ah, but I am." As he said this, Shirazi looked at Kris' face again, this time staring and tilting his head as if something on it had caught his eye. He pulled out a napkin, stepped forward, and placed it over Kris' ear as Kris cursed him and struggled against the restraints. "Oh, oh this is quite fortuitous. Most auspicious. You see I would have threatened to kill her, but this ..." Emperor Shirazi pulled the napkin away from the Kris' ear and looking over to Dara, said, "I'll ask you some questions, and you will answer them truthfully. I'm taking your silence thus far as an indication you're the reasonable one. If I'm correct, you're in luck and with your emperor's mercy, can be taken out of this little mess into which you've gotten yourselves. And make no mistake, he can struggle all

183

he wants," Reza held the napkin now soaked in blood up to Dara, "but he needs my help."

Dara felt sick. She looked at Kris, who had a dark splotchy patch she had never seen before on his neck. *What's happening? What's going on?* She looked him in the eyes. Her fear that something was wrong was confirmed by his reply.

"It's nothing, Dara, really. Don't listen to him!"

Emperor Shirazi laughed. "You're going to lie to the girl you obviously love and let her watch you die? To think, *I'm* the one who has the reputation for cruelty."

Dara, teary-eyed now and deciding she'd heard and seen enough, spoke up. "Tell me what's happening, Kris."

"He's dying. That's what's happening. He has igioyin, but not the way you know it. Something in his make-up—whatever it is that allows him to display his ... gifts—weakens the virus, making it less potent. He then burns the virus for fuel when he uses his abilities, but the usage of these abilities weakens his body, thereby leaving it susceptible to the ravages of the very disease which powers him. Poetic, isn't it? Of course, weakened igioyin means he doesn't get the standard mercy of being fine one moment and dropping the next. No, his body's gradually shutting down. He'll feel all of the pain. His continuous use after realizing he was ill has only accelerated the process—*yes*, that's *right*—has he told you *nothing*? Oh. Sad, maybe he doesn't care for you as you think. But you two lovebirds are in great luck as I said earlier. You see, I'm a fan of young love and because I'm rooting for you kids, I'm willing to provide him with a new lease on life in exchange for a favor. Which is really, quite the bonus; I mean, doing something for your emperor—your *Oba,* is already its own reward. I'm sure you'll be able to work out your differences with the new time you'll have together."

"Yo you psycho we're not doing any favors for you; you must be cra—"

"SHUT UP KRIS!" He went silent. Dara looked to the emperor, who was momentarily stunned by the sheer force of her outburst. "What would we have to do, what exactly are you offering?"

Recovering quickly, Shirazi ran a finger down the gulch below his eye, smiling. "Good, now we can get somewhere. I have little reason to believe you two criminals are any different from the rest of your ill-informed and uneducated generation. That said, I'm sure you've heard of the Nth and their activities."

"How can we not have," said Dara. "Their name is mentioned in the news anytime something bad happens anywhere in the world. It almost feels like they're everywhere at once, maybe even hiding under my bed at night."

"I'll excuse your ignorance and chalk up your glib remark to the fact you're too stupid to understand the real terror they've caused and the countless number of innocent people who have died horrible deaths at their hands." Emperor Shirazi let the weight of his words sink in.

Dara looked unaffected. "You'll have to excuse me when I say the terror of not knowing if I or my friends or family are going to die tomorrow at the hands of our own neighbors or one of the Ministry's beloved Pro-Ts has always been a far more urgent concern than the distant boogeyman threat of the Nth. Seeing them on the news doesn't make it any more real than the pain we suffer in Todirb which never makes the headlines."

Emperor Shirazi clapped. "Congrats. You've suffered. You're like the rest of the world. *Maybe* you should consider that if it weren't for the presence of the Nth your life wouldn't be as miserable. If it wasn't for the Unity bombings, there'd be no need for the vanes. They were conceived as the security measure with the highest chance of protecting the population after the attacks. You would have been able to roam free, have great lives, even—" he snickered, looking at Dara's cap— "attend Stuyvesant University. These were terrorists who created *igioyin as a biological weapon*, the *same disease* that causes you daily terror. Terrorists who stole

185

corlypses, an item we needed to create life-saving vaccines for you and your neighbors, and held them for ransom. It is only our vigilance that has given you any chance of survival. They've played a far greater role in making your life fruitless than you care to realize. Let's not waste anymore of my time with your sob stories, you should be under no illusions as to who your real enemy is here. You're being ordered to put your abilities to use for the sake of your union, for the honor of your crown. We've located members of the Nth we believe to be responsible for the Unity bombing and other attacks. They're spread out in different locations and they're planning something more sinister than even the Unity attacks, more widespread than igioyin. Our locations expert Emis Ptolemy Kabore will have the specifics. You will help apprehend them and phrin them to a location. Its coordinates will be provided to you by Emis Kabore. Your crystals will not be returned to you, but you will be given clypsars—which will allow you to access your power more efficiently than your shoddy jewelry and open phrinways just the same."

Kris and Dara looked at each other confusedly. What did the crystals have to do with anything? Did Shirazi not know about the sprezens?

"You will report to Lord-High Baroness Eaves Darcela." Shirazi gave a nod towards an emis who came forward and placed a strap embedded with what appeared to be corlypse fragments over Dara's free hand. Another emis placed a pulser to the back of Kris' head.

"Open a phrinway, child." Dara, still confused and not believing it was going to work, brought her arm up and opened her hand. Initially nothing happened, and she almost told Shirazi they needed sprezens to do what he demanded of them, but then, with suddenly the greatest of ease, a phrinway opened before her.

"Whoa."

"Yes, Mr. Arvelo. As I told you, your mere trinkets do not do your abilities justice." Shirazi nodded to the emis who

186

deactivated the strap and removed it from Dara's hand. "These will help you get the Nthns to the correct location."

"And what happens to them at this location?" Kris asked quietly, traces of insolence lingering in his voice.

"The only part of this mission you need concern yourselves with is the part where you do what I've ordered you to, and live as a result. Stop shaking your head. What is it, girl? You're beginning to annoy me."

"This doesn't make any sense. You told me he's dying and using his oyas are the cause. Why would we agree to help you?"

"Because I can help you, as I mentioned earlier." Emperor Shirazi motioned to an emis holding a vial and a syringe to come forward. "I thought you would have guessed. It was quite obvious. You should be getting on your knees in gratitude. If it weren't for the work of a brilliant scientist employed by us before you could *form sentences*, you wouldn't have this opportunity for redemption." He turned back to Kris, patting the squirming teen on the shoulder. "No matter, I'll administer it now so you can see it works."

"You're not putting a thing into my system."

"You're not really that stupid, are you? If you don't accept my offer do you think you're going to be a martyr? Do you think you're going to be a hero? What happened to your father? Does anyone remember him now, save for you and your mother? What do you think is going happen when *your girlfriend* starts to get sick? You didn't realize that was a possibility, a likelihood? You'll *wish* you'd made friends with me. But you're not thinking about that, are you? No, because you're inconsiderate. This aggression, this protectiveness, it's an act. You're nothing more than a typical selfish teenage boy, unexceptional except for your powers. What do you think will happen after you've defied us and you're dead? We'll lock her away forever; that's what. For treason. And we'll study her. We'll probe her. She'll help us make new discoveries into the abilities those like you possess. She'll

187

never have a free moment again as long as she lives. And you know," Shirazi looked back at Dara, "now that I think about it, if you're not going to cooperate we may as well start now—"

"Don't you dare touch her!" Kris screamed at Shirazi demanding and half pleading he stay away from Dara. Finally out of breath he said, "Okay. Give it to me—do it; go ahead; I'll take the dose."

"Ah, so you *are* smart after all. Good, I was getting worried. You see, your good health is tremendously important to us. As long as you maintain your end of the agreement, you'll find access to the kind of healthcare you need is available to you, both of you, whenever you wish. I think you'll also find serving your union will imbue you both with a sense of purpose that is nothing short of liberating." As Shirazi said this, he looked back at Dara, who suddenly wished the days Bivins was standing in her way were her greatest worry.

Emperor Shirazi motioned to an emis who injected Kris with a serum. Its effects were immediate. The bleeding stopped, the patches cleared up, and color returned to his face. Shirazi motioned to another emis, saying "Release them both." The emises looked surprised, as did Kris and Dara, but they followed orders nonetheless. "You see, I'm a reasonable ruler. I understand this is a lot for you to process. I'm giving you some time to think over my offer—forty-eight hours."

"What's to stop us from vanishing into the wind as soon as we get outta here?"

Emperor Shirazi smiled a genuine-looking happy smile as he stared at Dara, and directed his reply to Kris without turning to look at him again. "Oh, you'll make the right choice. Now, run along. I have to go protect those freedoms you take for granted. My emises will return you to Todirb. I've had Emis Kabore program into your clesses how to reach me."

* * *

She stared at him, tears in her eyes. He gazed back silently. It wasn't only that he didn't know what to say, it was that anything he could say felt stupid, inadequate. He thought of saying sorry but that was the worst thing to say when you've done something you can't undo. Sorry meant there was no solution. Sorry was defeat. He watched the pain on her face and saved the way it looked at that moment to his memory, so he would always remember that it was not Reza Shirazi, but he, Kristano Arvelo, who'd caused her this pain. Instead of apologizing, he asked her what he wanted *desperately* to know:

"What are you thinking?"

"I can't believe you didn't tell me, Kris. How could you go through this alone? And your dad ... why did Shirazi keep saying ..."

"It's been my problem since it started. I've *just* gotten to really know you. I wasn't gonna burden you, or anyone. You don't do that to someone you're fond of. I still feel this way, ain't nothing change that. It's my problem, not yours."

"I don't know why I didn't realize something was up. I guess I was too excited to realize or admit you helping was too good to be true. But you knew why it was happening, didn't you? That's why you helped me."

"Dara, it wasn't like that. I wanted to help you anyway. *For real.* The pain ... it hits me. It keeps me awake, reminds me *every day* there's no time. Around you wasn't the worst place to be when the end came. I knew this day would come, for you too. Sick or not. Because that's the only ending there is. Pointless."

"Your dad."

Kris nodded.

"But, he still fought for something, right? Now you have all these others following you and they have no idea why you don't care about anything. You got them following you into

189

things, places where you don't care if you live or you die, but what about them?"

"Dara *don't*—"

"I'm not done. Why do you talk to them, preach to them like you've got everything figured out? And you brought them together to follow you but you didn't have the courage to tell them? Did you think about them at all? For even a minute?" Having momentarily quieted Kris, salt from recently dried up streams tracing a crystalline path down her plum cheeks, Dara let her words find a resting place in the tension between them. She looked out in the direction of the lake towards the sky. It was the first time she could recall the sun hiding behind the clouds in this place, but everything else was as it always was when they were both younger. As they stood in the clearing beneath the trees, Kris—supporting his weight and seemingly his spirit against one, looked at her boldly.

"They know the stakes. I didn't hide nothing from them. Everyone joined cuz they wanted out of their lives as they were. I never sugar-coated it for anyone. You act like our lives are anything and it drives me crazy. All my boys, all those guys you mentioned could be dead a few hours from now and it wouldn't have a thing to do with me *or* you. What good would it have done to tell you or anyone? 'Hey I'm dying; can't do nothing about it; panic anyway guys. Be twibs.'"

"Kris, I'm being serious."

"*I'm* being serious. That bastard Shirazi confirmed what I knew and didn't want to admit to myself. And I don't trust him. I feel better, sure but who knows what's in that shit he gave me? We can't do this, Dara. Let me help you escape somewhere safe. Hell. We can stay *here* in the woods. They won't find us here. You know that, right? They'll *never* find us here."

"Are you crazy? Are you purposely forgetting everyone else? If this affects you, doesn't it them? What about your mom? What about me? I have people I care about there, *my*

190

family, *my* friends. No. We can't risk it. We'll help them, and figure the rest out. It's not you alone anymore and it stopped being you alone when you brought everyone together."

"I mean them too! We can start over here with everyone! Trees, clean air, water, animals for food, this is the perfect place. None of the cold we deal with in the Wall. No need to wish we were in the clouds. We can phrin a few more times to bring everyone here. I'll talk to Trev and we can figure out where the rest of the serum is. We can steal it for everyone else and begin again here. I'll tell Donzi, Envy. The crew won't have to keep phrinning and weakening themselves, and neither will you. We can't trust Shirazi, *you know that!* What if he decides we're his emises from now on? His lab rats? You know he wants to do it. You heard him. Hell, I *already am.* We'd be helping out the same people who've overseen our suffering for *decades.* Could *you* live with that? They took mi Papa—*I* can't."

"No, but you're choosing to gamble now? To take a stand when it would be most dangerous for us? You made it clear to me at every chance you don't believe in anything, so what difference does it make? You knew they caused our suffering before and I know they hurt you, badly, but you didn't want to challenge them then. It hurts to consider but if Shirazi's right—"

"Coño—"

"If Shirazi's RIGHT, then the Nth is a lot to blame; at least we'd get to do something about *that.* We know he needs us, and as long as that's the case we'll have access to the serum, and some leverage and we can plan. It's the only concrete thing we have in front of us, Kris, because running isn't an option and stealing serum is a pipe dream. And hiding? Here? What do we know about this place? I'm *still* not sure it's *real.*" As she said this she waved her hands around in the air for emphasis, and then stopped and sighed. "You know what I think? I think you drew a door once. You fell into it. And you've been running through it ever since. You

191

can do something else if you want to, but it's not only about you. I'm heading back." Dara opened a phrinway. She looked back at him one last time with pity and sadness in her eyes, shrugged and left.

As soon as she closed the phrinway behind her, Kris waited a couple minutes and phrinned back to his apartment. He messaged Donzi to come by. He closed his eyes as if doing so would help him sleep.

"What could you possibly want at five in the morning!? So extra!" Donzilana, yelling at her cles, was annoyed at Kris' text that came attached with an alarm. It littered her room with a cacophony of sounds until the clutter moved above her ears to her eyes and she could not see let alone hear over it. She deleted the alarm, which of course took longer than usual. *Never again. You're off the list of people that can send me that.* She was up. She still had on her clothes from the night before and annoyance quickly turned to joy as the smell of *him* reminded her ... but then she looked around, saw Envy had left, and her annoyance returned. *Who knows when I'm going to see him next?* Envy had promised her he was back for good, but his penchant for disappearing without warning for days on end before popping up without any explanation was not what she'd had in mind. She hissed and said aloud to the empty room, "You'd better be dying, Kill. As she got dressed she looked at the cap on her dresser and debated whether or not to tell him she was Laran. She hadn't told Envy yet because she didn't want him to know before Kris.

"Long time no see!" Kris said to her, beaming while squeezing her in his doorway as if they weren't supposed to be asleep like the rest of the world was at the moment. "Come in!"

"Ugh. Lay off the viz, Kill. Drug induced overexcitement is wild lose on you. Plus, it was already dumb when you said it yesterday."

"Damnnn, rompiendo mi corazon, hermanita," he said, while theatrically clutching his chest and falling back. "Like I would ever need to use vision. *Seeing* you is a drug enough to *me,* little sis. But you so cold. So cruel."

As Donzi rolled her eyes, she noticed his playfulness seemed a bit hollow and wondered if he'd finally figured it out.

He dropped the act when he saw she looked a bit off. "What's up? Did any Pro-Ts stop you on the way here? Please tell me they didn't bug you about the huv."

"Nah, not at all, for a change."

"Then what? Still mad at me? Because I got something to tel—"

"Nuh, I wasn't mad at you, I jus … never mind I don't know what was going on. I wanted to tel—never mind. You were saying?"

"Nuh, nothing, it can wait. Go ahead."

Promise not to be mad at me, okay? If I tell you this."

He smiled, "Sure."

"I'm serious, Kill. I need for you to promise me you won't get upset."

He stopped smiling and examined her face for a clue as to what she was about to say next. Nodding his head slowly he said, "Okay. I'll need you to promise me the same soon."

Donzi exhaled deeply. "Well … there's only one way to say this. Kill, I'm Laran."

Kris' stupor was that of a student who needed the teacher to repeat the question. For so long he didn't change his stance or expression that Donzi wondered if it were possible to be dead and maintain the balance needed to remain perfectly upright. "Kill?" It was more of a prayer than a statement or query.

"Tha hell? You don't even know … *who* that is. I've never introduced you two. I don't ever talk about him. I don't get what you're saying. In that case, I'm Dara. Cool. Fun game. Now let's talk about real things."

Donzi sighed. She wasn't sure if he was mad or genuinely unconvinced. It didn't matter which; she turned on her voicer. "Thanks for the opportunity, Kill. Brink what are you doing!!! Larceny 81 is the greatest tag on earth, and its mine."

Kris' heartbeat sped up and he felt the onset of another headache. He had to face that either Donzi was remarkably great at mimicking voices she'd never heard or she had indeed selected and generated Laran's voice and was telling the truth. "Why? How did I not notice?"

"A unisuit and beard's pretty convincing if done right. It wasn't the first time I'd worn it and I overheard one of the boys at school talking about how you had something going a few days before. I got dressed up and followed them because I wanted to see what you were up to. *Then* I saw the actual flyer where you'd included one of my tags. Maybe it was suspect but I felt like it was my chance to get closer to you, especially after Envy left. Be closer with my best friend."

"But why didn't you come to me as yourself?"

Laughter volleyed the back of Donzi's head against the wall. "You? Let me come out and traze with you guys? No buddy, I wasn't getting in that drag-out where you act like you're Papa and I'm your troublesome daughter who's gotta be set straight. I'm too old for that. We're the *same damn age.* Remember when you used to hit only the tunnels? When you first went trazing and I tried to come along? And you kept telling me it was too dangerous and ratted me out to Grandmoms, becaus—"

"I thought it would stop you."

"You thought it would stop me. But then I snuck out again. And that second time was where the Pro-Ts caught you and locked you up overnight. I was so scared for you— afraid you'd never come home. And I knew it was my fault— I *just knew* you wouldn't have been caught if I hadn't trailed you. When you came back I was so relieved. And you made me *promise you* I wouldn't sneak out again. You even let me still think it was my fault. So yeah, did you think I was gonna forget all that and hope you'd suddenly encourage me? You know better."

Having stated her case, she let out a satisfied exhale. The pause allowed her to look at Kris' face and notice the fissures in whatever force normally held him together. The longer she looked the more she realized this was something her words couldn't possibly have done.

"What's wrong? You were going to tell me something."

Kris sat, noshing on a toothpick and didn't answer her for a long time. When he stirred, it was to grab a tumbler, into which he poured a dark liquor. After returning to his seat, he took slow sips of the drink, marinating the toothpick in his mouth with it. "It's wild, isn't it? The rush is crazy." He was addressing Donzi but looking in the distance at nothing in particular. "Too good to be true. I knew that. You too. No way you didn't … you can feel it … every time we jump."

"Kill, *what is it?*"

Kris proceeded to explain everything to Donzi: His igioyin diagnosis, his fear she and the others could also have it, his guilt in their involvement, Emperor Shirazi and the cure, his plan to escape.

Donzi, listening intently, cast her vote with Dara. "There's a way for you to get better. That's all that matters."

"I'm so sorry I dragged you into this shit; so sorry I did this to everyone. But I—"

"You act like it isn't worth it to have these oyas at that cost when we could go at any time anyway. Every one of us feels this way; I know it. We've seen things we would never have normally seen. Things I still can't believe we've seen. We're the Kids of *Stolen Tomorrow*. What else would there have been for us, ever? I'm not afraid. Don't be afraid for me, bro, save it."

Kris took a deep breath as they both wiped away tears.

"Whatever solution there is we work together."

"Donzi I don't wan—"

"You can't tell me what to do. You're not doing that anymore. I may already be sick anyway or I may not. But I'm helping every way I can." She grabbed him, threw her arms around him before he could respond, and for a long time they embraced, as if the love and energy each exchanged would extend the other's lifespan. In this way, they resembled two hands clasped together beseeching Olorun, calling on Ogun, imploring Shango and all who would hear their silent cry floating beyond the barriers of Todirb Wall. Their cry, silent beneath the low hum of Kris' heater, the only sound in the room, was yet forceful and thunderous as Shango's own rage.

REZA

"WHAT ARE YOU DOING, Shirazi? We were specifically told to grab the corlypses and get the hell out of this Enugu-nowhere village. If you got any ideas about playing the idiot hero, save them for when I'm not around. I'm already on the emperor's shit list."

Reza did not speak, but lifted a finger to his lips to signal Emis Brouder to keep quiet. Brouder had a look of both annoyance and bewilderment but Reza moved quickly, pointing to a large black safe against the back wall of the oversized shed. More corlypses?

They moved stealthily towards it, scanning for more combatants, stepping over bodies of assailants. Satisfied the coast was clear, Shirazi pulled a scan and ran through combinations. The safe opened. Out fell not more of the sought-after crystals, but piles of leftover, unused weapons. As they sifted through a pile, Brouder let out a gasp followed by a "What . . .? I don't believe it."

Every last weapon in the safe belonged to the Institute.

"I'm lost. What are they doing in an Nth base of operations in Obinagu? These are official IPU weapons. No way to get them without authorization—makes you question if the whispers about Val … I mean, this is crazy."

"It's not crazy, Brouder. They were stolen. By fanatics. Quite simple, actually."

"Are you kidding? No way you believe that. How? These many weapons? And why would they need the corlypses to build weapons when they already have these—doesn't add up. If this is what it looks like, Emperor Martin lied to us about the origin of the Nth. If he's lying about that, he lied about Val. Shit. Shit-shit-shit! Thought it was dumb rumors

but think: her founding the Nth would make perfect sense—
their warriors, some of those guys—" Brouder looked at one
of the dead soldiers, "they fight like us. What if she's alive
and others left with her? Like Lison—they were close,
weren't they? He disappeared at the same time ... Val was
our best. Damn it, my head is spinning ... what do you think
she found to turn her against us like this? What's the emperor
covering u—"

"I have no idea what you're saying. Val's dead and I don't
plan on giving my mind leeway to roam on all sorts of half-
wit conspiracy theories," Reza said coolly. "It certainly isn't a
time to doubt the crown." He picked up one of the weapons,
a pulser and examined it as Brouder, who bristled at being
interrupted, pulled up his panel to document the find.

"Sorry Broud," Reza said as he fired one pulse at point
blank range into Brouder's temple. "There's a lot about this
mission I couldn't tell you." He checked Brouder's panel to
make sure no footage was sent, and destroyed it. He placed
four pulse bombs inside the safe, resealed it, and detonated
them. Reopening the safe, he found a tar like substance where
he'd moments ago seen scores of firearms. He checked
Brouder's vitals to make sure he was dead. Satisfied, he pulled
up his own panel and sent a message which read:

**Brd null. Corlypses secured. Weapon stores found, eradicated.
Charges set to vape compound upon extraction. Exploring further.
Have team on standby for extraction.**

He stored photos of the weapons and the shed and
checked it once more to make sure there weren't any
survivors hiding. As he nearly tripped over the body of an
Nthn on his way out, he took a look at the man's blank
expression, shook his head and muttered, "Biting the hand
that feeds you never ends well. You should have been grateful
for us, not our enemies, traitor." He spat on the man's face.
He put the pulser in his weapons sling, exited the shed and

got onto his maver, a hover-cycle built specifically for combat
and difficult terrain. As he rode out of the compound
through the blast-created opening in the once impenetrable
wall into a greater village, the redolence of rich soil after a
soothing rain greeted his nostrils on a light breeze. Then
followed a strange scent of *bread?* wilting to the aroma of
charred flesh. Staring at the still smoldering rubble, he noted
piles of former residences strewn about haphazardly. Years
from now, these heaps would be the playground of kids
who'd never know what truly happened there.

"Let's get started," he said to the bike as he rode slowly
towards the first pile. The village had already been looked
over once for enemy combatants by the pre-raid tactical team.
Reza was going through to make sure they didn't miss out on
any corlypses. Before he made it to the first pile, he found a
stunningly clear aquamarine tinted crystal fifty yards from the
opening at the base of a shrine to the goddess Yemoja,
untouched by the calamity. "Why thank you, kind goddess. I
don't know how we missed this the first time," he said,
chuckling while placing the additional corlypse into his bag.
"Idiots. If these people knew the value of what they had and
sold it instead of worshiping it...." He didn't know if it was
their fanaticism that drove the Nth to build compounds near
villages frozen in time, clinging to dead gods, but he thanked
them for their stupidity. It made finding them easier.

He rode on. When he got to the first pile, he scanned it
and found nothing. Moving from pile to pile uneventfully
convinced Reza there was nothing more of substance there,
and he was wasting valuable time. Nonetheless, he persisted
until he was hungry. As he grabbed his lunch from the maver,
he heard what sounded like a large object falling down one of
the piles, about a hundred feet away. He left his food,
activated his pulser and silently inched towards the pile from
where the sound came. *Probably nothing, but let's make sure.* He
held his breath, feeling as if it were somehow too loud. As he
neared the site of the sound, he heard something that sent his

heart racing. "COME OUT NOW! PLACE YOUR HANDS UP AND NO SUDDEN MOVES!"

Slowly from behind the pile stepped a beautiful, tall girl with long braided hair in a colorful, half-torn gown. She looked to be in her late teens or early twenties. She had followed Reza's order as best she could, but was unable to stifle her tears, and so she shook with her hands in the air as she cried.

Reza kept the pulser aimed at her. "WHAT ARE YOU DOING HERE?"

No response. More crying. Reza armed the pulser.

"I'LL REPEAT IT ONLY ONCE MORE THEN I'M FIRING. WHAT ARE YOU DOING HERE?"

The girl half-choked, clearly attempting to speak through the sobs.

"TAKE A DEEP BREATH AND SLOW DOWN. THEN ANSWER."

"I was," between sobs, "returning home, from work—"

"WHAT DO YOU DO?"

Silence.

Reza fired a shot at the ground.

"IF I HAVE TO REPEAT MYSELF THE NEXT ONE'S IN YOUR SKULL."

"I am a fantasaria. At least I was, for this town."

Shirazi snickered. "So you're a whore." She was silent again. He looked her up and down and began to feel an uncomfortable heat around the back of his neck. The sooner he killed her, the better. Noticing his pause, the girl spoke up.

"You saved me. You saved me. Oga, without you I never escape them," she pointed to skulls in the rubble. "They kidnap me when I young and they force me, Oga. Now I have chance to be someone better to start over. Oga, I'm grateful to you. I am in your debt. I thank you for this chance." As she said this, tears still in her eyes, she moved towards him seductively.

It's too bad. She might have had marginal value. Shirazi laughed, fired his pulser, and started back towards the maver. Before he could finish turning around, he found himself trapped in a light blue bubble. He looked back and saw the girl, unharmed by his kill shot. The bubble was the same color as the pulser beam. Did she *deflect the shot?* The bubble disappeared within seconds and he fired at her again, with the same result. *Stay calm, there's an explanation. Focus on the task at hand.* He tapped his cles for extraction then got out another weapon and fired, this one spraying a lava. The girl created a bubble around herself matching the brilliant orange of the lava in color and all his shots turned to rock and shattered against her force field.

Lunacy. He reached for a long slender rod at his side—*The Paralytics.* "Block this!" He pressed the mask setting on his blacker, flicked a switch on the rod and out shot two orbs, smoke clouds pouring out the moment they hit the ground near her.

Still enclosed in her bubble, she walked right through the clouds up to Reza, until she was face to face with him and said, "I'm not your enemy. I need your help. Please listen to me." Then she disappeared.

He looked around for her, bewildered. She reappeared (?!) by his maver. "STAND DOWN" Reza aimed his pulser at the maver and fired, reasoning the resulting pulse explosion would be great enough to disable her force field and take her down. *If this doesn't kill her—*

It was the last thought he had before everything went black.

"Wake up sleepyhead! Rip Van-Reza!" Reza came to in a gurney in the back of what he recognized as a phrinjet, the same one from which he and Brouder had descended to the compound hours earlier. The jovial and boisterous man greeting him was Captain Ruben Darcela, who had overseen the mission. The rest of the extraction team was there as well.

As Reza got his bearings, he thought for a moment he'd seen the girl from the village, smiling. He violently reached for a weapon, yelling "INTRUDER" before he was restrained by several of his team.

"No! Reza, it's okay. Reza! Look at me," Captain Darcela said as the other emises held Emis Shirazi steady.

"Why's she here?!"

"She saved your life, Reza. Explanations later. Calm down. Breathe." Getting this partial explanation seemed to subdue him, if it didn't exactly put him at ease.

He looked again and saw she was restrained, and left the issue alone for the moment. He remembered the mission. "Was the extraction successful? The corlypses ... the compound?"

"We got everything, Shirazi, impressive work. The compound was leveled as soon as we took off, you set the charges perfect. They won't be using these corlypses to build weapons anytime soon. Sorry about Brouder. We found his body amongst others in the compound. She swears she didn't kill him."

Reza nodded and said, "Another hostile surprised us."

Captain Darcela nodded. "Okay. Save your energy. Landing time is in two and a half hours. From there, Emperor Martin will debrief you." Reza nodded. "Get some more rest, he's going to talk to you about the girl anyway. No need to hear it from me, he'll tell you everything." Reza looked at Captain Darcela once more, debating whether to say something else, which he forgot as his heavy eyelids decided for him.

* * *

"Why couldn't she escape her pimp or madam with all the oya she possesses? Surely they couldn't have posed a greater challenge than you."

"I believe they asked her the same thing on the way here, Emperor Martin. I think its best you hear directly from her and judge for yourself."

"You believe what she told them, Reza?"

"I don't know what she told them, Oba. But I think after today, the dynamics of what I'm capable of believing have changed slightly. It's best you hear from her directly."

"Then *we'll* hear from her together and you'll tell me what ya think."

"Yes, sire."

"I got your text lines about Brouder. Sorry you had to do that, but you understand this mission could not be compromised in any way."

Emis Shirazi nodded. "It was my duty, Oba. I understand."

Emperor Martin, who was holding a lit cigar, had his feet on his desk and leaned back in his seat, far enough to fall, a habit that irritated Reza. Reza remained standing, though he knew the emperor would soon demand he sit. "Good. You locate anything on Val at all?"

"No, sire. But we found an artillery cache she funneled during her days here as a captain, and I think the fact we were able to get corlypses indicates she and her team were caught by surprise."

"Well, we can't let the others find out what she knows or why she's doing this. We gotta stop her before this gets further out of hand. I won't allow her and her goons to disrupt our work."

"I understand. Sir, you should know before Brouder died he did speak on rumors—he seemed to believe ..."

Emperor Martin took a pull of the cigar. "That's fine. It's human nature. Rumors are acceptable. I can live with that. Hell, we gotta expect them at this point; everyone in the Institute knows who she was. It's only proof that can be dangerous if you don't know how to get ahead of it. Once we stop Val and give 'em evidence she's been long dead it won't be anything but pure conspiracy gibberish...." He tapped the cigar lightly, knocking lose a modicum of ash. "So ... we couldn't get her, but she's gittin' desperate, sloppy, forfeiting corlypses, weapons and the like. This is progress. This is *good*. Have a seat, Reza. You been through a lot today and you did quite a bit. The crown is pleased."

Emperor Martin pressed a button on his desk and a large panel screen appeared above it, with the girl's face visible to him and Reza, who sat in the chair across from him. She was in a holding cell with her hands restrained, and hooked up to a machine where IPU doctors appeared to be running tests on her in the background. She winced.

Emperor Martin smiled. "Hullo Grace," he said. "Do you know who I am?"

She nodded. "They say you are Emperor Martin."

"Thaaat's right," he said, continuing to smile. "How you dé?"

A look of surprise, followed by a smile flashed across Grace's face. It was unclear whether she was impressed or simply amused at the emperor's token use of her homeland slang. "Fine, Oba. But I wonder why I am treated this way for saving your officer's life."

"We jus' have to be sure of some things, Grace. I assure you we mean no harm. Capn' Shirazi here," Emperor Martin ignored the astonishment on Reza's face at being addressed as *captain*, "informed me you were a fantasaria."

"Oh, that is what he said to you? Because to me, Oba, he simply said whore."

"A misunderstanding I believe. But it is *my* understanding you were pressed into service after being kidnapped at an early age and beaten. Now of course you'll appreciate, that with yer extraordinary oyas, it seems a bit hard to believe such a thing could happen to you, or at least go on for so long. For ten? 'Leven years, accordin' to Captain Darcela."

"If you'll allow me to explain, Oba. It will take some time but then it may make more sense to you."

"All the time ya need, *iya*, go ahead."

"Thank you, Oba," she beamed. "When we were on the plane, your Captain Darcela asked if there were others like me. There were, but they died in whatever it was that destroyed my village. And I am thankful to you for that. I am in your debt. You see, in my village, only one person can leave at a time, but they must always return within three days, or they will die a slow and painful death and the village would burn to the ground. Shortly after I was kidnapped at the age of nine, I was forced into the sex trade. My captors trained me to be a fantasaria. On the night of my twelfth birthday, I was to entertain a client when a wave came over me and Shango appeared to me in a vision saying: 'You are now joined together in fate; bound by this power I bestow. What you chose to overlook in weakness shall be your undoing should you choose to do so in strength. I shall leave you intact. Three days hence I shall return and strike you down forevermore. Choose wisely.'

When the vision passed, my client had disappeared, nowhere to be found. Like everyone else in the village, I ran outside in a panic, confused and scared, O. We all headed straight to the Babalawo's. His door was locked and he did not answer, but for several hours we waited outside while hearing the low tapping of his talking drum. When he stepped out, he told us before Shango left he had spoken with him a bit longer, and that the youngest fantasaria in the village must be sacrificed; sent out to work, and bring the money back to him to be held for the village, and the village must send a man out with the money earned by the girl and buy items for tribute to Shango. The two can never be gone at the same time, for only one may leave the village at a time, and each time one must return within three days or the village would be razed. In return, the Babalawo said we had now been blessed with fantastic oyas, bestowed upon us by none other than Shango himself, partly to protect the lone individual who was chosen to leave, and partly as a test. Over the coming days we showed power to travel through the village in an instant, faster than walking running or driving. There was a storm, an angry bitter vengeful wind, and trees were thrown around but they bounced off of us; we were suddenly protected by something we could not see. We were amazed and gave thanks and praise to Olorun, and celebrated for days.

It was not all joyous however. I was the youngest fantasaria, and after the large monies I brought back on my first trip out of the village, I remained the youngest. As the years passed, we grew more isolated as rumors flew throughout the city of Enugu about a "strange magic" possessed by our people. We became closed to the outside world—shielding our village with an illusion to cut down on those who would come to gawk and create mischief. The amount of times I was attacked on my trips outside the village grew in frequency and severity, though I was always able to defend myself.

Within the village, people were thankful for what I provided but resented me because I got to leave often while they had to wait their turn. They despised what I did for a living and only kept me alive because of what had turned out to be a curse for all of us. If it weren't for that spell and its conditions, they would have killed me long ago—they were not interested in suicide. Then one day I went out and returned moments before the third day was up, and the town was—" tears streamed down Grace's face as she struggled to keep her composure. "It was what the Babalawo had told us would happen. I knew it was my doing, but I wasn't in any physical pain, and I was still alive. I realized I was free. I wondered what could have done this; what miracle could have kept me alive while killing the rest of my village. And that was when your Captain Shirazi found me."

Emperor Martin was silent, save for the sound of expelling cigar smoke. When he spoke, he showed no emotion in his face or voice. "There was a compound by your village. Separated by a wall. What do you know of the proceedings behind that wall?"

"Nothing, Oba. We had too much concern for our own lives to worry about a world we could not see. I heard occasional whispers it was West African Union government, but that was all."

"Captain Shirazi was trying to kill you. Why'd you save 'im?"

"He freed me though he didn't know it. You freed me. I wanted to return the favor. I wanted him to know I was thankful."

"But you could have killed 'im once you knew he was trying to kill you and fled somewhere far away, where we'd never find you. Wouldn't you have been free then?"

Grace shook her head. "No, no, the only people I ever wanted to hurt were those who hurt me without giving me choice, those who took away my choice, those who took away my life. You freed me, sire. I am grateful." She smiled. "Praise Olorun. Praise Shango. Through you, they freed me."

"Okay, Grace, that'll be all." Emperor Martin shut down the cles and the panel.

"You believe her, sire?" Shirazi's voice went up like a question, but it was a statement.

"Reza, you recall—" Emperor Martin stopped and laughed aloud to himself. "Ha. Recall ... now *that's* rich ... Reza you know of the Miracle of Elegua?" Reza nodded. "I can still recall when these 'New gods' first appeared before us all those years ago. What is it now, 59 years?" He chuckled. "I'm old. I was five at the time. I wasn't even sure what I was seeing. But sure enough, there they were, warnin' us, offering us salvation, telling us Olorun sent children to earth thousands of years ago to intervene and save us from our self-destruction, and that he'd done so in different ways many times throughout human history. But Olorun grew impatient, and this—them, our vision of them was our last chance to wake up and save ourselves. I remember it, clear as the

207

moonshine I had for breakfast yesterday, and all the drama that ensued, because there was not a person alive at that time who didn't see that vision. Oh my, if you coulda seen the panic. Those who already believed praised the miracle and rejoiced. Others called it the devil's work. But ya know, some ah the same folks who called it blasphemy and trickery also said it was further proof of the power of their God. You name a religion, it splintered. At first, there was the peace of stunned silence but it was followed by madness … chaos. One big mess I didn't reckon we'd sort out any time ever, but my predecessors—they were smart. They saw what was coming—understood this future. They worked with the Ministry and we took hold of the narrative. Made sure our primacy was reestablished along the lines of the new order of things. Because no one alive on the day of that vision could deny it. We all saw it. And over time lotsa of people became followers and believers, flocked to those gods, converted as you know and since then there has been all manner of unexplainable mysterious occurrences … there's a point in my rambling somewhere I think."

Emperor Martin took a lengthy puff and blew a succession of smoke rings. "Ah, yeah, anyway, it was long before either you or our captive Grace there were a cosmic thought, but strange things have happened before and as a man of science I can't dismiss them—not when there's transcendent gifts backing them. So, while I don't necessarily believe all of her story, I do think something traumatic happened to her in that village and we saved her by turning those fellow villagers of hers into collateral damage. For that, she owes us a great debt and a creature like her—with her extraordinary oyas—is who we want to have with us. Them gates we got are one thing, but I've only ever seen them travel the phrinways. *Deflecting pulser beams? Shielding you and her from explosions?* This girl is a whole 'nother bag of goodies. If I had to wager a guess on the side of science my boy, I'd say her oyas have less to do with Shango and everything to with all them crystal fragments we found around the village."

"You think her power comes from corlypses, sire?

"Sure. She's no different from our gates in that regard— no corlypse, no oyas. Padrino confiscated a bracelet she was wearing, chock full of little corlypse chips. Bet if we strap some clypsars onto her hands we'll see what she can really do. You heard what she said about travelin' through the village. Wouldn't surprise me in the slightest if she's also a gate."

"Sire, I have one more question if you don't mind."

"Fire away, son."

"Was *Captain* Shirazi a mistake, or did you mean it?"

"I don't make mistakes, Reza. You earned yer ascension." As Emperor Martin said this, the IPU Captains' insignia appeared in blue over the breastplate of Shirazi's blacker. "Hell, all the good works you've carried out in your time here … probably the reason I'm emperor. You been through a lot today son, go get some rest."

"Respectfully, Oba, I rested on the plane ride back here."

The emperor smiled. "Very well. Come with me."

Emperor Martin walked over to a wall across the room from his desk. It didn't take Reza long to realize the emperor was being bio-scanned. The wall shifted shortly after, revealing an elevator. He followed the emperor into it. "You're a terrific warrior, Captain, maturing just as I knew you would. You're loyal, hardworking and best of all, yer quiet. You don't ask questions before following orders. *If* you ask later, you ask the right ones. That's what the world'll need in these years to come, the rarest of rarities in this day and age." The emperor examined Shirazi once more, as if making a final assessment. "You're ready for the whole picture. Goin' forward, I want you fully aware of your purpose here."

The elevator opened into a small empty room containing another elevator. Reza waited for the emperor's bio-scan to open the other elevator door and followed.

"A few months ago, I took you to sit in on the Royal Congregation. Bound by the crown's oath of secrecy, I'm sure there's many questions you've withheld since that gathering for fear of breaking it. However, as your emperor, I've long decreed you speak freely to me, mah' boy and yet we both know you don't." Emperor Martin smiled at Reza's slight look of surprise. "Oh, no worries it's okay. Today you'll get answers to those unasked queries. 'Haps it'll encourage you to be bolder bout what's on yer mind. I'm sure you've always thought of the crown as more symbolic, more ceremonial than anything else. I'm sure in the past when you'd addressed me as sire, or Oba, you were referring to my title as High Commander—moreso than Emperor. But that congregation, it opened your eyes, didn't it boy?"

"It did, sire—but I've always—"

"Let me finish son, don't interrupt your emperor. Fact is, in an ideal world—the emperor *should* be ceremonial. The IPU coordinates communications and actions between the civilized governments of the remaining world. Ensures the strongest union between the unions, so tah speak. We're the entity that'll prevent another Nightfall from devastating our interests; it's why our highest ascensions are reserved for the Decalaoba. But this world is far from ideal and so the full force of the crown must be shown when appropriate. That meetin', the mess in Enugu and why I sent *you* to clean it up and get those corlypses, it's all because of what you're about to see."

The door opened and they went through an emis guarded hall before they stepped into the wing of a hospital in what seemed like an entirely different building. Orderlies, nurses, doctors, patients being moved on beds in and out of rooms, all hurrying around uninterrupted as if a breeze came out of the double doors and not their emperor. Reza was shocked at what he perceived to be disrespect. He didn't hide it well.

"Relax, Captain, we didn't come down here to get our wangs tickled. 'Scuse me, nurse?"

"Yes, sir, Emperor Martin!" She bowed.

"I'm looking for Dr. Bekoe."

"Yes, Oba. I'll take you to him."

Dr. Kofi Bekoe, head of research, bowed, greeting them at the doorway of his office. "Good day Emperor, Captain. How may I be of service?" He was a tall man, gray and skeletal. The way his jacket hung off his shoulders, he resembled a standalone coat rack. He wore no expression. Reza sensed pieces of his face would have to be swept off the ground if it ever managed to contort into a smile.

"We're giving Captain Shirazi the tour, Kofi."

"Ah. Understood, Oba. Right this way. Captain, feel free to ask me anything."

They walked into a cold, dark room which lit up as they came in. Reza noticed people on metal carts lined up in rows from wall to wall. As the three made their way closer, he realized they were not people, not anymore—but shells. Many of them showed strange post-mortem signs of disintegration; lesions, bloody splotches, varicose veins enshrouding gradient skin tones. What had happened to these people?

"The bodies you see before you Captain, are victims of a disease we are calling *igioyin,* from a Yoruba term which expresses utter devastation. While igioyin cases have increased, it is not yet widespread, and our hope is that we can combat it before it is. Its victims simply drop dead without warning whether virus was present for minutes or *years*—no symptoms accompany it. Question, Captain?"

"No. Continue."

"This is the Crash Room. All our failures go here until they're cremated. We study the effects of our experimentation to determine what we've missed, and how close the patient may have been to surviving. Of course, there's only so long before the body's post-mortem processes render further study impossible. That's when we cremate."

They followed Dr. Bekoe to the back of the Crash Room and stepped through an adjoining door into a lab. Several patients of various ages, all in varying stages of disintegration were strapped to beds, hooked up to tubes and their faces were covered in masks of gel.

"The masks provide us with freeze frames of the effects on human skin at different phases of medication," the doctor said to Captain Shirazi. "It gives us a way to compare the physical effects of the body's reaction to treatment."

Unlike at the entrance to the wing, the doctors here stopped to acknowledge the emperor and Reza before being ordered to keep working. "This is where the bulk of human testing is done, Captain. We're in the process of creating a vaccine to slow the effects of the disease. We've managed to retard the mortality timeline by anywhere from a few days to weeks. These ones show *symptom*s; all the accelerated breakdowns we normally only find post-mortem, slow down and course through the body at an excruciating pace. And yet, they're still alive, unheard of years ago. Promising, though we're still some ways away from a cure."

They left the lab and followed the doctor down another long, emis guarded hallway, through five sets of bio-scan secured doors. They came to a lab which appeared at first glance to be empty, until the mannequin in a lab coat, startled by Dr. Bekoe's voice, turned around. "Dr. Ali."

"Oh, Emperor Martin! Good day, sire. I hope I may be of service."

"And, this is Captain Shirazi." Dr. Bekoe continued, "They'll be observing, but first tell them what you're doing." Dr. Bekoe looked around. "Where's Dr. Barrington?"

"You didn't see him on the way in? He went to the Crash Room to grab some samples. He should be back in a few minutes, but I can call." She tapped the cles on her shoulder for Dr. Barrington. "What I'm doing here is moving stabilized water over to a Parin chamber where we can apply separation to the strands." As she spoke, Reza noticed a glowing blue crystal submerged in liquid in a small clear tub on the counter next to Dr. Ali, and recognized it at once. Dr. Ali stopped talking and looked momentarily flustered.

"What is it, Suraya?" Dr. Bekoe asked.

"I think we're going to need another corlypse. This one's already weakening. I doubt it'll be effective beyond this week."

"Again? Doctor Ali, you must be cautious. I can't snap my fingers and provide you and Dr. Barrington with corlypses out of thin air. They are a struggle to obtain."

"I understand, but we're using them in the most efficient way possible."

"Acknowledged. Now as you were explaining . . ."

"Oh! Yes," Dr. Ali continued, "Igioyin has its origin in the water supply. It's active there before it mutates again in the human body and becomes almost impossible to fight. I'm trying to eliminate traces of it in the water—"

"And the need for a cure." Dr. Barrington burst in carrying a crate full of Petri dishes and vials, two large tubes tucked precariously under each arm, and a metal board keeping his chin from his collarbone. He hurried over to a counter to prevent certain calamity and set the items down. "It's far easier said than done; which is why I'm working on a vaccine. I'm Dr. Barrington. Good day sire, Captain."

Reza's gaze hadn't shifted from the tub. "What do you use them for?"

The others in the room looked confused.

"The corlypses. I see you use them. But what for?"

Dr. Ali spoke up. "Ohhhh. Yes, Captain, we use them to stabilize the virus in the water so we can reverse engineer and treat it. They also possess uniquely powerful immuno-enhancement properties. That's what I was trying to explain earlier. Sorry if I didn't do a good job of it."

"Without them none of this process is possible," Dr. Barrington added. "Captain, I'm aware of the integral part corlypses play in powering the weapons you use and of course that protection is necessary … but this work is going to ensure we survive at least a little while longer as a species, if we're successful."

"What's the likelihood?"

"That we survive as a species? If that's your question … the chances aren't good anyway, Captain. It's a miracle we've been around this long." Noticing Captain Shirazi didn't share his amusement, Dr. Barrington stopped smiling. "It's been promising, I assure you. I can't project a date for completion at this time, but I can say we've been having a steady string of breakthroughs lately."

"Like?"

"Decrease in the recurrence of certain strains. The virus has been slowed down in its mutation due to the stabilization process. If we can stop it, or render it dorman—"

"Right now, do *I* have igioyin? Have I been exposed? You say it's in the water."

"Oh yes it's possible, but you've been tested for it, haven't you? If not, you should, it's a time bom—"

"That's enough, Dr. Barrington," Dr. Bekoe said curtly. "I think he gets the point." He turned to the others. "Sire, Captain, Dr. Barrington and Dr. Ali must get back to work."

As soon as they were out of the lab and on their way back to Dr. Bekoe's office, he addressed Reza. "What they won't tell you, is they're within striking distance. They're close, Captain. To answer your question, no, you haven't been exposed. The water available to us in this facility comes from one of our dungeons; it's uncontaminated and amongst the many tests you received in your pre-screens was one to detect incubation." The doctor looked at Emperor Martin.

"Captain, Dr. Bekoe now reports directly to you and will provide you with weekly updates of his team's progress. You'll be responsible for overseein' his division, and you'll provide me with a monthly summary. Your bio-scan has been modified to allow you access to this wing."

"Yes, and, Captain, if you ever feel the need to come down and look around or check up on any of our work down here, you're free to buzz me at any time." The emperor nodded and Reza realized the emperor and Dr. Bekoe had made this arrangement long ago.

"Thank you, Doctor."

"Somethin' else I want you to see, mah boy." Having left the lab and hospital wing, Emperor Martin took Reza into an empty room several levels below, accessible only through bioscan, and turned on a panel, revealing several smaller screens of workers assembling pulser circuits and others placing corlypses on a conveyor. Others showed small—tiny labs, each with its own scientist hard at work. "None of the people pictured in these panel screens are aware of what they're working on, not even the labcoats—but they're all playin' an integral role in the future of our world. I know, Dr. Nanda knows—"

"The former royal Head of Medicine? I thought he was dead, sire."

"Yes Reza, he is. But his just as brilliant son Rashi is very much *alive*, secretly working on what'll be his greatest achievement. Ya see Rashi's dad discovered igioyin, and Rashi's dedicated himself to his daddy's life's work; it's really quite touchin'. This is the flipside of what you seen goin' on upstairs. Rashi is responsible for what you see before you— fine work he's done thus far. And thank goodness. No sense in his daddy makin' such a discovery if we can't take full advantage. Members of our houses around the globe, even the high lords with their upper-level clearances—don't know about this. They don't know it exists; they've only been made aware of the more obvious reasons we stockpile corlypses. And it'll stay that way. But when the time comes, it'll do the job that'll fulfill our mandate, and they'll be thankful. Such is the weight of the crown. Do you know what this is? Do you know what yer lookin' at?"

Reza, who'd studied each screen as Emperor Martin spoke, nodded. "Yes, Oba. I have some idea."

"Good. I call it Dialuz, and it may be the last weapon we ever need. I'll be long gone by then, but one day when it's complete, it'll be yer responsibility. And when it's time to do what must be done, I know you'll have the conviction."

"What of Minister Zhang, Oba? We're on North Emerian soil. Does he know?"

The emperor chuckled. "*North Emerian soil?* I don't give a damn if it's on Minister Zhang's backfat. Any place this palace sits is sovereign—property of the crown and the crown only. 'Sides, the screens you're viewing are in locales spread out over the various nations of the Global Union Alliance. Minister Zhang knows only what the crown tells him. My purpose, and perhaps someday yours, is to keep these secrets and bear these burdens so the Minister Zhangs, or Minister Whites, or Minister Olajides of the world perform the duties of elected leaders and continue to pacify the populace with the hope of choice. But don't look down on the limited power they have. Minister is still a colossal undertaking and a very important role; the secrets we keep would make it an impossible one."

"You're scared silly, ain't ya?"

"No, sire."

They were up the elevator now on the way back to the emperor's alcove. Reza wasn't lying. Maybe he *could* have been terrified, but he wasn't, not even in the playful fear-of-failure sense the emperor might have meant it. He felt ready—like the world was finally beginning to give him what he was owed, but he was also confused; hadn't the emperor *just earlier* reiterated Reza's barrier to ascension? Reza was a low-born noble; a red-vane orphan who'd earned his nobility through his service to the crown. He was no prince, no Decalaoba; he wasn't born into any of the ten ruling corporate dynasties. So why was he being given secrets and duties reserved for the chosen?

"It comes down to destiny, son. We've been selected by forces greater than even us, to determine the path of this world for everyone else and we either right the ship or we go down with it. Our planet, our species, we're a dying race of gluttons. We devour our resources; we devour our spaces; we devour the trust of our allies; humanity is eatin' itself. It's always been that way, sure, and maybe it got worse after Nightfall—that's what happens when ya destroy half the globe, turn folks into refugees—but we got wise, built clouds . . . we've always been able to adapt. This contamination thing is different; it's scary; this is *the planet* killing us, leaving us to die, our home becoming our enemy. We've kept the clouds protected up to now with igioyin-free water supply but who knows for how long that holds? They're *next*. What those geniuses are workin' on downstairs is gonna save us. And what Dr. Nanda's working on is our failsafe. For the *us* who can save the species. That's why we're important. We exist, you and I and the Institute—exist to ensure our most precious resource—human life, the human mind—the *right* human minds survive. I reckon that's what Captain Val couldn't grasp; that's why she went rogue and started that godforsaken Nth, but only some of us are gonna make it, and that's the way it is and has to be. We do what must be done. We lay our lives on the line Reza, to protect what's ours 'cause it's our birthright, it's our blood and it's our royal lineage that'll inherit what's left of whatever we leave to them. The best 'n brightest, the most well equipped; keep 'em around, keep 'em alive, protect 'em at all costs to give us a fighting chance. That's my mission and yours. The moment's chosen us. And we've accepted the honor." They entered his alcove and Emperor Martin walked back to his desk and sat, resuming the undisciplined recline that drove Reza crazy inside.

"Oba, is there something I'm missing? I'm honored you've given me these undertakings and I serve the crown at your whim but—"

The emperor chuckled. "But you're what? Not of noble birth?"

Reza nodded.

The emperor lit a cigar. "Well, I suppose it's time we had a bit of a discussion 'bout that." He rubbed his forehead. "I guess we can start with yer name. While yer birth name is indeed Shirazi, it is not your family name—Lyte is." Reza's eyes grew wide. As in Lyteche International? Was the emperor playing some kind of joke?

"You're the first-born child of your mother, Emperor Cyra Lyte. She had ya in secret and you were put up for adoption. Little's known of yer daddy, save that he was a common ruffian she was enthralled with when she was too young to know better, and that he died shortly after your birth. It wasn't a shameful thing to Cyra; but it was a turbulent time, and your family felt it could be used to derail her ascension. She decreed that your parentage not be revealed to you until after her death, at the discretion of the emperor. While my predecessor allowed me to recruit you, he felt it best to never divulge to you—or anyone—the true nature of your lineage. I, on the other hand have borne witness to your deeds, no doubt an example of your royal blood shining through."

A million questions flew through Reza's mind and he was unsure of what to say; his lips moved without command. "So that ... means ... I ..."

"You're Decalaoba. You have been since the day you were born. And my choice for eventual ascension to emperor. Yer unique upbringing will serve you well. You've had to fight for every inch of space all yer life, defy hopeless odds for each ascension. Even the ... mark on your face is a reminder of what you've had to endure. And that's good son, 'cause it won't be easy. You got much to still learn—polish

218

those rough edges a bit. You gotta become a leader the others'll *lay down their lives* for. 'Member, these folks who'll be following you are nobles and they were raised nobles; they're proud, all of 'em. And you'll have amongst them those whose claim to the throne is as great as yours—in some senses greater, 'cause they grew-up knowing they were the chosen and have been groomed for it all their lives. There'll be times you'll want to show force against them, *crush* them on your path to ascension. I advise against this, as they're merely testing your loyalty to the crown you'll bear. You want to turn them into your allies, not create powerful enemies within your future court. An Oba is only as strong as the respect he commands. Fear's a powerful tool, but it's best reserved for true enemies of the crown, not those who serve it. Understood?"

Reza nodded solemnly.

"Good. There's something I need you to do for me, son."

So, there would be no Q&A. "Yes, Oba, anything."

"The West African Union's Ministry has been on our back about Obinagu. They been houndin' me about a couple of employees who they believe perished in the destruction and their daughter who went missin' in the aftermath, something … Olumo or whatever, I think is the last name. They sent over full profiles and other information. Look into it and submit a full write up of your findings. What Ministry employees would be doing near that wretched village in the first place beats the hell out of me. Feel free to choose a team to assist if need be."

"Understood, sire."

60 O.O.

"Yer staring a hole in her big enough to phrin through. You sure Shango didn't bless you with oyas too?"

"I don't know what it is you believe you saw Oba, but I assure you I'm only looking at her because of the pattern on her blacker, sire. If it has come off as unseemly gawking or leering, I apologize." The confidence Reza tried to portray in his response was undermined by the sudden tremulous quality of his voice.

"Relax, Shirazi. I'm yanking your chain. Yer gonna have to learn to take a joke or two as you ascend through the ranks. The path to emperor is littered with foes—doubly so for you. Competence will get ya respect, but the way you interact with and treat others'll get you loyalty, and that's what you'll need. Loosen up a bit." Emperor Martin, who was standing beside Reza as he sat dissecting his lunch, patted him on the shoulder. "Anyway, those are the new trainee unis. Whaddya think?"

"Fashion isn't my strong suit, sire."

"Give an opinion, Captain."

"It looks, nice?"

"Well that wasn't so hard, now was it?" The emperor motioned to Grace. She walked over to the table with a self-assuredness that made the notion of her as a trainee in anything quite laughable. "Grace, Captain Shirazi is your commanding officer. You'll report directly to him, and address him with any questions or concerns you have during yer training and beyond from here on out. Am I understood?"

"Yes, Oba."

"Good. You're dismissed." As soon as Grace was out of earshot, Reza spoke. "Sire, are you sure that's a good idea? Captain Darcela normally oversees special cases and while I'd be more than happy to—"

"You question my judgement?"

"No, sire."

The emperor smiled. "Yes, Reza. It's a good idea, I assure ya. But you know what's better than a good idea?"

"No sire."

"An order."

"Understood sire."

It had been over six months since his initial encounter with the former fantasaria in Obinagu. It wasn't so much Grace's abilities, or her story, which he still found some aspects of (specifically any part involving the appearance of any Orisha) ridiculous and attributed them to paramnesia, that made Reza nervous about being her commanding officer. There was a rational scientific explanation for whatever it was the corlypses activated in her, and he'd find out what it was. Her beliefs and story weren't even that uncommon considering what he'd heard in his years of secondary school and academy training. He'd grown quite used to the fanaticism, and the eye-roll inducing ways many around him looked for, and found signs in mere coincidences, and often mistook incidental correlation for causation. He was even used to the irrational need for his mates to waste well over an hour each morning praying to gods that didn't exist. He had come to accept this as the price of excelling while sane in a world gone mad.

No, something else bothered him as he thought of Grace's beautiful long braids, glossy, perfect skin, deceptive doll face, and her curves that made her a landscape unto herself. Each time she rose she appeared to be borne from the earth anew, and this natural elegance she possessed reminded him doubly of his own ineptitude—or rather—hassles with the opposite sex. He'd known three girls his entire life; two at the orphanage he spent his early years in, one of whom was his friend around the time he acquired the burn on his face that was a point of pride. Her name was Saylona. They were playing and kept venturing further and further away and decided to explore a distant neighborhood even though it was late. She wanted to go home, but Reza wouldn't be friends with a girl who was afraid; Reza wouldn't like her anymore and she wouldn't have any other friends or people who would speak to her or people who played with her or people who cared. Bad people did bad things to Saylona and then burned Reza's face and Saylona disappeared forever and Reza showed off his beauty mark to all the other orphans and the headmistress and the director. Then there was his foster sister—Kaci, who was his second kiss in what was a generally awkward affair during his already awkward early teens. She would do things for him; leave notes and gifts for him—useful items and then one-day Kaci met someone else and she was confused and she stopped and he'd grown used to the gifts. Bad people did bad things to Kaci and Kaci didn't disappear forever, but Reza got sent back to the orphanage. After that he figured it best to focus on his academics and his future and not give a second thought to the inconveniences of lust and its byproducts. This turned out to be his path of least resistance, and by age sixteen he'd excelled so well he was recruited to join the Institute for the Preservation of Unity, the youngest recruit ever at the time. It was then-Captain Martin who took a chance on Reza despite objections from his superiors, saying the teen's callousness and lack of morals needed only minor tweaks, taking care to expunge the blemishes of his past.

Sometimes, laughing proudly to himself, Reza wondered: Would Emperor Martin have vouched for a child who *burned his own face?* Would he have broken from his predecessor, opening the boy's path to the crown? But Reza's temptation for others to know what he got away with was never greater than the power of his secrets.

Over the following years, his desire came and went, and he'd learned to view it as a quick distraction easily disposed of by delving into his work. But here he was now; he couldn't simply make her go away. To the contrary, he'd be seeing her daily as she *was his work.* He feared his inexperience would overwhelm him and impair his ability to control the situation and mentor her effectively. If he failed in this assignment it could be a significant roadblock to his ambitions. He knew he couldn't turn to anyone about this; not Emperor Martin, not Captain Darcela—one of the blue-blooded rival Decalaoba who'd see Shirazi's weakness as an opportunity, and certainly not Grace *herself.*

No one.

"I'll figure it out," he murmured as he picked at the leftovers of his meal.

"Figure what out, Shirazi?" Captain Ruben Darcela said as he walked by.

"Nothing."

"Sanity's always the first thing to go, Shirazi. When you start having conversations with yourself …"

"In that case I'm in great shape, if we consider you talk to yourself for an hour each morning in front of a bronze statue."

Captain Darcela snickered. "Watch it; no one here gives you flak on your godless kamikaze trip through life. That said, I never said I was sane." He knocked over Reza's drink and his laughter thundered as he walked away. "This guy, he's been a captain for like three seconds and already he's running his mouth."

Reza wrapped up the last of his food to eat later and took his mind off his Grace problem by thinking of his recently completed investigation on the West African Union Ministry employee deaths in Obinagu as he returned to his quarters. The WAU had notified Emperor Martin the official inquest found no wrong doing on the part of the IPU and their independent inquest concurred with the findings of the IPU's report; namely, that the employees' missing daughter perished along with them and was amongst the charred corpses in the rubble. Reza had done well again.

His thoughts turned to the secured corlypses. It had been a few months since he'd read an update from Dr. Bekoe on where their scientists were with a treatment for igioyin (as they rarely varied), or asked whether the corlypses were proving to be of any use, but he felt a deep sense of accomplishment. Everyone knew it was due to him that more were out of the hands of Nth operatives. But most

223

importantly, *he knew.* He would resolve the Grace thing as he did all else. At ease, the future *Oba* smiled to himself as he went to sleep.

* * *

October 93 O.O. – Present Day

"I don't understand why you would let them go, sire."

"All will reveal itself soon. As I recall, you were the one who was preaching patience before."

"I don't mean to be impatient, Oba. It's—you know we haven't had luck in a few years finding gates, and these two fall into our lap at the perfect time. With them we could be damn near all locations at once! We didn't send latchers to track their phrins—we have no idea of knowing where they are. I jus—I don't want us to waste any more time, Oba. Not when we can be more efficient."

On the subject of the gates, Captain Darcela was correct.

After Dr. Barrington's indications to Reza many years ago that igioyin was the origin of the gates' abilities, the Institute for Preservation of Unity began conducting experiments on red vane prisoners captured by Pro-Ts. For the past *ten* years, they sponsored monthly stealth missions where emises, disguised as Nthns, kidnapped red vane stragglers who'd had no access to verus, all but ensuring a high concentration of igioyin in their blood. All became subjects of experiments to determine if they possessed the abilities to turn walls into phrinways. The rare who did were used until they deteriorated beyond repair and discarded with all the rest back in the neighborhoods from which they were taken, all invariably believed to be victims of igioyin (a correct belief, all things considered). None lasted longer than a couple of years. In all the years of searching, Shirazi still had yet to find one who, like Grace, lasted and showed no ill effect. What disgusted Shirazi *more*, was over that same period of time, IPU Sciences

224

had managed to improve phrinway technology by a mere three miles bringing the distance covered by vehicle per phrin to thirteen miles. The best they had was latching—tech that, placed accurately could reopen a long distance phrinway used by a gate; a parlor trick in comparison. And here now were two gates, ready-made, theirs for the taking.

"I understand your daily agony. I understand your eagerness to find Vida, dismantle the Nth and put this all behind you. We will, but you must trust me now. I know what you've given up to remain active in the domain. The children will be back, and they'll do exactly what I want them to do. Latchers were not necessary in this instance. Tracking them is pointless; they need us. If they try to run, they won't get far."

"Okay ..." Eaves wouldn't be satisfied until she made every Nthn feel her pain, but she would make it happen with or without the child gates. She could wait a little longer. Or could she? A thought, the thought that kept resurfacing, the thought that left her alone less and less as the days went by and had begun to grow into a chorus seemingly louder at times than actual conversation pushed its way into this one.

"Sir?"

"Yes, Darcela."

"Are we making this too hard? What if we ... we already have a solution for all of this and we've been—"

Emperor Shirazi's look was stern as he cut her off. "No."

"But sire, *Dialuz* ... if we use it—"

Emperor Shirazi said nothing. Instead, his look grew more chilling. Eaves, though disconcerted, felt this was the moment to plead her case. "Sir, please, when I last mentioned it, you said it wasn't ready but we know that wasn't the case. What's keeping you from using it? Vida continues to elude us, we know the Nth are planning something devastating and we still don't know what it is yet, and those kids, if they won't cooperate, okay who cares? We solve all of these not to mention everything else it solv—"

225

"That's enough, Eaves."

A barely audible "Yes, sire," was heard as her shoulders slumped and she unclenched her fist.

"Its time will come. That time is not now. You've worked arduously. And now you stand at the cusp of certain victory. I see it. And perhaps you are anxious because you see it too. This is why you must remove your emotions *now*, lest you ruin all your hard work, to satisfy them later on. You want the Nth and Vida to suffer and be aware of their suffering, do you not?"

"Yes, Oba."

"You want them to know *you* are the architect of their suffering, do you not?"

"Yes, Oba."

"Good. Because we want to destroy our enemies by learning all their secrets. By capturing them, breaking them and showing them to be cowards. We don't want martyrs, Eaves. We have no use for martyrs. That includes Vida."

Captain Darcela made and held eye contact with Emperor Shirazi for a while before she nodded. "Understood, sire."

"Good. The boy is mouthy. You'll recognize him. He's as foolish as his father was and will likely meet the same fate. The girl is the wise one. Quiet and understanding of what's at stake. They'll be back. Get some rest. I'm staying here in the palace and will retire to my chambers. I think it's best you do the same. The next few days are going to be especially demanding."

"Okay. Goodnight."

An alarm went off as Emperor Shirazi entered his on-base resting chambers. Its panel displayed a reminder of something he'd forgotten over the years. "Barrington, you truly were one of a kind," he said, smiling as he went straight to the bathroom where he entered the code to unlock and open the mirror cabinet. He opened a small case labeled "Verus Ten-Year Booster," took out a small strip and placed it on his tongue, where it dissolved. After returning the case

226

to the reflective safe and locking it, he headed to the bedroom. His lavish resting chambers in the palace resembled those of a ruler who was never there, let alone one who was contemplating abdication. If retirement was indeed on his mind as he'd conveyed to Captain Darcela, he certainly didn't look it at the moment. He was energized, buoyed by maneuvers he'd made—not just the ones he knew would lead to certain victory in the decades' long fight against the Nth. Over the years, he'd followed the advice Emperor Martin had given him that fateful day he revealed Reza's lineage and path, building allies and using his position as Emperor and High Commander to grow his "court" to a level never previously seen.

Of course, some of the advice Emperor Martin had given him was nonsensical (Reza had found fear almost *always* trumped all other ways of gaining influence and support, especially amongst his one-time Decalaoba rivals within the Institute), but the rest had been spot-on. The late emperor had also given Reza all intel the IPU had of his family's company—Lyteche, which Reza's half-brother had been head of for several years. Reza's further research indicated his half-brother was covertly using the full force of the Lyteche empire to prevent Reza from ever being anything other than a name on an errant branch of the family tree. Patiently, Reza bided his time, focusing on growing the strength of the crown so it came (with him at the helm) close in stature to its corporate benefactors, if not quite in resources. With a long trail of savvy maneuvers, he was able to topple his half-brother and wrestle majority control of Lyteche—the most powerful of the Decalaoba companies. "The Emperor of Shadows" didn't want to be front and center however, so he would allow his brother to remain the public face of the company, even as Reza built a new Lyte Family compound atop the old one and prepared to settle in. This, was his final *ascension*. Yes, he would abdicate, as he'd told Lord-High

Baroness Darcela, but only to rule as even the most powerful emperor could not.

The Clouds would have their future ensured, Eaves would have her revenge, and the Union Alliance would have a hero: him. The late great Emperor Martin couldn't have done it any better.

The kids could be perfect converts after completing the mission. Reza had great plans for them. If they exceeded expectations and showed the proper gratitude and allegiance, they could avoid becoming permanent lab rats and perhaps get on the Grace track (especially the girl—who he'd decided had personal use, and would join him at Lyteche). Having access to two gates would prove invaluable. He'd also speak to Darcela about shuttering Dialuz prior to her ascension. There'd be no need for the protocol in the world to come, the world he was shaping. Success—ultimate power as he'd oft imagined it—was so close to his grasp it was overwhelming.

He sat on the edge of his bed, removed his blacker until all that remained was his underclothing, and laughed, triumphantly, the hardest he ever had. He fell asleep this way, with tears of joy still streaming from his eyes, mouth half open, legs hanging over the foot of his bed, and sometime during the night, found himself in a strange dream. He was still in the room, seated at the edge of his bed instead of lying back, and he saw someone, a silhouette in the shadows he could barely make out but still knew. He wasn't even aware when the dream began, it just was, and suddenly a terrifyingly familiar face was before him, but the voice was a strange match in his ears:

"You are a man consumed with hatred, Oga. 'Hatred for the present and its prisoners,' as you said once. Others put their hopes on you imagining a light. Eaves imagines a light, she follows it; but we know it isn't there, don't we? It's that hatred. It's that hatred from you always, Oga. Only darkness."

Reza found himself struggling to form words, felt the
dream-drunk delay of his speech, but pushed out: "No! No,
you can't. I'm close! It's mine! Wait there's … you must see
… I must …!" He was unable to form a complete sentence,
but like any good apparition in a dream, it responded to its
host's thoughts hidden in his gibberish.

"Ah! It's okay. I understand, Reza. Save your strength.…
Yes, I know. I know, and I can't let you go any further.
Enough has been done. Now, *still* all I can feel is the hate.
And I can't let that be … no further than me. Not anymore."

Reza thought he saw a flash—as the silhouetted hands
moved quickly towards him—*was that a blade?* He felt a sharp
stabbing pain, then nothing. The security cameras in the
morning found no visitors to his room. A thorough medical
examination revealed he'd suffered a heart attack. Declared
brain-dead, he was moved below the palace by a devastated
Eaves who decreed he be placed on life-support indefinitely,
attended to daily by a dedicated team of imperial medical
staff, and watched at all hours by emises whose sole job was
to remain below the palace and protect the empty vessel that
was once Emperor Shirazi. All were to perform the tasks
given to them by Eaves in secret; on pain of death.

A teary-eyed Eaves confirmed the rumors swirling in the
palace, announcing the passing of the Oba of Obas; Emperor
of the Global Union Alliance, High-Commander of the
Institute for Preservation of Unity, Reza Shirazi. The news of
Emperor Shirazi's demise would've been met with panic and
infighting amongst the ranks of the IPU had he not long ago
declared—to nary a dissension—his successor. Eaves had
been handling some of the duties normally reserved for the
high-commander for a while, as she already directed her own
elite units. She'd also been entrusted with protecting the
Institute's darkest secrets, as Shirazi was before her. While
Lord-High Baroness Darcela wasn't looking forward to
dealing with the bureaucracy Emperor Shirazi had navigated

so deftly, the transition was a heavy-hearted but smooth one. The new emperor's first order of business was to investigate a connection between the arrival of the child gates and the death of the former emperor, as Eaves was unable to shake the suspicion they were somehow involved. That the former emperor had initially released them without sending latchers to track their phrins did not ease her suspicions. However, footage of the emperor's chambers, the IPU Head of Medicine, and the gates' lack of knowledge or recognition when Eaves interrogated them in the late emperor's bedroom all said otherwise. It was enough to get her to drop the investigation, although she would forever hold his death against them.

"You see this uniform I wear? Before me it was worn by a man, an *Oba* who made it possible for you two ingrates to be safe. He made it possible for you to wake and exist in one of the greatest and safest unions in the world. From now on, you two will bow in reverence every time you see me in this uniform—in honor of the Great Emperor Reza Shirazi. He was one of the greatest men this world had ever known and ever will know. He gave his life protecting it—all so I could babysit you two—children as morally corrupt as the Nth themselves, fit for nothing other than early graves."

She looked at them, knowing they would play a key part in helping her get what she wanted, disappointed she couldn't execute them on the spot. The boy had the exact face of a former imperial artist who was cast out in scandal and whose life ended amidst experiments by the Institute in exchange for the protection of his family. The girl reminded her of Grace the way oranges might remind one of sunlight. She took another glance at the boy and laughed to herself, fully realizing the nonsensicality of her trepidation and understanding why the emperor had been so confident. *Olorun keep your soul, Emperor, you brilliant, beautiful genius.* Splotches and thick vine-like veins were growing around the boy's neck, and he was constantly reaching up with a wipe to remove blood from his ear. He hadn't received enough of a dosage for a full cure; they *needed* the Institute to survive.

As she touched her breastplate where the Dialuz Protocol (along with other codes) had automatically been transferred per imperial succession, she vowed to honor Emperor Shirazi's memory by not using it anytime soon. It was not needed. Her predecessor had thought of everything.

Reza had already instructed the children. They knew what they had to do. There was a dosing schedule along with written form of the commands he had given them. She had the boy given another weakened dose of the serum and calmed them both down with promises of the full dose once the mission was complete. It was clear they had no choice. Eaves looked back from the girl to the boy a couple of times and saw what they didn't have to say. The girl still didn't look sick and maybe she wasn't *yet* but it was impossible to tell at that time and it didn't matter if she was or wasn't because the boy *was*.

"If you follow anything other than my orders, you know what will happen. We're tracking and expect you to communicate with Ptolemy Kabore throughout the mission after completion of each task. Emises Browning and Padrino will accompany you. Arvelo, you'll be the only one fitted with clypsars. They'll be removed after each phrin and returned only for you to get to the next location. You're not foolish enough to put your girlfriend's life at risk, are you?"

They didn't speak during the first extraction. Kris opened a phrinway for the emises to walk into the location and they begrudgingly forced themselves to follow. There they found an Nthn. Immediate shock registered on the man's face; his mouth was covered before he could cry out. The emises injected him with a slow acting poison and Kris phrinned everyone to a holding room secured by other emises, where Emperor Darcela sent them back on their way while she interrogated him. All in all, it took about five to ten minutes. Then they were on to the next location to do the same.

When they got to the third location, the order was given not to bring back, but to kill the Nthn who sat bound before them while a panel was set up to beam the footage back to the holding room where Darcela sat with their second capture who cried, "I'm a scientist! Nothing more. I swear I don't know anything! I don't know about a Vida or who or what she is! Please ..."

Emperor Darcela replied, "I believe you. But let's make sure." Without looking towards the panel she added, "Arvelo, it's time to earn that antidote you've been receiving."

The emis nearest Kris handed him a pulser. The emis nearest Dara pressed a pulser against the back of her head. The remaining emises stood by the bound Nthn, a woman who only said, "I feel sad for you Eaves, and for these children you now have doing your work. But then again Reza never cared how things got done. Or what lies he—"

"Kris, shoot her now or watch *him* do it after he takes your girlfriend's life," Darcela said, pointing to the one the others called Berl, a towering, heavyset emis.

"No Kris! Don't! Don't listen to her!" Dara screamed desperately but Kris had drowned her out. His hands shook as he aimed the pulser, closed his eyes and fired. Dara let out a strident cry.

Emperor Darcela turned to the scientist with a look informing him he could be next, and he began spewing forth any and everything. Before nodding to the emises to close the panel, she thanked Kris. "Don't be fooled, these aren't innocent people. They're terrorists and traitors they deserve everything that's happening to them. You don't realize it, but you're becoming one of the good guys."

Kris, who was shaking all over, dropped the pulser which was picked up by Berl. He didn't open his eyes until he was looking away from the direction in which he'd fired. He could hear Dara sobbing. He threw up.

"Classic," one of the emises said, cackling. Kris felt the nudge of a pulser to his back and looked at Dara and saw one on hers. "Okay, let's go kids. We don't have time to wait for you to grow up." Kris opened up a phrinway to the next location and they were off.

OLA IYA

57 O.O.

"SHO FE JE ashewo?! Eh? You wanna end up a prostitute?
Ah, Omo de yi, ko kin gboro! You're a disgrace! Sho gbo mi?
You hear me!? A disgrace! (Hissing) O ru igi oyin!" You
should be embarrassed! Skipping class?! Vandalism!? You
think you are going to bring shame on me and your papa?
Running around pelu those losers like you have no sense.

Have you no sense? Have some pride! It is my fault for
allowing you to have such an easy life; a maid to clean up
after you, no struggles to speak of. You've had no
responsibilities. But I hear you now, omo de. From now on
you will do the maid's work, and she will be paid to see to it
you do. And you will still complete your studies and excel.
Sho gbo?! You hear me!? By the time you are done each day
your arms will be too tired to deface property, your legs too
tired to skip!"

Her mother's almost musical application of vernacular
moved rapid fire in between the cracks of the cane landing on
her hands so that Grace Ife, as she would one day be known,
whose cries came in rhythmic response to each lashing, had
the odd understanding of what it meant to be a talking drum
in the band at the parties she attended with her parents as a
child. "Obinrin o ti ri aye li le! Ma se sege si e lara!"

And her mother was true to her words that day, for Grace
had never received a beating so thorough, until her father
arrived later that evening, and having learned from her
mother that she had been caught cutting class (exposed when
Officer Babawale found her trazing the side of a condemned
building earlier that afternoon) proceeded to lay into her with
a series of insults so punishing, he needed not lift a finger.

And so the cane of his voice went, *Wai-Wai-Wai-Wai,*
punctuated by the neighboring tone of her wails. If there
were any musicians worth their salt living in the adugbo who
happened to be present during that interval, fortune had
clearly favored them with so many great opportunities for
inspiration, or, if they were shameless enough to press record,
free instrumentals for their next set (they did not even have
to open their doors). Grace suffered greater injury from the
internal humiliation brought on by her father's harsh words,
for there was nothing more viperous than the tongue lashing
of an angry Yoruba parent in Yoruba. Her greatest regret
besides the trouble she was in was she hadn't been able to
somehow prevent the news from arriving until both Mama
and Papa were home at the same time. *Oh well.*

As she washed the dishes and turned the house upside
down, jolting all clutter and dirt from the corners in which
they'd grown comfortable, her aches didn't throb so much as
knock, demanding to know when sleep was imminent, a
query that would undoubtedly never make it to her parents.
She completed her last homework assignment in time to
shower and dress for school, and was more awake and alert in
class than if she'd slept a full night. She was of the notion
however, that her outer shell had disappeared—perhaps
abandoning her to continue polishing the cabinets in the
kitchen—and that she was a glorious apparition, unburdened
of rude things like physical discomfort. As she received the
results from her calculus exam, she barely acknowledged the
instructor who muttered "Iranu. Nonsense … what a waste,"
as he sent another green check mark to her panel:

100/100.

The ire of her parents and teachers was justified. Grace
knew this. She was quite easily the brightest of her peers
which was almost miraculous, considering many of Nigeria's
most luminous, most privileged—the one percent of the one
percent—attended Gregory's College. On scholarship, she
was aware of the opportunity afforded her by her attendance

and she wholeheartedly wanted to make her middle-class parents proud, or at the very least, not bring enough disgrace for her ancestors to come wailing out of their graves, bemoaning the curse of the child too intelligent. But she didn't fit in—not amongst the nobility, who laughed about weekend trips halfway across the world in their parents' phrinjets, who gave her dirty looks when she walked by— noting that she didn't accessorize her uniform. Who, jealous of her awful, dreadful, *appalling* beauty, would spread rumors about her sleeping with all the boys she turned down. And she was restless; she couldn't read about a foreign land, real or imaginary in a novel, or watch news from abroad, or look at pictures in the old history panels with those intricate, indecipherable graffiti walls in the background without feeling them tugging at her, pulling something within towards these alien worlds unplumbed by her.

As early as she could remember, she'd look at Global Union Alliance maps and play with the holographic topography, enlarging it and standing in the center of whatever town she fancied that moment, tickled at the thought of it being that easy to travel. In real life of course, she had to have a passport, which her parents (both netline engineers for the West African Union), took care to lock and quadruple encrypt; travel profile (which she had to be eighteen to obtain and it would be restricted), and spends and other inconveniences that left a gulf between reality and her fantasy and not so much as a tattered rope bridge on which to cling. So she skipped class to spray-paint the beautiful scenes in her head wherever she could across the city, planning to check them off when she'd gone to each. Her attendance issues made her a "good" student, fine enough to (barely) retain her scholarship but not exceptional, as she should have been.

She'd also secretly taken a job in Ikoyi not too far from her school, working with her friend Kehinde who'd been in the same form as her—eleven, until he dropped out to make illegal profiles and the occasional passport.

"Nawa O! Girl, shouldn't you still be in class?"

"It's my last period, Kehinde, and there's a sub in there today."

"I don't get why you skip to do this. I know Mama and Papa Olumo are going to LIGHT THAT ASS UP if they find out you've been missing classes."

"Ha. Ha. This again? *Now* I realize you took geometry twice because of your love of circles. Your concern is appreciated but they already did last night."

"Girl you suicidal, eh? Go home! I'm not going to have them coming for me next!"

"Oh hush. They don't know I'm working and they have no idea about you. They only know I've been skipping. Come here, I figured out how to add the tag to each profile. It holds long enough that by the time anything is suspected, the user would have long disappeared."

"Yeah, girl, you so gifted." Putting his arm around her, Kehinde attempted to sneak a kiss and Grace pushed his face away.

"That's the quickest way to get my parents to come for you. Grow up, boy! You smell of brandy."

"It soothes the senses. You don't have to be so harsh. Why you vex? I got a little overexcited; won't happen again." He downed a shot as she shook her head. "See? Nerves soothed, Miss Olumo; no more funny moves. By the way, I have a meeting with the Oga soon. I'll talk to him and see if we can start paying you more."

"That sounds good. Maybe one day I'll meet this imaginary boss of yours." She studied Kehinde's smooth babyish face and bright, carefree eyes. "Why do you waste your time with this work, huh? You have everything, silver spoon boy."

"Would you like me to turn that question back on you, and waste our time some more?"

Grace nearly doubled over with laughter. "Please do! Who are you kidding? As if we are the same. There are no silver spoons for me. Even stainless-steel spoon is too much wahala."

"You may not be rich but pelu all that government work, I'm sure Mama and Papa Olumo don't hurt for spends, maybe ask them nicely instead of this shady business."

While intelligent like Grace, Kehinde didn't care for school and rarely did well despite his sterling attendance, possibly because his attention would wane within the first couple minutes of a lecture. His exam results had often provoked jeers and hisses from his instructors and chants of "Olodo! Olodo!" from his classmates, though they were slightly more complimentary when showing up at his parents' manor for his weekend long "Celebrations of Youth," or when they needed a fake profile to get into the nightclubs. He'd come into the world with a brother who died shortly after childbirth and the kids would often say he ate his twin but forgot to down the brains. One instructor informed him she'd made him a dunce cap over the holidays and he should remind her to bring it in for his school photo. She wasn't joking. His parents were Nollywood actors who lived on nearby Victoria Island. People often stopped him to tell him to "Greet them both for me, may they receive highest blessing," or to say "You know, in that last scene in *For Better, For Worse*, your papa could have had a better dramatic pause. Shebi, you will tell him for me?"

"Yes, sa." Or "Yes, ma," Kehinde would invariably say, not bothering to inform them that in watching those films, they'd seen his parents more recently than he had. He dropped out of Gregory's by sending a note authorized by both of his parents, saying he was moving north to stay with his cousins and would be attending private school there: "All the Best in the work you do for our children and keeping Nigeria whole. Sincerest Wishes, Janice and Victor."

The school administration had been so distracted by the autographed panel, the message and the accompanying photograph of the "Most Handsome Couple in Lagos," they didn't bother to call and verify its authenticity. If they had, the likelihood his parents would have answered or returned the call was nil.

His routine after dropping out got old quickly. Bored from staying home and watching movies, consuming large quantities of liquor alone, playing games and throwing parties every day for a month, Kehinde decided to get out of the house and head to Ikoyi. He didn't have any idea what he was looking for, maybe play some night tennis, find some girls, anything. He parked his father's McLaren huv. He lifted his trusty flask from the center console and with a sniff followed by a sip decided to go for a walk.

The nightlife in Ikoyi was, while still vibrant, a subdued version of what one could find elsewhere in Lagos. Here you could find the quiet rich, looking to blend in but still stand out enough to have a better time than the locals. There were billboards everywhere advertising various goods and services all touting, for a few easy spends, some upgrade or another to quality of life. Most common were priests and priestesses, each claiming to have been around on the Day the Gods Came, each claiming direct communion with Shango, or Aje or Ogun or Obatala or Oduduwa or Orunmila and so on. Some promised eternal life if you brought them one of Yemoja's crystals. All constantly insulting themselves, gleefully undercutting, all claiming greater connection than the others. Kehinde wondered how they all made so much money when they were eating each other. His preoccupation and amusement caused him to jump when a man bumped into him.

"Can't say "hi" when you see your buddy?"

He recognized the voice but couldn't recall the person behind it. He examined the face but didn't recognize it either. "Oyinbo?" He tried to think of all the whites he was acquainted with. "Aw, I'm sorry but I don't believe I know you." He took a swig from his flask and kept walking. The man jogged in front of him and stopped him again.

"And to think I thought my beautiful voice and magical green eyes were unmistakable." He pulled the navy colored hood of his tracksuit over his head, covering his face save for his nostrils and mouth and spoke again. "I'll give you three profiles but it'll cost ninety spends."

Kehinde punched the man then embraced him. It was the shady businessman he and his friends went to for illegal profiles. "Ha-ha! Olumide!? You fool. You know I've never seen your face until now."

"C'mon. That's because it's always during business hours, you sabi?"

"Yeah, ha. I know. What's up ah-whey? Let's get a drink." They ducked into a bar a few yards up the block and drank themselves into the friendships men forge when there are women, good music and plenty of alcohol, and all sorts of business ideas are suddenly within the realm of possibility, no matter how ludicrous they may seem when they're barely recalled in the harsh sunlight of sobriety.

Olumide, fueled by one drink too many, told Kehinde, "Listen brother, though you're younger, I look up to you, man. Your parents don't even know how talented you are, really. You should come work with me. You'll be the Oga in no time! Big boss man!"

"You think so?" Kehinde replied, the malt in his veins making him a believer.

"Ah-whey! No lie! Meet me at this address tomorrow, or whenever," he pointed to a map on a small panel. "It's right here on this road actually," he motioned to the street outside the bar. They drank and the rest was a blur, with Kehinde telling stories of his parents sending him gifts but never giving him money and never being home and Olumide going on about his aspirations to be a vessel for the Orishas, in between grabbing every girl who walked by and making

240

arrangements to meet up later. Somehow that night *did* turn into a connection. Olumide remembered everything when Kehinde decided to eventually follow-up.

So here Kehinde was now, several months into his employment with Olumide, looking at "Miss Olumo," the girl he'd liked since form nine; the girl who at some point per her request would be introduced to the "Oga" who'd made good on his word after all; the Oga who easily charmed girls, then treated girls poorly but always seemed to keep them. Kehinde saw his chance to make something happen with Grace slipping away, today simply being the latest in a series of rejected advances, and turned to her. "Why won't you go out with me?"

"You think you can just take what you want, eh? Nonsense. *Iranu*. You rich boys and your sense of entitlement. Oh Kehinde …" she laughed.

"What? What is it?" He responded, baffled.

"Have you ever *asked* me to go out with you?"

He stared into space and realized he'd thought too long. The answer was obvious. "Oh, uhm, no!" Silence. He connected the dots. "Oh! Uhm, will you go out with me?"

She laughed again. "No." She watched Kehinde's shoulders hunch a bit upon her response, no small feat for a guy who could be as arrogant as he, and decided to help him out a little. "Where?"

"Huh?"

Grace sighed, "Where would you like me to go with you?"

"Ohhhhhh…!" Kehinde finally catching on, grinned, buoyed by the confidence of short term memory. "I'd like you to come with me on a picnic."

"Sure, you idiot. I'll go with you on your picnic. On the condition you leave the liquors alone."

He barely let her finish before yelling "Deal!" and making a show of disposing of all drinks in the vicinity.

"See what happens when you're direct and not snively and creepy?"

"Na-wa oh! Why you insult me, girl? I was being smooth."

"You weren't. But it's okay. We'll see if you make up for it."

He did. The more Grace saw him, the more she saw he had a sweetness about him, a yearning to care and be cared for that he hid under his feral-cat bravado. She knew most boys with which she came in contact weren't what they seemed—always shouting down a mess of hormones and fragility to be "men" before their time. But he'd caught her by surprise with how different he was, and how their dreams aligned. He too yearned to understand and immerse himself in other cultures; he too sought answers to the mysteries of existence. In him she found a counterpart; she'd once felt this was impossible with another human being. And though she'd tried to cut down on her skipping to avoid conflict with her parents and had stopped trazing, she found herself increasingly prioritizing spending time with him in any way possible.

Coincidentally, it seemed she was no longer interested in meeting the Oga. Just as well, since Olumide was around less and less as time went by. Kehinde got lost in her presence and knew it, but he welcomed Grace's influence. It was something, to have a person who cared about him for *him*. Before long Kehinde could not recall the last time he'd had a drink. One day, she declared her love in the most casual, accidental of ways, but he knew her well enough to understand casual and accidental with her simply meant "secret plan." He smiled, nodded and locked eyes with her. Then he returned the same by accident also, hours later; they both enjoyed playing *the game*. A couple of days after that she was set to show up for work, but hours passed and she was nowhere to be found. The same thing happened the following day. Kehinde sent texts, buzzed her cles a few times daily, then stopped for a while. *Maybe she needs a few days to herself or something.*

After a week, he summoned enough courage to stop by her parents' where he was greeted with a smile and a swift kick by her father who said, "Ah, so you are the riffraff, the reason my daughter was missing school and neglecting her studies? The choices of young girls O, they'll never make sense to me. But it looks like we have finally separated the grain from the chaff. We have sent her off to where you'll never find her. You won't destroy her future along with yours. Now! Get away from my steps or my next kick will leave you without a bloodline! Idiot!"

"Odabo, sa," Kehinde said, as he wisely turned around and semi-crawled away, stomach in revolt from the greeting kick. No need to stick around for the goodbye one.

* * *

To ascribe a level of shock to what she was feeling would have been to acknowledge there was some way to quantify how her mind was processing what had not been considered, foreseen, anticipated, or conceived. Grace was still back in Lagos, as far as her mind was concerned, but her senses told her *where?* Enugu. Her parents had cut her out of the netlines. No profile, no fingerprint or eye scan access, no bios, period. She would live in this small village, Obinagu, in Enugu with her cousins. This backward village that nauseatingly clung to the gods in a way her sophisticated family in Lagos did not. Obinagu, the village shrouded in superstition and all sorts of silly folktales.

Why?!

She'd have no access to technology. Lyteche may as well have cut the power to the village. The instructors were paid handsomely to teach her a lesson and she would do her work on paper and hand it in the way it was done in the days of old: in person. She'd help her aunt and cousin with all daily

243

chores, and when she was done, she would study, sleep and do the same the following day. She hurt from not seeing Kehinde and each day it grew worse, but she did her best to bury her ache because Aunty Chibuike was a darling and needed her assistance, especially with cousin Amadi who was quite a handful.

As she collapsed into bed one day, seven or eight months after arriving, she realized she could only recall the outline of Kehinde's face and while she recollected *deeply* the feeling his kisses gave her, she couldn't remember how his lips felt against hers. She wondered if he'd looked for her, if he missed her; she smiled and laughed a little bit, at the idea of Kehinde, carefree Kehinde, searching high and low, dressed in old pirate gear, sailing from land to land until he found her. She yawned and barely had a wink of sleep before she was up again, only this time she wasn't in the room she shared with Amadi, who'd been sound asleep on the floor when she went to bed.

In the place where she found herself, she saw a large shadow with a green and yellow light around its edges growing larger and larger, so she ran. It appeared to stop growing, but one of its arms kept extending in her direction the faster and farther she ran away. She headed down a cavern which had a bluish-white aura illuminating the cave. She saw Kehinde, in full pirate gear, and laughed hysterically while continuing to run. She looked back once and saw to her horror that the shadow's arm had extended into the cave, growing more pronounced in the relative darkness, winding behind her, coiling down the stairs. She laughed harder. As she descended to the bottom of the cave, her heart punched as if it were looking for a way out as well, but there was only a wall and nowhere else to run. As she backed up against the wall, the silhouetted arm touched her face, and it stopped and stayed on her face for a moment. She heard a scream and the arm slunk away, no—ran, was sucked—pulled away, faster than it had pursued her.

She opened her eyes, and was in a meadow and all was still. She opened her eyes again and was back in the cave. Then she opened them again and was in Linton City, capital in the last remaining stronghold of the former Eurhacian Union, and then she was in the stunning, ever shrinking rainforests of Madagascar and then shivering in the permafrost of the North Emerian Union and on it continued until it was nothing but an uninterrupted stream of places popping up, spinning around her and being replaced, as if they were sad planets drawn to a sun which promptly had business elsewhere. She felt herself growing tired; could you be that in a dream? And the stream slowed, until she was standing in a room quite different from hers back in Lagos and the one she was sleeping in now. There were statues in each corner, four in all, and they all looked like they were not sculptures, but sentient beings frozen with the life still very much in them. Each was accented with bold, unforgettable colored markings; from school she remembered it was a way to identify the gods. She recognized them as four of the most powerful gods; Shango (red and white) God of Thunder, Eshu (black and red) the Trickster God and Lord of the Crossroads, Orunmila (green and yellow) the God of Prophecy, Yemoja (blue and white) Goddess of Fertility and the Sea.

Grace would later recall the identical recognition and terror in their bronze eyes appeared as if they'd only realized they were being captured at the exact second it was too late. A white pigeon, tall enough to look her in the eye, landed a few yards away and in doing so drew attention to the absence of a roof. As it began waddling towards her, all five and a half feet of it, she felt no fear, no panic, only calm. It stopped directly in front of her. They locked eyes; it took off through the roofless ceiling, and she followed. The house receded, becoming at first a canary on a golf course, then the faded yellow tip of a strand of dying grass, and finally a fleck of sand indistinguishable from the sea of green.

She asked no questions about how she was flying or where she was going, simply grateful for the lucidity of the dream. It was only what transpired when they landed minutes later that led her to the question of when exactly the plane between reality and fantasy was shattered. They were back in Lagos, outside an old familiar abandoned building on Awolowo Street in Ikoyi, the pigeon now normal-sized and at her feet motioning its neck and beak towards the window. She knelt to see more comfortably and easily, and looked through the window to see Kehinde hard at work designing new profiles. She was overjoyed to see his face, but what made her heart smile the most were the photos he'd displayed of the two of them in her absence. It was overwhelming. She had to speak to him. She lifted her hand to knock, but found her fist repelled before reaching the window. She attempted it again, the same thing happened. It bounced off an invisible field. She turned to the pigeon and saw a taunting smirk. With all her strength, she punched as hard as she could and managed to break through enough to get Kehinde looking in her direction, and running towards the window. Before they could make eye contact, he was gone.

And she was back in her bed.

It was time for school. The day passed in a blur, but none of her teachers noticed as she'd mastered autopilot eons ago during her life as a Lagos schoolgirl. She spent the day trying to figure out how to get back to see Kehinde, retracing all the steps she took in the dream and then laughed at herself for being so stupid when it came to how she felt for a guy she may not remember in a couple of years. *I can't just close my eyes and fly.* But she couldn't stop thinking about the dream. When she had finished helping Aunty Chibuike with the chores, cousin Amadi with his schoolwork, completed her own homework and anxiously listened through another one of her Aunt's stories about the time the gods visited, she told her she was going to bed early.

246

Cousin Amadi had finished his homework with several hours to go before bedtime and was playing outside with the neighbors' children. Grace got into bed, closed her eyes and tried to fall asleep while thinking of the scene from the night before. She found herself outside the same window, only this time the room was empty, and she was definitely not in a dream. She went around to the hidden entrance at the side. The unlocked door powered off easily. She let herself in. *Kehinde, carefree Kehinde.* To her disappointment, the photos from last night were missing but she sat on a couch, waiting to surprise him. After an hour or so, the door switched off and she heard the unmistakable heavy clod of Kehinde's footsteps. As she readied herself to surprise him, preparing to jump into his arms, she heard a lighter more fleeting set of footsteps—akin to the sound of rain on a window sill, and the soft giggle of an excited girl. She recognized that giggle; it belonged to a girl Grace had often teasingly called the president of the KFC (Kehinde Fan Club).

"Kehinde, you're so funny, Oga."

"We'll see if you're still laughing on the couch."

By the time Grace could think to hide or disappear, they'd already seen her. No matter, she pushed past a shocked Kehinde whose hands were up the girl's blouse. She was sure he called, and chased after her, but she ran until she realized she'd started dream-traveling again. She kept going until the tears stopped streaming and her eyes were clear and dry. When she got back to the village, she gave her aunt a generous hug.

Her aunt was surprised. "Pikin, wetin be dis?" She said this half-laughing, nearly bowled over by the child.

"Thank you, Auntie—for everything," Grace replied. She considered telling her of the strange dreams and the travel, but it would've resulted in a trip to the Babalawo, and there was no telling what would come of that.

* * *

Grace didn't look back. She became an example for her little cousins and her classmates, and all her teachers pointed her out as the benchmark. She kept up her exemplary attendance but on weekends and when she had free private hours on weekdays, she explored. She went to her room, or to a "friend's house" or to the nearby igbo, and closed her eyes and woke up everywhere her heart had desired since childhood. She still got out her sprezens to traze graffiti from time to time, mostly in places others would never see— delighted at the unusual glow that accompanied and lingered afterwards. She was occasionally curious about the walled off compound near the village, but she'd heard rumors it was Ministry property and the days of bringing shame to her parents were behind her, so she put it out of her mind entirely and carried on with her explorations of the greater world outside. She found when she arrived in places with a dangerous climate, a protective field, like a bubble, formed around her, keeping her warm or cool as necessary.

If she ever found herself in grave danger, threatened by animals or men (they rarely differed), out from her hands without warning would come strange beams or electrical pulses—but mostly she'd disappear to another location or turn herself camouflage and hide. She learned she could travel without closing her eyes quite accidentally on one of the days she was escaping an attacker (one of the men who had gone mad when she showed up somewhere the likes of her had never been seen and decided he must have her at once). As she was running, she waved her hand in front of her and a phrinway(!) appeared with the igbo by her auntie's house in view. She ran through and the phrinway closed behind her. Was *that* how she'd been traveling all this time? Her old schoolmates, the royals—who needed their parents' vehicles to do what she could at a whim—would have died from the envy. Safe, she sat on the closest tree stump and gathered herself before walking home through the woods.

She collected things from everywhere she went and created a hiding place in the igbo by the house where she'd come back and look at them whenever she couldn't travel. She especially enjoyed her mini collection of rare crystals, clear, with their light blue tint a nod to the goddess who reminded her she would always be the girl from the City by the Sea.

Whenever her parents came to visit or she had an especially demanding course and chore load and couldn't find time to get away, the walks through the woods to get to her hidden travel treasures became as precious and exhilarating as the travels themselves. And they visited her more often now. As far-fetched and ludicrous as the possibility once seemed, her parents were pleased with what she'd become, and so when the time came for her to attend a university, they approved of her choosing to attend the prestigious Linton Economics School—far away from home, trusting her judgment had improved.

Of course, she could never tell them or the rest of her family about her oyas. They would have accused her of witchcraft and what they'd do after was unpredictable enough for her to know better. She did, however, enjoy feeling closer to her parents than she had in years.

As she began her first semester at LES, studying philosophy and public policy, she wasn't as surprised by how easy the coursework was for her as she was by how much she missed her family. So when she received word Aunty Chibuike was ill, she, despite their protestations, insisted on taking the first flight to Nigeria and joining her parents and Aunt. As she shoved and pushed amongst the airport crowd towards a taxi, she overheard a few people speaking in Ibo about Enugu. It wasn't good news. She heard the Ibo words for "fire" and "explosion." A wave of panic washed over her before logic kicked in: *Enugu is a big place, relax.* She was able to flag down a cab. The driver, a portly elder gentleman in striking red and black agbada, smiled as he helped load her things.

"Ahh you na fine-fine girl; you should not be carrying these heavy bags. Where dey your prince?"

She laughed and responded "Wetin I need prince for, sa? I have you." He chuckled as she entered.

"Where to, pikin?"

She responded "Obinagu."

He went silent long enough for her dread to creep back in. Then he smiled. "You know there is adventure premium for that, pikin. And I will have to drop you a few miles from the village as I do not want to be cursed with juju."

Grace rolled her eyes. "How much?"

"Three times the usual fare."

"Three times! Are you mad? It's not like you drive the thing; you just sit there like a sack of gari and make sure it doesn't go haywire. Normal fare!"

"Twice the normal fare."

"Abeg O! 1.5!"

"1.8! and that is final or you can find someone else to take you."

"Fine!"

As the cab began its weightless glide away from the airport, rainfall punctuating the silence, she took in the natural scenery and climate of home. She had missed the freely existing trees and hills, the pockets of sky that still opened up occasionally to bathe the land. Linton City, as the capital of the former EU was breathtaking, but as a clouded city had a synthetic beauty which never let her feel quite in tune with the world. In Linton, she at times felt outside of herself. Here, there was a silent harmony; it was easier to just be.

The cab driver interrupted this harmony, humming a tune she recognized from primary school as a battle prayer to Ogun for protection.

"Now you are going to war?" Grace was annoyed.

The driver chuckled. "Don't mind me pikin, I simply enjoy certain melodies."

"Nonsense. You old mugu. Keep believing whatever nonsense superstitions you want about my village. I'll get out here."

"Pikin, we are barely halfway, we are in the middle of the igbo …"

"That's fine, comot! Comot for road!"

After he complained about the spends she gave him and threatened to hold her luggage for safekeeping as a "courtesy," she paid him two trips worth of fare.

"Nothing personal little iya," he said, grinning devilishly. "But you know I must have my national cake. I too must chop."

She pointed to his protruding belly and politely suggested if he must chop, that was the best place to start. She hadn't wanted to phrin back to the village as she was wary of arousing suspicion if she were seen arriving. However, she couldn't shake the overwhelming anxiousness and feeling that each second she waited was somehow making something worse. *Please Olorun. Please, I beg of you, let everything be okay.* She grabbed the couple small bags the cab driver called luggage, waited until he disappeared from view and, having not been able to confirm any news about the explosion on the netlines during the ride in the cab, opened a phrinway. Her heart sank. As she looked on through the opening, stunned—she faced the remains of a smoldering Obinagu. *No. this isn't real. It can't….* She rushed through the open doorway.

She ran to the place where her Aunt's residence once stood. It was no less a ruin than the others around it. *Okay this doesn't mean anything.* "It doesn't mean anything. Hello? Ma? Aunty? Hello Amadi? Papa? Hello?" She desperately began flinging aside the rubble, calling for her relatives, praying for a response. Praying that Olorun heard her prayers and they were okay. She continued like this until she got to a necklace that she'd last seen on her mother.

251

No ...

She flung away more rubble faster, more desperately, until she shrieked.

No!

She vomited. She turned the village upside down ignoring what she'd seen and couldn't process; that Mama, Papa, Aunty, Amadi, and all her other cousins were gone. Their neighbor, Okafor the fisherman who'd always offered words of encouragement, was gone. His wife Adaku—who'd taught her how to make the sweetest tasting puff-puff—and their two daughters, *gone*. The Babalawo—Olamide, *gone*. Her prayers did not spare her loved ones—no special protections were granted by her words of faith; but how could they be? When even the Babalawo met the same cruel end? She wanted to do something—*anything*, yet all she could do was cry; a despair containing all the heartbreak, hopelessness and helplessness of everyone who'd ever suffered heartbreak in her time and all the times before. She collapsed at the heap of the charred remains that were once her loved ones, closed her eyes hoping to wake up where they were, trying her hardest to imagine and follow them where she could not go in her present state of existence. It was then that she *knew* they were gone.

Finality.

Clarity.

So she chose the other thing, the other way, finding a blade amongst the rubble with which to slit her wrists and was close to it when she heard:

"COME OUT NOW! PLACE YOUR HANDS UP AND NO SUDDEN MOVES!"

* * *

Reza Shirazi saved her life that day, even as she had reluctantly saved his. Only in the moment when her body involuntarily protected her against his weapons did she know

252

she had to live. She had to find out what happened to her family and the rest of the people of this village she'd felt more at home in than back in Lagos, and she had to know why. She had to find out the truth so that the truth survived, so that the contents of the lives of those who'd been buried beneath the charcoal remains of the village were not replaced with lies scattered across panels and repeated as gospel. And even if the lies were repeated as gospel, there would be her who knew the truth, who would pass the truth on to others so their souls—their good, sweet, exalted souls would always have a proper home on this plane of existence.

And those she now helped—the evil creatures who had, in place of eyes, tunnels leading to emptiness—the soulless demons who called themselves men—who did this, they would face justice. That was her oath and prayer. But she understood it wasn't simple and that what she'd have to endure to get there—the waiting and the near complete destruction of her old self—would be one of the hardest things she'd ever have to go through in all her days, and that only a patience inconceivable at that moment would see her through. She created a new back-story for herself; at first it started as a quick desperate lie in a moment of self-preservation—but then she grew it; grew it into a detailed lie too irresistible not to believe—a lie that fed the egos of the enemies she now allied herself with by painting them as her glorious saviors. A lie that had roots in the stories people told about Obinagu and her understanding of the line between superstition and reality. A tale whose believers grew the further one got from Obinagu. She inhabited it. It didn't matter who she'd been prior. Reborn in this new reality she was Grace Ife: daughter of tragedy in a celebration of life.

The hardest thing to get used to was their arrogance; the stupidity she had to feign and the gratefulness she had to show, the constant unwanted advances she had to tiptoe around and the willingness to subjugate herself again and again when she could have destroyed any of them. *Not yet.*

KIDS OF STOLEN TOMORROW

This is the only way. She was given clypsars—hand straps that harnessed the power of the corlypse chips embedded in them, allowing her to tap into her abilities, according to Emperor Martin. The emperor said this was because the corlypse was the source of her oyas. That may have been so, but the corlypse looked remarkably like it belonged in her crystal collection in the woods. She soon found there were others who possessed a similar ability to travel (all given clypsars) that the Institute for Preservation of Unity knew of, and worked with—read: locked up and experimented on. But there was no one like her, no one with the mastery or the abundance or assortment of oyas. Reza suspected she was holding back but she only allowed so much to ever be gleaned from all the tests they ran on her—barely more than what she'd displayed during their first encounter. The presence of her oyas meant more IPU poking and prodding of the others to see if they could duplicate Grace's gifts to any extent and she somehow felt responsible.

Emperor Martin had called them "gates" and sometimes "human phrinways." She never knew the names of the other gates, not their real ones, because it was forbidden for them to talk amongst themselves. Still, they got to know each other well just the same because they were brought together for impossible tasks and each time they survived, they gained new knowledge of one another that under normal circumstances would have taken years. The smoldering desperation of those moments forged understanding she was unlikely to forget in her lifetime.

She no longer dreamt often, and when she did, she rarely remembered. Occasionally, she'd wake up in the village in a heap of rubbish that was once her room. She would scream and phrin herself back to the palace, unable to sleep for the remainder of the night, but ever more focused during the day. Captain Shirazi consistently pushed her limits during training, as if he were looking for her breaking points physically and mentally—not to set them as boundaries, but to cross them.

It always felt like underneath his line of "making you the most efficient emis you can be," there was a cold, cresting rage never quite manifesting tangibly enough to be sure it was real. She wasn't allowed to use her oyas during training, though a new enhanced blacker was worn by Shirazi to protect the captain against her reflexive and sometimes involuntary outbursts. She eventually got over the suspicion he despised her and came to appreciate his part in helping make her a more efficient instrument of vengeance. Sometimes, if she allowed herself to admit it, she enjoyed his company. He wasn't emotional, he wasn't friendly, but she respected he wore no mask for what he was, at least not as far as she could see. Others constantly remarked on how he was hard to read and tough to quantify but to Grace there was no mystery: He cared only about how his work could advance him, and his interactions with her, the other gates, and the emises were integral to this and so a necessary inconvenience. The others would never see this about him because it was too horrifying to admit. *Probably,* she thought, because they had more in common with him than they cared to examine. *Tunnels for eyes ... leading to nowhere ...*

To nothing.

When he approached her she was initially surprised. It never occurred to her that he thought that way—that he had time to think that way. Then she was scared, and confused. He was eerily polite about the whole thing, never aggressive, but he didn't have to be. She was in his house, under his rules and the sheer danger of a "no...." She never had a choice because he'd removed it the moment he "asked." The first time, she had to hold her breath and make gentle passionate eyes belying the willpower it took to overcome the scent of his flesh and she cried for a long time afterwards as soon as she was alone. From then on, she found herself dreading each interaction with him; every training session never knowing when his desires would "politely" manifest themselves again and she would be involuntarily aroused by his sweaty, clammy touch. She was angry that her physical functions had betrayed her and that she wasn't strong enough to stop him. *This is your fault. You're letting this happen. You could stop this today if you wanted.* But she knew, that for all her oyas, this wasn't true.

The event bringing their encounters to a close was so sudden and unexpected she would have considered it a gift from the Orishas had it not also been so devastating. During a mission with the other gates where they were transporting weapons for a restock, the eldest one (by Grace's guess), a burgundy haired bright copper toned woman she'd nicknamed Ember—collapsed, causing her phrinway to close and the weapons cache halfway through to split, setting off a current that rendered the weapons useless. Grace ran over, beating out the other gates and the one emis who didn't head over to the weapons. When she got to her, Ember was convulsing slightly, with blood rushing out of both ears and large purple splotches all over her neck. Attempts to resuscitate her at the scene failed and Emperor Martin ordered her transported to the medical wing for additional measures. A week later, another gate—the boy she called Baby Jimmy—he couldn't have been older than seventeen in her estimation—dropped dead with the same mysterious symptoms as Ember.

Grace was placed in quarantine with the other two remaining gates for twenty-four-hour observation daily. Tests were run on her and the others, blood samples were taken and every question she had was stonewalled. She was scared, yet felt she wasn't quite as terrified as she should be. She was physically healthier and stronger than ever, and the quarantine meant no worries about now High-Lord Shirazi's advances. Still, each day she wondered if and when she would meet the same fate as her fallen comrades and occasionally whenever she felt particularly vulnerable or in slight pain it was accompanied by a spike in terror. In these moments she—oddly—thought of Kehinde, the boy who once broke the heart of a girl who no longer existed. Perhaps it was the

recalling of his carefree essence that brought her some
semblance of peace. After a few months of the isolated
observation she was released.

"A clean bill of health, I've been told, congratulations,"
said High-Lord Shirazi.

Grace vomited.

"Someone get over here and clean this up!"

She followed him down the dreaded path to his private
quarters. She painstakingly removed her clothes as he
dimmed the lights. He motioned her to keep them on. She
breathed an internal sigh of relief. To her surprise, he only
wanted to talk. She sat in the chair across from the bed and
he sat at the foot of the bed. His face was blank as always.
"How do you feel about returning to domain work?"

"They said I am healthy, Oga. I feel normal. Should I
not? How are the others?"

"No. No, I am simply checking up on you. You were,
after all, locked away in our quarantine wing for a significant
length of time. Your surviving comrades showed no signs of
infection. Now, domain?"

She bit her tongue to avoid speaking her mind, and
instead followed with "Yes. I will be glad to get back to
helping our team. I am ready, Oga."

"Good." The high-lord stood. Grace flinched. "On
edge?"

"No Oga, I—I am still getting used to interacting again."

"Oh good. Take your time." The high-lord paced around
the room. "Our doctors studied them. Your dead comrades,
the other gates. All of them. It wasn't only you."

"I know."

"They—you showed exposure to what caused those
deaths. You also showed infection. However, your blood cells
fought it back each time they were exposed. You were
released because they believe you to be immune and the
disease appears to only infect those like you—with your
abilities, so the threat of contagion on this base is

nonexistent. You'll be periodically observed for potential new developments. Not for as long. Nothing you aren't already used to."

"Yes, Your Grace."

"Any other questions?"

"No, Your Grace."

He nodded his head towards the door, sitting back on his bed as she saw herself out.

She could have cried from the relief.

The next time she was called on a mission, it was only her. This was unusual, but she did not ask any questions. She was given orders to go alone, which never happened. There was always at least one other gate and they were always accompanied by at least two emises. After closing the phrinway behind herself in a cave in the new location and beginning the search for another corlypse, she was startled to find the phrinways reopen and three emises come through them, with no sign of the other gates. One of the emises, holding a large diamond shaped object, entered some code into its keypad and the phrinway closed after him. The emises oversaw the search as usual and not a word was mentioned of what had taken place.

"You're not eating." Reza walked up to Grace who'd been sitting alone in the cafeteria.

"High-Lord Shirazi, what happened to the others?"

"We must keep everyone safe."

"What does that mean, Oga? On yesterday's mission three emises phrinned, but no gates accompanied them. How is this possible?"

"Grace, it's been seven years since I found you. You've been a fine soldier: loyal, protective, quick thinking. I'm not sure how you can be all those things and still be naïve, considering your background. We've done what needed to be done. Finish up; you have to rest for your next mission."

258

* * *

75 O.O.

As Emis Eaves Darcela sat across from her at the IPU's headquarters, Grace thought back to her own childhood days of twirling around in holograms of foreign cities wishing to be in them—what would that little girl have thought about her wishes coming true in a fashion that likely brought the gods to tears of laughter each cosmic happy hour? *I should have told that girl to stay away from such foolish dreams.*

She saw the pain in everything about Eaves—knew it all too well—and wondered what childhood dream brought her to the same hell.

"What is it you feel you can offer as a domain emis?"

As Eaves answered, Grace thought how odd it was she, who still felt like, and knew she would always be an outsider, was interviewing a third-generation IPU emis—the bluest of bloods. A *Decalaoba*. Had she gained *that much trust* in sixteen years? No matter. It was ceremonial anyway. Eaves would be assigned to domain before the end of the day. As far as a true formal introduction however, it served its purpose. "Better circumstances than under the ones which we met, Emis Darcela. You look well."

"Better. But I still look terrible, Captain."

Grace laughed. "Comparatively," she said, still smiling. "The one thing to be careful about here is not to let your anger be your overwhelming driver. In what we do, it would be foolish to pretend it isn't a factor and it helps to push us at moments we have nothing else. But don't identify with it so closely you can't separate yourself from the rage. You're gifted, but out in the domain the stillness within is what brings you home after each mission. Make it your base and return to it whenever you feel lost to the fury."

"Thank you, Captain." Eaves was dismissed and Emperor Shirazi entered Grace's office shortly after.

"How was she?"

Grace smiled at the emperor. "Oba, we both know the interview was a mere formality."

"More than that, Grace. I want her to report directly to you. You'll be responsible for most of her training. It's important you're comfortable with her."

Like you were with me?

"I understand," She said before adding, "She has the greatest motivation there is to be successful. She'll learn fast."

"Be sure she doesn't rush where patience is needed."

Eaves found Grace to be someone in whom she could confide. Often, Eaves felt isolated. The feeling of family she'd had with her fellow nobles and civilian comrades went away on the day of the Unity attacks, when she no longer felt cocooned from the terrors of the world. From that day, she felt exposed no matter where she was and it was an exhausting existence. The closest the cocoon came to returning was when Captain Ife was around. Grace understood the implicit games their male co-workers tried to play, the subtle and occasionally overt attempts at undermining her work and would often flash Eaves a knowing smile followed by a chuckle as she easily thwarted their attempts. She was *so confident, so unshakeable.* Eaves would often forget that Captain Ife was also a gate, until she'd phrin them somewhere unexpected for her training, or effortlessly put down an assailant during a mission in the domain. Her oyas gave Eaves fleeting feelings of invincibility, knowing no one could hurt her with Grace around. It was Captain Ife who provided the first glimmer of hope, the first true clue in the mystery that had become her personal life's mission to solve.

78 O.O.

"You've become quite the resource, Emis Darcela. It's been great to watch you grow under Captain Ife's tutelage. Your father would have been pleased."

"Thank you, sire."

"You know, when you were a baby he would bring you around here all the time. He always wanted you to devote your life to the service of the crown—take up the royal charge. He knew you would. Clairvoyant man your father was ..."

Not enough to save himself.

"Enough of my rambling. Captain Ife has disclosed to me that during a corlypse recon mission she found something she felt would be of interest to you. I was opposed to you finding out because I don't believe you're ready despite your progress, but she stated her case in your favor quite compellingly. I'm also of the belief she'd tell you herself if I attempted to keep it from you. She's convinced you can handle such information. We shall see."

Eaves knew there was only one thing Captain Ife's findings could be related to for Emperor Shirazi to be so reticent and unwilling to disclose them to her. She quivered.

Emperor Shirazi called Grace into his alcove. For a moment, Eaves thought she saw a look—was it *fear?*—on Captain Ife's face and a slight shudder as she brushed past the stone-faced emperor.

"While entering a previously thought-to-be-unexplored cave on a corlypse recon in a remote region of the South Emerian Union, Captain Ife and her team came upon a signature pattern similar to the pattern you recorded in the Lorzan file the day of the bombing. It was used to lock an entrance further down in the cave, and she and her team were unable to proceed further. It differed slightly from the Unity bombing pattern and didn't appear to trigger anything; although I believe it doubled as an alarm. She copied the file for verification. See for yourself."

Eaves would've cried out, if all words hadn't trampled themselves in the stampede from her throat. The signature was an exact match. The same signature she'd nicknamed "Vida," for what was taken from her the day of the bombings. When she was able to gather herself enough to make a sound, she quietly said, "How? Who?"

"We're hoping you can help us with that."

Grace added, "Can you decipher the pattern? Unlock it?"

"I can try." Eaves, noticing the emperor looked unimpressed, quickly added, "Yes, I can definitely unlock it. I'll need some time but it can—it will be done."

Grace looked at Eaves and appeared to be making calculations in her head. "If you can, then I would like you to come with me so we can find out what's being hidden in that cave. Can you be clearheaded? You'll be my responsibility but I'm not a babysitter. We don't know what to expect, and I need you at your best so we can be ready no matter what."

Eaves nodded. "Yes, Captain, I can. I assure you."

"Good. We leave in an hour."

The prior missions Eaves had been on with Captain Ife during her training were all vital, with high stakes and real, deadly consequences for failure. Against the silhouette of the current undertaking they were infinitesimal, trivial. As Eaves followed Grace through a phrinway, anxiety so traveled through her that her entire body vibrated. Her teeth chattered, caught in the quake of the relentless shiver. Grace looked back at her piteously and smiled. It was enough to calm her nerves and return her focus to the mission. They had phrinned into a thicket of bushes and she was kissed by mosquitoes in the embrace of the nighttime humidity. "They think you're cute," chuckled Grace.

"They don't bother you?"

"I grew up with them." Chopping through the brush Grace added, "You'll get used to it. We have a long hike ahead of us."

Eaves wondered why they weren't at the cave's entrance. Why hadn't they phrinned there? She nearly stumbled down a ditch trying to figure it out.

"Careful. Something about this region affects phrinning and latching; it messes with aim. Blame eshu's fickleness. This is the closest I can get us safely. We'll have to follow the signal being given off by that signature. We should eventually find our way back to the cave. It's good exercise. Watch yourself. Pay attention, Emis Darcela, and stay close to me. There's steep terrain coming up and if you slip, I may not be quick enough to save you."

She found herself struggling to keep up with Grace for the first few miles. Still, she was surprised at how much easier it was than she had expected. Her daily conditioning sessions with Captain Ife had put her in decent enough shape that by the time they hit a steep rocky stretch above the trees, she was gaining her second wind. They hiked for several hours without incident before Eaves' body registered the pain. Once it did, every step shot up her ankles and shins directly to her knees where it lingered momentarily before tearing through her hips and back.

"Soon," Grace said, right as it was becoming unbearable. And then, "Here."

Eaves collapsed in the booth of a small limestone balcony dug into the edge of a cliff and watched Captain Ife, following her eyes to a large cave on the other side of a canyon at least a mile across. The captain nodded. The gulf was bridged by a thick steel rope, the sort of rope used for sliders, which few could operate competently or safely. Before the landing on the other side, jutting out from the cliff were large spikes. Someone on the other side of that canyon didn't want any visitors.

"Captain are we ...?"

Captain Ife laughed. "Emis Darcela, did you bring a slider? You see any with me? We'll phrin; this is a good spot for me to aim from. It's nearly dawn and you're tired. Get some rest first."

Eaves, who wanted to leap over the canyon right then and snatch whoever was hiding in that cave and drag the person across the basin floor and up the side of the cliff but was too weak to protest, simply nodded and drifted off to sleep.

A pain in her neck roused her out of her slumber, and she rubbed it. *How long have I been asleep?* It was at least midday judging by the position of the sun. Captain Ife was absent, but she'd left her pack. Eaves helped herself to a few items in it to quell her hunger and headed back the way they'd come, looking for the captain and silently praying she hadn't gone off to capture Vida solo.

Moving cautiously down the slope, she'd covered close to two miles when she heard it:

"agchhhhhyyyyrrrraaahhhhhhhh …"

It took her several seconds to realize the sound was human—likely an eternity for the person emitting it. Eaves picked up her pace, moving diagonally in the direction of the voice. She was fully prepared to see someone wounded and was ready to help. She did not expect to see a gasping corpse, burned all over—save for the face, and she expected, least of all, for that corpse to be Captain Ife's.

"Pleeeeeahhhhse, someone … hehhhhlp …"

All the memories of her time spent by Ruben's lifeless body, her time in the hospital holding out hope for Blue, the moment her fears were confirmed—all of these things came back at once—and she was overtaken by an overwhelming sadness that left her unable to cry and instead allowed itself to be wrapped—squeezed by the anger that followed it. She looked Captain Ife in the eyes and quietly said, "I'm so sorry. I'm so sorry, Captain. We can save you. We can save you. I'll call back, we'll get you onto the carrier and—"

"No. it's okay." Captain Ife, always—even then, still trying to be a source of calm, replied.

"Who did this?! Where can I find them? How can I help?"

Captain Ife, last bit of life in her eyes, spoke: "My pack." With one heavy exhale, she was gone.

Eaves touched Grace's neck to check for a pulse but the moment her fingers made contact with the Captain's skin, the body turned to dust—a glowing, golden sand that scattered on the wind. Eaves throat went dry and her heart ran laps as panic and terror closed in on her. She had grown close to someone and, only four years after her entire world was yanked from under her, lost her too. What would she do now? How could she hope to survive in a domain determined to break her? Against an enemy who left her helpless? Destitute? She cried, and as she tasted the saline on her lips she saw the image of a weak *pathetic,* emis—a girl in a hospital bed, begging Grace, begging Emperor Shirazi, begging the doctor—for news on her beloved Blue.

No.

She stood, wiping the last of her tears. There would be no more overwhelming terror, no paralyzing fear. She hiked back in the direction of the cliff to their campsite at a pace that showed little regard for her personal safety. She slipped twice, bruising her knees in the process, yet hurried on. When she reached the booth, she grabbed Captain Ife's pack and emptied out all the contents onto the smooth limestone surface and examined them for something—anything that might give her a clue. She picked up item after item and threw them aside, not understanding how any of these things could help or to what the captain had been referring. She regarded the miniature statue of Shango before laughing harshly and discarding it. "Once again, you've failed to justify anyone's faith in you," she said, flinging it into the canyon. She noticed a cles, but as Captain Ife had advised her on the hike up, it wouldn't work until they'd returned to the arrival site. She strapped it around her waist in case she made it back down.

She was about to give up when she noticed something about the pack itself. It was made of image thread—similar to the material of blackers. Of course! It was practically a camera. She attempted to preview images by scanning the bag with her blacker, hoping the mini-panel on her armband would play whatever files it captured, but she had no such luck. Perhaps they'd be able to recover some footage back at the Institute and find out what happened, but Eaves would get no answers at this moment. She sat, staring across the chasm to the cave entrance and screamed.

"Again!? Again! What do you want from me Eshu?! I know this is you—I hear the laughter! What penance am I paying? What past life am I being punished for?! Answer me coward!" The echo—hollow, empty—was her only reply as she ignored the tears that begged she no longer be revisited by tragedy for her supposed best attribute. Her eyes remained trained on the cave. *I need a way across that canyon.* She stared across the impossible distance and depth as if her determination were enough to carry her across unscathed. A slight breeze blew, enough to knock a small stone loose a few yards away and roll it towards her foot. She looked down to kick it away for disturbing her focus and saw scrawny haphazard letters carved into the limestone by where she'd slept:

CELA GO HME LIV 2 FIHT

She began packing the items she'd emptied and placing them back in the captain's pack, copying all the data from it to her blacker.

Moved by the last order of the now-departed captain she'd admired, Emis Eaves Darcela grabbed the pack and headed back down to the arrival site. She reached it in time for nightfall, and noticed the cles was glowing. She signaled the palace, and waited quietly while an extraction team arrived.

* * *

"You're even more beautiful than I recall."

Grace hissed. She laughed. "Fi mi sile! Stop that nonsense, Olumide. You know I've always been immune to that kati-kati you call charm."

"You know I'm getting famous now—"

"Ah, yes. Do you want me to stick out my palms and transfer a few Naira to you so you can pull out cards and give me my fortune? Should I call you Prophet Carbo? 78 O.O. is a young year yet, with many upcoming lessons to humble you I'm sure—so don't be silly Olumide. Where's Tunde? Shebi you helped free me for a reason."

Darcen smiled a bittersweet smile and looked towards the door of the adjoining room. As Grace headed towards it, out came Tunde, short, muscular, hydraulics in his stride and a smile surely plastered on since birth. He wrapped her up in a hug and picked her off the ground before saying a word to her, then planted a kiss on her cheek that lingered enough afterwards to feel like foreplay. Grace demurred, pushing him away. "Tunde! Behave! I don't recall us ever being that familiar."

"Maybe not Miss Olumo, but seeing as you're our hero I figured that sort of welcome was the least I could do."

"It certainly is the *least*," she said. "As for this hero nonsense, you're merely the lesser demon. Rebels or no, you're both Decalaoba."

The Awolowo brothers bristled. Darcen spoke. "Well, it is a necessary step towards bringing them down. Shebi, that is what you want? You can call us lesser demon all day, but you've seen firsthand their evils."

"Yes, and I've also seen yours."

Tunde chuckled. "Eh? Iya? You say seen as if you were not a participant. You clearly understand our effectiveness if you do not agree with our methods, or you would not be

267

back here now so soon after request to help us with the next phase."

Grace smiled ruefully. "As if I haven't rejected many of your past overtures. I'm not without my skepticism; the Kehinde thing … I haven't seen or spoken to him in years. Surely, he's forgotten me by now, and if I recall he used to work with Darcen—Olumide. Is Kehinde somehow involved in this? A partner of yours? Is *that* why you wanted me out permanently? I don't see how it benefits you to no longer have me as a mole in the IPU."

Tunde's laugh was quick and hearty. "I assure you iya, while I share your skepticism on the Kehinde thing too, he has not forgotten you. He's no partner but we stay in touch and when Olumide let him know you were coming home, he demanded to see you. Sometimes it's good to be around old friends, that's all. As for that IPU business, we needed you out of there and back here helping us with this full-time— protecting our researchers, using your knowledge to help them. We are at critical juncture and you will ensure our success, and of course, secure your vengeance. It was the only way. Besides, one can only hide amongst the enemy for so long. It was simply a matter of time before your life was in danger."

"Hogwash, Tunde. Iranu logic. I could return tomorrow and they'd praise it as a miracle." While true, the thought sickened her.

Darcen laughed as an oddly expressionless Tunde rubbed his chin. "I still don't know why the other one had to live," he replied.

"Tunde be serious. If they were to buy me as truly dead she had to see me die. How else to convince her and give them what was needed to never look for me? Had we killed her there's no one to tell that story, just IPU searching ceaselessly maybe suspecting me and bringing more heat on you guys. You want that relentless loon of an emperor to have more fuel? Shebi? I thought *you* were the master strategist. Why must I explain this to you?"

It was Darcen who spoke up this time. "Iya, no need to be rude. Even self, for all your joke about my profession, shebi, it was us who got you to safety. Is that not a miracle?"

Tunde chimed in. "Should you not thank your lucky stars the great Darcen Carbo is protecting you? What gods came when they destroyed your village, eh?"

Grace's hands turned bright amber as she stepped menacingly towards Tunde. "You mean my village they destroyed because of **YOUR** nearby compound?"

"Wait, you don't—mama, I didn't mean anything by that, I apologize. But you know we are still taking risks to protect you. It's not like those disguises of yours make our jobs easier despite what you may think. Remember, you're helping us, but getting a great deal out of it as well … we are helping you.…" As Tunde fumbled toward the end of his sentence, the door opened and in poked the head and shoulder of a man in military duds.

"Oga, apologies if I'm interrupting, but you said to tell you when we're ready." Tunde and Darcen looked at Grace, whose hands were no longer glowing, and she gave a nod. Tunde motioned and the driver, accompanied by two armed guards, led Grace outside to an armored wheeled vehicle. Noticing the look on her face the driver said apologetically, "It's the only way to move undetected, madam."

She laughed. "Oh, it's okay, I just haven't seen one since I was eight or nine." As she sat in the back, two guards on either side of her, one in the front seat next to the driver, she realized she'd never traveled so slowly in her life and the boy—*no, man, he's a man now,* she was going to see … it had been ages. What would he look like? Would he still recognize *her?* Eternity, to see someone she hadn't seen in forever.

And then they were there.

There he was. She'd wondered if we make long lost crushes better looking over time in our heads because of age and distance, and she certainly had thought she had. One look at him was all it took to see that in the place of the romanticized nervously charming boy stood a more impressive man, albeit one whose joy had clearly seen too many sorrows. The carefree brightness had been exchanged for a certain determination written on the lines of his brow, made irreversible by worry and punctuated by the resolution in his eyes. *So life has taught you some difficult lessons too eh, Kehinde?*

"Aye, bay bee, you don put on some nice curves, figa eight now," Kehinde said, grinning, and for a moment she saw a flash of the playful, carefree boy.

It was strange, to hear him fall into the flirtatious cadences of their teen romance, reminding her of a lighter time—of who she *was*. Could she still be that? Lifetimes had happened. *It would be foolish ... unrealistic....* But a sense of longing urgently took hold of her—to be in that time—to relive that era as if the past twenty years had been bliss unbroken. To feel, or at least try. *Could that be?* In front of her—could that be a key to her own un-breaking?

She leaned over and whispered. "I've always had curves buh-buh. I was too busy running circles around you for you to catch up and see." She lightly slapped him. He stumbled back feigning serious injury as he rubbed his face.

"Oh, you've stooped to flopping eh buh-buh. Are you a footballer now?"

Taking her slick retort in stride, he embraced her and began walking her into the house. He motioned for the driver and guards to leave after he tipped them.

"Shebi, it is still Nigeria. Everyone must chop," he said to her as she rolled her eyes at the large wads of Naira he'd handed them. "Now come love, we have catching up to do."

"Oh, do we? How many of those party girls have you been chasing, eh?" She asked him this although she was somewhat mum on that part of her own life, not ready to tell him the past stories of Shirazi (and certainly not of the

270

emperor's most recent assault—the final straw prompting her decision to escape), for fear Kehinde might do something rash and be killed. She would probably never be ready. After his answer, she moved the conversation on to work.

"Ah, so you wanna know what I do? You first, ma! They told me you are like Vice Emperor Agent Superspy now. Shebi, that's like Queen? Should I bow, Empress?"

She laughed. "Don't be silly Kehinde. Yes, I served the crown, but as a Captain that's all, and not anymore. But I hear you na Mr. Big investor now, eh? Shower-shower the money over here." He smiled, then went silent, clearly wrestling with something. "Kehinde, what is it?"

"I know our last meeting wasn't on the greatest of terms but why didn't you come see me after Obinagu? Why didn't you let me know what happened? I have resources. I would have been there for you."

"Kehinde that's not fair. How could I? We hadn't seen each other in over a year by that time. Besides, you were such a carefree boy then. I think you're just looking back with the eyes of an overly sentimental man. Still, I *did* miss you, but we were just children and I had to bury those feelings—all feelings in the aftermath of that tragedy to make it through. Sometimes in weaker moments through the years, the thought of you helped, but I became what I did to survive and to be able to have this conversation with you right now."

He was quiet for a long time, looking at her, and stroking her cheek with his thumb as his palm cupped the side of her face. He looked as if he saw a little more of the girl he knew in this woman. "Okay."

"That's it? No more interrogation?" She said as he opened up a bottle of wine and poured it into two glasses.

He smiled as he handed her one. "You're here now. It's time to rejoice."

She looked at his glass apprehensively. "You're fine to drin—"

"Yes." That was a long time ago, Miss Olumo.

They laughed and drank and laughed and drank until they couldn't anymore, old friends reliving an idealized past with the promise of a suddenly better future. As she settled her head into his chest while they swayed to both the soft music playing in the background and the song of youth relived in their heads, she felt, for the first in years, safe. She pursed her lips and blew air slowly across his chest while running a finger up and down his bicep. As the thoughts swirled and her sense of balance disappeared, not quite sure if from the wine or the vertiginous heights to which he'd brought her that day, he calmed her with a single kiss to her forehead. And suddenly she was spinning in that good way that only he could make her, unable to keep off each other anymore than their predecessors who mated out of instinct—primal draw out of urgency, out of an innate need for survival; energy flowing from one to the other like branches flow from trees, like leaves flow from branches.

By the time they were done, a shaking, smiling, breathless mess of dew drops and tender flesh, hours had passed into the early morning and it was time for Kehinde to head to work. "I'm canceling my meetings and staying in."

"Don't you dare," she said. You're Mr. Big-time Oga because you're hard-working and you don't need people seeing that change."

"Are you sure?" he said, kissing her neck.

"Yes. Now go bring home the bacon!" She said, laughing as she smacked him on the rear end. Kehinde shook his head and got dressed, stopping for a slow kiss on the way out.

It was all Grace could do to not jump him again right there. She sat in a glorious stupor for a few hours before getting up and sending a message to Tunde:

I'm Home

The reply read:

Good. We can begin?

272

She smiled to herself before sending:

We can begin.

* * *

Those were the happiest days of Kehinde's life. Days he'd thought to be long past when Grace had seen him with his "fan-club" girl and disappeared for what he thought was forever. Sure, he had been a kid then, but he knew they should have been something. Looking at them, one could know. After Obinagu—the tragedy he'd recalled vaguely from news wires but heard most about from superstitious whispers—it didn't occur to Kehinde there might be a connection to Grace until Olumide reached out to him a few years after she went missing. How could it have? Kehinde had thought she'd gone to a top school, found a great job and was out living the proper life of a Gregory's Alum. She had no need or desire to contact Kehinde ever again—what for? She probably had a family of her own … and he had his own worries.

Olumide informed him Grace's parents had died in the Obinagu blast and though he and his brother Tunde were unsure where she was, she was still alive. He didn't say how he knew but eventually he produced proof. From then on, he promised to give Kehinde updates on her in exchange for information on some of the clients with whom Kehinde did business. It was a worthwhile trade, but he grew impatient over time and demanded to see her. Olumide continually said he would see what he could do, but never promised anything.

It was the passing of Kehinde's parents that led to Grace's return. After years of Tunde and Olumide sending updates without being able to do more, Kehinde inherited a warehouse in Port Harcourt. The Awolowo Brothers were attempting to make a deal with him for secret access to the warehouse—with the freedom to make any alterations they saw fit, and suddenly, they "found" her. Kehinde, no believer in coincidences, lit into them for their duplicity but he couldn't hold a grudge. It didn't matter how it happened, he wanted her safe.

With him.

Hell, the Awolowos could have kept the warehouse for all he cared.

* * *

She sat, tears streaming, twisting the luminous coil on the ring finger of her left hand, its stone's glow Aurora Borealis in a bubble, a thing that could never truly be held. Her mind raced back to those humid Lagos evenings when the sun, weary after another arduous day, was writing its goodbye messages on the walls of the rooms of those who'd been brave enough to let it in. It was on one of those many evenings when the windows sat open and the curtains were drawn for the slightest breeze, and they, she and he, sat atop a bed which sat atop a floor which sat atop a building which sat not atop, but deep inside the marvel that was Lagos, amongst the smells of egusi stew, fried plantains, jollof rice, moin-moin, puff-puff, chin-chin, suya and sweat and earth. And then there were the sounds that assaulted your ears from morning only to blend into your consciousness throughout the day so that by the same evening the children playing—the talking drums, the errant saxophone wails, the Afrobeat bands, the wind stations, the huv races and police chases, and ambulances, the ajas barking out of excitement, the ajas barking out of boredom, the chickens squawking, flopping, running every which way—were the steady hum of existence that enhanced one's love of the moment.

It was on one of those too perfect evenings he turned to her and said, "It's been a long time since I've been happy, let alone this happy . . . longer than I can remember. There's

274

only one way I could possibly be happier or more content, and if you feel the same...."

Even recalling it now, she could never quite hear the rest of his words, or her response.

She smiled and wiped another tear away and left the note and left the ring and left.

"My dearest Kehinde, Love and all apologies, but I cannot be the woman you want. I cannot be the mother you need to raise and nurture your children. I care for you dearly, but I will nev—"

He thought it was a joke when he saw it. *That one, she don have serious sense of humor. April Fools early paah pa....* He searched all the rooms in the flat and found many of her things missing, but she'd never kept too many items around anyway. He clessed her, but didn't get an answer or a voicemail—simply a "Netline Invalid" error. He tried the number several more times while also sending countless text messages. *Remain calm, it's nothing,* he told himself; but in truth, panic had taken over after the first try. He didn't trust the authorities when it came to his affairs, and they had never shown competence in handling matters of missing persons prior, as kidnappings typically turned into ransoms paid for the dead. As the minutes without a response grew, each second seemed to stretch to house minutes of its own, and Kehinde could not see himself in terms of anything beyond the desperation of that never-ending now. At wits end, he made a call to an old friend.

"Ah-whey! I never know whether a call from you is a great thing or a terrible one. Keeps things interesting. How you dé?"

"She's gone."

Silence at the other end.

"Where?"

"If she said, would I be calling you? Help me find her."

"Kehinde you know you're my comrade but I wouldn't even kno—"

"What'd you do the first time? How'd you guys find her then? Do that." He attempted to sound calm and in control, but he was pleading and there was no disguising it. "Whatever you guys want or need, just find her."

"We can try, brother—"

"Don't try! Find her!"

"Ah-whey listen to me! We'll do everything we can, but you have to know if she doesn't want to be found, there's little anyone can do. But we will try. Okay? Hello?"

Kehinde had disconnected the cles. Tunde turned to Darcen and said "She left him a goodbye note and gave him back the engagement ring."

"Have you heard anything from her?" Darcen asked nervously.

"Nothing yet, aburo," Tunde replied.

If she's gone ..."

"No need for panic, aburo. Kehinde is a man of his word. Unpredictable as this development makes things, the man understands the value of a contract. Miss Olumo has done what we needed and she'll reach out when she's ready. I'm sure of it. There's work to be done." Tunde stood, embraced his brother, and left.

* * *

Oluwadara Abiola Adeleye was born on December 16, 78 O.O. to a woman incapable of motherhood. She was, several months later, left on the doorstep of a man who, in a depressive spiral, mismanaged his business, wealth and inheritance and fled Lagos—cloudless city, crown of Nigeria, seat of the West African Union, land of natural tropical climate on a planet where such a thing no longer existed—for the biting permafrost and simulated sun of Yorkland Province, seat of the North Emerian Union. When Kehinde Adeleye saw the baby's face, he knew and wept, but for the first time in a long while his sorrow was mixed with joy—a

276

bitter kola nut joy, but joy nonetheless. He picked her up and he held her with the same affectionate embrace he'd often held her mother.

Kehinde was reinvigorated, dedicated to finding his child's mother and uniting their family. He was dedicated to making sure Dara would have the best grades and be the student he never was. At least in this way, she could choose her fate and rise up from the life his failures had brought her. Buoyed by these goals, for the first five or six years of her life, he was able to stop drinking. But as the hopes of finding her mother faded and the bills piled up and the hours piled up at work and he was less able to see his daughter, he felt the pull again. There was something comforting about an old familiar friend from a time when he was less himself, and that's all Kehinde wanted to be; less himself. He got so low he was willing to give up what was left to disappear, go to sleep inside the bottle. He was willing to forsake what he loved, his whole world because he couldn't see another way. He was a coward. He knew he was. But he didn't quite know how to fix it.

* * *

October 93 O.O. – Present Day

Dara stood, unsure what to think of the power of prayer in the face of their suffering but resolved to let go and hope it was enough. Kris came over and hugged her, both of them ignoring the jeers from the emises. They were still here, together, and that alone was a *miracle*, she reminded herself.

"We'll get through this," Kris whispered in her ear. She nodded, comforted, although she got the sense he didn't quite believe his own words.

"Enough. Let's Go!"

Berl barked as the location of their next phrin came up on the panel. As they moved through the bright shifting colors of the phrinway, Dara found herself indifferent to the staggering beauty she witnessed each time they headed towards a new destination. Instead, she looked straight to the task ahead thinking, *two more* …

Kris did the same.

They arrived outside the doorway of a dark, empty, dusty room—part of a warehouse that looked like it had never been inhabited, and the emises looked at each other, confused. Berl removed Kris' clypsars and they walked in. A phrinway opened and more emises came through it, confusing Dara until she noticed a large diamond shaped object in the hands of an emis who entered some sort of code into the object's keypad and watched it close the phrinway behind him. Berl used his cles to call Emperor Darcela for permission to proceed and sweep for combatants, which she granted while advising caution. They found a door at the far end of the room, which Kris was forced to switch off. Berl nudged him down the dimly lit staircase into a well-furnished not-so-dimly lit laboratory. Standing not too far from the bottom of the steps was a tattooed young man in a light green lab coat, smiling as if greeting long lost friends.

"I thought you'd never arrive," he said.

Kris stared in disbelief, the emises looked further discomfited, and Dara laughed. In the background, one could hear Emperor Darcela on the cles saying: "Panel Now! What the hell is going on? Who's there?"

It was Envy.

TJ

"I-3437 PANEL LOG entry. All previous statements and IDs fully confirmed, current and applicable. Today's date is Sunday, January 15, 75 O.O. The time is 1617 hours, Central Union Base Time. Updating progress on Program Irunmole. There have been some startling findings since the last session, rather promising. Myself and Dr. Ali … we've made significant upgrades in the purification process. Of 368 mutating strains, 124 have been combated effectively. Unexpected boost in continual residual effect: We've noticed upon the deletion of the 124, 63 additional strains become dormant in the human body. This represents an increased immunodefense response rate of approximately sixty-six percent from the first observation of this phenomenon in entry I-2437. However, larger concentrations appear to be showing diminishing returns. Remaining active strains still eventually overwhelm the immune system and the subject's body shuts down, but overall much improved. Perhaps changes will need to be made in the initial stabilization process. Further research necessary. The time is now 1619 hours on Sunday, January 15, 75 O.O., this log is complete."

Thomas Barrington was exhausted. It would occasionally happen like this. He'd have a day of unforeseen progress, a surprising breakthrough but instead of being energized, he'd be spent from the anxiety caused by worrying about the setbacks surely coming. Dr. Ali had grown tired of reassuring him and so whenever she noticed the body language change, the return of the forehead creases, the slumped shoulders, she'd say, "It's only the end of the world, Thomas."

He'd sink further and reply, "I know, and there's nothing we can do, is there?" Her sarcasm was lost on him.

279

As he exited the lab, having changed into his street clothes, she wondered if he had any family at all, anyone with whom he could at least share the emotional burden of their work, since voicing any part of it outside the lab was forbidden. At work they were prohibited from talking about their personal lives, but she got the feeling he wouldn't have if they could. He was a loner *through and through*, she decided.

"Goodnight, Dr. Ali."

"Goodnight, Thomas." She insisted on informality.

He didn't like it, but he knew it didn't matter. Dr. Ali was as strong-willed as the strains they were combating and far more stubborn. He'd long since given up requesting she comply. He walked a few blocks down to the wind station on Utica Avenue, followed at a wide distance by the same two emises who always escorted him to make sure he got home safely. He often got the sense their protection was more of a threat than a comfort, so he made it a priority to never give them the opportunity to put his suspicions to the test.

He lived a quiet, uneventful life outside of his work, never marrying or socializing—save for occasional visits from and to his younger brother, George. George was always the impulsive, streetwise, outgoing popular one, capable of making friends with a complete stranger in minutes, traits that mortified the elder Barrington brother. It also explained, Thomas had reasoned, the lightning quick manner in which he'd had a child with a Haitian woman he barely knew ("I'm fostering unity amongst the Southern Icelands, Thomas!"), who turned out to be more ill-equipped to be a mother than George was to be a father—no small feat.

"He looks like you Thomas," George would often remark after the child's birth. Thomas didn't see the resemblance— save that the boy's umber shade was more like his uncle's than his father's golden tone, and often wondered if George did simply because he'd chosen to name the boy "Tommy" (the boy's mother had agreed with a nonchalant "whatever").

The first time he held little Tommy, he was in the midst of a heated conversation with George about medical costs while the infant kept touching the same spot on his thermer. Thomas, annoyed, was about to hand the newborn back to his father when he noticed it: the child had closed the open buttons in closest proximity to his hands—a task which for *a toddler* took considerable comprehension and motor skill. It was then that Thomas looked at the child—really looked him in the face for the first time and saw the boy was wide awake. Tommy did not look with the overwhelmed wide-eyes of sensory overload in a foreign land, but rather of a traveler who understood the culture and the customs from prior visits long ago and was simply attempting to recall the language.

It took him five years to do so.

Tommy did not cry, even shortly after being born.

He would make a sound best described as "neh" which coincided with one need or another of his. He would repeat this sound in groups of three, evenly spaced apart until the nearby adult gave him the requisite attention.

George loved his son, but "dat boy dumber dan rocks, ya ere me? E fi gwan become janitor e lucky," is what he constantly told his brother. "Why e can' talk? E jus make dat neh sound all de damn time." He'd taken to calling the boy TJ, hoping adding the junior would somehow make him smarter.

Thomas would nod and say, "Don't worry George, in good time," constantly reassuring him over this period. "He's normal. It takes a while for some." Thomas, meanwhile, had let the boy know, "I see you and I recognize your awareness." Early challenges and tests issued to the boy by Thomas confirmed his brilliance. He now saw TJ's birth as a miracle, as an opportunity to leave a legacy he otherwise could not.

The sheer random probability of the boy possessing such a level of intelligence was almost enough for Thomas to believe in fate. Thomas considered himself the preeminent scientific mind of his time and was aware the work he was doing for the Institute for Preservation of Unity was not only groundbreaking, but paradigm shifting—the opportunity to make such a great contribution to science came around once a century or so. Yet, here he was, beholden to his bosses at the IPU—a mere government labcoat who would see no recognition for his efforts, not even a footnote in the brilliant work that would simply be credited to "IPU Sciences Division." It made him fume thinking about it, regretting his choice to go into the "safe and secure" world of Ministry-sponsored science, and he felt a growing desire to in some way, ensure history would know of his contribution.

He'd been given the chance early on—when he was a mere first year research student at Stuyvesant University—to work in the risky private sector by a secretive firm promising he would be at the forefront of his field and have unlimited resources. Ultimately, his concerns about their motives outweighed his desires. Now, he could realign his path with greatness once more. He risked imprisonment for treason if he dared publish any journals about his work and no information was "leaked" to the press without bioscan verification for Ministry tracking, so those were non-options. If, however, Thomas' suspicions about TJ's capabilities were correct, the boy could serve as a human storage unit for his research data until he figured out a suitable plan.

Thomas' suspicions proved correct. He spent the next few years during visits communicating with little TJ non-verbally (they had quickly developed their own system consisting of an amalgamation of modified sign language, nodding, and abridged Morse code), and sharing with him everything about Program Irunmole; the supply, who commissioned him, the secrecy, the danger, and of course, the science itself. It was refreshing to be able to "discuss" the science and nature of his work with someone outside of his work, someone who could understand, someone (though he would never fully admit this) whose comprehension may have been greater than his own.

282

It was through these communications he knew TJ had the capacity to speak since age one and had simply chosen not to. *You'll be no janitor,* Thomas thought as he looked at the boy. *I have something greater in store for you.*

TJ's first word was "Georgie," a deliberate move to appeal to the paternal instincts and needs of his father to be loved and adored by everyone, even by his son, the future janitor. TJ soon displayed the normal intelligence of the average unexceptional kid his age, a relief to his father and a pleasant development to his uncle, who'd wondered if the child had any inherited impulses or traits from his dad and required a larger audience for his genius—traits that would have placed them all in jeopardy, and more importantly, ruined his plans.

As TJ moved through grade school, bringing home Cs and Ds with the occasional surprise B and the obscure A, and getting trips to the firing range or cage fights or exclusive strip clubs from his dad as a result, he and his uncle Thomas continued their private sessions. Sometimes, when there was an unsolvable question stalling progress, Thomas would joke about how everyone was happy because the running crack was once they found a treatment, they were disposable. In this way he could talk around the problem without directly asking for help. TJ would quickly pick up on this and subtly steer the conversation in a direction that led to Thomas discovering the solution for himself. TJ would then change the subject as if the discussion had never happened, so important was their relationship to him.

In a world where he otherwise felt utterly alone, unable to relate to children his age and the adults he came in contact with on a daily basis, his uncle's intellect was a refuge and his longing was compounded by the fact that he never knew when they were going to visit him, or when he could stop by. Sometimes it was a couple times in a week, sometimes in a month, sometimes three or four months went by without a visit. As TJ got older, the visits were less and less.

"Uncle's busy, Tommy. Doctors gotta work a lot or they don't make enough," his father would tell him.

TJ would act out by getting into fights at school, or insulting his teachers—fully in control and aware of the source of his frustration and deliberately choosing to give way to the impulsive actions that followed when unchecked. In late September of 85 O.O., four months before TJ's tenth birthday, his uncle came by with a gift for him, a holographic V-Cube-7.

George laughed. "You think that kid can fi try one a dem? Come on Thomas, he no genius, he no doctor, he ain't you. Boom Ba-Ye the way he troh dem hands maybe, but no you … hah."

Thomas noted that George seemed quite proud of his son's pugilistic nature.

"It's okay. I'll teach him how to solve it. Anyone can learn how; *you* could if you wanted."

"Ah yes, clever big brother always lookin' out yah?" George downed a shot of rum. Thomas turned to the boy.

"Tommy, what's with all the fighting?"

"I dunno, Uncle T … I get angry sometimes. Kids test me."

"Don't make things harder for your father. He tries you know."

"I know. Sorry Pops, I'll try to be better."

George smiled, downed another shot, grabbed up TJ and put him in a headlock. "You'd better! The fighting's fine, child. We might have a little champ on our hands! I'll be taking you to Disco's gym soon, have you knockin' everybody out! Now go hang with your Uncle T. I gotta run out and handle some business."

As Thomas pretended to show the kid how to solve something he could've solved a thousand times mentally the moment he saw him bring it out, TJ picked up a nervous energy from him, and they communicated in their code once again:

I'm close, Tommy. It won't be long now. When I first started, I was worried that all I would've accomplished was further improving the lives of a few at the expense of many. But this one, this changes things, Tommy. All will benefit. I can't help but be thrilled at this, the scientific implications and general applications for humanity are mind-boggling. You will have a great part to play soon, Tommy, wait and see. This is an early birthday present and a celebration gift. I can't stay long today, but once my work is officially complete I'll come back here, and the three of us will celebrate properly.

Once the Cube was solved, TJ saw why it was the perfect gift. It transformed into a hologram of the three of them, from TJ's eighth birthday, when George had wanted to take TJ to another strip club and Thomas had instead insisted on the Museum of Modern Art and on paying for it. That trip was the closest he'd come to experiencing communion with other geniuses in physical form; so many snapshots into the minds of the brilliant of ages past. Each sculpture and painting seemed to say to him, "We understand. It's madness, noise, chaos all of it. This was our way of getting through, find yours."

George wasn't thrilled at first but by the time they had gone through all the nude exhibits, he perked up. "Not bad, big bro!!! Look the boy's smiling! Split image of you I swear...."

When he returned home, George noticed the different photos from that day on each face of the Cube and laughed. Below the rotating Cube was the static caption: 'Always remember your humanity.'

"Man ever with the sentiments! You gwan make de boy soft Thomas! Good pics though."

And that was the last time he saw his uncle. A week before TJ's tenth birthday, in January of 85 O.O., Thomas Barrington Sr. was struck down by an errant self-driving huv whose programming went haywire. Pro-Ts came by to notify George. It was on the local news the following day, with comments from a few of his "patients" lamenting the loss. Tommy would later recall finding this especially strange but unsurprising.

He had never truly dealt with the concept of grief or loss before. He knew his mother had left them, abandoned him, and he knew he shouldn't feel too great about it. He remembered wondering early on if it was because she hated him, but she was never an entity in his life besides giving birth to him so he tended not to dwell on her. With the death of his uncle, he attempted to manage intellectually by telling himself that these things happen, and it makes sense to feel loss but that's merely due to the synapses formed from that person's presence in your life telling you they should still be there.

He thought he could, by being analytical about the whole affair, detach himself from it, and forestall or bypass an emotional response. But he was unable to keep it going. Overwhelmed by emotion, he did what ten-year-old boys do when something hurts: cry. The funeral was difficult, replete with (out of place) testimonies from "patients" whose lives Dr. Barrington had saved, and George being visibly moved by how important his older brother was. TJ shed a few tears but was better able to control his reaction to the pain by this time. He wanted to get out of being part of whatever purpose the façade had served and grieve alone. He understood the reasons for the secrecy, but he wished his uncle could somehow have been publicly acknowledged for his true greatness. *He saved you, you greedy, ungrateful idiots. He may have saved us all! And the world will never know.* When they got home TJ gave George a big, genuine hug, and they sat in silent understanding, the two of them having had something in common all along.

There would be no more visits from his uncle. No more outlets for his intellect, no relief from the mundane day-today trivialities he endured. With the only person to whom he could relate gone, there was no place for him. He was lost.

The fights went up in frequency, the suspensions increased, his grades plummeted and he repeated a year in the apathetic red vane instructional system, a feat that took *considerable* effort for legitimate imbeciles. He now followed his dad to the strip clubs willingly and to the gyms to watch the boxers and mixed martial artists and sometimes spar. He started drinking and smoking—robbing people or selling illicits whenever he needed quick spends. He earned the nickname Envy from the robberies; often taking (on top of the spends) things his victims seemed to specifically hold dear. He wanted to find something—anything—to relate to, but he knew he'd never belong anywhere. He picked fights with kids older and bigger than him because he wanted to get hurt. He sought the pain, the jolt, the distraction.

He held the secret hope that one of the kids could and would kill him, something that wouldn't happen at the gyms because they loved and respected his pops. Invariably, they all failed to cause any significant damage and so, disgusted, he would embarrass them. He became infatuated with the old-time way of getting tattoos after getting a couple on his fists, finding relief in the constant sting of the needle. After he turned thirteen, he used them to mark the passage of time and began to get one for each kid he beat up. His father, once happy to have a partner in crime, was now worried. TJ's grandmother, who came from the Southern Icelands to live with them when Thomas Sr. passed, tried to help provide guidance through a softer touch, but there was little she could do.

Just shy of his fourteenth birthday, he had the good fortune of picking a fight he didn't win. The victor of that fight, Kris Arvelo, would eventually become his best friend. While TJ couldn't open up fully because Kris wasn't scientifically inclined, he was clever and possessed an intuitive brand of intelligence TJ could respect.

287

It was through Kris he met Donzilana, and she changed everything. He was taken with the way she took old-time words, phrases and mixed them with her own—taken with her upside down, inside out way of viewing everything, never having met anyone who thought or talked quite like she did. She teased him about his nickname, revealing a tattoo of his namesake she had on her back of the Jealous One's Envy mural running along New Grand Concourse ("You *hate* that you can't steal it, don't you? You love it, you want it, but it's mine ... don't Envy").

Between his friendship with Kris and his attachment to Donzi, he'd found home and he loved them both dearly for that. He still fought and was generally mischievous, but it was more out of habit—mostly to take on bullies, protect his friends and it occurred less than before. As he gradually grew more comfortable with them, he relegated the years with Uncle T to the back of his mind and fully embraced who he was with them as his identity. He didn't have to be the sad kid destined to be forever alone and not connect. He didn't *have* to use his gift to do something great; after all, that didn't work out so well for Uncle T. He was perfectly happy to stay the third musketeer.

As often occurs when we've made up our minds and settled into something comfortable, life jolts us out of whatever formation we've established and challenges us to make whatever adjustments are necessary or abandon the formations entirely. It wasn't too long after Envy had shoveled the last pile of dirt onto those early formative year memories with the late Dr. Barrington that, while Grammy was out shopping, he and George had a visitor at the house, late one March evening in 91 O.O. The visitor introduced herself as Dr. Sarah Alison, and she looked panicked about something.

"Ye lost gal? What you wan fi tern up at mi door for, interruptin! I'm a private citizen, livin' a quiet life, yi ere me now?!"

She shook her head—walking around repeating something that Envy couldn't quite make out but sounded rhythmically like something his uncle used to communicate to him during their exchanges. Envy stayed in his room, eavesdropping, and eventually he was able to make it out: "Once you're done, you are through; they box your things, and soon you're news."

The last part he'd once heard his uncle say verbatim, albeit jokingly. He poked his head out of his room to sneak a peek at the woman.

"What yer on dere babbling bout gal? Git out! Git out a ere!"

"I'm so sorry, I shouldn't have come here. It took me a long time to find; I know about—"

Envy saw a look of horror wash across her face.

"I'm sorry—I shouldn't have done this. Nice to see you, bye!" and without another word, she showed herself out.

"Strange gal …" said George as he closed the door behind her. "TJ, where you at?! Dishes boy!" Envy stepped into the living room, bike in tow. "I'll be right back, Pops. Hanging wit Donzi. Later tonight though, I got em, for real." He calmly strolled past George out the door. When he got outside, the woman had gotten far down the block in a hurry but was at perfect following distance. He got on his bike and riding close to the throng across the street, managed to stay out of her line of sight, which proved handy because she seemed to have the sense she was being followed and looked back every minute or so. She maintained a brisk walking pace but never broke into a run which allowed him to glide along patiently in the bike path grooved into frozen sludge.

She'd worked with his uncle; that was clear. But where'd she come from? What did she have to say and why now? She was obviously already taking some kind of risk by coming to see them, so why turn back? She went up onto the wind platform at Willoughby and Myrtle station. He went up on the elevator and stood on the platform next to her waiting for the wind shuttle. He placed a note in her pocket, got on the same car, watched her get off on her stop, got off two stops later, and rode over to Donzi's.

He didn't think she would show up the following day on the same platform, but he went anyway. She walked past him in the crowd never looking at him and placed a note in his coat pocket. They got on two separate cars. He got off two stops earlier this time and bought something. When he got home he read the note:

> I don't know why you would
> How you could
> But it was a mistake
> Nothing,
> Sorry.

The next day, a woman named Dr. Suraya Ali, who looked remarkably like Dr. Sarah Alison, was found dead from a self-inflicted pulse. Her patients were devastated at the news.

Three days later, Envy was hanging with Kris and Donzi at her house.

"It's getting late. I should head back."

"You're kidding right? This is like afternoon for you."

"I got something I gotta handle."

"You've been acting real weird, *real sus* lately, you okay?"

"I'm fine. Got some things to sort out."

"Okay, I'm here if you need me, babe."

"GAAAG."

"Shut up, Kill!"

He got his bike from outside Donzi's and was riding home when a note fell out from under the handle bar. He picked it up:

> It's as far as tomorrow
> Early as a mile
> Keeps coming back

Twice before
Stay away

He didn't know what they knew, or how they found him, whoever they were, but there was only one way he was going to get answers.

He showed up 5:28 AM the following morning at Myrtle-Willoughby and waited on the same platform he'd met Dr. Alison. He was there for an hour. Five shuttles went by and no one showed. He was leaving the crowded platform as the sixth arrived. He felt the pinch of a needle in his neck followed by the sudden inability to form words, sounds, or control his movements. He grew weak.

He felt two individuals, one on each side, usher him through the nearest shuttle doors, and sit him down as one sat beside him in the crowded car holding him down and the other stood in front of him, one foot on each of his. He never quite passed out but he was teetering and couldn't recall much of the ride when they'd arrived. He certainly did not remember how he got to the room where they were questioning him now.

"Why were you meeting with Dr. Ali?" Envy saw the pulser pins charged on the table next to him and knew this wasn't to be a friendly neighborhood Q&A.

"Who's Dr. Ali?" he replied. The current from the pins ripped through his flesh, poking through every inch of skin with the jabs of a million vibrating needles. "AGHGH! SHIT"

"Why were you meeting with Dr. Ali?"

"You mean Dr. *Alison*? I don't know. She came by my house a few days before she died, and left without explaining anything. I was trying to find out why."

Silence.

The man interrogating him asked the next question in the form of a statement. He would do this often over the period of the interrogation.

"You know her."

"I don't."

Needles. "C'mon man!"

"How."

"I don't know her! I think she used to work with my uncle. He was a doctor. She showed up to my house the other day looking a mess, said her name was Dr. Alison, muttering something I couldn't hear. Then she said it was a mistake, apologized and left. I followed her because I wanted to know what mistake drove her to show up in the first place."

"And—"

"And that was it. Next she's on the news, dead. Like my uncle."

"WHAT WAS THAT FOR!"

"Being less than forthcoming will only cause you more pain. You communicated with this woman. Tell us about your exchange.

"I gave her a note to meet me and tell me what was important enough for her to come see us while apparently putting her life in danger. Probably to do with you assholes—" *Goddamnit*

"No deviations."

"She showed. She disappeared quickly but she left me a note."

"And the note said what."

"That she was sorry. She implied that she couldn't help me."

"What were the exact words?"

"I don't know man. I told—"

More needles.

"OKAY. It said: 'I don't know how you could, but it was a mistake, nothing. Sorry.' And that was it, man. That was all, I swear."

The largest of the two men (a gargantuan creature whom it seemed a disservice to classify merely as man) who'd kidnapped Envy uncuffed him and moved the pulser pins far away from him at the table. The man who'd been asking the questions broke into a smile, shook Envy's hand and apologized. "We didn't kill Dr. Ali. Contrary to what you may believe, we were on her side, as she was on ours. I'd been following her from afar to protect her."

"Rousing success, I see," Envy said dryly.

"Yes. Clearly, we lost her. She disappeared right after the meeting with you. You can understand why we suspected your involvement. But she didn't leave anything in those final words to you to indicate that you were involved. And we've watched you since. We're satisfied. You can go."

"Wait ... get the hell outta here. That's it? She was important enough for you guys to rough me up and damn near kill me, and she worked with my uncle. I want to know what happened to her."

"We don't know kid or we wouldn't have roughed you up."

Envy was silent for a moment. "What was she involved in? Why was she working with you? Who in Eshu's name are you?"

The giant turned to the interrogator, "May I strike him? In the face? Break it? He's overstepped."

The interrogator raised a hand. "Maybe, but not yet. He raises an interesting point." He turned to Envy "You mentioned she worked with your uncle—that she was a 'doctor' like him."

"Yes."

"What do you know about what your uncle did?"

"Not a damn thing. And let's chill for a sec. You've told me you were on Dr. Ali's side, but I don't know what that side was, or who you are. You've told me nothing and done nothing to give me reason to trust you, besides you know, kidnapping and torturing me."

"We didn't kill you, did we? We're the good guys, kid. You can trust that."

"Oh, not killing. *That's* where you set the bar. Meanwhile, *King-Kong's* over there asking permission to break my face."

"Nobody appreciates manners these days," muttered the giant.

The interrogator walked up to Envy and stared into his eyes for about a minute before reaching his hand up—as if to touch Envy's cheek. It was slapped away.

"Are you crazy? Don't touch me. If it wasn't for being drugged and restrained earlier, I woulda knocked ya'll out." The giant lunged but was stopped by the interrogator.

"It's Okay 98," he said to the giant, waving him off again. Turning to Envy: "Perhaps we went about this a tad aggressively." The interrogator held out his hand "I go by Val 7. My real name—and I'm jeopardizing myself by telling you this—you should be appreciative—is Marvin Lison."

Envy didn't shake it.

Marvin smiled. "My large friend here is 98. So, you want to know more? Fine, but understand this is a gamble. If what you learn of us becomes a problem for you then we'd have to take measures as you'd become a security risk to us."

Envy looked over to 98 who was sneering. He smiled back. "Whatever man."

"Dr. Ali came to us about her IPU research, hers and your uncle's, six months after his death. We had approached her about their work several years ago. We'd also unsuccessfully approached your uncle—years before Dr. Ali—that's a story for another day. Anyway, initially she declined, but never exposed us. I still wonder if it was out of fear of what they'd do to her if she revealed she'd had contact with us, or out of an innate sense what they were doing was wrong."

"Wrong?"

"Yes. We offered her the opportunity to research the right way, to put her knowledge to use for the greater good early on, but she was new then, too scared to allow our message in, too shocked to believe we were telling the truth.

294

Most of all, I think she wanted to believe what they were doing was right."

"So then after my uncle—"

"She got suspicious and terrified she would be next."

"Wait, wait wait wait wait ... what the hell? What exactly happened to my uncle?"

"You've gotta have some idea by now, kid."

"I'm serious man. We were told he died in an accident. It was on the news. I went to the funeral. With my dad. There were patients there, people who spoke about him, people who he'd helped, everything. I cried for days. I need to know what you're saying."

Val 7 sighed. "I'm saying your uncle didn't die in an accident. He was murdered and yes, we have proof."

"Why, because you did it?"

"Don't be an asshole."

Envy relaxed a bit. To finally hear someone else say what he'd believed all along was momentarily freeing.

"Dr. Ali had begun to have doubts long before your uncle died but she hid them well. In what they did, if there was even the *perception* someone questioned or didn't see things the way the Ministry does—"

"Wait, he was IPU—what's the Ministry got to do with it?"

"Don't play dumb with me. A kid as sharp as you knows nothing worth killing scientists for happens without your government having a hand in it. The emperor's IPU is sponsored by and operates with the blessing of all Ministries. Anyway, Dr. Ali realized her open admiration for your uncle placed her at risk, and she knew she couldn't keep helping such an entity. She reached out and began working with us to help replicate the work she and your uncle did for the IPU and tried to give us some clues on his later work he'd kept from her."

"Until she was probably found out."

"Likely after she came to see you."

Envy who'd been standing since they'd unchained him,
sat back down. "I don't understand why she came to our
doorstep. How'd she know about us? Why put herself in that
kind of … did she finish helping you guys? Was she close?"

"She wanted you—his family to know what she thought
happened. To her it was worth dying for."

"Except she never told me anything, anyway."

Val 7 smiled. "But it's more about what *you* told her
though, isn't it? I'm sure you've figured out that's why we're
here."

Envy ignored Val 7's comment. "You present yourself as
benevolent. You talk about the Ministry and the IPU as if
they're evil. *Is it that simple?* What is it that you were doing that
was so good compared to what Dr. Ali and my uncle were
doing? Why was it bad they were working for the IPU and
not you? Why did her loyalty to my uncle put her in danger?
Why was he murdered?"

Val 7 smiled. Envy looked for menace but could find
none. It was pure . . . satisfaction? Had he been waiting for
these exact questions?

"Why don't we talk about the wind station where you met
Dr. Ali. Did you notice anything strange, unusual?"

"Nope."

"Two people on that same platform collapsed and died
while you were meeting her. One beforehand. Another that
night. These don't register enough to be news anymore. You
didn't see them as out of the ordinary because they're not.
We've accepted igioyin as our cross, as the sacrifice we make
in this life. But we have no idea what we're sacrificing for, and
that makes it absurd to believe we must suffer in the first
place, simply because we have. There was a time we didn't
have to fear such an end; when tragedy wasn't continually
rationalized and explained away as something 'Olorun wills';
when we all had a say no matter how small it was, about some
things."

296

"What, the time before the gods? Are you gonna take us back there? Do I need a blacker that absorbs tachyons?"

"Don't be a dick."

"Then what exactly?"

"Dr. Ali and your uncle were working to protect the Ministry's glorious cloud people. You know, those people you never interact with, yet are somehow supposed to believe they have the same struggles as you. They were synthesizing an inoculation that would need to be administered only once, *ever*. Instead of weekly—which only benefits those in the clouds who can afford such an expense and leaves your loved ones in the red vanes suffering. Igioyin as a contagious, infectious disease with no cure is a myth. But even the glorious green and blue vane inhabitants have been deceived. The weekly vaccines they're given are of marginal efficacy; enough to only suppress a disease that could have been eradicated. This keeps the coffers of the Ministry overflowing. Ever wonder why all the Ministry's officers and councilmen and women live in the green vanes, including those who serve the wretched reds? Where do you think they get their wealth?

The true source of your suffering over the years was your government's decision to suppress the truth and focus on only a small segment of the population, the elites; wealthy noblemen and women along with the somewhat well-off civilians, the so-called "betters." This, at the expense of the larger community long considered expendable competition for resources ever since the war made many lands eternally barren and uninhabitable and we made the transition to an automated society. You see the crowds of hungry unemployed who wander because there's no place for them, no demand for whatever labor they might provide."

"Zombies." Envy added, nodding. "But how's the Ministry the enemy if they recognize this? Aren't they simply operating efficiently?"

"Spoken like the boy who would be Minister."

"I'm questioning what makes *your* view the right one. We get the opportunity to live full length lives then what? We'll spend a longer time being miserable. It doesn't change the number of purposeless masses who waste away or become lawyers fighting for scraps. Everyone from the lessers wants a shot at the betters anyway. No one truly believes they've got one but it's that tiny shred of hope that at least keeps us—"

"Brainwashed, kid, that's all."

"Yeah, but we act like it wasn't the Nth who put us in this predicament anyway. Igioyin was their biological weapon and boy did they—"

98 punched a wall. Val 7 raised his voice.

"That's the Ministry's propaganda machine at work! Yeesh. The Nth didn't create igioyin. Don't feed into the nonsense. Don't be one of those idiots who recognize evil only after history decides! Do you have any real idea who the Nth are? What they do? No matter. Another day perhaps. Look kid, it's not my mission or place to tell anyone what their purpose is or how to figure out their life or what to do with it. But it *is* my mission to give them as fair of a shot as possible. And that means finding people like Dr. Ali, like your uncle. Extraordinary people who knew something was wrong and wanted to fix it. People who were looking for a way."

"Can we go now?" 98 asked Val 7. "His face annoys me."

"Patience, my large friend. Soon."

Envy looked around the room. It was plain, blank. No character or purpose he could discern other than the one it served at the moment. He looked at Val 7, aka (or was it formerly?) Marvin Lison—a name disclosed for trust but equally meaningless to Envy. A man who seemed to be demanding something from him while expecting nothing at all. He took a deep breath. "Did Dr. Ali help you complete your mission? How far along are you?"

"She did not. She provided notes for our team and was in the process of decoding them for us. It could take years to decipher them without her. Her death sets us back a while."

Val 7 produced a panel showing notes provided by Dr. Ali. Envy examined them, recognizing not only the handwriting but the formulas structured in the way only someone who'd worked closely with his uncle would.

"And if … if …" He drew a long breath. "If I had access to notes—my uncle's—and had the means to decode them, what would that be worth to you?"

"Get the hell outta here. May Olorun strike you down for your lies. You're messing with me, aren't you, kid?"

"I'm not; why waste time? I'm serious."

Val 7 nodded and turned to 98. "And *that's* why we don't always do things your way."

He said to Envy, "So let's pretend you're telling the truth and have what we need. What is it you want?"

"Protection for my family and my friends. I want this buried as deep as it can possibly be—no connection between this and my normal life. I want to be able to go back home without there having been any suspicion about my whereabouts. I want to remain as "normal" a kid as possible. And I want the first permanent inoculation. It's a miracle I'm still alive and I want all of this as soon as possible. I don't care what it costs."

"For your family and all your friends? Protection? It may be impossible for all of them. There are a lot of unknowns, kid. I can't guarantee most of what you're asking."

"Should we do this? You already know I won't help you if you can't meet my demands. Let's not waste each other's time. What I'm doing carries large risk and is impossible without me. If you want to kill me, you should go ahead."

98 snarled. Val 7 waived him off.

"We'll take care of it. What are you going to do about your family in the meanwhile? You'll likely be gone a long time. Months, years."

"I'll leave my pops a note—let him know I'm striking out on my own. He thinks it's about time anyway. Only Grams might miss me but she's headed back to the Southern Icelands soon. Either way, it won't be a problem."

"If you say so. But rest assured, we *will* be monitoring that situation closely."

"As long as the protection and the monitoring are done by someone else other than you two, fine. This is my family. We don't want another Dr. Alison situation on our hands."

98 punched the nearby table, splitting it in two. Val 7 sneered. "Oh, you're going to be a joy to work with aren't you, kid?" Val 7 then produced an uncrumpled note and handed it to Envy. The handwriting was his. On the note was one of the formulas used in his uncle's work with Dr. Ali. "You wanted her to know, didn't you? What were you hoping for?"

Envy looked at the note he'd handed Dr. Ali forty-eight hours ago, made eye contact with Val 7 and replied, "So you knew this whole time."

Val 7 nodded. "You're not the only one who can play dumb, Tommy Barrington. What were you hoping for?"

"She'd risked a lot coming to our place to try to tell us something. I wanted her to know she wasn't alone."

IGBO OLUWA

Present Day

"YOU GUYS ... THE SHOCK on your faces ... I'm the one who should be shocked, you know?"

Envy had stopped smiling, and Kris felt as if he were a ghost above the room floating and witnessing the reunion between them without feeling one way or the other. Dara had calmed down and was the only one who seemed capable of action or words. "Kris wake up!" she shouted as she grabbed the pulser from the holster of the emis beside her and shot a beam at Berl as he lunged towards Envy. Berl yelped as he was struck in the back and fell over, scattering his pack of clypsars, prompting Kris to grab them, snap a couple onto his hands and throw a couple over to Dara. These were batted down by another emis who fired his pulser. The shot narrowly missed Kris who somersaulted out of the line of fire and attempted to open a phrinway for them to escape through. Out of the clypsars came not a doorway, but two bright beams, much larger than anything from the pulsers.

"Whoa, what the——?" Kris glanced at his hands as one of the shots knocked the emis back towards Dara, who moved out of the way, allowing him to fall over. She ran towards Kris while firing her pulser at an emis behind him. Together, Kris and Dara fought and held back the emises while Envy half-watched and threw items into a bag. More emises appeared to arrive out of nowhere and one of them disabled Dara's pulser. Kris fired more blasts from the clypsars, but with Dara disarmed, they grew overwhelmed and the emises began to surround them.

"Dara, I can't hold them back!" Kris weakened as he attempted to increase the rate of his shots which only grew sporadic in response, and he began to miss. The emises closed the remaining space.

"No ..." Dara, who had difficulty breathing, saw one of the emises reach for a fleer and overcome with fear, she panicked. *This can't be how it ends....* A cloak of tranquility enveloped her, and it was as if she were a passenger in her own body. Everything went dark and when she came to, Kris and Envy stared at her as if she were an alien.

"What is it?"

In response to Dara's question, Kris hurriedly opened up a phrinway, and pushed Envy and Dara through. Once Kris was on the other side, he closed it.

"What the HELL was that back there? That was insane!" Kris nodded as a breathless Envy said what he was thinking.

"What do you mean?"

"Dara, you shot blasts out of your hands out of thin air, without sprezens—without these," Kris said, pointing to the clypsars on his hands. "I've never seen anything like that before ... and the blasts, yo—you hit like fifteen emises ... unreal."

"I don't know what happened ... I ... things went dark." But she knew it had happened once before, when she attacked Vida and a glowing sprezen had formed from seemingly nothing. "Besides, what about you? Those beams you fired ..."

"Yeah, we got more oyas to learn, looks like. Where the hell are we?" They looked around. They had jumped into what appeared to be a cavern whose walls glowed like the inside of an active volcano but gave off none of the heat.

Dara opened another phrinway and they stepped into an abandoned building. "We're in the Southern Icelands now. They saw us phrin. You saw that weird diamond thing with the numbers they used to reopen our phrinways, right? They might have been able to follow us. Don't want to risk it."

Envy's disorientation did not prevent him from addressing the matter which brought them there. "So that's what your 'missions' were? Secret IPU-sponsored attacks? *That's* why you guys would sneak off? We expected company at the Port Harcourt lab but not enemies ... what are they paying you? If it's money you need, I can help. Olorun keep, briz. I thought I knew you, Kill. You're a good dude. This isn't you."

Dara jumped in before Kris could say a word. "Funny thing about knowing someone, it tends to pay off with unwelcome surprises. There's only one person here who has to explain anything. Considering you've been outed as an Nthn, and we saved your life at the expense of ours, you'd better start telling us something that makes sense."

Envy looked at Kris who'd been watching them both in silence. Kris nodded slowly. Envy looked back at Dara. "I'm not an Nthn, and neither are any of the other people who were victims of your mission today. We were a team of scientists the Nth put together to produce a permanent single dose cure for igioyin—"

"Considering you caused it—"

"I used to think that too. But it's not true, Dara, at all."

"Then there's the laughable part about you and science."

"It wasn't the Nth. And it wasn't some viral epidemic spread through exchange of bodily fluids as they always told us. They lied to us. It's the water. It was contaminated long ago, years before any of us was born. Normally, when you've been exposed over generations to something, your genes develop a mutation to adapt. But the strain wasn't static. It kept evolving, fast enough for that natural immunity to never occur. It was too fast, smart—too stubborn. So the IPU assembled a team to come up with an inoculation—a permanent treatment, knowing eventually the private supply of water enjoyed in the clouds would run out and leave them exposed. That's how verus was born. But there was a problem. Verus required an expensive weekly dose which ended up being a big financial benefit for the Ministries of the Global Union Alliance. My unc—"

"I don't get how you know all this, man," Kris interrupted. "What does any of this have to do with you?"

Envy looked down, kicking pebbles at his feet. "I didn't want to disappear on you and Donzi. You guys helped me through the toughest part of my life. Around you, I found a way to relate to people in a way I thought was impossible. It was okay for me to relax and enjoy that side of myself."

"The non-terrorist side?"

Ouch. He looked back up.

"Kill, I'm not a terrorist. I know who you think the Nth are—"

"If there's one thing we're learning today, it's not to *know anything*. Information briz, facts only, please." Kris wasn't pleading. He was being polite. This was an order.

"I'm trying to explain it in a way you'll understand and believe me. It's a lot."

Dara spoke up. "I don't know about understanding, but it's going to take a hell of a lot for us to believe you."

"My uncle was a scientist for the IPU. He did some good, but he also did awful things for them, the best and worst of which was coming up with verus to combat the igioyin strain in the water supply and being a part of the cover up. They had him working exclusively on this treatment for the clouds so once their strain-free water ran out, they could be protected against the contaminants of our impure source, and they could enjoy their quality lives unabated while we suffered here. No matter what you want to think about me, the Ministry is the enemy, actively looking to eradicate those who voted for their protection."

Kris laughed. "*Who are you* ... man? Rocking lab coats, using big serious words out the blue— 'eradicate,' 'contaminants,' you don't talk like that briz ..."

"My uncle during this time—he needed someone to vent to, and he opened up to me.... It was therapy for him—he was under a lot of stress ... who knows? At first, he thought he was telling a little kid what amounted to gibberish but I

304

comprehended *everything*—the calculations, the science of
what they were doing, the applications and implications. To
me it was fun; like a new puppy or Holo-towns were, I
imagine, for many other kids. He wasn't perfect; I realized
eventually he was using me and probably didn't have the best
intentions, but he was the only one I could relate to
intellectually."

He removed his lab coat.

"I know it's strange. I thought I was normal for the few
years of my life, and then I started to be around others my
age. I soon realized it was more likely I was the outlier and
not them. Preparatory was horrible. The amount of effort it
took to play dumb was daunting, but I had no choice. The
things my uncle told me were perilous, and let me know what
kind of wicked we were dealing with. Even if he hadn't asked,
I never would have shared his secrets with anyone. I'd
occasionally have nightmares where I was forever an
imbecile—unable to recover, with all of my mental faculties
atrophied from lack of use. But when he came by, I was
alive—conscious in a way everyone only dreams of, in a way
everyone secretly fears. Then one day, he was *gone*. My
intelligence had given me an illusion of control and it was
now telling me loudly there was nowhere to run where
anything would make sense. And I was so scared because of
what had happened to him. After he died I didn't bother
looking for anyone to relate to. I sank into myself and gave
up. My pops came from and believed in the streets and yeah,
he wasn't the greatest role model, but there was nothing else
for me so why not be like him, you know? That's how I
became the dude you knew." He shrugged. "That's how I
became Envy."

"When you disappeared then, you were helping …
them?"

"Everyone. *Us*. I was working for them, but I was helping
all of us. I made a deal with them that I could come back
after significant progress was made as long as I assisted—and

I believe in the work. You know igioyin could strike any of us at any moment and it does. The clouds needed it treated and they've got the money—they're happy with that, but the rest of us need something bigger, something to reverse the effects, combat the damage already done, something we can afford. Not a treatment—"

"A cure," Dara interjected, looking at Kris.

"How do you know they're not using you, like the IPU and Ministry did your uncle? That it's not some cure for them to make off with and kill the rest of you? And don't tell me you trust them."

"No, Kris, it's nothing like that. It costs too much in time and resources for it to be for a small group. It's inefficient. It would be a colossal waste. The underground warehouse in Port Harcourt—the one near the lab you found me—it's huge. It has everything. I've seen the scale on which they intend to reproduce and it's massive."

"Hmm," Dara grunted. "Where are you with this cure?" She asked.

"My uncle already had it figured out before he died. He told me he never revealed it to anyone except me, but I always wondered if they somehow found out and that's why they killed him. We have it, and we're working on making a version of it we could provide to everyone and quickly. We have something . . . we have something that can mimic an airborne pathogen; fast spreading, easily contagious. We needed time to test it and work out some of the side effects . . . we were doing that ... we were in the final stages but since you guys were able to get to *me* I'm guessing that . . ." he looked up at Kris.

Kris nodded solemnly. The orange glow of the cave walls reflecting off his face seemed to impossibly—add more gravity.

"How many?"

"Everyone except you and two others we were supposed to get." He could hear resentment in Dara's voice still.

"What do they know?"

"Not much from what we heard, but we're not sure. One of your guys swore up and down he was a scientist . . ." Kris looked away and trailed off.

Dara picked up without missing a beat. "But when he was tortured he gave a story sounding nothing like yours and everything like a terrorist's."

"Ah. I'm sorry I screwed things up for you guys. Didn't mean to put you in danger, but there was no way I could've known. I know it's a lot to ask but I need your help getting back in contact with—"

"Oh, as if we haven't done enough? Best of luck to you. May we never cross paths with you again, Olorun willing."

"Dara, you know we can't do that." Kris chewed on a toothpick without looking up at either of them. His tone indicated a resignation to fate more than enthusiastic support for an old friend.

"But you—we have to go back. We can still fix it. Otherwise we went through all that ... everything we did— things we can't ever forget or undo—for nothing. I *know* we can save you. We have to try."

Envy could tell Dara was struggling not to cry. *What else was going on?*

"What would we tell her? We've already crossed the line. There's no way to go back now; you know this. We made our final choice the moment we saw Envy. And I'm glad because we're free now, Dara. We can get away from this—we can protect everyone . . . we can do it now. If what he's saying is true, we can help people like where we're from—a lot of them. That's what you've wanted this whole time."

Dara smiled and shook her head. "It was a dumb plan then and it still is. I don't want you to die."

"No one's dying. We'll get everyone to the place and we'll figure this out."

"Wait, what are you guys talking about? Why would you be dying? What's wrong?" Envy looked puzzled.

"Long story but yeah, Envy, I am. That's how we ended up wrapped up in this shit. The point is you can help others and that's all that matters. I mean, you *can* help others. *Right?*"

"Yeah, I can and I will—but what's causing you to di—"

"Igioyin," Dara interjected. "But not what you're treating. Something different. He's suffering from some strange extended version that has to do with his phrinning."

Envy smiled "That's it? No, no that's not what I mean. This is good—really good. The cure that my uncle created came from similar hosts—uh sorry! People. What I mean is Kill—he has the cure in him, or at least the ingredients and all I need is for you guys to help me get back in contact, then I can get to one of our labs and we can either try the cure already made or make some alterations based on Kill's unique physiology. It works out perfect as I'd be able to finish assisting with the delivery phase of the Nth's plan and we can get the cure airborne."

"And how exactly do we get you back in 'contact'?"

"Get me to a secure location where I can send a message to Val 7. From there, I'll get coordinates of where I can meet with him. He's my go to in the Nth."

"I don't trust it."

"Yeah, Dara, but no time to argue is there?"

Dara addressed Envy. "We still have to grab our friends and family and get them to safety before Darcela and the IPU get to them. We're not letting anyone else suffer because of you. Afterwards, we can figure out how helping you will help us."

They spent the next few minutes formulating the rudimentary workings of a plan. Kris contacted Trevin, explained the situation to him and had him get the Kids of Stolen Tomorrow together at the Quarters so they would be ready to go upon Kris and Dara's arrival. They began by searching for Kris' mother as she—being at work in New Stuy, would be the easiest for Captain Darcela to locate.

Kris opened a phrinway but before they could enter he yelled, "No! Ma!" Dara could now see Kris' mother who was being bound by two emises and surrounded by at least ten others, fully armed. Kris' mother, who was able to see and hear him through the opening shook her head. Dara and Envy had to pull Kris away as the remaining emises in the room fired a pulser beam through the phrinway towards him.

"Close it Kris! We gotta go!"

As Kris struggled with them he heard his mother yell "Run! Save yourself, I'll be fine!"

He closed it.

Envy tried to comfort him. "I'm sorry man, but we'll get her, Kill, I promise you. We'll find her and stop them."

Kris didn't look up. He simply said, "How?"

Dara hugged him and kissed him on the cheek. She opened a phrinway and they went through, immediately finding themselves in her living room with her father passed out on the couch.

"Damn he's heavy," muttered Envy, as the three of them moved Dara's father through a newly opened phrinway to a place more stunning than Envy could have dreamt. He was reminded of the book he'd read in the Quarters the day he returned, while waiting for Kris. But *those* words, as much as they'd brought a verdant oasis to his purview, did not prepare him for the breathlessness he encountered as he observed the splendor before him. "What the hell is this place?"

"The place of our dreams," Kris said quietly.

"I mean are we in wild South Emeria somewhere outside the Union? Or below the East and West African Unions? Hidden deep? I've been to those places, Kill, the air's not as clear as it is here."

"We know as much about this place as you do, and we don't have time to waste talking. Dad, Dad, wake up!" Dara gently shook her father until he woke, mumbling at first until brought to fully by the inescapable sunlight.

"Eh? This is Igbo Oluwa?! Dara, where is dis place?"

Dara shivered, having heard that ... *Igbo Oluwa* ... before. "Papa, Kris is going to stay here and watch you. I'll be right back. You're safe here. He'll explain everything."

Kris gave her a look of disbelief, but he understood. It was better he be there, lest her father be a danger to himself, or something unexpected happen. He nodded and watched her push Envy through the phrinway to the next destination.

"I have to at least send them a message about the others on my team. They should be told we've been hit, possibly revealed to the IPU. They can put contingencies in motion if they know," Envy said as they went through.

Dara smirked. "Envy, aren't you supposed to be this great intellectual mind? In your urgency to make contact, have you considered an organization as powerful as the Nth already knows what happened? You think they're depending on *you* to report? Anyway, that's not the priority. It's not the deal. We get everyone to safety before we reach out to them."

"I don't take anything for granted, and it's more about the help they can provide *us* if they know what's going on. Trust me, these *are* the good guys and they have more resources at their disposal than you can imagine."

They had gone through three phrinways without Dara stopping in any of the places. "That's the thing, Envy. I don't trust you. Some of what you've said seems true, but I'm mostly tolerating your presence because of what you've meant to Kris. Even if I could put such trust in you, there's the issue of the people you work with. No, I'm fine with trusting our abilities instead."

"Extraordinary as your oyas are, this isn't something you can do alone."

"It's not up for discussion. Let's just get through this—carry out the plan as agreed." In the fourth phrinway, they came upon Envy's dad in bed with a scantily clad younger woman draped around his waist. "Ahh man, Pops, really?"

"Tommy! What you doin interruptin' a good time? We're just gittin started!"

Dara helped Envy quickly push both of them off the bed
through the phrinway onto the grass of the Igbo Oluwa as his
dad yelled obscenities and the color left the woman's face.

"Thanks."

"No problem," Dara replied, chuckling. "Good to know
my papa isn't the only embarrassing one."

As they opened the fifth phrinway, Envy noticed Dara's
face and posture crumble before he saw it: a younger girl he'd
bumped into a couple of times during his second year at Ron
Ed. "Nic—" he heard. It was less a name and more a heavy
exhalation. The girl was on her back, eyes wide open, mouth
agape with blood overflowing. The boy next to her, whom he
remembered from a few classes, now had a thick shell of
black crust, courtesy of a fleer, undoubtedly.

Envy ran to Dara who'd jumped through to grab Nic; he
began hugging her, trying to drag her back through the open
phrinway. "You know you can't; they're gone. We have to get
the others, whoever's left. Please. I know it hurts. But you
know there are others."

Dara, tears streaming, pushed Envy back into the
phrinway and eventually, followed. "I'm so sorry Nic ...
Jess." Closing it, she took a deep breath as the tears
continued flowing and opened a new phrinway to the
Quarters where most of the Kids of Stolen Tomorrow were
gathered.

"Get in!" She yelled. They dropped everything and
complied, following Dara through the next phrinway. As they
arrived on the other side, there was a collective gasp.

"Whoa, what's this place?" It was the normally silent
Trevin. Envy's dad was still shouting in the background as
the woman with him tried to calm him down.

"Pop shut-up! I'll explain later," Envy yelled.

Dara's father noticed something was amiss. "Where's
Nicole? Your friend and her brother, aren't you going to get
them too?" He hugged Dara as she ran to him and sobbed.

Envy, clearly shaken up by what he'd seen, looked at Kris, who'd been sitting next to Dara's dad. "We've gotta find Donzi. I couldn't live with myself if they—"

Kris said nothing, as Laran unmasked and tapped Envy on the shoulder. More gasps. Donzi, full disguise off, planted a strong kiss on Envy's lips silencing his questions. "Kill just found out. I was gonna tell you and everyone else at the right moment."

Kris watched Dara and her dad for a while longer before he realized something. "Where's Flick?"

Trevin seemed to be the only one who heard. "He quit. He said he felt he was betraying the gods. That it wasn't his path to fool around like we had been. I tried to get more out of him but he wouldn't say anything else and vimmed out."

Kris' expression was somewhere between tired and fed up. "You know where he went? His life could be in danger."

"Nuh. I was tracking him but it went dark about an hour before Envy and Dara showed up. He was last in the South Emerian Union, somewhere around Bahia."

A throat was cleared and a hoarse voice spoke softly. "We don't have time to chase him and still save others. Whatever pushed him to choose, he made a choice. Let's respect it," Dara's voice, shaky initially, was steadying."

"You okay?" Kris said to her.

She shrugged and said, "I have to be. We'll fight. Gotta make sure they can never do this to anyone again. Envy you ready?" He nodded. "Okay. I'll need a few minutes. Then we can go." She got up to gather sticks, grass and flowers to build a small shrine to Nicole and her brother Jess, while Kris addressed the small gathering. He told them of the threat the IPU posed to them and all outside the clouds, and he revealed his condition.

He allowed the initial shock of those who were unaware to sink in. "We here because our lives are in danger. I take the blame 'cause a lot of foolish selfish shit I did put us where we are today. But this is the safest place we could be—so know this is only the beginning for us. We'll grow stronger. Our eyes have been opened," he looked over to Envy as he said this, "to the extent of the IPU's evils. We're putting an end to the Ministry's deceit."

Dara walked over to Donzi and Envy and called on Brink to join them. "I'm taking Envy back over to the Wall to meet with his guy who's supposed to help us get a cure for Kris and everyone else outside the clouds. He trusts his contact but I think it's best we play it safe—"

"You don't have to ask, we're down," said Brink.

Kris spoke up. "There's some things we need to show you. Everyone should be as protected as possible and I think we've discovered some oyas that'll help with that. Get your sprezens and meet me over in that clearing." He walked over towards the circle of trees by the lake as the group grabbed their sprezens and followed.

Donzi, sprezen in pocket, simply kept her arms wrapped around Envy, who was contrite. "I'm sorry, Dara, for your loss, for the part I've played—"

Dara put up her hand to interrupt. "Too many apologies going around. Don't waste time feeling sorry for me or anybody. Just help this go right."

Dara and Kris spent several hours showing the rest of the group how to repeat consistently what they'd done out of desperation, to surprising success. Dara—to her astonishment—found she no longer needed sprezens or clypsars to send blasts and Kris found he could fire consistently with either clypsars or sprezens with the same intensity. He also quickly found that both Dara and Donzi were better shots than he. After they were as satisfied as they were going to be with their new oya, Kris stayed behind as agreed while the rest of the KoST accompanied Dara and Envy. She opened a phrinway and they were off—first to a secure location where Envy messaged Val 7 and received confirmation of the meet. "Half an hour at the Myrtle-Willoughby wind station, we're good to go." They let twenty-five minutes go by before Donzi opened a phrinway to Myrtle-Willoughby.

"Crap." Brink said aloud what they were all thinking as they stepped out from an alley near the Myrtle-Willoughby wind station and noticed heavy Pro-T presence everywhere.

"The Ministry really got the word out, didn't they? We're stars! You think they'll recognize us? Maybe we should pose for photos."

Envy couldn't tell if Donzi was nervous and putting on an act or being her usual carefree self. He decided to play along. "Me and Dara are probably famous, but not you yet, sorry babe. You gotta do more."

Donzi laughed in response and, sprezen already loaded, sent a blast a hundred yards down the street away from the wind station that sent all available Pro-Ts scurrying towards it. "How about that? You think that's enough?"

Envy chuckled.

Dara did not. "Enough flirting. Let's go! We don't have time to waste!" Dara, focused as ever, raced across the street and led them up the station platform. "Do you see your contact? Do you?"

Envy calmly looked around. He grew frantic as the meeting time approached. Marvin Lison (or Val 7 as he preferred) was nothing if not punctual. Envy was surprised Val 7 hadn't been on the platform waiting for them when they arrived. They stayed until the meeting time had passed. Val 7 was still unseen.

Dara snickered. "I knew not to trust it."

"Hey Dara, c'mon that's not fair," Donzi responded, visibly annoyed.

"We can argue back at the place!" Dara yelled as pulser beams flew towards them and she produced a protective bubble.

"Agreed!" Donzi fired a blast, sending a crowd of Pro-Ts tumbling back down the platform.

314

"Look out!" Brink yelled, sending a blast to counteract a fleer beam. It was coming from emises. "Shit. We definitely gotta get outta here."

The diverted fleer beam destroyed the concrete awning of the station platform, sending chunks everywhere, and Dara opened a phrinway, pushing Envy through and sending one last blast at Emperor Darcela's men as the Kids of Stolen Tomorrow escaped back to Igbo Oluwa.

As she tumbled through the phrinway back into the clearing, Dara roared at Envy. "I knew it. I knew it wouldn't work. I knew there was something off. You're so full of it. AGHH!" She sent glowing columns towards the sky which dissipated as lightning and left thunder in their wake.

Dara's father jumped up and ran towards her, tackling her as she ranted at Envy. "By Shango! Omode! Calm down now! Wetin be this craziness, pikin?"

"Tell them," she said to a crestfallen Envy. "Tell them!"

Kris watched the faces of Dara, Donzi and Brink and already knew what Envy was going to say.

"Val 7 didn't show. He confirmed a meet when I messaged him. But he wasn't there when we arrived. We waited as long as we could but then we were attacked by Pro-Ts and IPU. Something must have happened."

"So ..."

"I know how to make a cure for you Kris, but if I can't get to my lab ... I need corlypses. I need Parin chambers ... time ... I need a lot of things."

"And everything you grabbed when we first got you?"

"That was the dispensation system—I was testing its mechanics. There was no actual verus being used ..."

"And all those others your buddies were supposed to help?"

With each question Kris asked, Envy seemed to sink further under the weight of what had occurred. "They have to have been telling the truth about that ... as I said before, the scale is too massive and the delivery system is real—there's

315

no way it could be anything else … no … way …" he fell to the ground, defeated.

"I'll believe it when I see it," Kris replied.

Dara and Donzi ran to Kris, enveloping him in an endless embrace. "What are you going to do?" A teary-eyed Donzi asked.

"What else can I do? Keep moving forward," Kris responded.

* * *

Emperor Darcela smiled despite growing angrier the longer her captain spoke. Those thoughts that the late Emperor Shirazi had warned her against began creeping in again. *If you can get them back here … all of them … Dialuz. It would be so easy …*

No. She would stay the course. Emperor Shirazi had been right. *I promised him.* She could hear him even now. *Make them suffer. Show them to be cowards. No martyrs.*

"Was there anything at all you didn't screw up?"

"Emperor, we were able to record the exact coordinates of their phrinway exit."

"Well why didn't you lead with that?" Emperor Darcela ordered a team over to Myrtle-Willoughby to place latchers on the coordinates provided by the captain and recreate the opening. "You'd better hope they're still on the other side of that phrinway when we reopen it, Captain."

* * *

Still attempting to adjust to the new land in which they found themselves, the Kids of Stolen Tomorrow once a week sent two of their members (one of them always being Trevin) outside the Igbo Oluwa to a temporarily secure location to find any clues they could on Kris' mom from the netlines and get an update on any news related to the Ministry/IPU and the Nth. They'd had no updates on Kris' mom but it was in the third such week of this search they discovered someone on the Willoughby-Myrtle wind station platform had recorded footage of the KoST versus the IPU and the resulting carnage which had gone viral. It didn't take long after for Trevin to find the Ministry's edited version of the footage in the context of many news netcasts painting the KoST as the latest members of the Nth. They were branded as the first in a long line of human weapons to be unleashed upon the unsuspecting public, their first attack occurring on the platform where countless civilians died, including two blue-vaners in Todirb Wall on a charity visit.

"No. No! We can't let them do this! The public has to know exactly who they're dealing with." Dara was fuming. *Vida, is this what you meant by my greater path? Because the further along I get, the worse it seems. From future minister to common terrorist. Ogun would be proud, eh?*

But that was it, wasn't it?

Dara jumped up, full of energy.

"What can we do?" Brink lay in the grass, staring at the sky.

"Kris, Trevin, Envy, Brink. Brink!" Dara yelled.

"Huh, what?"

"Never mind, Brink. Trev how good are you at hijacking net—"

"Great! You don't have to finish the question, trust me— Kill has asked me a million times. What are we trying to do?"

Dara smiled. "Olorí-iré."

* * *

"What the hell am I watching? Get me Emperor Shira— Get me the emperor—NOW!"

Minister Corlmond was witnessing something that could not be happening. For the past few minutes, she, like all of the North Emerian Union and most of the Global Union

317

Alliance, was "learning"—via netline feed—of the part she, the Minister, and her counterparts in the GUA, had played in ushering the unions' poorer citizens to certain death while subsidizing extended life and protection for those under the clouds and exploiting the wealthier cloud inhabitants. She watched her government and the imperial Institute for Preservation of Unity be labeled merchants of death in front of the entire world. She listened as calls from other angry GUA leaders who'd been similarly implicated came in, all threatening to move the IPU palace to the next union on the list and cut its tenure in the NEU short.

"This failure is yours and yours alone! Repair it!" Said Minister Edward Kabore, head of the West African Union. The unabridged version was rich with infinitely more colorful words and phrases and was echoed in sentiment by Minister Esquivel of the South Emerian Union.

"Emperor Darcela is on the line, Minister."

"Emperor, what is going on? You got some kids plugged in to the waves and netlines leaking all sorts of classified information, saying there's a cure, saying we forced the weekly inoculation and suppressed the cure, and saying they have what we kept for ourselves! I got the GUA on my case about this and we're gonna have to increase Pro-T presence for Shango knows how long. How did they get ahold of the information? What's this nonsense about a cure? You know what? Forget it for now. Just get them off the air."

"I'm working on it, Madam Minister. We're as livid as you and are taking care of it. I'd like to meet with you ASAP, Madam. We have a resolution."

"Uh-huh, well you'd better."

"Why can't you find them, Toley? You're supposed to be the best at this." Emperor Darcela's band of emises working around the clock to reopen the phrinway at Myrtle-Willoughby had been at it three weeks with only marginal progress. Now the escapees dared broadcast, openly taunting

her on the netlines. Darcela's anger was replaced with a wave
of knowing calm.

*I will see them again, and they will suffer. But you were wrong
Reza. This is the time for Dialuz. Without drastic action, Nthn
presence will continue to strengthen, spread. Maybe to the blue vanes. I
can't allow that. Ogun will have his offering.*

"Whoever's doing it is better than good, Emperor. The
addy's changing trillions of times per millisecond. It's
impossible to trace them. Looks like they uploaded the file at
billions of mirrors. Service providers are taking them down
but they keep migrating … I can disrupt the signal though
and get it off the air, heh-heh."

"Can you replace it with anything?" Darcela asked.

"Yeah, heh-heh. *Anything.* Even the image of me using
those drones to blast that girl and her brother. Crissspy. Heh-
heh." His unsightly fangs knocked against each other as he
tittered incessantly. "Whatever it is you want, Sire."

"You'll show no such thing. I don't know why you're
pleased with yourself when you couldn't even get to Dara's
father in time. I'm meeting with Minister Corlmond. Disrupt
it for now and I'll give you the feed replacement orders
soon."

* * *

They knew they wouldn't have control of the feeds
forever. Trevin saw they were working against impossible
odds and he made this clear to everyone. Still, by the time the
links were cut their message had gotten out to millions of
panels and there was a sense of relief. "We're uploaded
everywhere too. The Ministry will have to chase after any and
everyone who wants to share. Should keep their hands full."

"Trev, I need to send an untraceable message to
someone," Envy requested. Trevin looked over to Dara. She
nodded.

319

Did What I Had to.
If you're still out there,
Your Move.
The world is waiting.

* * *

"On this day, November 17th, 93 O.O., the hijacked broadcast you all witnessed featured a gang of terrorists who are the latest weapons of the Nth. They're dangerous, as you may have observed during the portion of the broadcast where they showed their ability to manipulate certain energies. They're the same teens responsible for the wind-station tragedy. Don't be fooled by their statements on water supply or igioyin. It's merely a diversion and an attempt to curry sympathy in the wake of their atrocities. The treatment available is what we've provided. There's no vast conspiracy to keep treatment away from you outside the clouds. We've always made it available to all. There's no miracle cure in existence for this terrible, catastrophic disease. Don't be fooled by their image as crusaders of good as they've attempted to paint themselves. They're not messengers of the gods. They're liars attempting to manipulate you and sow the seeds of discord. They're terrorists. They're dangerous, unhinged. They have killed before and will likely kill again. We are working in concert with the rest of the members of the Global Union Alliance and we've sent the IPU and an elite Pro-T team to apprehend them. If you should see them or have the misfortune of coming into contact with them, remain calm and hold '9' on your cles. Help will arrive shortly. Their claims in the broadcast are unequivocally false and were deliberately made to cause disruption. I've promised you, from day one as your beloved Minister that I'd work to protect you, and I've not wavered from that commitment. Today, my resolve is strong as ever, and I know we can do this together. To uphold my promise of keeping you safe,

320

we're placing a Safety and Unity Protection Edict in effect. While the edict is active, all citizens must be in their residences by 8 PM, save IPU, Pro-Ts and other emergency personnel. If you're stopped by protection personnel, as always, please cooperate. Remember, this is for the good of all of us. Unity everlasting and may Olorun bless the North Emerian Union and the Global Union Alliance."

"Edict. They love to get cutesy with the words. Who said anything about being messengers for the gods? I don't know what we watching this for anyway."

"Relax Kris," said Dara. "We're heading back soon." She turned to Envy. "Anything from Val 7?"

"Nothing. But it was a long shot anyway. You were right about them. Let's go."

"We did a lot of good today. You stepped up, E. Whatever happens, glad you're with us."

Envy, Kris, Dara, Trevin headed through a phrinway and into four different phrinways as a security measure before finally arriving in the Igbo. Donzi ran to Kris and hugged him, followed by Envy. Dara walked back to her dad and sat next to him. "Never a boring minute with him," Donzi said to Dara. "I know like all of your family history and still want to hear more."

"See, Dad?" Dara said to her father. "It's way better when you don't drink."

"It is not as if I have a choice here, omode," he replied, grinning.

They sat in the clearing staring at the darkening, multi-hued sky as deep, sonorous blues began to seep into the oranges and soothe the fiery pinks. This might have been one of the great days of Dara's life, if it wasn't for the loss of Nicole and the always present worry about what would become of Kris. She fell asleep, as did the others.

She awakened to the smell of smoke and was up on her feet, looking around, gripped by fear. She began tiptoeing towards the smell to avoid waking and alarming the others. A voice startled her when she got to the clearing:

"No need to be scared, omode, Olorun has provided for us. This is reason to rejoice." Her father was cooking the meat of several small animals over a fire.

She savored the smell. "How did you—?"

While turning the meat on a spit, without looking up at her, he replied. "There are many things you don't know about me, omode. Your mother and I would occasionally get away to a place like this. We'd spend days there at a time and bring only a tent and a few snacks. Her Papa had taught her to hunt, or so I believed. We ate well, well. There are many fish here also. This place is fine. Igbo Oluwa. We'll eat well, well here too."

"Dad."

"Yes?"

"What is Igbo Oluwa?"

"Oh! Ha, sometimes I forget your Yoruba is not what I'd wanted it to be. Igbo Oluwa is the 'Forest of Miracles.' It is a name given to a place where many wondrous, strange, magical things happen. Your mother and I called the other place Igbo Oluwa because it was a great place to get away, especially during a period of turmoil. I particularly call it that because it was where you were conceived. I think we're going to have to build some shelter here eventually. The weather reminds me of Lagos; I get the feeling rains will be heavy. We'll need something for then."

"There's a cave here, Papa, a spacious one in case we need shelter." She thought back to the time she saw herself in the cave, recalled the loud laughter of the dream and shivered. She heard a noise in the brush and turned towards it, alert.

"Chill Dara, I'm only here to steal the food. Daaaamn Mr. A! Fancy exotic meats? You know what this would cost in New Stuy? We can't get this in Todirb." Kris had awoken and the rest of the crew followed, shuffling over to the clearing.

They enjoyed the food and drank water from the river. Over the coming days and weeks, they discovered Dara's dad was correct. It *was* a place of miracles and abundance. Fish, rabbits, hyraxes, aardvarks, gazelles, boars . . . there was plenty.

The Kids of Stolen Tomorrow found their oyas not only worked in the Igbo, but were more controlled and steady, less explosive and intense. When hunting, this was useful as they could be precise and not worry about accidentally cooking the animals during the hunt. The kids did the bulk of the hunting while Kehinde fished and showed them how to prepare the food over a makeshift spit. For a full month they sacrificed to Eshu at the shrine at night, so he could take their messages of thanks and of protection and guidance for Nicole and her brother to the other gods. Each morning the sacrifice would be gone, replaced with the message written in the dirt: *I will not undo you. Your words remain true.*

Envy built a boat, complete with steering apparatus to explore downstream, and all sorts of clever contraptions to add conveniences to their daily lives. They no longer endangered themselves by going to the outside world for news updates. Trevin phrinned there monthly to run quick netline searches for Kris' mother—the only activity worth the risk.

They found berries, mangoes and kola nuts, and eating these became little events of their own to pass the time. Dara and Kris found themselves wandering off and exploring new parts of the land, places she hadn't seen in her dreams or he in his childhood escapes there. The Igbo had done much for Kris, who had once welcomed the inevitability of his early death, as it appeared to reverse his disintegration and revitalize him physically, but he'd remained, to her frustration, quiet as ever. It was during these excursions she found he would open up to her the most, perhaps buoyed by the novelty of different surroundings, or, conversely, thrown off

323

by them and in need of the assurance further closeness could provide.

One day in particular he said, "So Trevin found a potential location for mom and verified it as much as he could. I haven't mentioned this before because it's a trap. I've tried to live, but I can't be happy. Not when I know I didn't do all I could. She's still out there, and I'm here, hiding like a punk. I look at this place and maybe I should be grateful but all I can see is my moms isn't with us. Every day it eats at me."

Dara placed an arm around him. "You're not a coward. She told you to run. We all saw it. You saved your life and all of ours by listening to her. She's proud of you." Dara said this hoping the truth would be enough. But his pained expression was her clue it wasn't.

"I'm gonna do something about it," he said as if she hadn't said a word.

"What happens if you start to get sick again? I don't think it's a coincidence you've been fine here. Do you think she'd want that? To be the cause of that for you? What about Donzi? She's healthy, safe. You think she wouldn't drop everything to join you? Do you want that for her too? Think about it."

He said nothing more, but she knew he'd be going back for his mother. They sat for hours in silence before making their way back to the clearing. Kris tried to object to her coming along but Dara was having none of it. They decided they would wait until nightfall when everyone was asleep and phrin back.

THE ILLUMINATED HALLWAY

Your Move.
The world is waiting.

VAL 7 CLOSED THE PANEL on his cles on November 17, 93
O.O. and advised 98 to stop punching things around him.
"I'd prefer it if you'd sit still occasionally, 98. You might find
you can do miraculous things, such as think." 98 grunted and
sat. Val 7, who'd had this conversation with 98 several
hundred times a day in his estimation, had come to realize he
was much too amused by it to care it never worked. He
showed 98 the message and said, "It appears our young
friend, the newly minted celebrity, now gives orders."

As 98 scowled and got up again, Val 7 put his hand up.
"No, no, 98, I'm clearly exaggerating. It's a joke. And no, we
can't go find him to break his face. You saw his new
comrades. They're impressive. A very strange sort of kids—
with oyas, gates … not worth the hassle."

98 grunted again and sat, but not before staring at Val 7
as if he were considering him for a stand in.

"Grow up, 98."

"What's the little twitface want?"

"You saw the broadcast. He wants to rush us. But the
kid's right. It would have been time soon anyway."

"Are you going to tell Val 3? He'll be mad,"

"*Tell him?* He knows. They all do. It shouldn't be a
surprise either. I'm headed to a meeting with him and the
others. Can I trust you to stay here and keep quiet for a few
hours?"

"I'm no child; maybe I hurt you, go instead."

"Don't be a fool."

"Yes . . . I can stay."

As he grabbed a few items and left, Val 7 recalled his last meeting with Val 3—a month ago—right before the aborted wind station meeting with TJ (and the so-called Kids of Stolen Tomorrow) at Myrtle-Willoughby, and shook his head. *This was my fault. I should have ignored Val 3's orders and met with the kid anyway.*

Val 7 wasn't surprised at the level of calm that greeted him as he stepped outside. The day's broadcasts had been a lot to digest and this was likely the brief moment of peaceful indecision before total chaos. Then again, this was New Stuy; Den of the content. Faithful followers of the Ministry. The thought of there ever being any reaction within its borders was wishful at best. He had three hours to get to and from the meeting before the edict kicked in and Pro-Ts would start asking questions. As he neared the border gate, he noticed the Pro-Ts there were too preoccupied with authenticating the flood of entrants from Todirb Wall to pay him any attention as he moved in the opposite direction. He overheard one of the desperate entrants yelling.

"That's right! Bivins! I don't *live in Todirb are you insane?* I only teach there! Let me through! New Stuy is my ho—"

What kind of madman would teach those kids, he thought, making his way into the Wall without being stopped for a single query. Once outside the cloud, a red flash came from his cles that was gone as soon as it had appeared. Location confirmed.

Two hours thirty-seven minutes.

He chose a wheelie taxi over the wind station. While slower, it would be easier to know if he were followed. He had the taxi drop him five blocks from the meeting place.

Two hours nine minutes.

One hour fifty minutes.

He arrived at a dilapidated storefront and looked around before entering. No one had tailed him. He walked straight to the back of the store and went through a door down into the basement. He scanned in.

"Look who's got time for us today! Surprise, surprise! The great Val 7!"

Marvin grumbled under his smile. "I'm early, Val 3. I need to speak to you in private."

"Not quite but that's fine, 7!" Val 3 turned to the room full of Nthns: "One moment, Vals! Seven and I will return shortly." They stepped into an adjoining room.

Val 7 spoke first. "I told you we shouldn't have bailed on picking up the boy. I could have gotten him quickly to safety."

"Nonsense 7, it wouldn't be the right move at all—way too dangerous. We already had to destroy the warehouse and lab in Port Harcourt because the boy was discovered. We weren't going to risk someone of your importance. And furthermore, it was an order executed properly. What do you have to gain by questioning the chain of command?"

"But ... abandoning those in need? That's not who we are—we're supposed to take care of our own."

Val 3's smile lessened. "That boy is *not* our own, 7. He's the nephew of a former IPU scientist, a man who assisted the IPU and Ministry in the atrocities they continue to commit daily. The boy's uncle is a big reason we had to carry out this operation in the first place. Spare me that line of simplistic reasoning."

"*That boy,* TJ, by the way—proved his loyalty to us. We shouldn't have left him hanging. The fact they exposed everything before we were ready to is our fault. It puts pressure on us for the timetable."

"What'd I tell you, 7? We've been over this before. The boy provided us with everything we needed, and is now a liability. It was best to let things sort themselves out."

"Well they have now, 3. Sorted themselves out. And it doesn't look great *for us*, especially if we don't deliver soon and I can't be the only one who feels that way; I'm not. I know for a fact the next room is full of others who agree. Again, this isn't who we said we'd be—not when we're invoking the name of the gods and claiming to be protectors of the innocent. You forget, I knew Val from the beginning. This is *not* what she would want."

Val 3 laughed and gave Val 7 a friendly jab to the shoulder. "You worry too much, old friend. No one's going to dishonor the original Val's name. Don't be ridiculous, 7! This works out fine. As a matter of fact, it improves the timetable for everything."

"I don't follow. How so?"

"Oh, don't you worry. I'll be addressing that momentarily. Come on. Let's keep our comrades waiting no longer!"

"Sorry for the delay. Val 7 had some *very* legitimate concerns about our timetable in the aftermath of the day's events. I'm sure you all do. We all saw the memorable display of those kids, and it's certainly inspiring to know those extraordinary youths believe in our cause. That's partly why Val 1 and Val 2 requested I call this meeting today. You see, the actions of these ... these ... Kids of *Stolen Tomorrow* have merely helped our timetable rather than rushed it, as the Ministry was exposed—if only briefly. Contrary to what may have been believed amongst the ranks, we see this as a positive development. They've made things easier. It's now up to us to capitalize on what these brave teens have done. I'm letting you know I've received orders to—pending a message delivered to the media from the one and only Val 1—move release of the airborne verus to tomorrow. All will receive the cure. Everything's in place!"

There was further discussion with the room full of Vals and Val 3 answered all queries thoroughly, acquitting himself with ease. Val 7 noticed the looks of surprise on the faces of his fellow Nthns; but all in all, they were overjoyed.

"You *sure* they're not bothered by the Barrington kid and co. revealing the secrets, front-running us?"

Val 3's look was suddenly serious. "Not bothered at all, 7. While it was unexpected, we look at it as a blessing in disguise. Bet you didn't expect that, did you?"

"I didn't know what to expect, but I figured we weren't quite prepared. I'm glad I figured wrong."

"You had every right to be worried, 7. You've always been a pretty smart one. But now you can relax. Enjoy! Let's celebrate and prepare for the next step."

One hour seven minutes.

Val 7 watched his timer. He'd have to catch a huv back to beat the edict and avoid the Pro-Ts, but he had some time to celebrate. He was happy as his comrades but he felt strange about the unexpected surprise. There were so many obstacles they'd overcome to get to this—a point that, if he was being honest with himself, he often thought may never happen. But now, here they were, on the precipice of truly being heroes, enacting lasting change for the better—perhaps justifying the actions they took to get here—some of which still gave him nightmares. It was, indeed, quite an uplift. Lost in his exhilaration, he smiled so widely he almost didn't notice the others around him falling off their seats to the ground, some twitching, convulsing before final stillness, and as panic crept in upon recognition of what was happening, he could do nothing about it. His eyelids grew heavier, his breathing became difficult and he slid off his seat into quiet, peaceful darkness.

* * *

94 O.O.

"How many? Next emis who gives me a wrong answer will join the casualties." Emperor Darcela was struggling to hold herself together. It had been for naught: The Vanes, the Unity Protection Act; the sacrifices: Ruben, Blue, Grace and countless other lives. It was all happening again, and this time it was because she miscalculated—misjudged the seemingly ironclad leverage she'd had over Kris and Dara. She was too focused on the Nth to see the greater threat before her. *I should have taken greater precautions. Maybe sent only the girl.* And now they'd unleashed an attack deadlier than the Nth—with all their secret cells and encrypted netlines—had ever conceived. She'd underestimated the kids, read them wrong, thinking *she'd* turned them into killers. No. To bomb inoculation centers was an act which required cold blooded savagery that could not be taught. Once her emises found "KoST" tags at the scene of multiple imploded inoculation centers, it was kill or capture and whichever took place no longer mattered to anyone. Even *the Nth* publicly disavowed any affiliation with the so-called Kids of Stolen Tomorrow in the wake of this tragedy. It was the first time in recent memory Eaves had seen the Nth distance themselves from acts of terror. Nthns had their limits apparently, which made these kids something darker.

"1,422, Your Majesty. 283 wounded. Igioyin treatment facilities in green, blue vanes all hit and a few red vane buildings hit by pulse bombs and that's only here in the city. There are reports coming in of similar attacks in Carolanda, the Southern Icelands, the WAU, the SEU . . ."

How are they alive? The boy especially . . . he—they, should've been back, begging for my help.

There was cooperation from all vanes all over the world as if they weren't separated by impenetrable clouds, armed guards, socioeconomic standing, cultural differences and general disdain. The Global Union Alliance was now truly an alliance for perhaps the first time since the end of the Nightfall War.

"Toley! Put it out on the netlines: if Kris Arvelo ever wants to see his mother's face again, he and the girl better turn themselves in. The rest of you! Anyone who so much as flashes a sprezen is to be captured and locked up, fleered on site if they make a move. Understood? We have Pro-Ts and our emises in other nations under the same guidelines. No one escapes. If you find the ringmasters before my team, bring them to me alive. Secure them, transport them back to the palace, and notify me. There's not a place on this globe they can hide now that the world has seen their glamour shots."

* * *

Dara, who'd fully believed she could not be shocked or surprised any longer, stood unable to comprehend what she was seeing. *Was there a war?*

"Damn, did we do this with that broadcast? This is lunacy . . ."

The warehouse was barely intact and several buildings in the general vicinity that were once firm pillars of IPU intimidation had withdrawn into themselves and left only remnants of their external shells for prying eyes. Kris was overwhelmed by the rubble and tried to push to the back of his mind what the destruction had placed in front of it. *She can't possibly be here.* The warehouse, intriguingly devoid of a Pro-T presence outside, still felt like a place they could get some answers. They phrinned inside and found it deserted. Walking by the dungeon where Shirazi had once held and threatened them caused Kris to shiver. They searched the space and found nothing. There was no sign the IPU had ever operated out of there apart from a few terminals; no signs his mother or anyone had ever been held captive there; no clues as to where she may be held right now.

Kris sent blasts at the terminals and walls in a fit of anger and frustration.

Dara didn't stop him, but she spoke up. "We still have other places to look. We'll find her. I know we will when you're ready."

Kris didn't stop but he turned to Dara. He yelled "We *are* finding her!" as he let another blast fly, as sirens and alarms went off, moving outside of the building to fire at it.

Dara, understanding, joined and together they did their best to make the warehouse resemble its forlorn, wrecked neighbors. They waited.

"It's when you want to see them they take their time," said Dara, as emises and Pro-Ts began swarming in, a hive executing its lone directive. Kris and Dara did not resist, and were soon reunited with the woman who could lead them to Kris' mother. They were both hit with paralyzing pulses and their hands were bound.

"You cowards are displaying uncharacteristic bravery, showing your faces, attacking a dungeon in my domain. Wonder what brought you out your rat holes? I guess you really do like your mum, Arvelo. I was starting to wonder ..." Emperor Darcela walked up to Kris, touched his face, tugged on his ear and squeezed his cheeks. "Well, *you're* looking alive. Maybe your friend wasn't lying in that broadcast after all." She pressed a fleer hard to his forehead and laughed. "Waste of cure if you ask me. I can undo all that healing right now. All I have to do is open this—"

Unfazed, Kris barked, "Where is she?"

The emperor stopped smiling and put the fleer away. "Oh! Well didn't take long for you to make demands, huh? *El bastardo desagradecido.* I guess you only come out to see me when I have something you want, don't you? How do you know she's alive? We could have tortured her slowly before bringing her to a merciful end. You've seen me do it. You know I enjoy it."

Kris, restrained by chains and several emises, could only threaten.

"And what are you going to do in this state? You two should have never come out of hiding. You're going to suffer for what you've done. Once I'm satisfied with your pain, I'll kill you both. I'm going to let you watch each other die but not before the realization your 'Kids of whatever' ends with you. A special treat for you first, Kris. By the way Dara, how's Nicole?"

Two Pro-Ts brought out Kris' mother as Dara struggled against the restraints and emises who held her. "May Shango smite you, *bitch*. I'll see to it—"

Emperor Darcela slapped Dara and laughed. "Cover her mouth."

"Ma! We came back to get you." Kris was unable to hold back his tears as he laid eyes on his mother, who looked as if she hadn't eaten in weeks.

She smiled at him weakly and said, "Mi pequeño mundo, te amo … you shouldn't have come back."

Emperor Darcela aimed a pulser at Kris' mother. "There's nothing you can do is there? Powerlessness is fun, no? Say goodbye, Kris."

"No!"

As Emperor Darcela fired the pulser, a phrinway opened and the pulse wave was deflected by a blast coming out of it. Kris' mother was pulled into the phrinway. Taking advantage of the split second of confusion and surprise, the masked assailant who emerged from the phrinway was able to free Kris and Dara by disappearing, reappearing from another phrinway directly above them and sending another blast flattening the emises around them. Dara and Kris felt themselves being pulled into a phrinway as well, confused by all that had transpired. Kris' mom, Kris, Dara and the masked assailant found themselves back in the clearing of the Igbo Oluwa.

As they attempted to make sense of the wild sequence, Kris' mom was the first to speak. "I don't know what just happened, but you saved my son. Thank you, may Orunmila bless your path as has been done for us through you." The assailant nodded, blacker and helmet-mask still on.

"Donzi?" Kris thought aloud but was soon answered by a stirring in the group sleeping yards away. Kehinde, along with Donzi and Envy followed the commotion to the point of origin. Dara's heart leapt initially as she thought Vida had come to her rescue once more; but now able to see the assailant's full stature, she was somewhat disappointed.

Kehinde realized what had taken place and was not pleased. "You, bright as you are, you let this fathead boy drag you into his nonsense after you told me you would stay here? You are lucky you are not dead. And you," walking over to Kris and smacking him upside the head, "I do not care whether you can make laser fire rainbow rain from the sky, if I see you around my daughter alone anytime soon, I will personally break all your bones and sacrifice what remains of your tattered frame." He turned back to Dara. "So, you are saving his life if you stay away from him."

Dara, about to reply, was interrupted by the masked assailant. "Kehinde, they showed great bravery and because of them, his mother is alive. I'm sure you can appreciate this as a parent and be proud."

Mr. Adeleye was silent and Dara was not sure she could interpret the look on her father's face but she had a feeling it wasn't good. He quietly said to her and the others in the clearing, "Please, leave me and this person to speak alone."

Soon Dara and Kris and others were back by the sleeping area, wondering what could possibly be going on. Kris hugged his mother and set about getting her food and drink. Dara sat watching them for a few minutes before preparing a soft sleeping spot for Mrs. Arvelo. The rest of the camp stirred and began normal early morning movements as conversation continued in the distance. Mr. Adeleye's raised tone indicated quite often theirs was a conversation the way a towering inferno and candlelight were both considered fire.

As Kehinde finished and made his way back to the group, the person he'd angrily engaged followed anyway despite the clear impression it wasn't his wish. Kris, shocked, looked at the person then looked back at a stunned Dara. Did she see it? Did she realize the mystery person was her *ibeji*? Her *twin*? They were spitting images of one another . . . was he the only one who noticed?

334

"Since she's bent on disobeying my request, I have no choice but to tell you. My pikin, my dearest Dara, this woman who has come here to stir trouble is the lady who physically gave birth to you, and so is technically your mother."

Everyone got up and walked off into the clearing to give Kehinde, Dara and the woman privacy. Dara stared at the woman without saying anything, eventually nodding.

"He's right you know. You've grown into a beautiful young woman without any help from me. I'm so impressed with you and proud of all you've done. It would be silly to expect you to call me Mama, but you can call me Grace, or Ms. Ife. Or (she looked at Kehinde, who looked away) Miss Olumo."

The woman's smile seemed genuine, as if there was true pride stemming from their relation. She moved towards Dara but Dara stepped back, studying the woman's face. She could see a radiance and joy but to her it was distant and inaccessible—like reading stories about the sun's warmth earlier in her life. Dara wasn't angry. She simply didn't know this woman.

As if reading her thoughts, Grace spoke again. "I know it's a lot to process. I know I seem alien to you, and I wish I had been a big part of your life, but I will give you all the time you need. I don't regret everything I did that kept me away from you and your father because it was in the interest of keeping you safe and giving you a life that was your own."

After another long silence, Dara spoke. "Why are you here now? How did you get here or know where to find us?"

Grace laughed. This was a topic they could discuss. "I'm similar to you, Dara, as you've seen. I can move between walls, places and worlds. This place, *Igbo Oluwa*, as your dad calls it, is home of sorts to those with our oyas. It is replete with the energy of the gods and a source of equanimity. Within this land all our imbalances are corrected—mind balances with body, body balances with soul and we are brought back into harmony. The same pervasive forces we find out in the world are here too, in abundance. Fear, lust, greed, deceit and so on, they have their role within the land but they are absorbed by the faith, hope, and perseverance stemming from love until they're reborn as expressions of it." Grace turned to look at Kehinde, who hissed. "I must apologize to you both, not only for abandoning you, but also for not revealing myself sooner, but I love you and I've always watched over the two of you—when I could—from afar. I've wanted for you to have a life that was all yours—"

"So you left." Even if it were true Grace loved her, Dara didn't think one could abandon one's child and get to make grand proclamations of their love for the child or were entitled to wanting anything from her. It seemed strange and silly. She was baffled. "The only thing I want from you is to know how you found us. But it seems you won't even tell me that."

"But I *will* tell you that and more. If you care to know, or listen, I can tell you of the terrible event which caused the destruction you saw and why you must remain here for now. I can show you how to learn what transpires on that side without exposing yourselves to danger. And I can tell you why you have the gifts you do and the reason you were given them. I'm here to help you, omode. If you can give me some more of your time, you won't have to be bothered by me any longer."

Dara looked over to her father.

"The woman is many things I shall not say, but in such matters as these, she has a tendency to speak the truth. It's okay to hear her, pikin."

"My reappearance in your life is something decreed by the gods themselves, as certain events coalesced, alarming them enough to make their presence known to me. To tell you what has been revealed to me, I must tell you the story of your oyas."

336

Dara incredulously shot another glance at her father, who nodded again, this time more convincingly than the last. She would give this woman her undivided attention.

"Ninety-four years ago or so, the Orishas returned to the earth to intervene—for the last time—in mankind's flight to self-destruction. Though they succeeded, they knew the nature of humanity is such that humans would always return to the brink. So, in parting, they decided to leave a gift: men and women who would serve as the champions of the gods on earth, with oyas bestowed upon them by a disease, a dreaded scourge that would cause the swift, catastrophic deterioration of the immune and nervous system. The plague we know as igioyin. That plague, while killing many who weren't quite developed or equipped to handle it, gave others unimaginable, nearly limitless oyas, such as those you and your friends have either demonstrated or seen demonstrated. The purpose of those with these gifts is to intervene where the gods no longer choose to—when humanity's existence is put at risk. Some with the oyas still suffered—igioyin tore through them, though at a much slower rate—and that was due to Eshu's stipulation; that the chosen who declined the path set by the gods while still using their oyas would suffer a fate worse than those who are merely ill-equipped. Those who found their way eventually ended up in Igbo Oluwa and, finally aligned with their purpose, found themselves healed. And still, many things had to go right, even if one possessed the gift. If they were not exposed in some way to Yemoja's Crystals in some form early on, the oya would never be activated. You may have sometimes heard these crystals referred to as corlypses. It is my belief the sprezens you and your friends often wield, contain trace amounts of the crystal—enough that the use woke what would have otherwise remained dormant. I once wielded sprezens myself and sometimes, out of nostalgia—will show that form. However, the crystals are crutch of sorts. Exposure to the Sea

Goddess' crystals must occur with each use—this was Yemoja's stipulation.

But there was an exception. Dara, out of the chosen, you, I, and another—many years younger than you, were given something rare: the ability to use our gifts without ongoing exposure to the crystals. We were chosen it seems, as a failsafe. Of course, there is a toll taken in other ways, such as your body forcing you to recharge by shutting down after extensive use, but you will grow adept at managing this over time as your mastery increases. You'll find our oyas in particular, grow exponentially with each use."

"If what you say is true, why us? Why you and I specifically?"

Grace smiled. "My dear Dara, I want to say it is because we have suffered. And *my* how we have suffered, but many have suffered as much, and some worse. So, I do not know. No god has ever answered that question for me, and I stopped asking long ago. You will find with time the 'why' shall cease in importance to you as well. As to why I am here, my plan was always to reveal myself to you, when you were ready. Many things have occurred which have hastened this. There is something you must see. Over in the cave—Olumo Cave as it was named on the day it came to be—near the bottom, you can view events in a space of time through the Illuminated Hallway. It's occasionally how I kept track of you, and it's something I can show you how to do."

Dara followed the stranger who was her mother into the cave with Kehinde walking with her, holding her hand, and Kris, whom she'd called over her father's objections, on her other side.

"Eshu, please tell Olorun we are grateful for the blessings bestowed on us this day and those before. Guide this journey and protect us. Shield us as we place our eyes where they cannot be seen." Grace turned to Dara. "The energy in the cave acts as a cloak, and allows you to view through the Hallway without running the risk of being detected. It turns

TRAZER

the phrinway into a panel of sorts instead of a doorway, giving us windows where there are walls." Grace opened a phrinway to nowhere in particular and they were transfixed by the way various glowing colors collapsed and melted into each other amorphously and unexpectedly formed concrete divergent paths. She touched a path on the screen and the image of several bloodied people screaming and crying at the base of a giant pile of rubble came into focus. The image was followed by a news anchor reporting above the caption "Inoculation Centers Attacked Worldwide: KOST Terror Group Still at Large, Nth Claims No Affiliation," followed by stills of Dara, Kris, Envy and Trevin from their original broadcast.

"I don't understand," said Dara, and Grace proceeded to show them piles of rubble that made the buildings by the warehouse look like crumbs. They viewed devastated neighborhoods (even in the clouds!) along with ongoing protests against them and all trazers and gates. In many of the neighborhoods shown, "At What KoST?" tags were prevalent, mirroring the phrase on some of the protesters' signs. Dara looked away from the image of a few young trazers whose lifeless bodies were being paraded.

"No. Don't turn away. You must see it all and understand what has happened."

"What *has* happened? How did we—how are we responsible for any of this?" Kris had uttered Dara's exact thoughts.

"Someone saw your broadcast as an opportunity to place this tragic attack on your resumes."

"Who? Who would do this and why would they blame us?"

"I have my suspicions, pikin," Kehinde said, as he looked at Grace.

Kris and Dara were both silent for a while until Dara spoke up again. "The cure? Envy—*we*—mentioned a real cure for igioyin. We told people it was coming in our broadcast

339

because Envy worked with the Nth to create a cure for all affected. They were supposed to have re—"

"To this date there has been no release of a cure by anyone, and the attacks have wiped any momentary support your group might have had."

"Envy ..." Dara rushed out of the cave back to the clearing followed by Kris.

Kehinde and Grace, staring after her and at each other, stayed back in the cave. "What little faith the children had left is gone. I, on the other hand, have always known better than to trust you ... or your people."

"Kehinde, I know you're angry and I'm sorry. You may never trust me but you should know I haven't worked with them in a very long time—years. I don't know what this is and it's not to do with me but I will find out for the sake of our child."

"Envy!"

Envy, who'd nodded off next to Donzi was startled. "What? What's up?!"

"Val 7, the Nth—they never came through!"

"What do you mean, Dara? What happened?"

"When we went out there to save Kris' mom it looked like a war had taken place. We know why now. What's happening is the cure was never released, and we're the enemy. *We're* the Nth now. *We're* the terrorists."

"That's lunacy. I know I didn't get to finish helping them perfect the airborne delivery, but there was enough in place. To start saving people; enough to start making a difference. That's what the Nth always told me we were doing. I know Val 7 never showed, but the only possible move—only logical thing to do was to release the cure. Dara, it doesn't make—"

Dara took Envy's hand to pull him off to the cave as the rest of the group followed. Grace ran through the panels in the Illuminated Hallway as the group watched in horror and stunned silence.

Envy spoke, his voice shaking, "I didn't . . . I can't. I need to go back there. Let me try again, let me get in touch with—"

Grace interrupted. "No one's going back there. Not right now. No one is leaving this place anytime soon. You've seen all that's there and you've all done all you can. It isn't safe for any of you." She looked at Dara and Kehinde. "Now what comes next will be difficult, especially in light of what you have just seen, but you *must hear it*." She turned to the rest of the group in the cave. *"All of you."* Grace made eye contact with Dara, who nodded, and she resumed.

"While I do not yet know who attacked the inoculation centers, and while the Nth's delay in releasing a cure is bewildering, they are the least of our concerns. I learned and discovered many things over the years in my travels, with the gods guiding me in one way or another. For a long time, I thought following the path meant destroying the IPU from within—but this was my own external quest for revenge that I twisted to suit my beliefs. In that quest, I *did* discover things, things which led me to what I believed my real path was to be: helping the Nth to cure igioyin, hoping in this way to provide greater life for those in the red vanes. And so, I poured myself into that—helping find willing scientists— scientists like you Tommy—and protecting them, giving blood samples, and locating corlypses for these people who wanted to use them to build a cure for the impoverished, as opposed to the IPU who stockpiled them for the crown's weapons and for the Ministries who already had treatment for the clouds and cared not to share it with all. I believed *that* was the action which would save humanity from the brink. Yet even to this day, I am still learning. When I communed with Orunmila, I was informed the danger was imminent; that while aiding in the cure of igioyin was a noble task, a greater danger would soon render it moot. His only clue to me was to 'Follow Yemoja's streams' and I would find my answers. So, I began to again track corlypses. And then I tracked the others tracking corlypses. And in this I discovered the IPU amassed corlypses not because they need them to keep treating the clouds for igioyin—they had more than they would ever need for that years ago—and not even to bolster the standard arsenal they've used to terrorize the innocent. No, it was because they'd built last of all pulsers—a strange, monstrous, lightless pulser, and they needed massive amounts of the crystals to power it. It's called Dialuz. And if deployed, it can kill entire red vane populations within seconds."

There was a collective gasp.

"How?"

"It uses shadow-pulse blasts as a delivery system to send a wave of highly-potent weaponized igioyin through the atmosphere of each red vane, making it immediately toxic. The separated atmosphere of the clouds would remain protected, leaving blue and green-vaners unaffected. Once I discovered this, I believed by killing Reza Shirazi—"

"Wait, *that was you?!*"

"Yes, Kris. I believed by killing him I was killing many birds with one stone, saving you and also putting a halt to the life of the person most likely to use it. But—"

"You were mistaken."

"Yes, Dara. I was."

"Unsurprising."

"Ah! Ah! Omode! Show some respect!" Kehinde's voice boomed and was followed by the sound of him smacking Dara on the back of her head. "What she is telling you is serious and you'd better keep quiet because you won't get this information from anyone else!"

"But why? All those people. Why would anyone, no matter how deprav—"

"The Nth place most of their bases in the red vanes; their supporters are red-vaners. Sure, they may manage some hidden operations in the blue vanes, but destruction of the red vanes would all but wipe them out. Dialuz was built primarily with this in mind. In killing Shirazi I thought I'd delayed its use by many years and bought time to eliminate it. Instead, I have the inkling I have merely hastened its dawn by giving power to the person who intends to use it soon."

* * *

Emperor Darcela, replaying in her head the ambush of a few weeks ago by the mystery Nthn and subsequent getaway of Kris, Kris' mother and Dara, stood impatiently looking over the shoulder of Emis Ptolemy Kabore. He held a latcher in his hand, furiously running numerical sequences on the diamond shaped object's keypad at the Myrtle-Willoughby wind station in Todirb Wall, which had been closed off for repairs since the emises' months-ago run-in with the Kids of Stolen Tomorrow. Repairs had yet to begin.

"I think you're wasting my time Toley. We've been successfully latching for years. And I've seen it done within minutes, seconds. What in Ogun's blade is the hold up? You started in October—it's MARCH—six months you've been working with them on this." It was getting to the point where Toley's usefulness could cease to protect him from her deeply held rage.

"Heh. That's the thing, Your Majesty. There's something unique about this frequency. Other latcher frequencies can reopen phrinways instantly without matching completely—usually all we need's a range. But this is unlike any other. It has to be exact and I don't think we've ever encountered anything remotely similar. But not to worry, Your Majesty, I didn't call you to waste your time heh-heh. Here!"

Before them was now a view of a place which did not quite look like any she'd ever seen.

Eaves, staring into the open passageway did not even feel the urge to silence Toley who, with his latest feat, had earned a few more years of life. They'd still had no luck in the search for Vida, but if Kris, Dara and others were on the other side of this phrinway, she could take her frustrations out on them in the meantime. She gave the signal for the emises on the platform to step in and the troops below to ascend and follow.

* * *

Another mad day settled into an exhausting evening.

Envy lay awake—as he had for the last several nights—attempting to figure out what variable in his equation went awry to place things in their current state. They'd put the perfect amount of pressure on the Nth to step forward and unveil the cure. The Nth had everything to gain by taking the cue—a legion of converts and increased influence. It should have worked . . . *it was set up perfectly*. Unless . . . the IPU had shut them down?

Could *that* have been it?

Did we ruin things by drawing attention to their plans?

It had never occurred to Envy, once things were in motion, that the IPU could stop the Nth; that their broadcast might have made things harder.

Arrogance. Foolish oversight.

He'd somehow forgotten to consider the outcome that had a higher probability than any other. He wasn't sure how many dumber calculations had been made throughout history with so much on the line (though the several historical instances of failed invasions of the rough, mountainous former Eurhacian Union came to mind as a close second). He was tempted to once again try to reach Val 7 but thought of Grace's warning and the danger it could put his friends in and decided against it.

I can make it again. I will. Recreate the cure, release system—maybe make a better one. I'll have to search. Trevin can help. It'll take time ... but I have that here.

Satisfied with his planned course of action, he fell asleep.

His eyes had barely been shut fifteen minutes when he heard rustling. Dara and Kris? He looked and saw them fast

344

asleep yards away; clearly it wasn't them. He heard the sound again. He was tired, but could not ignore it. He stood and tiptoed to the edge of the clearing expecting to find a restless and possibly hungry tiger or some other sort of wild creature. He was frightened by what he saw and bolted back to the clearing, yelling desperately for everyone to wake up.

"What—who's—" Dara had barely stirred before she had to deflect a fleer blast from the direction of the clearing. Scores of IPU emises and Ministry soldiers advanced upon the camp. Grace, who everyone assumed had stayed in the cave, phrinned into the middle of the camp and began ushering Kris' mom, Kehinde, Envy's dad, his companion, and the KoST through a phrinway. Dara resisted as did the rest of the Kids of Stolen Tomorrow.

"What are you doing? We're staying here. Ain't going nowhere, ma'am," Brink said as he sent blasts back in the direction of the clearing.

"Where'd you send them?" Kris asked.

"Somewhere safe," Grace responded, mask now back on. "You'll be able to find them easily using the Hallway later. I still think you all should go. This is my fight. She doesn't know it, but Eaves is here for *me*."

"That may be so, but if we don't all stand up to them together today, we'll never have a moment of peace again."

In the background Donzi was struggling with Envy. "You need to follow them!"

"No. I'm not going there unless you come with me. If you're staying, I'm staying."

"Stop with the foolishness. Get in there!"

Dara who overheard added, "Hey! Genius! You're no use to anyone dead," and together they used a field to forcefully push Envy through the doorway Grace had sent Kehinde and Mrs. Arvelo through.

Grace closed the phrinway and the group focused their attention on the advancing emises flanking Emperor Darcela, firing fleers and pulses their way. A wave of emises and

345

soldiers broke from the group and encircled Grace, who placed herself in a large protective orb. They shot blast after blast unsuccessfully as some glanced off the surface into the atmosphere, and a few appeared to be absorbed by the orb. Once the initial attack slowed, the orb glowed and the emises, confused and panicked, increased fire. The orb ceased to glow and there was a moment they could see clearly through it to Grace at the center, standing perfectly still. Suddenly, a wave of energy pulsed outward from the orb and flattened the entire unit of emises and Ministry forces surrounding her. As they lay unconscious, she moved outside their circle and opened a phrinway in the ground around the still assailants, causing them to fall through.

"Whoa. How'd you do that? Where'd they go?" Donzi, having fought off a couple emises of her own, had caught the tail-end of the drop.

"Far, far away. The headache will be the least of their worries when they wake u—lookout!" Grace bent a beam around Donzi to hit two emises approaching. One was knocked so far back he landed at the foot of Emperor Darcela, who unceremoniously kicked him out of the way and sent pulse beam and more emises towards Grace. Grace sidestepped the beam.

There's something familiar about the movements ... that quickness ... Eaves thought, observing the actions of the masked Nthn who dispatched emises a little too easily. It made her angry. "What the hell are you doing standing here? You're not doing anything blasting from over here. Bring me those kids!"

A swarm of emises left Eaves' side and descended upon Dara and Kris, overwhelming their protections with immense force and dragged them over to the emperor. "Reunited at last." She cackled.

Donzi cried, "No!" as she caught wind of what was happening but was knocked to the ground by one of the group of emises fighting her, Brink, and Grace.

346

Grace, who was next to notice Kris and Dara's capture, blasted the emis who felled Donzi, and with the help of Brink and Trevin, fought off the rest. Grace then pointed to the unmoving Donzi. "Brink, Trevin, get her to the cave! She can recharge there." She opened a phrinway around Brink, Trevin and Donzi.

Grace charged towards Eaves, deflecting blasts from the emises surrounding her, Dara and Kris. As she neared the formation, she tore off her tactical helmet-mask and flung it to the ground.

Im ... possible ...

Emperor Darcela froze and yelled at her troops to hold fire. The emises stopped and so did the camp, puzzled as to what halted the emperor who'd led the barrage from the clearing with unrelenting fury.

This is not real.

This is not real!

She marched up to Grace, staring at her, pulser in hand, using the barrel to touch her face. "No ... you died. I was there ... I watched your body disintegrate.... Are you an Nthn now? What did they do to you, Grace? What happened to your *face?* How ... how did you become ... *this?* What happened?" The latter two sentences were said with all the disgust Eaves Darcela could muster.

Grace said, beaming at Eaves, "I always knew you'd become so powerful and strong and respected. But you still let your pain consume you. It's here now, in all this," She motioned to the IPU and Ministry forces strewn about and the emises holding Kris and Dara. "These children are not who you think they are; let them go. They're not terrorists, Eaves, and this isn't the way, believe me. I once tried the same."

Eaves laughed. "It's a miracle old friend; it truly is ... and oh how I looked up to you ... I looked up to you so much. But you're wrong about them. Why don't we leave with them and the rest and you promise to disappear and we never cross

paths again? That's the best thing for everyone involved."
Eaves' face lit up. "Or even better—join us. Join me. Come
back—come home Grace … it's been a while. Things are
more dangerous than ever. Look around. We could use you."

Grace's smiled sadly. "You know I'm not going to do
that."

The hope in Eaves' look faded abruptly. "Hm. Then we
find ourselves without a path for compromise. I'm not sure
what brainwashing you've undergone or who you believe
yourself to be but it's clear the Captain Ife I knew died on
that mountain years ago. Pity. Because she would have killed
you. Good thing I survived to do it for her."

Emperor Darcela fired the pulser at point blank range
and the blast was sent off to the sky by a field formed around
Grace. The emises and Pro-Ts followed suit and the fighting
intensified. Grace blasted the emises who held Dara and Kris
to break them loose. Brink, who had returned with a
rejuvenated Donzi and Trevin, was grazed by a fleer and
yelled in agony as they struck down the emis who'd fired at
him. Grace avoided the emperor's flurry of blasts through a
combination of jumping in and out of phrinways and putting
up a new shield anytime one wore down. She struck Eaves
several times, forcing her back as Eaves' blacker bore the
brunt of the attack, but made no attempt to kill her.

"These are children, Eaves. They're not killers. They
didn't choose to be thrown in the middle of this."

"No. Lies! I've seen what they're capable of. They may
not have been killers at one time, but they are now, and
they're far more dangerous than you're willing to see. I
should've have known. I should have recognized it when I
saw the girl. It wasn't a coincidence she reminded me of you.
That's what all this is about isn't it? Saving your little girl? Tell
me traitor, how did you survive being burned to a crisp?"
Darcela fired another blast towards Grace, this one hitting
her blacker and pushing her back slightly.

"What is she waiting for? Why isn't your mo—Grace killing Darcela? Doesn't she know we're fighting for our lives out here?" Kris said this as he felled an emis who'd attempted to fire at Dara as she downed an emis who attempted to fire at Kris.

"Don't know but it doesn't matter because we'll get her no matter what happens." Confident as she was of this, Dara noticed Grace seemed to be weakening the longer the fight went on. While they'd made a significant dent into the force that first descended upon the Igbo Oluwa, there were still a great many to go, and any weariness or slowdown would mean certain death. "Kill!"

"Yeah, Dara?" He looked at her quizzically, puzzled at her use of his nickname.

"You can create fields around others right?"

"Yeah."

"And still manipulate them?"

"Like win."

"For how long?"

"How long you need?"

"Five minutes, maybe ten"

"Yeah, probably. Why?"

"One sec. Donzi!"

Donzi who'd deflected a pulse blast back into a group of emises and watched them collapse, put up her field and ran over to Dara. "What do you need?"

"Kill is about to put a field around—can you—" Kris was unable to hear the rest as he ran over to aid Brink and Trevin who were surrounded. He crisscrossed the blasts from a sprezen in each hand to send it wide and free them.

"Thanks, Kill."

"Just returning the favor, briz." They followed him back over to Donzi and Dara.

Dara gave them instructions. "Brink, Trev, I need you two to stand outside of us and keep off any attackers the best you can. Kill, how many of them could you put in a field . . .

right about … Now!?" As she asked they looked towards the rush of emises towards them, pulsers and fleers firing. Kris responded by placing most of the entire flank in a blast absorbing bubble, though he visibly strained to hold them there. Trevin and Brink deflected and picked off the stragglers, while Dara opened a large phrinway and was aided by Donzi in increasing the size.

"The great Captain Ife, weakened by blasts from a pulser? You're getting old! I guess we all are." Darcela laughed and fired another shot at Grace who was no longer jumping through phrinways and whose force field was giving way with each additional blast. "You would have been *me now*, you know?! Maybe you wouldn't have been emperor—but you could have been High-Commander! Emperor Shirazi trusted you—loved you more than any others—if it were possible for him to love. And you were the best!"

Grace laughed. "Ah Eaves, you are brilliant but after all these years you can't be this naïve! I was never going higher than captain. I wasn't born into your world. I was never one of you. It was always going to be you or one of the other nobles, not the 'trash' they 'rescued' from the village."

"You brought these kids together against us and what we believed in because you weren't homegrown? After fighting alongside us and seeing the evils we sought to protect the world from?"

Grace fired but only managed sparks which scattered and died before touching her intended target. "You have that wrong, Eaves. Those children had nothing to do with any of this, until Shirazi—whom you revered—yanked them in, threatened them, used them. He was no man of love; he was incapable. He was a man of incredible hatred and contempt. You'll *never* understand what he was … but I did! And you picked up where he left off. Are you proud of yourself? Would that girl who lost Ruben recognize what you've become?!"

"You have no right to talk about my father! Not after you abandoned me! I trusted you! I cared for you!"

"And I for you, dear Eaves. I always saw your good and I still do … that's why this rage, you can't … it's destroying you. Eaves, I know about Dialuz. I know you're in pain. But you must look deep within yourself and see what's happening around you. That pain you feel, that feeling that's driven you all these years, I know what that's like. But you have the power to put an end to the cycle of pain. You have the power to bring peace. *You.*" They had momentarily stopped exchanging fire.

"How do you know about Dialu—you know what? It doesn't matter. It has nothing to do with anything." Tears streamed down the emperor's face.

"It does, Eaves! I see the good person you still are—the great leader you have within, but she's being consumed by her pain. And if you let that pain win here today starting with these children, you'll have nothing left. You'll be empty. Millions will suffer and not just the ones you think."

"So, what, I let them get away with murder? They help the people who took away my father and I embrace them? You?"

Grace, who appeared weakened by mere conversation now, took several deep breaths. "No, not quite but we can figure something out. It'll be hard and I know there'll be sacrifices. I'm realistic. There's much you need to know. It's so much bigger than us, greater than us, and we can end this here. Please. You can end this."

As Grace said this, the protective orb around her faded completely. Her skin glowed and flickered. Her long curly hair wrapped itself behind her head into a single plat. She grew smaller and her skin grew lighter, and Emperor Darcela's eyes grew wide and wild. "No … no *not you*. Not you!" whatever distance remained between them when they stopped shooting and started speaking was closed as the emperor descended upon the still flickering Grace who'd changed back into herself almost as quickly as she'd involuntarily changed into Vida.

"I can explain," Grace said, weakly

"There *is* no explanation!" Emperor Darcela sent a blast which Grace barely managed to block. Thrown back several yards by its force, she flickered again into Vida form. Eaves ran after her. "*You* want *peace?* You, who dedicated yourself to evil *from the beginning? You who killed my father?* Who killed *the beautiful young man I loved?* All those lives … I never loved again because of you! *You* created this creature, this monster—this broken evil you see before you and—" Emperor Darcela smiled.

Suddenly.

Chillingly.

She reached over to her breastplate and keyed in a code while the still flickering Grace, who realized what was happening cried "No!" and fired at her. But the hands that once released debilitating beams barely mustered a spark. "Eaves, there's no coming back once you do this," she pleaded, crying.

"Don't You *Get It!?* I'm already gone! There *is* no coming back! You did that! But it's fine now. Every single red vane citizen on earth is dead, and that's *your* doing, Grace. That's *your* legacy. And now it's your turn. You can rest peacefully knowing I'll be the one to send your daughter and friends to join you at the crossroads."

"All those people Eaves … *lives, children* …" Grace, tears in her eyes, flickered into Vida again—

"PUSH, KILL! PUSH NOW!" Kris, sprezens at full force in both hands and all the strength his legs could muster, pushed the field containing the rest of the emises into the phrinway. He let go as Dara and Donzi rapidly closed it, and he fell to the ground in a heap.

"You okay!?" he heard them say in unison. He gave a thumbs-up before Donzi and Dara pulled him back on his feet.

There was a terrifying, blood curdling wail. It did not stop and only grew in fury and magnitude as the seconds progressed. The group looked over to the direction of the outburst to see Emperor Darcela, teeth bared with her gloved hands around the neck of a little girl and the child's feet kicking as she struggled.

Dara's eyes went wide. "VIDA!" She ran over, blasting the emperor several feet back. She held Vida in her arms and, ignoring the panic sweeping over her as she saw the bleeding from the chest wound made by a pulser blast said, "You're going to be okay."

Vida nodded and smiled. "You. Learned. Much. Olorí-iré," as she said this, her skin flickered and her body grew and changed shape until Dara was staring at Grace.

Dara could only muster a weak "How?"

"I needed ... to be able to protect you ... reveal your oyas but ... keep you safe. There were so many things coming you had to be ready for. I wanted to get the timing right. You don't know how many times I held back; and then I was afraid I would be too late. There's so much I wanted to teach you. I didn't want you to be caught up in ... in this ... violence." Grace coughed and flickered back into Vida.

"Yeah, well, that didn't work." Dara was crying.

"You say so now ... but over the coming months, you'll begin to see you have your freedom, something I never had, and that is enough for me."

"But it's not enough for me."

Grace/Vida coughed again and smiled. Dara noticed a bright object forming, glowing, in her hand. "Dara, you need to know something ..." she trailed off.

"What? What is it?!"

Grace was either too weak to speak or struggling to find the right words. Dara waited, an eye on the still forming object.

Grace exhaled heavily. "You need to stay in this place— all of you. For a long time. Until the gods make things clear and not a moment before. It's the only place you'll be safe. Don't worry about the Illuminated Hallway or things on that other side. Do not concern yourself with that world okay? Forget about that one. This is your home. *Promise me.*"

Dara nodded, teary-eyed. "Okay, I promise. We promise."

"Grow here, develop yourselves ... get to know the Igbo, and enjoy your lives. I once saw you here, in the cave, my beautiful daughter, long before you were born. In the cave, Olumo Cave. I ran into you in a dream, but my you've grown.... Your path is ... beginning. I'm proud. I won't be there to see, but...." The object, having cooled, was fully formed now and Dara's mother handed her a corlypse shaped in the likeness of the prophet-god Orunmila, accented in his trademark gold and green—markings which glowed while the rest of the object remained static.

"What's this?"

"A little help. Orunmila's wisdom shall be your guide—" A large pulse blast hit Grace-as-the-little-girl-Vida in mid-sentence, stunning everyone. Dara didn't need to check her vitals to know she was gone. She let out a gut-wrenching shriek and fired all she could in the direction of the pulse blast, a barrage impossible for the already heavily injured Emperor Darcela to survive. Dara fell to the ground.

Kris tried to console Dara but she cried and writhed on the ground saying only, "Get Papa. I wanna see Papa." Kris went into the cave and returned with Kehinde, his mom and Envy. Kehinde ran to Dara, and began crying as he embraced her and looked at the body that had, for the final time, changed back into Grace.

GLOSSARY

Babalawo – *n.* (Yoruba) priest; holy man, healer. Diviner of the prophet-god Orunmila and other Orishas.

Bisa - *n.* slang, used primarily in the northeastern red vanes of the North Emerian Union. Term of endearment; refers to the object of one's affection.

Blacker - *n.* virtually impenetrable bodysuit worn primarily for combat.

Briz - *n.* slang. originated in the red vanes of Yorkland Province, used throughout the North Emerian Union. A term of endearment; interchangeable with friend, brother, cousin. Can also be used derisively.

Bushwall Heights - green vane town which houses the IPU Palace (home to the Emperor of the Global Union Alliance and High Commander of the IPU), and Glory Tower (home to the Prime Minister).

Bushwick Heights - blue vane town. Home to the lower noble class.

Cles - 1. *n.* a device for calling; moves sound via phrinway technology.

2. *v.* the act of using a cles; interchangeable with call. *I clessed her but she didn't pick up.*

Cloud - *n.* slang. refers to blue and green vanes which are under the protection of Climate Limitation Atmospheric Organic Devices (C.L.A.O.D's), engineered to combat severe climate change. C.L.A.O.D's simulate sunlight and provide warmer temperatures in perma-frosted regions and cool temperate weather in overheated ones. The term cloud, which initially referred to the C.L.A.O.D's, is now a class distinction, as the impoverished occupants of red vanes have no such protection.

Clypsars - *n.* corlypse embedded straps placed on the hands of gates to enhance their phrinway opening abilities.

Corlypse - *n.* rare blue tinted jewels used by Babalawos to commune with the sea goddess Yemoja. Known to the scientific community for their immuno-enhancement properties, they are a highly sought commodity by both the IPU and the Nth.

Decalaoba - *n.* from the Greek *deka,* meaning ten, and the Yoruba *oba,* meaning king. Refers to the ten ruling houses of the corporate class and their members. Surviving sponsors of the Nightfall War, the once fluctuating number of corporations in this exclusive group has been static and locked for decades. An emperor may be chosen only from the Decalaoba.

Emis - *n.* entry level rank for an IPU operative, from the term emissary. A reference to the IPU as merely an international peacekeeping force and used to maintain that veneer to the general public.

Eurhacian Union - a collection of nation-states comprised of East Eurhacia and West Eurhacia. Virtually obliterated during the Nightfall War, only small pockets are habitable. Linton Province, home to Linton City and located in former West Eurhacia, is the lone major population center remaining. Many former Eurhacian citizens sought and found refuge throughout the GUA.

Fleer - a weapon that emits long wave bursts of concentrated radiation with minimal fallout. Contact with a fleer beam on human skin results in instant third degree burns. Exposure for more than a few seconds is fatal.

Floatshoe – *n.* (also *float-shoe*) a designer dress shoe, typically high heel, that hovers millimeters above the ground, alleviating stress on the wearer.

Gate - (Gates, *plural)* *n.* human beings capable of opening and traveling through phrinways. Gate can also be used to refer to a phrinway.

Glory Tower - the living and working quarters of the North Emerian Union (NEU) Prime Minister.

GUA - Global Union Alliance. Officially formed in response to the destruction left by the Nightfall War, the GUA is Earth's governing body. GUA refers to both the governing body and the member nations within. The seeds of the GUA were planted in the immediate aftermath of the Miracle of Elegua. The GUA recognizes the high-commander of the IPU as their ceremonial emperor.

Igioyin [eeh-geeh-oh-yeen] - *n.* tachy-degenerative disease of unknown origin. Simultaneously attacks nervous, endocrine, and respiratory systems rapidly, resulting in critical failure. While igioyin can be detected and lay dormant in the human body for years, it activates without warning and, upon activation, is immediately fatal. It is pulled from the Yoruba colloquialism signaling impending doom: "O ru igi oyin," which translates to "you have brought a thicket of hornets upon yourself."

IPU - Institute for Preservation of Unity, the international "peacekeeping" arm of the Global Union Alliance. A royal clandestine force, they are publically neutral, with a high-commander who serves as emperor of the GUA.

Latcher - *n.* object used to reopen phrinways closed by gates. Latchers work by being placed over the exact coordinates of the closed phrinway and cycling through algorithms until the right sequence is found.

Lyteche - a *Decalaoba* company, specializing in communications.

Marlsonne - specially trained singers for the nobility, performing anywhere from royal ceremonies to business events for the gentry. Not quite nobility themselves, Marlsonnes still see many of the same perks as a result of their talent.

Ministry - designation given to the governing bodies within each nation in the Global Union Alliance. Each ministry is comprised of a council. The popularly elected head of that council holds the title of minister. Ministry can refer to a specific one (WAU Ministry) or generically be a reference to all.

Miracle of Elegua - during an escalation of tensions between the leadership of the Emerian Union and the Eurhacian Union, the Prime minister of the Emerian Union gave the go-ahead to his generals to unleash nuclear weapons upon the Eurhacian Union, an action that would have sparked a chain of events resulting in the deaths of billions of innocents and humanity's extinction. Having observed the atrocities of these poor actors on the world stage long enough, Olorun and Iya Nla sent Shango, Ogun and Oya, to earth intervene; Yemoja decided to accompany them. And so they intervened, by freezing time and disabling all nuclear weapons and other weapons of mass destruction, removing all traces of them from earth.

Moog - *v.* slang. fail to do or complete something as a result of fear or a lack of confidence.

Bobby: Why'd you moog out Tommy? You told us you were gonna fight him.

Tommy: I was scared
New Stuyvesant - blue vane town. Home to
Stuyvesant University, the most prestigious college in
the North Emerian Union.
North Emerian Union - a collective of Nation-
States in Earth's northwestern region. Formed in the
aftermath of the Nightfall War, it is comprised of the
remains of the Emerian and Emerian Central unions.
Nth - organization dedicated to combating quality
of life disparity. Believers that the IPU and GUA failed
in their interpretation of the Miracle of Elegua, they
see themselves as the true followers of the Orisha
Doctrine and believe that lasting change can only be
achieved by force. To this end, they are staunch
worshippers of Ogun, the Yoruba God-of-War. The
Nth were established by Orisha Val, a former IPU
Captain who faked her death prior to spearheading
the first attack against the Institute. The IPU and GUA
classify the Nth as a terrorist organization.
Nthn - a member of the Nth. Nthns are highly
trained in hand to hand combat, speak a wide range
of languages and specialize in clandestine and black
ops.
Nuh - No.
Orisha Doctrine - (influences much, never
explicitly mentioned) the belief that the Miracle of
Elegua occurred not as a blessing, but a punishment
for humanity's crimes. First posited in the hours after
humanity was pulled from the brink, the doctrine has
gained momentum through the horrors of the Nightfall
War, adverse climate events, and the onset of igioyin.
Followers of the Orisha Doctrine tend to believe that it
is a chosen few who will move humanity back towards
the path of enlightenment, as the rest are otherwise

cursed. The Orisha Doctrine gave birth to the derisive term "Mirage of Elegua."

O.O. - *La Ti Odun Oluwa* [lah-tee uh-doon oh-loo-wah], a Yoruba phrase which translates to "Years since the Miracle." It sets the official calendar according to the number of years since the Miracle of Elegua, with events prior referred to as OTB (Olorun's Time Before). O.O. is the Global Union Alliance's official date marker, made worldwide after Nightfall.

Panel - *n.* a device for viewing video and other images. Panels take two forms; holographic and physical-tangible.

Phrin - *v.* to move through time-space instantaneously using a phrinway.

Phrinway - *n.* a connecting path through the traveler dimension. Modern science has been able to harness the phrinway for communication and rudimentary (yet still far advanced comparatively) travel. Gates are able to open phrinways by unknowingly summoning Eshu, the trickster god and lord of the traveler dimension. As a result, experienced gates have phrinway access that far exceeds anything current science has achieved

Program Irunmole [eeh-roon-muh-leh] - IPU operated, GUA funded program to combat igioyin; first through treatment of water where it first appeared, then through treatment in the human body. Verus is created as a result of Program Irunmole. Irunmole in the Yoruba faith are Olorun's liaisons between Orun (the spiritual realm) and Aiye (Earth).

Pulser - *n.* electroshock weapon that sends concentrated high voltage current at its target.

South Emerian Union - a collective of nation-states in Earth's southwestern region. Formed in the aftermath of the Nightfall War, it is comprised of the remains of the Emerian South Union and the Southern Icelands.

Southern Icelands - formally the West Indies, this group of islands were amongst the hardest to be hit by devastating climate change.

South African Union - comprised of the nation-states of south-central and southern Africa. Occasionally referred to as the AU, they initially opposed the formation of the Global Union Alliance.

Slant - *n.* a special needle containing a cocktail that immediately soothes sufferers of physical trauma without side effects.

Spends - *n.* money

Sprezen - *n.* a dispenser used for graffiti.

Swoop - *v.* slang. To eat.

Todirb Wall - a red vane town in Yorkland province. Home to Dara Adeleye, Kristano Arvelo, Donzilana Yang, Tommy Barrington and the Kids of Stolen Tomorrow.

Trazer - *n.* slang. graffiti artist. Originated in Todirb Wall. Used throughout red vanes in the GUA.

Twib - *n.* slang. a feeble, clumsy person.

Vane - *n.* zoning designation for towns in the Global Union Alliance, determined by class. Red vanes--the highest populated, house the impoverished, and are exposed to the elements. Blue vanes house the gentry (lower nobility), entertainers and general well-to-do. Green vanes house the exceedingly wealthy and high nobility. Blue and green vanes, in addition to pricey housing, bear a hefty cost of living tax due to climate protection of the clouds and the ready availability of verus. The separation of blue and green vanes from red is clearly marked by the armed forces at the border entrances to the clouds, as well as the clouds themselves; dome-shaped ethereal, yet impenetrable structures which make attacks from the outside virtually impossible.

Verus - *n.* inoculation for igioyin, must be administered weekly.

Vim - *v.* slang. to leave. *Vimmed out.*

West African Union - comprised of the nation-states of West Africa, Central Africa and the remaining strongholds of North Africa. Formed in the aftermath of the Nightfall War with the backing of Decalaoba giant Awolowo Industries, the West African Union spearheaded the formation of the Global Union Alliance.

Yorkland Province - *noun.* a sprawling city-state containing countless red vanes, the Blue Vane Stronghold, and the most influential green vane in the NEU, Bushwall Heights. Yorkland Province is the capital of the NEU, housing Glory Tower.

YORUBA TERMS

Plenty of online resources exist for official Yoruba pronunciations and definitions, such as the ones below:

https://en.wikibooks.org/wiki/Yoruba/Pronunciation, https://www.omniglot.com/writing/yoruba.htm, http://www.africa.uga.edu/Yoruba/alphabet.html.

This section is to serve as a guide for key Yoruba terms used specifically in this book and provide basic, visual, simplified pronunciations.

Gods Referenced

Eshu [ay-shoo] /eɪʃuː/ - the trickster and god of the crossroads. Colors: black, red

Ogun [oh-goon] /ˈogún:/ - the god of war. Ogun, when lowercase, or spelled oogun, means medicine. Colors: red, black and green

Olorun [uh-luh-roon], /plpɹún/ - the god of the heavens, often called the sky father. Olorun, Olodumare (the god of creation, also written Eledumare) and Olofi (ruler of aiye – Earth domain) are the three manifestations of the Supreme God.

Orunmila [oh-roon-me-lah] / oʊˈɹunmilæ/ - the god of prophecy. Colors: yellow and green

Oya [oh-yah] /oʊjɑ/ - the goddess of winds, lightning and tempests. Colors: many - brown, red, pink, white, burgundy, purple, orange

Shango [shun-go] /ˈʃæŋgəʊ/ - the god of thunder. Colors: red and white

Yemoja [yeh-muh-uh-jah] /jɛmʌd͡ʒæ/ - the goddess of seas, rivers and fertility; mother of all orishas. Colors: blue and white

Other Terms

Aburo [ah-boo-row] - n. younger brother

Awe [ah-whey] - n. fellow, friend, buddy

Dada [dah-dah] - adj. good. ex. *Omo dada lo je* [uh-muh dah-dah loh jeh]: *You are a good child.*

Egbon [eh-bun] - n. older brother

Elewon [eh-leh-wuhn] - n. prisoner

Fi mi si le! [fee mee see leh] - leave me alone!

Joko [joe-koe] - verb. sit; sit down.

Lagbara [lah-bah-rah] - by the strength of, for the strength of; by the grace of

Odabo [oh-dah-buh] - int. goodbye

Omode [uh-muh-day] - n. child

Ori Buruku [oh-ree boo-roo-koo] - 1. wicked one. 2. Ori which means head, may refer to one's destiny, or to one's make-up, which informs their destiny. Ori Buruku in this context refers to a person constantly beset with misfortune and hard-luck.

Oyinbo [oh-yeen-bow] - adj. Caucasian

Pikin [pee-keen] pidgin. - n. child

JOSEPH OLUMIDE ADEGBOYEGA-EDUN was born in Lagos, the then-capital city of Nigeria. A great-grandson of the First-Secretary of the Egba United Government, he was brought to the United States at age two when his parents came to study. Increasing corruption in the Nigerian government followed by the return of military rule thwarted their plans to move back and America became home. They set roots in Brooklyn, New York, a vibrant environment colored with graffiti and steeped in elements of hip-hop that left an indelible mark on the future author's consciousness.

The cultural influences and experiences of his homeland and the city of his early youth have been a strong source of creative inspiration for the author. *Trazer: Kids of Stolen Tomorrow* is his debut novel, and the first book in the Trazer Series. When not writing, Joe enjoys working on other projects with his creative partners LenStorm, 7Woundz and Soundz, and exploring the breathtaking wilderness of the Chesapeake.

CPSIA information can be obtained
at www.ICGtesting.com
Printed in the USA
LVHW02s2035130818
586831LV00003B/704/P